Angela Thirkell

Angela Thirkell, granddaughter of Edward Burne-Jones, was born in London in 1890. At the age of twenty-eight she moved to Melbourne, Australia where she became involved in broadcasting and was a frequent contributor to British periodicals. Mrs. Thirkell did not begin writing novels until her return to Britain in 1930; then, for the rest of her life, she produced a new book almost every year. Her stylish prose and deft portrayal of the human comedy in the imaginary county of Barsetshire have amused readers for decades. She died in 1961, just before her seventy-first birthday.

"Mrs. Thirkell is in triumphant form in her return to Barsetshire and its rituals. She is one of the subtlest of social historians, in that the reader can seldom be quite sure which of the county values she endorses and which she is laughing at."

—*Times* [London] *Literary Supplement*

"In this latest Thirkell chronicle we gladly meet once more the friends we loved and admired and laughed at in twenty-two preceding volumes."

—*Saturday Review*

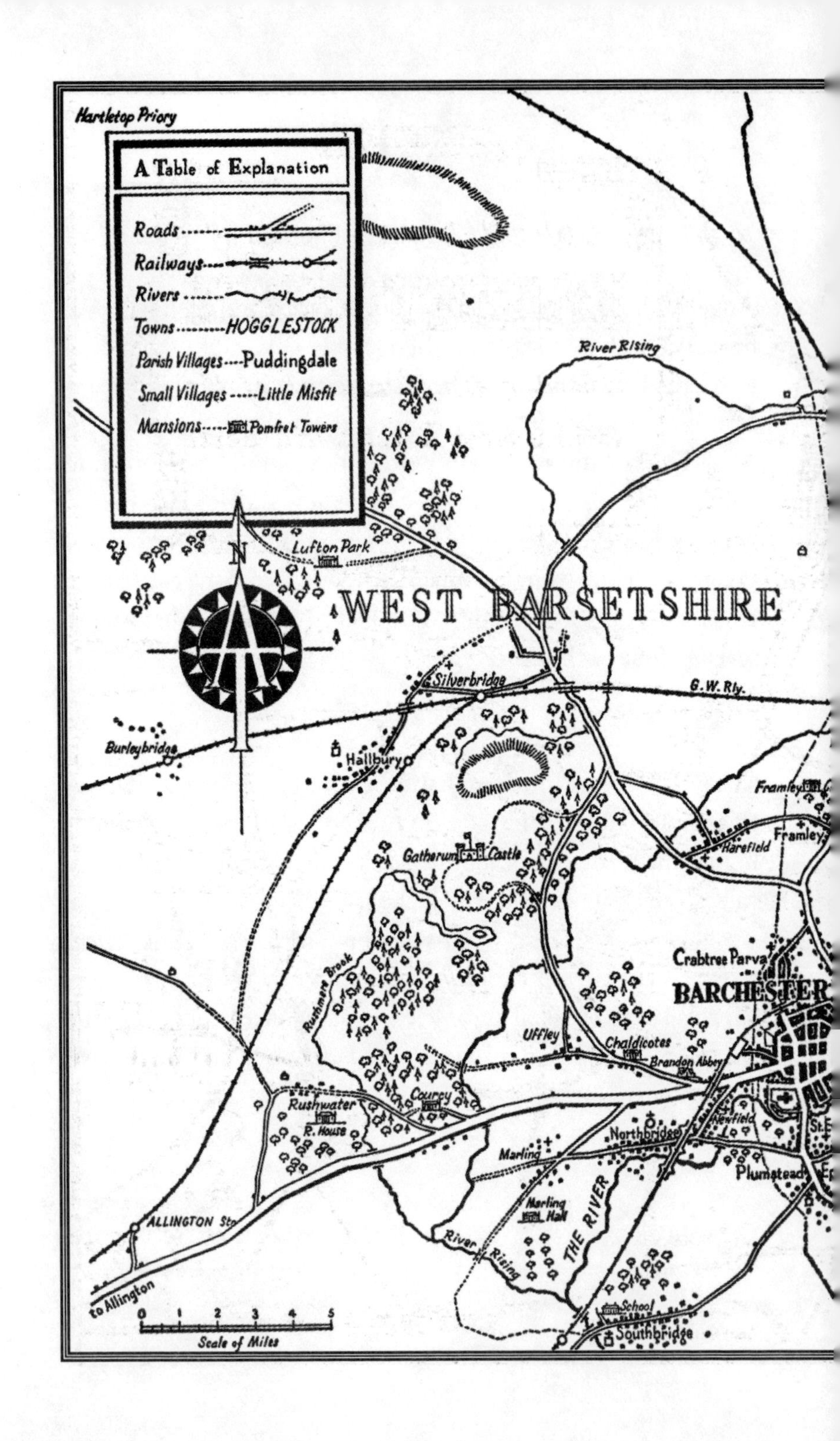

Hartletop Priory
A Table of Explanation
Roads
Railways
Rivers
Towns HOGGLESTOCK
Parish Villages Puddingdale
Small Villages Little Misfit
Mansions Pomfret Towers
N
Lufton Park
WEST BARSETSHIRE
River Rising
Silverbridge
G. W. Rly.
Burleybridge
Hallbury
Framley
Framley
Harefield
Gatherum Castle
Crabtree Parva
BARCHESTER
Rushmere Brook
Uffley
Chaldicotes
Brandon Abbey
Courcy
Rushwater
R. House
Newfield
Northbridge
Marling
Plumstead
Marling Hall
THE RIVER
River Rising
ALLINGTON Stn
to Allington
School
Southbridge
0 1 2 3 4 5
Scale of Miles

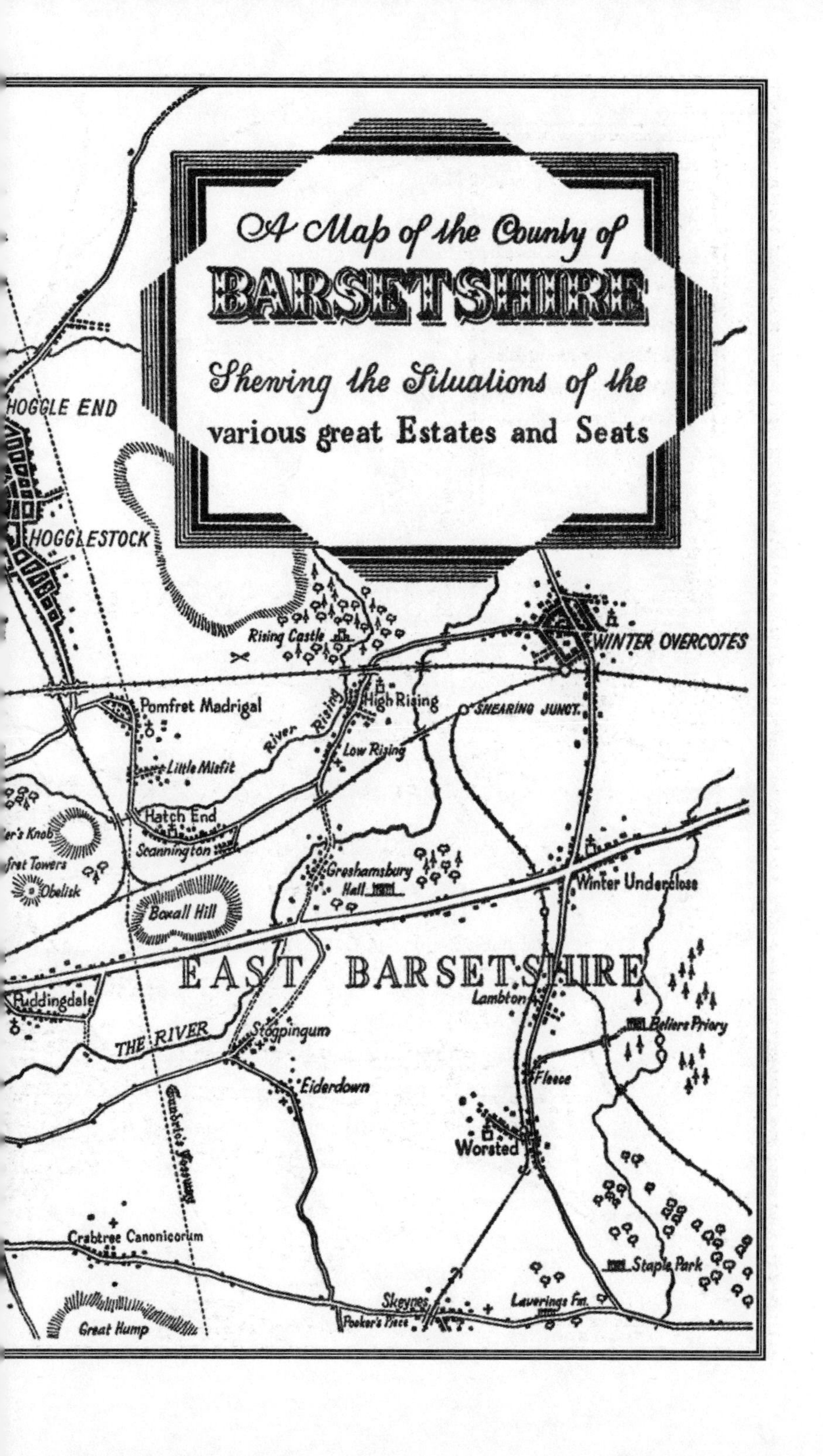

A Map of the County of
BARSETSHIRE
Shewing the Situations of the
various great Estates and Seats
HOGGLE END
HOGGLESTOCK
Rising Castle
WINTER OVERCOTES
High Rising
River Rising
SHEARING JUNCT.
Pomfret Madrigal
Low Rising
Little Misfit
Hatch End
Scannington
Obelisk
Greshamsbury
Hall
Winter Underclose
Boxall Hill
EAST BARSETSHIRE
Lambton
Puddingdale
Beliers Priory
THE RIVER
Stogpingum
Fleece
Eiderdown
Worsted
Crabtree Canonicorum
Staple Park
Skeynes
Laverings Fm.
Pooker's Piece
Great Hump

Other books by Angela Thirkell

Three Houses (1931)

Ankle Deep (1933)

High Rising (1933)

Demon in the House, The (1934)

Wild Strawberries (1934)

O, These Men, These Men (1935)

August Folly (1936)

Coronation Summer (1937)

Summer Half (1937)

Pomfret Towers (1938)

Before Lunch (1939)

The Brandons (1939))

Cheerfulness Breaks In (1940)

Northbridge Rectory (1941)

Marling Hall (1942)

Growing Up (1943)

Headmistress, The (1944)

Miss Bunting (1945)

Peace Breaks Out (1946)

Private Enterprise (1947)

Love Among the Ruins (1948)

Old Bank House, The (1949)

County Chronicle (1950)

Duke's Daughter, The (1951)

Happy Returns (1952)

Jutland Cottage (1953)

What Did It Mean? (1954)

Enter Sir Robert (1955)

Never Too Late (1956)

Double Affair, A (1957)

Close Quarters (1958)

Love at All Ages (1959)

HAPPY RETURNS

A Novel by

Angela Thirkell

MOYER BELL
Wakefield, Rhode Island & London

Published by Moyer Bell
This Edition 1998

Published by arrangement with Hamish Hamilton, Ltd.

LIBRARY OF CONGRESS CATALOGING-IN-PUBLICATION DATA

Thirkell, Angela Mackail, 1890–1961.
Happy returns : a novel by Angela Thirkell. — 1st ed.
p. cm.
ISBN 1-55921-255-1
I. Title.
PR6039.H43H36 1998
823'.912—dc21 98-11871
CIP

Cover illustration:
Countess Jean de Polignac by Édouard Vuillard

Printed in Canada
Distributed in North America by Publishers Group West, 1700 Fourth Street, Berkeley, CA 94710, 800-788-3123 (in California 510-528-1444).

HAPPY RETURNS

CHAPTER I

It will not, we hope, surprise our readers to hear that Lady Cora Waring, formerly Lady Cora Palliser, only daughter of the Duke of Omnium, wife of Sir Cecil Waring of Beliers Priory, was expecting what used to be called an interesting event. Not that the event was very imminent, but her ladyship was so puffed-up about it that her husband accused her of being a baby-snob. To which she replied that everyone was a snob about something and why not about babies, and her husband said they really ought to ask the Brandons to dinner and the Marlings too, by which he did not mean Mr. and Mrs. Marling from Marling Hall, but Oliver Marling and the Honourable Mrs. Oliver Marling who was Lord Lufton's elder sister.

"Va pour les Marlings," said her ladyship, "but why the Brandons, darling? They haven't asked us to dinner and I am all for etiquette. Brides *expect* to be asked," to which her husband replied contemptuously that she wasn't a bride now, she was a matron.

"Well, frankly, as that ghastly Harvey woman used to say, my love," said Lady Cora, "I can't stand Francis. Peggy is a pet and to see her dance the Tango with Francis was one of the high spots of my life—do you remember—oh no, it was before I knew you. It was at the Conservative do at the Castle two years ago."

"Well, if you want the truth," said her husband, "Francis

Brandon is an uncommonly good man of business. I have had some dealings with him in Barchester and he might be useful to me."

"One of your Utopias?" said his wife, for Sir Cecil was planning a kind of home for boys of naval men killed in the war, or in poor circumstances, using a part of the huge and hideous house inherited from the uncle whose only son had been killed in 1918 just before the Armistice, with the intention of sending them on to be trained for the navy. And such a plan required a great deal of planning, if we make ourselves clear.

"And what exactly *is* Francis Brandon?" said Lady Cora, and we may say that this is a question we have often shirked asking ourselves, so no one need be surprised that Sir Cecil also shirked it, saying that he thought in London Brandon would be called a financier, whatever that was; that he certainly was a chartered accountant and had a real gift for dealing with money. So then Lady Cora said six was a silly number and they must have another couple and as he was asking his man of business why not ask Mr. Macfadyen of Amalgamated Vedge who was buying all their kitchen garden produce so nicely, as Cecil Waring was fiercely reorganising the estate and like most landowners now was always looking for good markets. So then another woman was needed and suddenly, in a county where single women are far from rare, they could not think of anyone who would fill the bill until Lady Cora suggested Lady Lufton.

"It would be so convenient," she said, "because Mr. Macfadyen is her tenant at Framley and he could drive her over. And she can tell me how to run the W.I.," for the widowed Lady Lufton was a tireless worker for that excellent body the Women's Institutes and in spite of her sad, distracted appearance had a very practical mind where they were concerned.

So Lady Cora telephoned to ask everyone and everyone accepted.

It is always very interesting to know how people manage to give dinner-parties now and there are usually two answers. One is Money, the other the gift for finding people who want to work. Money the Warings had, as far as anyone was allowed by Them to have money; and not for nothing was Lady Cora the daughter of a Duke with American blood in her veins. From the day when she first visited the Priory (for her visit to the Priory School earlier we do not count) to see her betrothed after his emergency operation at the Barchester General, she had gathered retainers about her. Her first conquest had been Jasper Margett, the half-gypsy keeper-poacher, whom she had so subjugated that quite a large proportion of the rabbits and other game were now brought up to the Priory instead of being disposed of to the Black Market. Then by treating Nannie Allen, the strong-minded old mother of Selina Crockett, cook at the Priory School kept by Cecil's brother-in-law Philip Winter, as an elderly ex-Nannie should be treated, she had the key of the domestic question in her hand. Nannie Allen had ordered several village girls to go to the Priory and not (as they had meant to do) go getting themselves into trouble in Barchester with all them Poles and things; Mrs. George Pollett of the Sheep's Head, herself no mean artist, had produced a young woman who cooked with enthusiasm and some skill and had long nourished a wish to be with what she called *aris*tocrats and Cecil Waring maintained that crowds were at the back door every day like the French Revolution, clamouring to be allowed to work.

At Pomfret Madrigal Francis Brandon was pleased by the invitation, quite realising that it was a tribute to his business capacity, and his wife (having seen that her husband was pleased) expressed her admiration of Lady Cora's gifts as an actress and thought about a new dress, for Francis, to do him justice, was very generous in money matters and liked to see his wife admired.

At The Cedars the Honourable Mrs. Oliver Marling said to her husband that they might as well go and if the new bitch chose to have her puppies that night Podgens must just ring them up, for she had brought that old retainer to Marling with her as a kind of stud-groom for her cocker spaniels.

Lady Lufton at Framley was surprised by the invitation, for she was a sad creature who had never got used to being a widow and her son had once said of her rather irreverently that she would have been much happier if she had committed suttee, but she accepted the invitation as she accepted any county festivities that came her way, partly because her husband always made a point of so doing and also with a muddled kind of feeling that it might help her son. As for Mr. Macfadyen of Amalgamated Vedge, when his secretary gave him the message (for he rarely answered the telephone himself) he asked cautiously who else was invited and when his secretary, with one hand over the mouthpiece, told him it was the Marlings and the Brandons and probably Lady Lufton, he told his secretary to ring up Lady Lufton and ask if he might have the pleasure of driving her to Beliers.

But Lady Lufton was out at the Barsetshire Women's Institutes' Book Day, so he told his secretary he would ring her up later. Accordingly when he got back to Framley he put his car away, lifted the telephone receiver, put it down again, lifted it again, replaced it again, and went out into the garden and so through a wooden door which was left unlocked into Lady Lufton's part of the garden.

"Hallo, Mr. Macfadyen," said Lord Lufton, raising his tall self from a border where he was weeding. "Do you want mother? She's just back. She's been out at the W.I. all day. I say, what's this I've just pulled up? Is it a weed, or what?" and he held up a few pale green leaves with a dirty purplish flower, itself hardly better than a leaf, rising from them and long depressed-looking earthy fibres hanging down.

Mr. Macfadyen, who had long ago decided that the young lord, though well-meaning, would never make a gardener, said it was probably Macrobogonia Smithensis, but might be a variety of Phyllicallus Toddii; being a market gardener, he said, he would not presume to make a definite statement. And in any case, he added, it was not a flower for a gentleman's border and he would away with it at once if he was asked. Lord Lufton said as he had pulled it up it might as well go and threw it into the wheelbarrow where he was collecting his weeds, at which moment Lady Lufton came into the garden, her handsome, melancholy face more troubled than usual.

"Oh, good evening, Mr. Macfadyen," she said. "Ludovic, what shall I do? Lady Cora has asked me to dinner. Do you think she really wants me?"

This was one of the moments at which Lord Lufton, fond as he was of his mother, could willingly have killed her. What he wanted to say was If she didn't want you she wouldn't have asked you; and if to this he had mentally added the words And don't be a fool, one could hardly have blamed him. But he was a gentleman and held his tongue, which might have made him burst had not Mr. Macfadyen, who had put a poor opinion of the Southron intellect, explained in precise terms to her ladyship that an invitation sent in all good faith should be taken at its face value and certainly accepted unless the recipient had already a prior engagement. Only he said rather more than this.

"Then," said Lady Lufton, whose anxious spirit always looked ahead for difficulties, "I had better get young Podgens to take me. Or could you drive me over, Ludovic, and he could fetch me. Or perhaps if Podgens took me over, you could come later and take me back. Unless perhaps anyone else with a car is there, or . . ."

But before her son could kill her, Mr. Macfadyen, at considerable length, and rather as if he were speaking to a very nice, very young child, said he also had been asked and if Lady Lufton would allow him to take her in his car he would count it a privilege. Lady Lufton, who during her married life had referred everything to her husband, looked round piteously, as if in hopes that he might somehow still be there and answer for her. Lord Lufton knew this way of hers very well and though it irritated him he felt so sorry for her that he miraculously kept every trace of irritation out of his voice as he thanked Mr. Macfadyen and said his mother would be most grateful. Lady Lufton, still in a flutter, thanked Mr. Macfadyen and went back to the house.

"I had a mother myself," said Mr. Macfadyen thoughtfully, "and many's the time I could have hit her over the head. They are all the same, Lord Lufton."

"I say, I wish you'd say Ludovic," said Lord Lufton. "I still always think it's my father when people say Lord Lufton, and I am sure mother does. It's awfully kind of you to take her, Mr. Macfadyen."

"Well, well, I'm willing to say Ludovic," said Mr. Macfadyen, "if you will drop the Mister. Your mother is a fine woman, Ludovic, and you may well be proud of her."

"But I am," said Lord Lufton, feeling, quite justifiably we think, that he had done nothing to make Mr. Macfadyen think that he in any way underestimated her. "She has been marvellous. I mean none of us having any children and she does so want grandchildren, and not minding you being at Framley. I mean—I don't mean that—I mean—" and his voice tailed uncomfortably away.

"Don't try to explain, my lord," said Mr. Macfadyen with a touch of stiff courtesy which rather frightened Lord Lufton till he saw that the rich business man was amused. "Fine I know what it is to be turned out of your own house. Wasn't my own mother turned out of hers when my father was killed in the South African war and she with nothing but her pension. I was only a wee lad then, but I mind it well and how I determined to give my mother a home. And I did. And then she died and I came South and lived here, setting my wits against other men's. I have done well for myself," said Mr. Macfadyen, not without a certain dignity, "but I know my place and if your leddy mother lets me give her a hurl in my car I count myself honoured. Well,

I must be stepping," and with a kind of friendly half salute he went back to his own part of the house, leaving Lord Lufton amused, interested and, we must confess, faintly disturbed that their tenant should suddenly intrude his remarkable personality into their quiet rather dull lives. Then his thoughts turned, as they very often did, to the day when he had gone at Emmy Graham's invitation, she who was now Emmy Grantly, into Rushwater Churchill's stall at Rushwater and how from the gloom of the bull's stall he had seen a girl in the bright sunshine outside and had seen in her eyes that she admired his courage. Not for one moment did he think that she might have a higher opinion of him as a person. Courage was a thing: you could admire it without liking the person who showed it. And this he had faced for the last year, telling himself that the look had not been meant for him, could never be for him. But one may tell one's heart home truths till one is black in the face and it will walk straight over them, right through them, towards its own goal. He suddenly remembered that the bailiff Pucken wanted to see him about a cow, for he had now begun a dairy-herd in a modest way and had ambitions for the future. He pulled himself together and went away to the farm.

As the day for the dinner-party drew near, Cecil Waring told his wife that he felt rather like Horatius when the Etruscan armies had been summoned from east and west and south and north, to which his wife said not to be silly and remember he was a naval man.

"I'm more like Mr. Churchill in President Roosevelt's telegrams to him," said Cecil, "Former Naval Person," for the Admiralty had taken what he considered a biassed and unreasonable view of his health since he had been operated on at short notice the year before and had intimated that they could get on without taking too much of his valuable time. "I don't like it, Cora," he had said to his wife, who replied that she didn't either, as it made it far too plain that she was only his second best love.

But secretly she was thankful, for the day when she had driven a grey-faced Cecil, faint with pain, at sixty miles an hour to Barchester still haunted her mind.

"Well," said Lady Cora, as they waited in the hideous drawing-room for their guests, "this will be one of my last appearances in public I suppose," to which her husband said Not to be Conceited and kissed her with careful affection, for one of the very few things that ruffled his wife's equanimity was to have her party make-up disarranged. And considering how beautifully and unobtrusively it was done, we think she was right.

"English weather," said Lady Cora, who was drawing the curtains and taking a last look out of the hideous drawing-room windows at the lovely English landscape of garden, fields beyond, and on the far side of Golden Valley the high line of the woods, for since her marriage she had opened some of the big rooms saying, which is perfectly true, that it is far easier to keep big rooms tidy than small rooms; which may sound unreasonable but is, we think, proved by experience.

"'. . . and from the deluged park
The cuckoo of a worse July
Is calling through the dark'"

said Lady Cora, adding that though it wasn't July, the principle was the same.

Her husband asked what that was.

"Tennyson, my sweet," said Lady Cora. "You are too, too ignorant, as that odious little Clarissa Graham would say."

Sir Cecil protested, saying she was only a child, to which his wife replied that she was old enough to know better and a heartless little fool when a nice boy like Charles Belton was hers for the asking and content to wait upon her caprices, and whatever happened *she* would never desert Mr. Micawber and she put up her face to be kissed, which proceeding quite unmanned Marigold the village problem girl, now engaged to

Geoff Coxon whose father kept the garridge, and caused her to back into the arriving guests who were Mr. and Mrs. Francis Brandon.

Ever since the Conservative Do at Gatherum where Mrs. Brandon had danced so beautifully with her husband there had been a pleasant though not very deep friendship between the Brandons and Lady Cora, who liked them both but—and this is a trait more common in women than people will admit—on the whole preferred the wife to the husband. When pressed by her husband she said Mrs. Brandon was a gentleman and Francis wasn't and Sir Cecil said he thought he saw in a general way what she meant but couldn't possibly put it into words. In any case they made a very good-looking couple and if Peggy Brandon had any skeleton in her closet she had locked it up for the night. While Cecil talked shop to Francis Brandon the two ladies plunged into nursery intimacies and Peggy Brandon said rather shyly that if Lady Cora cared to have her Karri-Kot the twins would soon be too big for it, while Lady Cora, hearing that Number One was growing out of her bed said she had seen a couple of small ones in the north attic only a week ago, and if she would like one—. To which Peggy replied that she would simply love it as everything got more expensive every day and how people were going to manage she couldn't think. Lady Cora, who as the daughter of a heavily taxed landowner had been at close quarters with Confiscation, said she couldn't agree more and did Peggy know of any good Nanny who would be available say early in the New Year.

"I've asked our old Nannie Allen," said Lady Cora, "because if I didn't she'd be offended, but she doesn't know any young Nannies. She was nurse to Cecil's cousin George Waring who was much older than he is, only he was killed so long ago that he feels much younger now—I mean he was younger than Cecil is now—I mean—"

"I know," said Peggy Brandon. "If Fred was alive he would be much older than I think of him as. He was my first husband," she added, seeing that Lady Cora did not understand. "He was killed in Burma. But now I'm much older than he was—I mean older than he was when he was killed. It is very confusing."

"'The lads who will never grow old'" said Lady Cora, her thoughts going back to her brother Gerald who was killed on D-Day, enjoying every moment up to the last, and one Froggy, the penniless son of an impoverished peer, shot down and killed at Arnhem; and with the incredible speed of thought she had mourned them both, found and loved Cecil and was back in the present, observing that her charming guest did not understand what she had said.

"Only a bit of poetry," she added and then, all in a bunch, in came Lady Lufton, squired (for we can use no other word) by Mr. Macfadyen and followed by Oliver Marling and his wife, and conversation aided by sherry became general.

Dinner was then announced by Marigold who, thanks to Lady Cora's good advice and Nannie Allen's scoldings, was looking much more presentable, having cut down on the lipstick and coiled her naturally golden hair into a bun, so that she looked really pretty, and was walking out quite steadily with Geoff Coxon. Owing to nearly everyone being husbands and wives the seating had given Lady Cora some trouble, but finally she had got it right, putting herself between Oliver Marling and Francis Brandon, which she ungratefully called Bearing the Brunt, while her husband was provided with Lady Lufton and Mrs. Brandon. Cecil had maintained that at a round table there was no top or bottom so it didn't matter who sat where, which his wife said was silly, as wherever The Waring sat *was* the head of the table.

By this arrangement Oliver Marling found himself next to his mother-in-law, to whom he remarked upon this fact, adding that he could never think of her as one. However they got on very well as both were good amateur gardeners and Lady Lufton rather more than an amateur and she talked away, quite confidingly, of what a help Mr. Macfadyen had been and how he had given her a rare specimen of a Himalayan plant just like a primula: so like in fact that she was never sure whether it was the English one or the other way round, at which point she became confused and rather helpless, till a twist in the conversation made her turn to her host, leaving Oliver to Lady Cora, who remarked how well his wife was looking, to which he replied that he quite agreed and that, if he might say so, she was looking very well herself.

"I expect it's the baby," said Lady Cora. "I've often noticed that the women who don't look quite *ghastly* before they have a baby look their very best. My sister-in-law, Silverbridge's wife you know, looked perfectly magnificent all last autumn. Even handsomer than she usually does," to which Oliver, now quite Benedick the Married Man, said if it were possible for Lady Cora to look more handsome than usual, she had done it. And as he spoke his eyes wandered to his wife Maria, across the table.

"Penny for your thoughts," said Lady Cora. "Or am I a brazen-faced hussy?"

Oliver said Not at all and looked slightly confused. Lady Cora laughed; a mocking laugh but a very kind mockery.

"Then I'm right," she said, in a lower voice.

"One has hopes," said Oliver and then was ashamed of himself for being affected; a state of mind which was quite foreign to him before the Honourable Maria Lufton had taken him in hand.

Lady Cora looked at him and sang softly in her attractive husky voice ". . . flüstern vom Bräutigam und vom nächsten Jahr."

"Do you sing Schumann?" said Oliver, almost forgetting himself (a rare occurrence with him) as he took in the meaning of her words.

"Why not, my sweet?" said Lady Cora. "If I had a voice I could sing *anything*. But I haven't. Only a trick. Only a trick. What some clever man who wrote songs called a petite voix de compositeur. Shall I sing to you after dinner? It's a pity Silverbridge isn't here. He accompanies me too divinely, even if he doesn't know the notes. I can only fudge the accompaniments. And how are the dogs?"

Taking this as a sign that music was not to be further discussed Oliver said they were very well and he really did know some of them from the others now and Maria was expecting a telephone message from her old groom at any moment about some new puppies, to which Lady Cora replied that in her young days they would have said the bitch had littered and none of this fuss; after which they got on very well.

Perhaps the most enjoyable conversation, though everyone was enjoying the evening, was the one in progress between Maria Marling and Mr. Macfadyen. He knew almost all there was to be known about gardens and a good deal in an amateur way about dogs. Maria knew almost all there was to know about dogs and was an enthusiastic amateur gardener. So absorbed were they by these subjects that Oliver told his wife when they got home that evening that at one moment he had distinctly seen Mr. Macfadyen demonstrating the correct manner of planting Manypeeplia Upsidownia with a piece of potato for a flower bed and the salt spoon for the seedling, and Maria explaining the points of her hopeful Marling Matador by kneading her bread into the likeness of the future champion. All of which, said Maria indignantly, was quite untrue; as indeed it was, but the willingness is all.

Meanwhile Peggy Brandon was getting on very well with her host, who having a very good-looking wife thought but poorly of women who were not good-looking: though he was always courteous to them. So courteous indeed that Miss Pemberton, the joint author, with her lodger Mr. Downing, of the great Provençal Dictionary financed by Mr. Walden Concord Porter of the United States, grimly stated her opinion that his courtesy was almost an insult. But she did not mean it for, as she later remarked to Mr. Downing moult gent monstran cortez, iceluy mostran cor; though it was to her mind Lord Silverbridge, Sir Cecil's brother-in-law, who was de cortez tout confaict.

Cecil Waring thought that from time to time her eyes wandered to her husband and put it down to wifely affection, though, come to think of it, he added to himself, they had been married now for at least five or six years. Or was it a curious anxiety? But none of his business anyway, so he asked Peggy about her family and Pomfret Madrigal, a bit of the county he did not know, and Peggy prattled about the babies and their old friend Sir Edmund Pridham and the clergyman Mr. Parkinson and his wife.

"They have *so* little money," she said, "and they are so good. The people in the village even go to church on Sunday evenings sometimes, which shows. I did hope Mrs. Parkinson would let her children come and play with ours, but she didn't seem to like the idea. I expect she was afraid of Nurse."

Sir Cecil said that he had never met anyone who wasn't afraid of Nurse, or Nanny as the case might be.

"Except Cora," he added. "She treats Nannies exactly as if they were human and they always adore her. I expect you know we shall be wanting a Nanny this winter. Do think of us if you hear of anyone," and Peggy Brandon said she had already promised Lady Cora she would, and then she had to turn to Mr. Macfadyen of whom she made a complete and immediate conquest, nor was his admiration in any way lessened when he offered her a cutting of Jinglia Teakettlia and she had never heard of it. Then Lady Cora collected her ladies and took them away, while the men remained to drink some of old Sir Harry Waring's port which Cecil had brought to the light of day only just in time. Oliver and Francis, who each in his own way would have dearly loved to pose as an authority, could not pretend to any great knowledge of port, though they reverently enjoyed Sir Harry's choice, but Mr. Macfadyen appeared to have considerable knowledge of the subject and became almost eloquent about it, also lauding the wines of an earlier age when Edinburgh society knew and chose its clarets, and spoke learnedly and at what some of his audience considered unreasonable length, of vintages now unprocurable, of a Scots pint and a tappit hen, expressions of which the younger men were ignorant though they would have died rather than confess it. Then came Francis's turn, when some question raised by Cecil gave him an opportunity to show off a little on the subject of exchange and devaluation.

"It is a pleasure," said Mr. Macfadyen in his measured way, "to hear a young man who quotes the best authorities. If I'm not mistaken the man George Schwartz used just about those same words in his article last Sunday. He has the root of the matter in him, forbye that he makes me laugh, Sabbath or no Sabbath. Follow him, Mr. Brandon, and you will not go far wrong."

"Touché" said Francis, not quite at ease and rather unkindly hoping to confuse Mr. Macfadyen; far from which Mr. Macfadyen, remarking "Trop d'honneur, monsieur," raised his glass and gravely drank to Francis, while bestowing upon Sir Cecil and Oliver Marling something uncommonly like a wink. "My mother was half French," he added. "It is an old friendship between the Scotch and the French."

For one moment Cecil, who saw the whole situation getting unexpectedly out of control, wondered if he would as a J.P. have to arrest his guests for breaking the King's peace, though what a J.P.'s powers were he was not quite sure, when everyone began to laugh and Mr. Macfadyen and Francis fell into very interesting and well-informed talk about the financial situation in general; which talk we shall not attempt to report as we have not the faintest idea what it all meant, a position we share with the host who though very intelligent was not a specialist and presently took his gentlemen to the drawing-room.

Lady Cora had doubtless made her own plans for the rearranging of the party; it is one of the duties of a good hostess. But any private arrangements she might have made were entirely disconcerted by Mr. Macfadyen who came up to Lady Lufton and with a kind of bow asked if he might sit by her.

"But of course," said her ladyship. "If you are quite sure," she added with her usual indecision in social matters, "that Lady Cora doesn't want you to sit anywhere else."

"If she does, she will doubtless ask me," said Mr. Macfadyen and sat down beside his landlady.

"You know," said Lady Lufton, looking at him with mild interest, "I don't think we have sat down together before. We have met in the garden and you were so kind. But you are so busy I didn't quite like to ask you to tea. Besides, you don't get back for tea, do you?"

"Not often," said Mr. Macfadyen. "There's not much in a cup of tea for a bachelor to come back to. I go to the Club as a rule. One meets useful people there. I did wonder if you would come and see how I am keeping my side of the house, but I thought maybe Lady Lufton would not like to see a stranger in her own home."

Lady Lufton, who though sad and anxious was not wanting in commonsense, as the Barsetshire Women's Institutes well knew, said of course if it was Germans or Russians, or indeed *any* kind of foreigner, she added, one wouldn't like it.

"But when you are our tenant and keep the garden so *beautifully*, Mr. Macfadyen," she added, "it seems silly not to meet more. Perhaps you will let me come to tea one day now. I believe you come from near Perth, where my father-in-law still had a place when I first married, and that makes it rather comfortable." So Mr. Macfadyen sat down beside her and told her, though not at all boringly, about himself and his long line of ancestry, with a farmer and a minister in each generation, going back to a burgher of Perth at the beginning of the seventeenth century, which pleased Lady Lufton because her people had always farmed as well as riding to hounds and being J.P.s and she asked Mr. Macfadyen how he came to be such a good gardener.

"If your ladyship knew the gardens in Perthshire you would

not ask," said Mr. Macfadyen. "And you will have noticed that before His Majesty's present Government—and a Monstrous Regiment it is—had harried the landowners, just as those breekless, cattle-lifting Highlanders used to harry my people in Perthshire, in every big place in England you would find a Scotch gardener. I worked about the policies of Auchsteer as a lad, that was away up north under Ben Gaunt, just by Loch Gloom, and I brought back my earnings to my mother, poor thing, every month. And if old Methven, the head gardener, wasn't pleased with my work I had to do it again. So when my mother died and I came south to seek my fortune I sought it under a good Scotch gardener and I found it. But it was in marketing, not in growing. And here am I, making a fine sum of money every year for the Labour Government to tax. Labour, do I say? White-collar Labour. Trade-union officials and sic-like that have never fyled their hands with honest work. I beg your ladyship's pardon," he added, with a smile that changed his rather grim face and made it suddenly very pleasant.

Lady Lufton said she was very sorry about his mother, because she knew how dreadful it was when people died, because then they were dead; which statement appeared quite reasonable to Mr. Macfadyen and he looked very kindly at Lady Lufton as if she were a seedling that needed special care.

"I know what I would do if I met any of the Government," said Lady Lufton.

And what, said Mr. Macfadyen, would her ladyship do, and he looked with a kind of amused admiration on his landlady.

"I have thought about it a great deal," said Lady Lufton earnestly. "If I had to shake hands, I should take off my glove and when I had shaken whoever's horrible hand it was I should say 'It is cheaper to wash one's hand than to have one's gloves cleaned'," at which Mr. Macfadyen, after the second's hesitation incumbent upon a good Scotchman, laughed so much that everyone wanted to know why.

"But that is Atavism, if that's the word I mean," said Lady

Cora. "I remember my grandmother telling me how the dowager Lady Lufton of her mother's time met the Great Duke of Omnium—you know, the one that nearly disinherited my ancestor Planty Pal because he flirted with that very old Lady Hartletop when she was Lady Dumbello—at a party the bishop's wife had in London, though why in London I don't know, and she absolutely *loathed* him because he wasn't virtuous and they got so close together in the squash that he had to bow to her and she made her crinoline as big as she could and did a court curtsey and simply *annihilated* him."

"A very just comparison, Lady Cora," said Mr. Macfadyen, "but you will observe that there is no member of the Government here to be annihilated—more's the pity," at which most of the guests couldn't help laughing, though in a very kind way, and Sir Cecil said it reminded him of the story, only he knew he would get it wrong, of the man who said to a Scotchman about another Scotchman that he wouldn't see a joke if you fired it at him out of a pistol, and the Scotchman said "But you can't fire a joke out of a pistol," at which the company laughed again, but not so much and Mr. Macfadyen sat and looked at them, quite kindly, till they stopped, when Lady Cora, feeling a little guilty of guest-baiting, asked Oliver if he really wanted her to sing some Schumann.

Everyone said yes. Some, including the Brandons who were not much given to classical music, from politeness, the others from a real wish to hear her sing.

"I wish Jeff were here," said her ladyship, hunting among the music. "I can fudge it, but he really plays. Oh, here it is," and she set a volume of Schumann on the piano. "It was *Der Nussbaum* we were talking about, wasn't it?" she added to Oliver. "I know it all right, the tune I mean, but I'm afraid I'll boggle the accompaniment a bit. I can't think why Cecil can't play the piano like Jeff. It would be so useful."

"If you would care—" said Lady Lufton nervously. "I do know them pretty well. I used to play for," and she named one of the singers in whom the tradition of the German Lieder singing still lingered. "He was a great friend of my mother's," which offer surprised everyone, even her daughter Maria who being splendidly immune to music had never paid any attention to her mother's piano playing.

"If I would *care*," said Lady Cora adding in her enthusiasm, "*My Lamb*!"

Lady Lufton, entirely unmoved by this form of address, sat down at the piano, ran her fingers over the keys as novelists used to say, and looked to Lady Cora for a sign.

"Look here," said Lady Cora. "I'm not good enough," a statement which profoundly surprised her husband who had never yet known his wife be anything but superbly self-confident.

"Oh yes, I am sure you are," said Lady Lufton, which command as it were Lady Cora meekly accepted.

It occurs to us at this point that George du Maurier in Trilby describes his heroine as singing this same song and with magic in it. We cannot compete with him and shall only say that Lady Cora with her moving husky voice and Lady Lufton with her accompanying had brought some of their hearers very near to tears. Cecil Waring's eyes were fixed on his wife. The Marlings were looking at one another as if they each cared for the other a good deal—as indeed they did. And though it was not at all the kind of music the Brandons were used to, being devotees of the newest dance-music on gramophone records, and though neither of them knew German, something of the beauty made them very quiet. There was silence when the song had ended. Then Mr. Macfadyen asked Lady Cora if she knew any Scotch songs.

"Thousands," said Lady Cora, perhaps a trifle jauntily to cover her feelings. "You forget we are partly Fifeshire."

"It was not Fifeshire I was thinking of," said Mr. Macfadyen. "My mother was from Ayrshire. You would not be knowing Crail Toun?"

"*I* do," said Lady Lufton unexpectedly. "I had an Ayshire

nurse when I was little. Does it go like this?" and she half said, half sang a verse of that strange song with its mysterious double refrain of words whose meaning has long been lost, while Mr. Macfadyen sat spellbound.

"I think some drinks now," said Lady Cora to her husband, for a drawing-room must not have too much emotion. Lady Lufton quickly left the piano and resumed her usual look of being a little apart from the world though very ready to deal with county duties; which was just as well, for Lady Cora, feeling that a complete change of atmosphere was needed and one that would include the Brandons, began to ask questions about the Women's Institutes and what she might best do to help the very small branch at Lambton and so sensible and so interesting was Lady Lufton's advice that Peggy Brandon joined them to hear what it was all about.

"Of course the real head of the Lambton W.I. is Mrs. Needham, our Vicar's wife," said Lady Cora. "She is quite wonderful, especially when you think that her husband has only one arm. In fact she runs everything so well that all I have to do is to be their President and find people to talk. The one thing I will *not* do is to go for an Outing to Bournemouth in a motor coach from 8 A.M. to 8 P.M. in driving rain. I feel that the future Bart wouldn't like it."

"And the present Bart would forbid it," said her husband. "Do you know Mrs. Needham, Lady Lufton?"

Lady Lufton said she did and gentle though she was she nearly added From the Zeal of Mrs. Needham Good Lord deliver us, for the eighth child of the Deanery's tireless zeal was apt to flatten out all who came within her orbit. And then Lady Cora asked Peggy Brandon if they had one at Pomfret Madrigal, to which Peggy replied that they had and that the village people ran it almost entirely themselves, which Lady Lufton greatly approved and said she would like to come to a meeting.

"Oh, I *do* wish you would," said Peggy. "Our vicar's wife is the secretary and she is splendid. They are frightfully badly off and have two small children and are expecting another, but she never seems to mind. And her husband is so hard working and good."

"And frankly such a bore," said Francis, laughing. "They are one of Peggy's enthusiasms;" and his hearers did not feel comfortable.

"Could you possibly come to our next meeting?" Peggy went on with hardly any change in her voice. "Mrs. Morland is going to talk to us."

Lady Lufton said she had once met Mrs. Morland and liked her very much and would certainly come to the talk and say a few words if Mrs. Brandon thought they would like it, which pleased Lady Cora who had an organising mind and liked to see things happen under her guidance, and then the party began to break up. Cecil Waring, interested by some of Francis's remarks, asked him to come to lunch at the County Club one day soon. The telephone rang.

"I would wager sixpence that it's a crossed line again," said Cecil Waring. "Palmyra Phipps at the exchange has been on holiday for a fortnight and high time she came back. Hullo? Oh, it's you, Palmyra. Did you have a nice holiday?"

"Ever so nice," murmured Lady Cora as her husband exchanged badinage with Miss Phipps. "What is it all, darling?"

"Oh, thank you so much, Palmyra," said Sir Cecil. "Yes, they will be delighted. Yes, the dinner-party went off splendidly. Oh, it was your auntie that made the flan, was it? Tell her I had three helpings. And look here, Palmyra, if you see Margett anywhere, tell him the gutters want cleaning again. Yes, her ladyship is very well. No, I hadn't heard about Mr. Palmer's Alderney. Splendid. Good night. And that," he continued, putting the receiver down and addressing the company, "is the blackmail one has to pay for a decent telephone service. Ten minutes of chat when one would do. Oh, the message was for you, Oliver, at least for Maria. Your man couldn't get us, some muddle on the line, so he very sensibly rang up Palmyra. Your cocker has puppies; two black and a golden: one dog two females. End of message."

But instead of thanking him Maria ungratefully wanted to know whether it was two black bitches and a golden dog, or a black bitch and a black dog and a golden bitch, or—

"That's all," said Mr. Macfadyen.

"But look here, I did algebra in the Navy when I was a midshipman and I'll never forget it," said Cecil Waring. "Permutations and combinations. If you have three numbers you get six changes out of them."

"But not if two are the same," said Mr. Macfadyen.

"Well, hang it, they may *look* alike," said Cecil, "but they're different. I mean if you have xyz for your letters, there are three different letters."

"Conceded," said Mr. Macfadyen kindly. "But supposing you have two x's and one y, what then?"

"Have the two x's got to be the same thing?" said Cecil, who was beginning to see defeat staring him in the face but like the Royal Navy would not admit it.

"As a matter of pure argument, though mind you it would be an entirely fallacious argument," said Mr. Macfadyen, "there is no law against one of your x's being one thing and one being another. But there is the very good law, known to Euclid and other mathematicians, that one thing cannot be two different things. Let me make it clear. Say you call your two females x and your dog y. How will you know which x is which?"

"Well," said Cecil grudgingly. "Perhaps you are right. Yes, I see. If I say one black bitch, one golden bitch and—which of them was it that had two colours? I mean which were the two that were females?"

"The females are the bitches, you idiot," said Lady Cora.

"Yes, I know," said her husband rather crossly. "But which is the black one?"

"Well, darling, that is what Palmyra did *not* tell you," said his wife.

"If Lucy were here," said Maria Marling, alluding to her husband's younger sister Mrs. Samuel Adams, "she would say it was Rot. Come along, Oliver. We ought to be going and the sooner we get back the sooner we shall know whether the bitches are dogs or not and what colour if any. Can we give anyone a lift? Thank you, Cora. It was a heavenly party. Did Oliver tell you?"

"Not in so many words," said Lady Cora, "but bless you, it's bursting out all over him."

"Well it's not bursting out over *me* just yet," said Maria, looking almost enviously at Lady Cora. "But give me time," upon which there was a great embracing and kissing and Oliver said they really *must* go, as did the rest of the party.

"Tired, darling?" said Cecil Waring to his wife when he had seen their guests off from the hall door.

Only nicely, Lady Cora said, and what fun about Oliver and his wife and what a bore that Francis Brandon was.

"Admitted, as our nurserymaid used to say when Leslie and I were small," said Cecil, remembering his nursery days with his sister before his parents died and he went to sea. "But extremely intelligent in his own line and very useful to me. And a very pretty wife."

"As pretty as can be," said Lady Cora. "But I don't like to see a wife watch her husband to see if she is pleasing him," at which her husband protested.

"Oh yes, men all hang together," said Lady Cora, "and don't contradict me, or the future Bart will be born with a grievance against you. How very interesting it was to see Mr. Macfadyen come out of his shell. I'm glad Lady Lufton has him for a tenant. She might easily have had someone ghastly like that awful Geoffrey Harvey. Do you remember him the day I first met you, when we all came to look over The Lodge to see if it would do for Jeff and Isabel?" But this was merely a rhetorical question, for Cecil would never to his dying day forget his first sight of the girl who was standing in the sunshine on the gravel sweep. The sun had been in his eyes, but her elegant nylon-clad legs, her perfect figure, and her sleek dark head had conquered him even before he saw her face. "If only that poor Ludovic would get married. He looks so lost and wretched," but her husband told her to stop planning everyone's lives for them and come to bed.

"What a very pleasant evening," said Lady Lufton, as Mr. Macfadyen drove her homewards in his extremely comfortable car. "I don't know when I have enjoyed myself so much. I think it is charming of those young people to ask me."

"If I may say so, I feel much the same," said Mr. Macfadyen. "About myself, I mean. May I say something to you?"

"Oh do," said Lady Lufton. "But I do hope it isn't that dry rot again," for during the previous winter dry rot had been found in a room of Mr. Macfadyen's wing and though the builders swore they had stopped it, it moves in a highly mysterious way and like the common cold is one of those ordinary ills against which Science is powerless.

"No, not the dry rot," said Mr. Macfadyen. "It ill fits me perhaps, Lady Lufton, to presume to give you advice, but if you would go about a little more you would give pleasure to a great many people."

"But how?" said Lady Lufton, surprised and a little bewildered.

"Just that it gives your friends pleasure to see you," said Mr. Macfadyen, "and secondly, though I should have put it first, it does you good. I'm a plain man and I speak plainly. You gave great pleasure to everyone this evening and look all the better for it."

"Oh, the piano," said Lady Lufton, who appeared to be relieved that she could shelter behind that instrument.

"Ay, the piano, if you wish to put it in that way," said her tenant. "But I was thinking of you. It is not for me to intrude upon your private life, or to belittle your loss. And also—you said I might speak—what about your son?"

"Ludovic?" said his mother.

"The young lord," said Mr. Macfadyen. "He does his duty. He

sits in the House of Lords and has to be a lodger, so I am informed, with an elderly female relation. Not much of a life for a youngster. And he does all he ought to do here, on the estate and in the county," and he paused.

"And lives with an elderly mother," said Lady Lufton, with no bitterness, no resentment, but a weariness which for that one evening she had forgotten.

"I would sooner have lost half my money," said Mr. Macfadyen, careful not to exaggerate, "than that you should think I meant that," and as they were now within the gates of Framley Court he stopped the car in the drive.

"I didn't think you meant *anything*," said Lady Lufton, which non-committal statement appeared to help Mr. Macfadyen who continued, "Heaven forbid that I should criticise anything you do, but your son will marry some day and——"

"I am always wishing that he *would*," said Lady Lufton. "I should quite like to live at the Old Parsonage and then I could have the grandchildren over to play in the garden. There is a very good bank to roll down. But he doesn't."

"And I will tell you for why," said her tenant. "The callant is carrying a very heavy weight. His duties first. Then his grief. And then your grief. And he will never tell anyone. You told me I might speak freely."

"Oh yes, oh yes," said Lady Lufton. "I have been selfish," she said quite simply. "You see, when his father died, I was lost. Quite, quite lost. I do my Women's Institutes and try to keep up the place and think all the time if it is what would please my husband. And I suppose you would say that it doesn't please him to see Framley Court such a sad place. I expect you are right," at which simple avowal Mr. Macfadyen was in two minds about killing himself for his odious interference except that there was no way of doing it and not much room in the car to do it in.

"Will you do me a great kindness, Lady Lufton," he said, "and forget that we had this talk and forgive me, for it was well meant; and worse I cannot say," he added grimly.

"But I didn't *not* forgive you," said Lady Lufton, in mild surprise. "I only felt rather like the queen in Hamlet when Hamlet has been so really dreadfully rude and she says he has turned her eyes into her very soul And there she sees such black and grained spots As will not leave their tinct. And I am thinking how I can alter it."

She appeared to be so pleased with her literary allusion that Mr. Macfadyen hoped he had not hazarded his pleasant new relation with her in vain. He started the car again, drove up to her door, got out and gave her his hand to alight.

"I am *most* grateful," she said. "I will find out who Ludovic likes and ask them to dinner and make him look in the cellar. My husband knew a good deal about wine. You don't think I ought to give up the Women's Institutes, do you?"

Her pleading upturned face under a chill summer moon made Mr. Macfadyen feel that he had been a brute and she was an angel. But he only looked down at her and said that if he could help in any way, in *any* way, he repeated, she only had to say the word.

"I can't reform myself, you know," she said. "I'm too old. But I shall remember everything you said. And I shall ask everyone if they know of a little flat for Ludovic instead of that cousin. I suppose we could afford it."

"I am not in a position to judge of that," said Mr. Macfadyen. "Your lawyers would know, doubtless."

"I don't think lawyers know *anything*," said her ladyship with some vehemence. "Whatever you want to do they say is wrong and they take *weeks* to answer letters and then make you pay for them. I suppose I'm stupid. I really oughtn't to go on like this. If only—"

She stopped and Mr. Macfadyen thought, compassionately, that what she might have said was, "If only my husband were alive."

"Well, good night and thank you again for driving me. It does make a difference to go in a comfortable car," said Lady Lufton as she gave him her hand. "And you really will ask me to tea; won't you?" and then she went into the house. Mr. Macfadyen put his car away, went to his comfortable study or library or whatever one may please to call it, and with a comfortable whisky and soda sat down to deal with some letters. They were not business letters for, as he often said, when he shut the office door behind him he left his troubles there and very often by the next day they had solved themselves, but he had a considerable correspondence of a friendly nature with the great growers of fruit and vegetables, not only in England. And, as every successful Scotchman has, a perpetual trickle of letters from aunts, uncles and cousins of every degree in Scotland, to whom he was familiarly known as Jock o' London and by whom he was expected to honour the kinship by pecuniary help to the seventh degree of relationship. All these he dealt with, kindly in most cases and firmly in the case of his father's stepsister's nephew's son who had gone to the bad in Glasgow, consorted with what were little less than enemies of his country and appealed at least three or four times a year for financial assistance; usually once after the August Bank Holiday and once after Hogmanay, with lesser demands round about St. Andrew's Day and any other public festival that struck his fancy. The last begging letter from the unpleasant Rob McGuffog was lying on his writing-table. He read it again carefully. He considered his own past life in which he had striven to give honest service, to improve in his trade, to keep his mother in what comfort he could and be beholden to no man; and then after some thought wrote a letter to Messrs. Jarvie and Keelevin, Writers to the Signet, in Glasgow, empowering them to pay five pounds yearly, as from the present date, to Robert McGuffog of whose address the police would always be able to inform them, together with the information that any further demands upon the donor would result in the withdrawal of the allowance and the return of all letters, unopened, to the sender. This was a step that he had for some time been contemplating and what drove him to take it that evening more than at any other time, we do not quite know. There are moments when we feel that our kindness is only weakness; that to be bullied or blackguarded into charity is not true generosity; and that one might, even if a passably wealthy man as far as They have let us, spend one's earnings to better advantage. And the possibility of Rob McGuffog turning up at Framley, probably the worse for liquor, was one which he had often thought of with considerable distaste. If one had a kind landlord, it would be a poor return for his kindness to let that worthless Rob try to beg from him, as he would certainly do. And if for landlord he sometimes read landlady, it would be no more than Canning when he wrote that for Europe he might be desirous now and then to read England. After which he sat for some time apparently thinking of nothing at all till he suddenly realised that it was late and he was cold; and so went to bed.

Meanwhile Lady Lufton had gone upstairs to her sitting-room (for the drawing-room had been closed and dust-sheeted for some time now), where she found her son writing letters. As he got up to welcome her she suddenly—whether as a result of her talk with Mr. Macfadyen or because she had, as she so rarely did, been out in society and enjoyed herself, we cannot say—saw him with a fresh eye. Mothers, and we speak feelingly, are apt to have a kind of general impression of their children which becomes a fixed image. Because John or William was at one time like this or that, we go on thinking of him as he was. He changes, we do not notice the change or we rationalise it (if this pretentious jargon means what we think it means) and expect him to remain as, at a given time, he was. But mothers are veritable ostriches in their powers of self-deception. Now Lady Lufton had come to her road to Tarsus and in one moment the old Ludovic, the boy for whom she and her husband had thought and planned together, was not there. In his place there was a young man, not unlike their image of him, but as his mother with a pang of remorse saw, for the first time, a young man looking too sad, too burdened for his age.

"Darling, how tall you are," she said, sitting down by the fire.

"Not taller than usual, I hope," said her son, letting his long self down into a chair opposite her. "It would be too, too Jack and the Beanstalk," which phrase, most unlike his usual way of speaking, was obviously an echo of one of Clarissa Graham's affectations.

"No, not taller," said Lady Lufton. "But tall enough. I sometimes wonder, Ludovic, if you get enough to eat."

"My dear mamma!" said her son. "Of course I do. You always keep a good table, even under reverses. Excuse my way of speaking," he continued, "but it's the way Charles Belton and I talk sometimes, just for fun."

"I know. Just as your father and Old Canon Thorne, though of course he was *much* older than your father, used to talk like the Regency," said his mother, which her son said was pretty vague, but please she *must* not think he was starved, because he wasn't. Look at the eggs and the pig and one thing and another, he added vaguely.

"I didn't quite mean that," said Lady Lufton, "I was thinking of when you are in Buckingham Gate with cousin Juliana."

"Well, she *is* rather a stingy old beast," said Lord Lufton cheerfully. "But one can always go to a pot-house for a decent meal. The real difficulty is that one can't ask anyone to see one. I mean one wouldn't expect her to give one's guest a meal or anything, but of course she has my ration book as I live with her, so I can't get tea or sugar. It would be rather nice to have cups of tea sometimes. I did ask once, but she didn't at all like it, so I didn't ask again, and I didn't want to say anything or she might have written you one of her stinkers. But she's a good old thing on the whole."

Lady Lufton's sad, stormy face grew sadder as he spoke. Mr. Macfadyen's words rang in her mind. She looked at her son again as he sat between lamplight and firelight, seeing not the young man, inheritor too young of his father's title and responsibilities with all that the war might have meant behind him, but the little boy, the son after two daughters, outside whose nursery door she had often listened quietly lest his nurse might be unkind to him, whose night nursery door she would very gently open when he was asleep to reassure herself of his precious being. That little boy: and she had been false to her trust. Tears stung her eyes; but this was folly and she brushed them away so quickly that Lord Lufton, looking at the flames, did not notice.

"I have been thinking," she said, "that perhaps cousin Juliana doesn't quite understand young men. If we could manage a little flat—only then there would be the question of a housekeeper for you—I'm sure we could manage it somehow—there is some jewellery in the bank—"

"Oh, I say, mother, you can't," said Lord Lufton. "The girls ought to have that."

"Never mind the girls," said his mother with unusual spirit. "These are things of mine; quite, quite private. I shan't wear them again and they would be your wife's in any case."

"But what about the girls?" said Lord Lufton.

"Can you see Maria or Justinia wearing jewels?" said Lady Lufton. "Justinia only likes what she calls dressmakers' jewellery and Maria never wears anything except her grandmother's pearls. Now, my dear boy, do be reasonable."

More touched than any son would like to admit, Lord Lufton said anyway Parliament was having a nice long holiday and when he had to go back to that awful London he would look about for some digs, only he was afraid Cousin Juliana would be rather annoyed.

"Let her," said Lady Lufton with unusual spirit. "Your father was the kindest person I have ever known, and how he came to have such a selfish cousin I cannot think."

Lord Lufton gave his mother a heart-warming hug and asked what the evening had been like. Very pleasant indeed she said. Maria was looking very well and so was Lady Cora and it had reminded her of Italian Old Masters. Her son asked what ones, to which his mother replied that if he ever read his Bible he would know what she meant.

"Do you know, mother," said Lord Lufton, "the girls and I always thought grandpapa had written the Bible."

His mother, who had long ago stopped being surprised at anything her children did or thought, asked why.

"Oh, I suppose it was because he read the lessons in church," said Lord Lufton. "And on Sunday morning he often said he must go over the lesson, so we thought he was correcting his homework."

Lady Lufton said she supposed everyone thought about things in a sort of way they could understand, at least, what she meant was——But her son begged her not to explain.

"I have a kind of idea, right at the back of my head, mother," he said, "and if anyone interferes with it, it will vanish. But I *think* I see what you mean," to which his mother very sensibly replied that if it was *really* an idea then it would come back again, and they must go to bed.

Lady Lufton had enjoyed her evening so much, and it was so long since she had enjoyed anything, that she found it difficult to settle to the boring task of getting to bed. She had often, as many of us of an older generation do, envied the young who drop all their clothes on the floor, don't bother to clean their faces, and fall into bed, there to spend a refreshing and dreamless night. But one cannot do this by wishing to. To anyone who has been taught in youth by Nurse, or Nannie, or Nana, to fold her clothes neatly, put her shoes side by side, wash her hands and face (if she had her bath in the morning), or have a bath (not to lie soaking in but really to *wash* in), it is normally, mentally, physically impossible to leave one's bedroom like the morning after an air raid and one's pillow messed with powder and lipstick. As Lady Lufton, pleasantly tired, conscientiously put everything straight, removed what we can only call her token make-up, brushed her hair and made all suitable preparations for bed, there came into her mind a horrid picture. Not long before her husband's death, he had asked her to invite Captain Fairweather R.N. for the night, as the gallant captain was giving a talk to the Framley Sea-Scouts, a small but devoted band who practised their seamanship on the river and had a week somewhere on the coast every summer. Some mention had been made of his wife, daughter of Mr. Birkett the ex-Headmaster of Southbridge School, and she was included in the invitation. Those who have known and disliked the beautiful Rose Fairweather do not need to be told what Lady Lufton's old housemaid, one of the Podgens family, thought of that ravishing creature. While the guests were seeing the gardens with their host after breakfast, the housemaid had asked Lady Lufton to come and look at the room. It was a revolting sight. Lipstick on the pillow and sheets, powder liberally strewn everywhere, nasty bits of cotton wool lying about and, incredulously counted by Lady Lufton, no less than fourteen bottles and jars and containers of various kinds.

The old housemaid, removing the guests' sheets, had said darkly that it would take more than soap to clean up *that*, my lady, and Lady Lufton had gone downstairs, really shocked, to find Mrs. Fairweather looking like an angel in an Italian picture; and if she was also quite incredibly silly, doubtless a good many angels are. It takes all sorts to make any kind of world. What Captain Fairweather thought, no one would ever know. It was the opinion of his mother-in-law that he had completely subdued his Rose from the day of their marriage to adore him and eat out of his hand but had thought it wiser to leave her one outlet for her incurable and revolting untidiness, behind the scenes.

Mr. Macfadyen was as good as his word and asked Lady Lufton if she would have tea with him on the following Saturday, convening also Mr. and Mrs. Samuel Adams, for Mr. Adams had acquired the controlling interest in Washington's

Vimphos, Corbett's Bono-Vitasang and Holman's Phospho-Manuro, though Mr. Holman was the nominal owner of the combine; and to a man interested in market-gardening, as was Mr. Macfadyen, artificial manures were of considerable importance.

The afternoon was cold and stormy, which most people will agree was a good thing, effectually checking, as it did, the English habit of taking tea out of doors, or in a horrid garden-room, under conditions of acute cold, draught, damp and discomfort. So it was to Mr. Macfadyen's sitting-room where a comfortable fire was burning that the Adamses were shown by a quiet elderly maid.

"I say, Mr. Macfadyen," said Mrs. Adams, whose abruptness of manner had been slightly softened by marriage, or at least so those who knew her best maintained, "do you mind our bringing Grace Grantly? Her father's our clergyman and she awfully wanted to see your garden. You know her mother has got Miss Sowerby's Palafox Something that old Lady Norton wanted."

Mr. Macfadyen said any friend of Mrs. Adams's was welcome and shook hands kindly with the uninvited guest.

It is some time since we have seen much of Grace Grantly. At the time when Mr. Adams first took the Old Bank House at Edgewood she was in the last stages of her Barchester High School career. She had now firmly learnt shorthand and typing, had refused to learn economics on the reasonable ground that they were silly, but had plunged deeply into civic and county matters and at present had a job at the Barchester Central Library. There was good blood and there were good looks in the Grantly family, who usually married one or other or both of these qualities, and there was that indefinable thing, breeding. Of all these Grace, so her old friends observed, had a very large share. It was not the cold, vacant beauty of the Griselda Grantly who had married the Lord Dumbello of the day, as is told in county history; it was not the late-flowering quieter beauty of Grace Crawley, the poor parson's daughter who had married old

Archdeacon Grantly's son; perhaps something of both, added to her mother's excellent gentleman-farmer background of a family which, like Mr. Wickham's over Chaldicotes way, had kept the noiseless tenor of its way not without the quiet distinction that often accompanied that manner of life; for accompanies we hardly dare to say, now, though we would like to say it with all our heart. But at any rate Grace had become, from a hoyden at home and an uninhibited rebel at school, one of those young women who help to preserve tradition and the deeper decencies. All of which, rather unreasonably, though we think we see what she meant, made Mrs. Grantly feel that Grace would never get married.

Then Lady Lufton came in, a little nervous, but far less nervous than she would have been the night before her talk with Mr. Macfadyen which had had a very good effect on her, making her feel that there were still things she could do to help people, and greeted Grace very kindly, placing her at once.

The tea, provided by Mr. Macfadyen's Scotch housekeeper, was as good as the Lufton cows' milk and butter and the housekeeper's scones and cakes and home-made jam could make it, and so liberally was the table spread that when Lord Lufton accompanied by Charles Belton came in, there was a silent feeling of relief, for by long privation all our older stomachs have become so shrunken that we can only be really greedy with our eyes. The younger generation likes its devitalised food for it has never known better. Yet it still has immortal longings in it, almost unknown to itself, and when the two young men had begun upon the good food, they ate like shipwrecked mariners, to the grim pleasure of the housekeeper as she brought fresh tea.

"I say, Lord Lufton," said Grace.

"Yes, Miss Grantly?" said Lord Lufton.

"Oh, all right, Ludovic then," said Grace. "Have you any spare books? I mean books you don't want?"

Rather taken aback by this sudden request Lord Lufton said

why, adding that there were no less than three copies of Creasy's Decisive Battles of the World somewhere about the house and as far as he was concerned she could have them all.

"Miss doubtless needs them for curl-papers, my lord," said Charles Belton, who had been rather quiet.

"Oh, shut up, Charles," said Grace. "It's not curl-papers. It's the Barchester General. They're having a Book Drive Week and we've all sworn a kind of oath at the Central Library to get as many as we can. Only they must be the kind of books people in hospital would *like*."

Rather amused by her enthusiasm, Lord Lufton asked what kind of books.

"Oh, you know, the kind of book you'd like to read if you were in a hospital," said Grace. "*Not* War and Peace," she added with some violence. "I think Tolstoy's *ghastly*."

"Faith, my lord," said Charles, "the wench speaks well. If ever I open one of his musty tomes, sink me!" and he took an imaginary pinch of snuff and flicked his jabot.

"I say, that's wrong," said Lord Lufton indignantly. "You're being eighteenth century, not nineteenth. You ought to have said, "Ouida, Miss Grace. Or Pater perhaps" and burnt with a hard gem-like flame," at which Grace and Charles had the giggles while the Adamses looked on with a kind of benign want of comprehension and Lady Lufton felt that she could talk just like that if she liked and do it better.

"If you really want some books, Grace," she said, "we will look for some after tea and after Mr. Macfadyen has shown us the house. You shall all come back to my half and have some sherry. You had kindly offered to show us your improvements, Mr. Macfadyen."

Obedient to this hint their host got up and took them over his part of the house. Lady Lufton had come prepared to feel melancholy, though this to her did not present much difficulty, thinking as she so often did of the old un, as her daughter Justinia had once irreverently said, but when she saw how very slight the changes were and always, she had to admit, for the better, her heart almost sang to see the rooms as they used to be before the war, taxation, her husband's death and then ever fiercer and more senseless taxation had turned them into cold sheeted and shuttered corpses of what they had been. The floors were well polished but not too slippery. The old furniture shone and its brasses were like gold. Curtains had been mended and in some cases replaced with very suitable material. The rather primitive electric lights which had lingered as things so often do in an old family house, at least fifteen or twenty years behind their time, had been discreetly replaced. Outside, even in the cruel light of a grey cold autumn dusk, the lawns were velvet, the flower beds still showing colour, the hedges trimmed.

"I hope you like it, Lady Lufton," said her host. And then, looking at her, he saw that her eyes were wet. "I beg your pardon, my lady," he added. "I have been inconsiderate. I had thought to have given you pleasure, but——"

"Oh *please*," said Lady Lufton. "It *is* pleasure. It's only that I thought how my husband would have *loved* to see the place like this, instead of going to bits under his hand. And you have had the Canaletto cleaned, haven't you? We couldn't afford it," but so simply was this said that no criticism was implied.

Charles Belton, looking back from the doorway, thought what a very good figure Mr. Macfadyen made in that room; not quite a Raeburn perhaps, but better than a Watson Gordon—more like a Chantrey bust of himself perhaps, with a good forehead and the lines of work and purpose in his face. Mr. Adams, who under Mrs. Belton's guidance had acquired a better and sounder taste than his wife Lucy would ever have, was also impressed by what this Scotch gardener, like himself of lowly birth, like himself having owed and repaid much to his mother, had done, and he generously expressed his feelings, which certainly pleased Mr. Macfadyen, though he had no intention of showing it. Then they all went to Lady Lufton's quarters. Here she and the older guests talked in her sitting-room while the young people went book-hunting. It was of course inevitable that the two men, with various business interests in common, should find each other better company than the ladies, but Lady Lufton, who had been a well-practised hostess during her husband's life, rushed between the men (tropically speaking) like a well-trained sheep dog and having driven Mr. Macfadyen into Lucy's pen as it were, herself cornered Mr. Adams with whom she had a very satisfactory talk about the clinic for occupational strains and pre-natal stresses established by him at his Hogglestock works and Lady Lufton said she would come and talk to them about the various forms of emergency crib, from the bottom drawer (if one had a chest of drawers) to those very large stout cardboard boxes in which our everlastingly kind trans-Atlantic cousins were still, with unparalleled kindness and generosity, sending food to the rationed and overtaxed serfs of THEM.

"But, if you will excuse my saying so, Lady Lufton, there was never anything to beat those old Japanese dress-baskets," said Mr. Adams. "My old mother—and when I say old, I'm a lot older myself now than she was when she died, poor creature—had one of those baskets and I spent a lot of time in it when I was a baby. And if my old Dad came in a bit the worse for liquor which to do him justice was pretty well every night, she'd whip me up in the basket and shove it through the fence. The woman next door had lost three children with the scarlet fever and she'd look after me. Life's a funny thing, Lady Lufton, and that's a fack," and Lucy, whose wifely or third ear heard her husband while she was talking to Mr. Macfadyen, knew that he was moved, because except under the stress of some emotion he never said Fack now. And then, as their talk flowed gently on, she returned her attention to Mr. Macfadyen and each saw every reason to admire in the other a person of intelligence with an apparently inexhaustible capacity for hard work.

The younger people then came surging back with a large

wicker clothes-basket full of books and making a great deal of noise.

"It's awfully kind of you, Lady Lufton," said Grace. "We've got a marvellous collection. I expect you'd like to see them first in case you want any," but Lady Lufton said if it was the books in the green dressing-room and the attic she knew she didn't want them.

"There's a whole lot of Miss Braddon," said Grace, "and some Rosa Nouchette Carey and a whole lot of Nat Gould. And there's a lot of bound volumes of the Strand Magazine. Can you really spare them?"

"If Ludovic agrees," said Lady Lufton. "They are his books now," at which words her son became crimson and damp with embarrassment, but managed to say that he would love Grace to have them, but only if his mother approved, so Grace, who was very practical, accepted them on the spot. Lady Lufton then asked after Grace's parents and her elder sister, now Mrs. Colin Keith, formerly a worker at the St. John and Red Cross Hospital Libraries when Lady Pomfret was County Organiser.

"Oh, she's very well, thank you," said Grace. "Oh, if you know anyone who wants bed and breakfast and would mostly be away at the week-ends, will you remember her? They bought a house because it was cheap and in good condition, but it's too big for them even with the nursery, so Eleanor's going to take a lodger. She'd rather have a man. I'd rather have a woman," said Grace, "because one could ask her to do sitter if they want to go anywhere on Nanny's night out, but they think a man. They are both awfully nice and they would give the lodger dinner if he wanted it when they're alone and charge a bit extra. I don't think they're asking enough," and she named a price.

Mrs. Adams then collected her husband and Grace and took them away. Lady Lufton thanked Mr. Macfadyen with what he considered unnecessary gratitude for so simple a thing as keeping her house in decent order and so he too went his way. And later on Lady Lufton and her son had some very good rabbit stew for supper.

"Which is really one *great* advantage of living in the country," said Lord Lufton, "because rabbits cost nothing," to which his mother replied that there might not be rabbits in London, but then they couldn't eat all one's young vegetables and some fresh wire would be needed down by the hedge. Lord Lufton said he would see to it and then asked in a tolerably good imitation of an offhand manner what his mother thought about what Grace had said about her sister wanting a lodger, and then felt he might have put it more elegantly. His mother said wistfully that it did sound nice and she was sure they could afford it because even if it was nearly twice as much as Cousin Juliana was asking it did mean he would get more to eat. And not that beastly Kornog for breakfast said her son, his tongue suddenly loosened. If there was one thing, he said, he couldn't *bear* it was what people called cereals. They were so cold and one had cold milk with them.

"I *know*," said Lady Lufton, "and people always forget to crisp them in the oven and they are like damp leather. Juliana must have an inside like a millstone. I know Lady Bond told me that when Juliana goes to stay with her there is such a *fuss* about her getting the right kind. But she is a kind of cousin of your grandfather's and I wouldn't like her to feel offended. Her father was that old Lord Mickleham who married a Victorian beauty with lots of money, a Miss Foster," and though Lord Lufton was highly uninterested in his cousin's family he listened carefully, because whatever anyone may say families do matter, and the sooner one gets them by heart the better. And on this they went to bed, both vaguely comforted by the hope of a change of lodging for the young lord.

CHAPTER 2

It happened a few weeks after the Warings' party that Mr. and Mrs. Miller decided to ask a few friends to dine with them in their commodious Parsonage of St. Ewold's in the parish of Ullathorne. A hundred and more years earlier Ullathorne Court, the great house of the parish, had stood in real country and when the Ullathorne gorse was to be drawn the followers of the Barsetshire hounds knew they were in for a good run. But after the death of old Squire Thorne and his elder sister Miss Monica the place had passed to distant cousins who had sold a good deal of land on the Barsetshire side and so, little by little, the town had covered the woods and fields, and what had once been a country church to which young couples from the city would often walk out on a Sunday for the afternoon service, which was then at three o'clock, was now the church of a large respectable suburb of the better-to-do workers. Many of Mr. Adams's higher staff; accountants, heads of departments, technicians (to use a horrible neologism which has at any rate the advantage of embracing pretty well anything and not binding one down to accuracy), lived there and many of his co-father-in-law Mr. Pilward's staff from the brewery; and there was a tennis club and a bridge club and an amateur theatrical club and every thing handsome about it. And instead of corn now growing where Troy town stood, there were asphalte and concrete and streets and shops where corn once grew and cows once grazed, and St. Ewold's had been improved. Let us leave it at that.

The vicarage had been lucky in that the glebeland had not all been sold to the speculative builder and in summer it was still possible to sit in the garden and not see a sign of a red roof, so well was it guarded by its trees. It was in fact quieter now with motor buses than it had been with the once new-fangled horse tram, and the main road for roaring motor coaches was nearly a quarter of a mile away. In the days when Mr. Arabin was vicar, before he went to the Deanery, there was a back room upstairs from whose window one could look across the river and across the fields, beautifully studded with timber, to the city and the cathedral with its white heaven-pointing spire. All this had gone, swallowed up in suburbs; only, after the leaves had fallen from the great elms—many of which themselves had fallen by age or the axe—a glimpse could still be caught of the spire, especially on a day of heavy dark grey thundery summer clouds when one shaft of sunlight touched its tip.

Owing to the activity of Archdeacon Grantly, at that time the rector of Plumstead Episcopi, the house had been put into excellent order for Mr. Arabin and apart from the bathrooms which had later been made out of two small bedrooms, it still looked much the same. The cellar had been so well re-roofed, re-walled and re-floored that a hundred years or so had shown very little deterioration, but the kitchen range had long since been bodily removed, boiler and ovens and all, and a gas cooker installed, with a coke furnace in the scullery for domestic hot water, so that when Mr. Miller said indeed, indeed his lines had been cast in pleasant places, we think he was speaking the truth.

Nor was he less lucky in his church which had escaped the earlier stage of Neo-Gothic restoration owing firstly to its secluded position and secondly to the temper of the incumbent the Hon. and Rev. George de Courcy, and finally had been protected by the age and determination of the last vicar, a Mr. Tempest, of good Barsetshire family and with private means, who had utterly refused to have a Children's Corner or to use the Revised Version or Songs of Praise, had given a handsome silver cross for the altar to replace a very hideous brass one and had put the fine old lectern, removed by his predecessor to make what he called a Vista, back in its right place, besides replacing some green glass by white glass at his own expense. And when we add that the church had a chest of unusually beautiful vestments and some fine communion plate, we do not wonder that Mr. Miller said Indeed, indeed the Lord had blessed him in his latter end, though the Dean, who had a considerable fund of common-sense, said a man of Miller's age had no business to be talking of latter ends yet.

Although Archdeacon Grantly had expressed himself very strongly on the necessity of a long table and had even offered to pay the cost of enlarging the dining-room to that end out of his own pocket, his offer had not been accepted. A round table still stood there, though the room was otherwise a good deal changed. After Mr. Arabin's translation to the Deanery it had remained much as it was till a wealthy vicar had panelled the living-rooms and staircase in pitch pine and hung Arundel prints everywhere. To him had followed a devotee of Morris wall-papers and furniture of solid uncomfortableness. The wall-papers were of such good material that no vicar liked to change them until between the wars a cheerful incumbent from the North had white-washed everything and introduced several of those immense easy chairs made of sham leather for elephants and hippopotamuses to lounge in. These he had taken with him to his next cure of souls and his successor, Mr. Miller's predecessor, a bachelor and a student, had felt quite happy so long as he had a bed he could sleep in and a few chairs he could sit on and put books on. So when the Millers came they had a free hand and as neither of them had any particular taste and each valued comfort chiefly for the other, the house never had much character of its own. But this was made up for by the shining goodness and kindness of the Millers who were so much liked that the church was filling again. Indeed there was almost a snobisme de'église in the parish and the fashion of having one's visiting card in a little brass frame on one's pew had crept back into use, including that of the secretary of the local Golf Club whose card bore the interesting legend, "Major F. G. Baker, M.C. with bar."

The occasion of the dinner-party was the twelfth anniversary of the Millers' wedding day and being a dozen seemed to make it a rather special occasion, though Mrs. Miller said a baker's dozen would be even better. To which her husband, whose admiration and love increased with every year, said she looked younger now than she had on their wedding day, which indeed was possible, for twelve years of steady happiness had certainly not aged the ex-companion Ella Morris, and having no children (not that even the most Gampish inhabitants of Pomfret Madrigal had expected them to) seemed to her almost a kindness of Providence, for her husband was the rising of her sun and its setting. For him she bore with unwilling or over-zealous young women who came calling themselves cooks and left her almost worthy to be called such; for him she was President or Secretary or Treasurer of almost every committee interested in good works; for him she exquisitely mended, washed and ironed his surplices, cared for the vestments and cleaned the church silver with slow patient care; for whatever people may say about labour-saving silver cleaning, there is nothing like the slow, patient circular rubbing that gradually almost melts the surface of the silver till it is fluid and all inequalities of scratch or slight dent are equalised.

The party was to be purely clerical; the Dean and Mrs. Crawley, Canon and Mrs. Joram, Colonel the Reverend Edward Crofts and Mrs. Crofts and lowest in the hierarchy the Reverend Theodore Parkinson and Mrs. Parkinson from Pomfret Madrigal. And if any of our readers have been thinking that Mr. Parkinson's name was Edward on account of his being

Teddy for short, we may say that we had occasionally thought the same thing ourselves, but Something told us that it was Theodore, just at seven p.m. on a Sunday evening as this at present leaves us.

Mr. Parkinson has improved a great deal since we first met him as a theological student at a Deanery dinner-party in the summer of 1946. Partly owing to his determination to be worthy of his high calling, partly because his father had been a bookseller in a small way which gave his son something to look up to, and a great deal because his wife, the ci-devant Mavis Welk, daughter of a highly respected undertaker, was so shiningly and unselfconsciously good that almost any man would have been the better for her company. And now with Harold (after grandfather Welk) and Connie (after Mr. Parkinson's mother) and the shadowy third who was to be Ella after Mrs. Miller or Josiah, greatly daring, after the Dean, Mrs. Parkinson had as much as it is good for one woman to do. Her various older women friends who had noticed this tried in different ways to help and Mrs. Parkinson was truly grateful to them, but kept a kind of independence. Like Mrs. Amos Barton she worked from morning to night with never a word of complaint, but unlike that lady she had good health and a cheerful disposition, and as for dying in childbirth and leaving the unfortunate Connie to look after her father (and probably never be married herself in consequence), we may at once say that no such thing is going to happen, for Mavis Parkinson was not the woman to allow it.

Only one thing might have marred a friendly relationship between Mr. Parkinson and his nearest neighbour Mrs. Brandon, now Mrs. Joram, which was his modern church leanings. But with great good will on both sides a modus vivendi had been evolved. Mrs. Brandon had gently stopped coming to the Morning Service because she said it was no good going if the clergyman did it all wrong, and went to Evensong instead; and Mr. Parkinson stuck to the old and well-loved form of Evening

Service. Since her marriage had taken her to the Close the Parkinsons had missed her greatly and all the more that Stories was not as pleasant as it used to be. The Vicarage children played with Francis's children and Francis was a churchwarden and did all he should do in subscriptions, but when Harold Parkinson was found making faces at his younger sister and frightening her and explained it as making faces like Mr. Brandon made at Mrs. Brandon; and when the Parkinsons had dined at Stories and noticed that Mrs. Brandon was not only pretending not to notice her husband's sometimes distinctly offhand way of addressing her, but at the same time trying to smooth what he said away, the Parkinsons felt what they hoped was not a Pharisaical gratitude for their own domestic happiness and peace.

As was inevitable when two or three of the clergy and their wives were gathered together in one place, the talk fell upon the Palace and its projected cruise to Madeira, a subject which had exercised the whole of the Close for some time and had by now spread over most of the diocese. There was a general opinion, pretty freely expressed, that anything which removed His Lordship and his wife from the Palace for a few weeks was in the nature of an Act of God, taking that phrase in a grateful spirit for benefit received rather than—as we are too apt to do—bracketing it with battle, shipwreck, famine and the Labour Government.

If, said Mr. Miller, Providence, moving in ways not understood by us, did see fit to make war break out—which heaven forbid—indeed, indeed it would be a crowning mercy to feel that His Lordship was safe in Madeira.

"Excellently put, Miller," said the Dean. "And if, which again I say God forbid, the war should last for some time, the benefit would be even greater. And his lordship's gifts would not be wasted for there is, or was when I was there, an English church."

Colonel Crofts said that on one occasion when he was on leave from his regiment in India he went home by the Cape and had found that the Church of England in Madeira, at any rate at that time, was not very well attended, to which Canon Joram, who had also visited the island, added that the little cemetery was at that time rather neglected.

"It would be rather wonderful," said Mrs. Joram in a religious voice, "to think of a Bishop being buried in Madeira. I mean it would raise the standard—at least I don't mean that, but I mean if a bishop was buried there they would *have* to keep it tidy, wouldn't they?"

Mrs. Crawley said not if it was the Madeirans or Madeirese or whatever one called them, who did nothing as far as she could see except row about in boats bothering people to buy things, but doubtless the English colony would do something. Like Keats's grave, said Mrs. Joram, adding reflectively that she wondered if bishops *really* ordered their tombs before they were dead.

There was a brief silence while some wondered what on earth she meant and others what the answer was, and Mr. Miller as host felt responsible for a remark which might hurt Mrs. Parkinson. Not that he suspected her for a moment of being snobbish about her father's hieratic, well-ordered profession, but he wondered if Mrs. Parkinson would think that he was uncomfortable and so feel uncomfortable herself. Which is just the silly, self-tormenting kind of thing we all do again and again, judging ourselves (quite unreasonably) more hardly than we judge our friends.

"I mean not St. Pancras, but something rather like it," said Mrs. Joram in a voice of earnest self-explanation.

The Dean's bushy eyebrows almost stood on end with exasperation. "Our dear friend," he was just beginning in his most cathedral voice, evidently prepared to blast his old friend with an allusion to fools in their folly, when Mrs. Parkinson, going pink in the face, said nervously, yet with a little air of authority, "St. Praxted I think Mrs. Joram means. I did Browning the year I left school."

Whether Mrs. Parkinson had slightly confused the name with Thaxted, where practices characterised by her father as

ROMISH go on, we shall never know, for the Dean who much to the Archdeacon's annoyance considered himself and indeed was an excellent man of business and intromitted, as the Archdeacon had bitterly said, in diocese affairs with what old Canon Thorne had called an acharnement of ultra-viresity, felt that the situation must be dealt with, as he had dealt with the thousand situations of his busy and useful life, besides enabling him to indulge in one of his favourite hobbies, conversation arising from, or more often forced by him towards his own excursions abroad.

"Ah!" said the Dean. "Our old friend Santo Prassede! How well I remember that day. Spring in Florence! Ah," but before he could think what was to follow, his wife unkindly said that Florence wasn't in Rome and Mr. Miller, being a good host, said Indeed, indeed, it seemed not improbable that we might have to face another General Election before long, which universal solvent at once attracted the whole company. Had the Parkinsons not been present, the talk would have been unconfined, but no one knew what their politics were and no one wished to hurt their feelings, so everyone was careful. But in spite of their carefulness Mr. Parkinson was silent and though his wife smiled very charmingly her smile did not seem of any particular colour. The Dean, who always said he liked a hearty exchange of opinions, with a mental reservation that the opinions should be the equivalent of his own, noticed Mr. Parkinson's abstention and bent his bushy eyebrows more than once in his direction.

"Well, Parkinson," he said across the table, "we haven't heard what your views are. Nor your wife's."

"Now, Dr. Crawley, don't be a bully," said Mrs. Crofts, who had always kept a warm place in her regards for the Parkinsons because her husband had coached Mr. Parkinson in Latin when he was a theological student. "Tell us what *your* views are."

The Dean said, rather crossly, that his views were the views of all men of good-will, to which Mrs. Crofts replied that most people really were full of good-will, but it came out in different ways. Some were Buff and some were Blue.

"Like Pickwick," said Mrs. Parkinson unexpectedly. The Dean said "Ha" but appeared not altogether displeased.

"I am," said the Dean, preparing to enjoy himself, "a Churchman first and foremost. His Majesty the King is the Supreme Head of the Church and Defender of the Faith—" at which there was a kind of murmur of God Bless Him, for the nation had for a short time been united under the shadow of His Majesty's ordeal, grasping at every word of hope, keeping vigil about His palace, praying for Him in churches publicly, each continually in his own heart privately, "—and," the Dean continued, not displeased with the reception of his words, "by that I stand or fall. Never shall my vote be cast for men who have, some of them in their earlier years, some during their whole career, openly derided a monarch precluded by his very kingship from reply and uttered words of contempt for the whole British Empire; men who now allow any lesser breed without the law to spit upon the Flag of England; for Britain," he added, "I will *not* say."

"And what is so humiliating," said Mrs. Joram, "is that one doesn't know exactly what they are."

There was a second's silence while the party grappled with this statement.

"That, my dear Mrs. Joram," said Colonel Crofts, "is a remark worthy of our friend Mrs. Morland. And higher praise in one way of speaking I cannot give," he added, not wishing to hurt the speaker. "But, if I may use almost your own words, I don't know exactly what you mean."

"I think I do," said Mrs. Parkinson, going pink in a very becoming way. "I mean when people say Persians one thinks of Alexander the Great and people walking sideways shooting lions with arrows."

Mrs. Crofts said she quite agreed, for which support Mrs. Parkinson looked grateful. And, said Mrs. Crofts, when people said Egyptians she always thought of people who were quite flat sideways and had a full-face eye in a profile face and little striped aprons and rather horrid. Or, added Mrs. Miller, children with flies in their eyes, which enabled the Dean to get in a few words about a conducted tour in a dahabeyah (or however it is spelt) up the Nile. And then the talk returned to the prospects of a General Election, and the great question of whether it was a Good Thing or not, and everyone talked at once till the decorous clerical party became almost rowdy, with the exception of the Parkinsons. This Mr. Miller, in his strong benevolence of soul, very soon noticed and asked Mrs. Parkinson under cover of the Dean's booming, whether she took much interest in politics.

"Oh *yes*, Mr. Miller," said Mrs. Parkinson. "Father belonged to the Conservative Club at home and I was a Young Conservative and so was Teddy. We had some splendid discussions and once a gentleman came down from London to address us, and he said he'd never had an audience ask such intelligent questions. We didn't get away till after eleven that night and the last bus had gone and I had to walk home, so Teddy said he'd see me to the door, so really, you see, we have Mr. Churchill to thank for it. We did think of calling Harold, that's our boy, Winston, but Teddy said better not in case it seemed stuck up, so we called him after Dad, but we gave him Winston for his second name. It's a lovely name," and though the name, apart from its glorious associations, did not seem to Mr. Miller as wonderful as all that, he felt sympathetically that the Parkinsons had done the right thing.

"And when we came to talk it over," said Mrs. Parkinson, continuing her artless tale, "we thought it was just as well we'd decided to call him Harold, because the boys at school might have called him Winnie and he'd have felt it."

"Poor little chap," said Mr. Miller, "so he might. Boys can be very unkind. I know my name, Justin, was quite troublesome to me at my prep. school. Dustbin they usually called me till I blacked two of their eyes—I mean two eyes of two of them—at least it was one eye of each. I hope he is happy at school. Where is he?"

"Oh, the village school," said Mrs. Parkinson, "but he's going in for a scholarship when he's old enough and he *loves* fighting. Father is quite a boxer," which description of a highly respected undertaker interested Mr. Miller very much and he told Mrs. Parkinson how he had rowed stroke for Lazarus when he was a young man.

"But there has been a sad falling-off under the present Master," he said. "Men reading P.P.E., and preferring hikes or rambles or tea with female students to rowing or cricket."

Mrs. Parkinson asked what P.P.E. was as she'd like to get it at the library if it was nice, which so flummoxed her host that he was rather glad to be claimed by Mrs. Crofts; but his kindly liking for Mrs. Parkinson was increased. And then he asked Mrs. Crofts how things were going at Southbridge. If, said Mrs. Crofts, he meant the Vicarage, everything was well in hand and her husband could really do with a curate if people *would* go on wanting to be visited, to which Mr. Miller replied that if they got the curate the people would probably stop wanting to be visited.

"All the same," he said, "I think it is a pity that visiting has gone out. Old Canon Thorne when he was Vicar of St. Paradox, the church near the castle mound, used to keep two curates at his own expense with instructions to do nothing but visit, and every Monday they came to lunch and had to tell him what they had been doing. "Visit, visit," he used to say. "The church can look after herself if you look after her people." But of course he had private means," and he sighed wistfully, though not for his own, as they were quite adequate and luckily under a Trust which was of an active and progressive nature so that Mr. Miller, who would happily have invested, as so many of us have done, in Government Bonds which are not only heavily taxed but have a rapidly falling value, found himself not at all badly off except that They took far too much of it.

"Still," said Mrs. Crofts, at once wishing to cheer him, "even if you had the curates they couldn't do much good if they did call. All the women are doing the housework and haven't time to talk or be talked to, or they are out shopping, or fetching their children from school, or doing a part-time job. By the way," she added, seeing that Mr. Miller still looked a little depressed, "have you heard about Mr. Birkett's book?"

Mr. Miller said no bad news he hoped, for the late Headmaster of Southbridge School was much liked and had become by sheer force of character a considerable person in Barsetshire.

"Why did you think it might be bad, Miller?" said the Dean, most unfairly deserting his partner for possible scandal.

"Indeed, indeed, I was not conscious of such a thought," said Mr. Miller, "but in these times, with what I can only describe as men of bad will in high places, one often wonders," and then, not seeing any particular end to his sentence he stopped, not embarrassed but rather helpless, which made his wife look at him with a protecting love that twelve years of happy marriage after years of separation had been strengthened.

"I daresay," said the Dean, "but one must wonder *something*," which might have been considered a little brusque, though not ill meant, but he, owing to his position as head of the anti-Palace faction, was privileged.

"It was only that his book is to come out this autumn," said Mrs. Croft, hastily adding before any further intromissions could take place, "You know Lord Aberfordbury, the one that was Sir Ogilvy Hibberd."

There was a general murmur to the effect that though knowing quite well who he was no one of the company cultivated his acquaintance.

"Well," Mrs. Crofts continued, "he is the kind of very religious person that isn't religious at all. You know what I mean, Edward," she said across the table to her husband, who said his wife meant that his lordship arrogated to himself the right to be religious in his own way, which included preaching subversive doctrines which people called Lay Sermons in well-known churches and even cathedrals.

"And Mechanics' Institutes," said Dr. Joram, veiling his dislike quite unsuccessfully under an archaism.

"His Lordship," said the Dean, skillfully suggesting that he used the title in poorly veiled contempt, "did once occupy the pulpit in the Cathedral. Not with my good will, but it would have been impolitic to insist upon my right to exclude him. After he had preached with what I can only call arrogance, self-righteousness and Leftism, he was leaving the cathedral and stopped to congratulate the choir on their rendering of the anthem."

"How *dared* he!" said Mrs. Joram indignantly. "He hadn't even paid for his seat."

"The choir," said the Dean, unmoved by this outburst, "were patriots to a man. Without one word they walked past him, looking straight in front of them, and out by their own door. The Precentor who was near at hand said he had never seen a man so put down."

"But that wasn't very kind," said Mrs. Parkinson when the hum of applause had subsided. "I mean I daresay he was really sincere."

Most of those present were touched by her simple faith but the Dean, who liked snatching brands from the burning, said firmly that a man like Sir Ogilvy Hibberd—he begged that gentleman's pardon, Lord Aberfordbury he should say—was constitutionally incapable of being sincere. Besides, he added, it had come to his certain knowledge that his lordship's son, an ungracious young man, was a Director of the National Rotochrome Polychrome Universal Picture Post Card Company and drawing a salary beyond the dreams of avarice, which salary was in large part, and doubtless with the connivance of the Commissioners of Inland Revenue, so heavily charged with Expenses against his earnings, that he paid about a third of what he ought to have paid in income tax, which reminded Mrs. Crofts very pleasantly of a booklet, published by a very reputable newspaper some years previously, with the full list of capital investments of each member of a Socialist Government.

"What *is* Socialism?" she said, suddenly, but the Dean said rather crossly that her question was like Tolstoy writing a book called What is Art, which led to a very pleasant general discussion of Impostors and Humbugs in all walks of life. Mrs. Parkinson on being pressed as to her particular form of humbuggery said she pretended she adored excursions with the Women's Institute, but really she always felt sick in a motor coach all the time, while Mr. Parkinson said he far too often said there was some good in everyone, which he secretly knew to be a lie about some people.

"And mind you," said Mr. Parkinson, who was vastly enjoying his evening, "I know I hadn't ought to say it, but there are some people that I don't *want* to find good in. After all, we say in the General Confession that there is no health in us, so I daresay other people think it too—about us, I mean. And sometimes I can't help thinking it about them. Or leastways, I do try not to think it, but there it is, so I *have* to think it. It's all very difficult sometimes, sir," he added, turning to his ex-coach Mr. Crofts.

The Dean said Evil was a force to be recognised and fought, so if one saw Evil, or felt Evil one ought actively to dislike it.

Like the three monkeys, said Mrs. Parkinson sympathetically to Mr. Crofts, who after a minute of complete bewilderment seized her meaning and smiled, thinking as he did so what a very nice couple they were becoming; and good Christians he added to himself, and would willingly have said it aloud, for his was the straightforward simplicity that one finds not infrequently in an old soldier and he was as little self-conscious about his faith as a man can be.

Mrs. Miller now rose, looked at her ladies, and began to shepherd them to the drawing-room which was comfortable and highly undistinguished, for neither she nor her husband had any particular taste and were barely conscious of their surroundings provided they had chairs and tables and fires and those things required for the level of every day's most quiet needs by sun (when available) and electric light. But just as they were going across the hall there was a slight scuffling from the kitchen quarters and through the service door came Mr. Wickham, the Noel Mertons' agent, with a peculiar bulge in one of his pockets.

"Good evening, Mrs. Miller," he said. "I hope I am not a nuisance, but I saw old Attlee was speaking tonight and I had a couple of rabbits I thought you might like, so I left them with your cook—she's not a St. Ewold's girl but she seems to understand rabbits all right. Where does she come from?"

Mrs. Miller, who took Mr. Wickham as calmly as she took everything else, said she was from Grumper's End, but she was a Bodger, not a Thatcher.

"Plenty of Bodgers when you get up into the beech woods," said Mr. Wickham. "You get 'em in Bucks too. They were the fellows that rough out the wood for chair legs and so on—live near the woods mostly and camp out there when wood cutting is on. I had a word with her and she's going to do those rabbits in red wine. I had half a dozen bottles with me that I got cheap off a fellow in Silverbridge, Clem Stringer, you wouldn't know him. Horsy fellow that drinks. His great-uncle or someone got into trouble over a cheque in Silverbridge, years ago that was."

By this time Mr. Miller, hearing a noise in the hall, had come out of the dining-room. He greeted Mr. Wickham warmly and said they might as well all go to the drawing-room together and listen to the nine o'clock news. Not that Mr. Miller was a wireless addict, nor was his wife, but being as unselfish as people can be while remaining human, and knowing that large numbers of people looked upon 9 p.m. as an almost sacred hour, he made a point of as it were forcing the wireless upon visitors, barely taking a denial even if they didn't really want it.

"You know the P.M., if one can call him that, is speaking tonight," said Mrs. Crawley. "I do wish he wouldn't mumble so. I wonder what he wants."

The Dean said abstractedly the croaking raven was bellowing for revenge, and then made a rather servile and entirely insincere public apology for applying such words to a gentleman who could only be described as a bleating and rather inaudible sheep.

"Now then, Dean," said Mr. Wickham, taking from the pocket of his shooting-jacket a bottle of Cointreau and putting it among the coffee cups, "you know as well as I do he means business this time. General Election probably. They've stood out against it till even some of their own chaps are a bit sick. The Cointreau's all right. Got it from a pal of mine who lives in Jersey. He's got a working arrangement with Customs and Excise."

The whole party acquitted itself manfully over the liqueur, while Mrs. Miller like a good hostess kept her eye on the clock and at two minutes to nine turned on the wireless, for it was one of those machines that like to take their time and purr like a large lion for some time before they begin to give voice.

What the news was on that particular night we do not know, nor really did anyone else, for the anticipation of what might be to come made it impossible to care about Persians or a Greater Atomic Output; and the anxiety about His Majesty's health was lulled.

When the news was finished the Prime Minister announced that Parliament would be dissolved on October the fifth and a General Election would be held on October the twenty-fifth, and for once his unimpressive voice gave unfeigned pleasure to a great many people not only in Barsetshire, but all over the world: excluding of course the very large number of people to whom it gave no pleasure at all. Mrs. Miller turned off the wireless.

"Well," said Mr. Wickham after a slight pause, "I daresay he means well."

"And a more damning remark you couldn't make," said Colonel Crofts, to which Mr. Wickham replied that was exactly why he had said it and he would have to be getting busy.

"Are you standing, then?" said Mrs. Parkinson.

"Lord bless you—sorry if I'm trespassing, Parkinson—" said Mr. Wickham, "but I wouldn't stand for the best heifer at the Royal Show. It's a mug's game. Look at Adams. He was an M.P. and he chucked it. He's a business man and he knows what's what. But I'll do a good spot of electioneering. I'll show 'em what's what," to which Dr. Joram replied that if Mr. Wickham splashed the drink about too much he might find himself in trouble. There were, he said, very definite limits to the amount of bribery and corruption at which the law would tacitly connive.

Mr. Wickham, after reinforcing himself with another Cointreau which he characterised as syrupy cat-lap, said that he was perfectly fly and too old a fox to be caught treating people after hours, and he supposed he ought to be getting on.

At that moment the telephone rang.

"It's for you, Mrs. Joram," said Mrs. Miller. "Your man wants to speak to you."

"I cannot *tell* you how nice it is," said Mrs. Joram, not hurrying to the telephone, "not to have to think something is wrong with one of my grandchildren when the telephone rings. When I was at Stories with Francis and Peggy, I always thought something awful had happened if anyone rang us up when we were out together. It never did of course, but one does feel so sick. Yes, Simnet, what is it?"

The peculiar cracklings and splutterings that too often represent the voice of a friend, or in this case a trusted servant, burst out of the earpiece.

"Oh dear," said Mrs. Joram, removing the holders a little further from her ear. "How very sad, Simnet. Still I daresay it is just as well. We must all do what we can you know. I am sure the Dean will be most interested. Good-bye. And three guesses," she added to the company, with what her son Francis used to call her mysterious mischief face.

"Now, what *is* it, Lavinia?" said Mrs. Crawley, who as the

Dean's wife and a prolific mother and grandmother felt she had a right to make the demand.

"Oh, it's the bishop," said Mrs. Joram and paused, partly we fear with a view to making an effect. "But he doesn't *have* to vote, does he, because he's in the House of Lords," at which preposterous suggestion even the least politically minded had to laugh.

"Nobody has to vote," said the Dean, rather sharply, "but it is every citizen's duty to vote."

"And in Australia they're fined if they don't," said Mr. Wickham. "For the Federal election that is. When I was on the Australian station a pal of mine, Tom Buckley up at Baroona, one of the best, got fined good and proper for not recording his vote. And as he had to vote in order of preference for seven fellows that he'd never heard of and didn't like if he had, it seemed a bit hard. But Jim Brentwood at Garoopna and a fellow called Troubridge, I've forgotten the name of his station, and I put up the money to pay it and then we put up as much again for a few drinks and made a night of it. Those were the days."

"Yes, yes, Wickham, doubtless they were," said the Dean rather crossly, "but we are waiting to hear what Mrs. Joram has to tell us."

"Me?" said Mrs. Joram, in unfeigned surprise. "Oh! Simnet you mean. He only rang up because he heard from one of the Palace servants that the Bishop had cancelled his cruise because of the election."

"Silly old bloke," said Mr. Wickham. "What difference would it make?"

Mr. Parkinson, getting hotter and pinker (we mean physically, not politically) as he spoke, said that whatever he might think privately about anyone, he didn't see how they could act differently than they did when it was a question of principle; and of one's duty, he added. Most of the party, respecting his serious view of the matter, made no comment. The Dean remarked in an abstract way that anyone who was, if his son-in-law the

Reverend Thomas Needham who had once met the Bishop on the steamer from Portsmouth to Ryde could be trusted, entirely allergic—a neologism which he would not have used except for a person so eminently suited for it as his Lordship—entirely allergic, he repeated, to the motion of a ship, had a very clear case for avoiding such an experience again though, he added, he thought his Lordship might have been better advised to obtain a postal vote and, having set his hand to the plough, for after all a ship was as it were a plough of the ocean, leaving a furrow behind it, not to have withdrawn it; all of which led to an extremely ill-informed conversation about postal votes and how various people had become disfranchised, or disenfranchised, at the last election by making a muddle of it.

"Excuse me," said Mr. Parkinson, somehow making his voice heard through the clamour, though he had not raised it, "but there is one point—" and he paused.

"And what is it?" said Colonel Crofts, very willing to help his protégé.

"Well," said Mr. Parkinson. "His Lordship is a Liberal."

There was a respectful silence.

"Well," said the Dean. "Thank you, Parkinson. That point had quite escaped me. Ha!" which majestic monosyllable reduced his hearers to awed silence, except for Mr. Wickham who said that unfortunately a Liberal vote had exactly the same value as a Conservative vote. It wouldn't be a bad idea, he said, to make a law that it took two Liberal votes to equal one Conservative. It might learn 'em to see sense he said.

"But, Mr. Wickham, that wouldn't be fair, would it," said Mrs. Parkinson, at which everyone began to laugh, but so kindly that Mrs. Parkinson began to laugh too and then the conversation was quietly steered by Mrs. Miller from controversial topics; not difficult when all those present had pretty well the same loyalties.

"And I must say this for the P.M.," said Mr. Miller, always the kindest of men, "he did say that we all earnestly pray for his

Majesty's speedy restoration to good health. And so we do," at which words there rose a kind of loyal murmur and the words God bless him, earnestly spoken.

"I know what it was like when Teddy had the pewmonia," said Mrs. Parkinson, her eyes a little misty. "It was touch and go the doctor said and I couldn't help thinking how awful it would be if he died, just when the people were getting quite keen on coming to church. There wasn't much time for praying with the children both so small and we'd only just come to Pomfret Madrigal, but I did my best and then the telephone was out of order, oh it was dreadful. And I really hadn't time to go to church but I did pray in the kitchen and then Mrs. Thatcher from Grumper's End sent her niece over to help, so I felt quite ashamed."

Before this artless tale everyone felt moved without quite knowing why, unless that simple goodness has a shining quality to which we are not quite accustomed, a quality that makes us conscious of our own shortcomings. Mr. Miller and the Dean began to discuss Mr. Fanshawe's small and scholarly work on Tibullus lately published by the Oxbridge Press; Colonel Crofts and Dr. Joram compared notes on the fertility rites in Mnganga-land and Sikkim; while Mrs. Joram got herself up to date about Grumper's End from the Parkinsons. Mrs. Crawley and Mrs. Crofts talked about Mrs. Morland's new thriller from Madame Koska's dress shop, while Mrs. Miller went to see about tea for her company, ably seconded by Mr. Wickham who had a knack of knowing at once where everything lived in other people's kitchens; while he attributed to his naval experiences. Not that she was servantless, for she had a real cook who lived in and two cheerful girls from the Housing Estate; but they went home at night and the cook went to bed and locked her door in case anyone should try to Get Her; a fate which she expected in every place and at every time, from her bedroom or the scullery at the Vicarage to the crowded bus stop outside the Barchester Odeon and the very well-lighted bus that brought her home.

But so far not a single fear had been realised and it would have been an unusually courageous ravisher who cast his eye on her as she was extremely plain and the same size all the way down with ankles that overflowed her sensible shoes.

Mrs. Crawley, as senior matron present, asked Mrs. Parkinson several searching questions about her young family, expressing great approval of what she heard and also of what was obviously to occur in the Parkinson family. So kindly did she ask about the two children and the shadowy third that Mrs. Parkinson was emboldened to ask whether, in the event of its being a boy, she thought the Dean would mind their calling him Josiah, adding rather timidly that they could call him Joe for short, to which Mrs. Crawley replied that unless the Parkinsons had anyone in mind with stronger claims, the Dean would like to be one of the godfathers, which made Mrs. Parkinson go pink with pleasure.

"And—I know you won't mind my saying this—" Mrs. Crawley added, "I have so many grandchildren that I can usually get clothes that are grown out of before they are in the least worn out. If you would care—" and Mrs. Parkinson, almost crying with gratitude and the very good dinner and the Cointreau, said it would be like heaven not to have to worry quite so much about the children's clothes.

"Because the prices go up all the time, Mrs. Crawley," she said earnestly, "and with shoes it's *dreadful,* because Connie's feet are quite a different shape from Harold's and shoes wear out at once. I do think a government that calls itself Labour did ought to think about children's shoes, Mrs. Crawley. I do hope the new baby will be a girl because she can wear Connie's things, but if it's a boy he'll have to wait so long for Harold's, because Harold is growing all the time. And I've cut up everything I could, Mrs. Crawley, for nice frocks for Connie and you'd love her, I'm sure. I suppose you couldn't come to Pomfret Madrigal could you and see them. Our Women's Institute is having a Meeting this month and Mrs. Morland is going to tell us how to write books. I wish I could write a book, but even if I could I don't think I'd have much time, with the children and Teddy. And I think father will be there. He would very much appreciate meeting you if you wouldn't mind. You know he's an undertaker—a very respected one."

Mrs. Crawley said, quite truly, that it seemed to be the one profession left where people were properly trained for their job and took pride in it, which pleased Mrs. Parkinson very much.

"Thank you so much," said Mrs. Miller to Mrs. Crawley when that lady told her about the invitation. "That young couple are as good as they can be and it isn't easy for them. Justin thinks very highly of Mr. Parkinson, but she's the better man of the two I think. I wonder what Mrs. Morland's talk will be about," to which Mrs. Crawley, who was very fond of her old friend Laura Morland, said whatever it was it certainly wouldn't be about what the gifted authoress said it would be about, as she was quite incapable of sticking to the point.

CHAPTER 3

Any doubts that might have been felt as to the imminence of a General Election were by now dissolved. In the first place by Mr. Attlee's broadcast though even this did not wholly convince the extreme right wing and Sir Edmund Pridham, doyen of the county in years and good service, said the worst of fellers like that lot was that you never knew where you'd get 'em; a statement whose truth became an Act of Faith with all rightly thinking men, though most of these would have had to admit if pressed that they hadn't an idea what Pridham meant. In the second and far larger place by His Majesty's Proclamation of the Dissolution of Parliament.

The Times, always majestically cautious, contributed leaders on Links with Canada, India's first General Election, Constituencies with peculiar names, the Manchester Dock Strike (recommending that the workers should be more loyal to their union leaders and the union leaders show more confidence in the workers) and Guy Fawkes; the square article on the top right-hand corner of the same page was about the Monsoon season in the Himalayas with special reference to Mount Everest which was as usual in process of being attacked by a reconnaissance party one of whom in this particular instance weighed fifteen stone and appeared to have been used as a half-way house when fording torrents; while light relief was afforded by letters on such diverse subjects as the wages of Hotel Staffs, Share-

Owning Democracy and Birth Rate in Asia, in each of which it was conceded that while on the one hand there was much to be said for one side yet, if the matter were looked at with the judicial eye, there was much to be said for the other side. The Lord Mayor received the president, vice-presidents and members of the Fédération Internationale de Football Association (sic) at the Mansion House and the ship of state, temporarily captainless and rudderless, lurched on her way as usual, while Sybil's Nephew easily disposed of Stymphale (a French horse, poor fellow) at Newmarket and—according to the *Times* Racing Correspondent—his victory, together with that of Monarch More, gave great pleasure to their father, Midas; though what their respective mothers felt was not mentioned.

By an extraordinary piece of good luck Mrs. Crawley was having a small sherry party at the Deanery on that afternoon, namely Saturday October the Sixth Nineteen hundred and fifty-one, which enabled all right-thinking (in every sense of the word) people to enounce the most loyal and in many cases quite addle-headed sentiments. But for the moment even loyalty was temporarily obscured by the horrid news that Lady Pomfret was bringing the Hon. Mrs. George Rivers, the rather unloving wife of a cousin of Lord Pomfret's and author of a number of very successful novels on the rewarding subject of Not So Young Woman Has Comeback With Young Man.

"It isn't Lady Pomfret's *fault,* of course," said Mrs. Crawley, explaining the situation to some early arrivals. "They always have her to stay because she is a relation—at least her husband is. Her daughter married that nice Lord Harberton down in Shropshire and her son is a sort of artist. He belongs to the Society of Fifteen and they have exhibitions somewhere."

The Archdeacon said he remembered the young man once at Pomfret Towers. A very uncouth person, he said.

"I wouldn't even say uncouth," said Mrs. Morland joining herself to the party. "I would say, just horrid. I mean rude and selfish."

The Dean inquired, with a tinge of scholarly sarcasm, what exactly was the distinction that their dear Laura was proposing to make.

"Well," said the celebrated novelist, settling her felt hat (for the county was by now in its shabby tweeds and its last year's autumn hats) more firmly upon her very tidy hair, "I think uncouth is too *good* a word. I mean it isn't nasty enough. A person could be uncouth and yet you could rather like them, but Julian Rivers you could not possibly like. He has a rather soft beard that never gets any longer," and she looked round for sympathy.

Sir Edmund Pridham said he quite agreed. If, he said, a young feller must have a beard, let him *have* a beard. In his father's time a lot of young fellers had beards, pretty well all of them in fact. His own uncles, old Alfred Pridham, had never cut his beard since it first began to grow.

Mr. Miller from St. Ewold's said Indeed, indeed, a Nazarite, which caused Sir Edmund to glare at him for contempt of court, but he was naturally tolerant to all those weaker than himself and merely asked why. Nazarites, said Mr. Miller, did not allow scissors to touch their hair; and when he said scissors he must be understood to mean any form of steel, or other metal, or indeed anything capable of cutting.

Sir Edmund, rather ungratefully, said why hadn't Miller said that before. "Read it in the first lesson only last year," he continued, "but my memory's not what it was. Where the dickens does it come? Sounds like the sort of thing St. Paul might say, but he'd only be the second lesson. Meddlin' feller. Tellin' women not to cut their hair. He'd have liked you, Mrs. Morland. Just his style," at which the well-known novelist, who was a modest creature with no particular idea of herself, said she hoped not, because she was sure he bored everyone *dreadfully* about his missionary journeys.

"Excuse me, Sir Edmund," said Mr. Parkinson who had come over on his bicycle, "it's Numbers, chapter six, about the fourth or fifth verse. I did ought to know exactly, because I was reading it last week, but sometimes one forgets."

"That's right, Parkinson," said Sir Edmund, relieved that this point had been settled. "But why the dickens were you reading Numbers last week? It's not in the lessons for last Sunday."

Mr. Parkinson was heard to say that he had got as far as that; and then looked round helplessly.

"I know!" said Mrs. Morland. "You *read* the Bible! I've been meaning to read it for *years*. I mean right through, and then start at the beginning again, but there are so many places where one gets stuck, like Numbers—I don't mean *your* bit, Mr. Parkinson, but those long chapters about families and the ones about their journeys, though I suppose now with aeroplanes they could have done it all quite quickly. But it is really so *useful* that we *ought* to read it."

She pushed some straying hair back and looked round, as one who has nailed his thesis to the church door.

"What do you mean useful, Mrs. Morland?" said Mr. Parkinson; not at all unkindly, but much attracted by the peculiar thoughts and expressions of the popular novelist, which of course to her old friends were so familiar that mostly they took them for granted as part of dear Laura.

"Well," said Mrs. Morland, assuming a serious, even studious look, "I mean things that are *useful*. Especially in Proverbs. There is one that says that anyone who blesses his friend with a loud voice, rising early in the morning, it shall be counted a curse to him, and I always think of that when Stoker is banging things about in the kitchen long before breakfast. Only it is more a curse to *me*, which isn't fair."

Her audience were by now enthralled, waiting to hear more. The Dean remarked that there was a verse about braying a fool in a mortar with a pestle, but he did not wish to appear to apply those words to their dear Laura, because he felt that no amount of braying, or indeed anything else, would make her foolishness depart from her. Mr. Miller looked agitated, for his gentle mind did not quite understand the state of extremely friendly warfare in which the Dean and Mrs. Morland lived. Mrs. Morland noticing this, as consciously or unconsciously it was her business to notice the trifles that make up our lives, and wishing to reassure Mr. Miller, remarked, "My desire is that mine adversary had written a book" and looked round as proudly as a cat with her kittens to see the effect produced.

The ensuing silence was broken by the Archdeacon, who was celebrated for having no sense of humour though an excellent clergyman and highly efficient man of business, asking why: adding that his admiration of the book of Job had always been tempered by its extreme improbability.

"Well, because I would hope that someone would give it a bad review," said Mrs. Morland, sticking firmly to her point. "Not that I have any adversaries so far as I know, except of course the Government, or ought one to say the late Government, but if I had, it would be a great comfort to see it slated; and by a very young man who was very conceited and knew nothing, or by a woman who was obviously a Mixo-Lydian or something of the sort," at which point she began to laugh and her hair sympathetically began to shed its pins, just like Tittymouse and Tattymouse.

"I'm only an old feller," said Sir Edmund, "but I've read my Bible every night and every morning, all through the cubbing season too, and there's another text I often think of: Oh that my words were written: oh that they were printed in a book. You know, Miller," he continued, addressing his old friend as one who might have some influence in higher quarters, "I've written my recollections of the Boer War, but no one will look at them. I don't say they're literature, but it's all Bible Truth. I've sent them to one or two of these publishing fellers but I don't believe they read them. I'm a simple kind of feller, but I *would* like to see it in print. Well, that's the way the world goes," and then Lady Silverbridge, she who was once Isabel Dale the writer of very good thrillers under the name of Lisa Bedale, came in and all attention was turned to her. Not altogether because she was a Countess and very beautiful and had supplied an excellent baby who would in the course of time be Duke of Omnium and had every intention of producing more scions of the ducal house, but because her husband had been nursing Barchester ever since his marriage, as the formally adopted candidate of the Conservative party.

"Jeff is coming if he can," said Lady Silverbridge to Mrs. Crawley, "but he has a meeting. I do wish one knew what was going to happen," and there was a kind of general murmur of assent to this, in the middle of which Canon Joram and his wife, formerly Mrs. Brandon, joined the party. The Pomfrets followed hard upon and the atmosphere became political with almost more noise than talk after the fashion of most parties.

When everyone had had some sherry and the original guests some more sherry, for the Dean was generous with his wine partly by nature and partly, we must admit, to show how poorly he thought of the Palace who had turned the beautiful mahogany wine-cooler into a receptacle for some very dull ferns, the Dissolution of Parliament inevitably came up again and the noise became as deafening as only a small party of well-bred people can be. Mrs. Crawley asked Lady Pomfret whether Mrs. Rivers was coming, to which the Countess replied that Mrs. Rivers had gone to the Liberal Committee Rooms and would come on as soon as she could.

"Not my fault, nor Gillie's," said Lady Pomfret resignedly. "You know what Hermione is like. She says one ought to know both sides before one makes up one's mind, which I call silly. The thing is to stick to what you've made up your mind to. No, Dr. Crawley, don't say prove all things. It unsettles one and it is no good being unsettled. Hermione is simply being *extremely* trying and it does worry Gillie so."

"Look here, Lady Pomfret," said Octavia Needham, eighth child and (rather to her parents' relief who ought to have taken matters in hand earlier) youngest daughter of the Deanery, wife of the Vicar of Lambton, "I'd like to speak to Mrs. Rivers when she comes," and the zeal of a long and determined line of clerical ancestry burned in her eye as she spoke. "I've been talking all over the place for the Conservatives and I know all the answers."

And, Mrs. Crawley thought dispassionately, that was exactly why Octavia, though respected and slightly feared, would never be greatly loved by her fellow citizens. Still, to her one-armed husband she was perfect, and if he could bear her, and if her increasing likeness to the Bishop's wife in dress and manner did not apparently dim his affection, she was not unworthy of it, being a most devoted wife and sensible mother, bringing up her young to be cheerful, self-reliant citizens of the Brave New World, and would almost certainly land Tommy in a Bishopric, as a good daughter of the parsonage should. And then she turned to meet late-comers, Noel Merton and his wife from Northbridge, she who was Lydia Keith.

"You will forgive us," said Noel in his deep pleasant voice. "I have only just got down from London."

"It's Morristown, isn't it?" said Mrs. Crawley.

"How flattering of you to remember," said Noel. "Yes, I was allowing my possible future constituents to heckle me in a large cinema with an average of twenty buses and trolleybuses per minute shaking the building to the foundations. I cannot think why I am doing it."

"Ambition," said Lydia his wife; not unkindly, not critically; rather with a loving dispassionate attitude to a child who wants his own way. "We don't know if we want to get in or not," she went on, as Noel passed further to speak to the Lord Lieutenant, the hard-working, harassed Earl of Pomfret.

Mrs. Crawley was as fond of Lydia as she had time to be of anyone outside her daughters, with their husbands and their children, and her two sons, both advancing rapidly in their University and Schoolmastering careers, carrying their wives and children along with them. And Lydia had been Octavia Needham's great friend at the Barchester High School. Mrs.

Crawley had sometimes wondered if all was quite well with Lydia and then, as Noel was now a K.C. and high in his profession and Lydia looked handsome and well, she decided not to think of it.

"We saw Mr. Wickham in the Close," said Lydia, speaking of the Northbridge agent. "He said he might look in later and he asked me to give you a bottle of frightfully old brandy. I put it in your little sitting-room because it's too good for a party."

Mrs. Crawley thanked her and said they would open it later when some of the people had gone and thought inside herself that Lydia would not be the worse for a thimbleful. But guests saying good-byes claimed her attention and Lydia passed on to find Octavia. By now the crowd had considerably diminished and one could almost hear what one's neighbor said. Simnet, the Jorams' invaluable butler, who had lent himself to the Deanery for the occasion, came to ask Mrs. Crawley if he could do anything else.

"Yes, Simnet," said Mrs. Crawley. "Mrs. Merton has left a bottle of old brandy, a present from Mr. Wickham, in my sitting-room. Will you open it?"

"Thank you, madam," said Simnet. "And, if I may make the suggestion, not bring it in till the party had slightly diminished. It is—" and he named a date which our ignorance forbids us to mention, and without waiting for an answer made a kind of major-domo's inclination expressing that he knew his place and being the best butler in the County (where alas very few were kept now), would always see that the gentry kept their proper place too.

"By the way, madam," he added, looking towards the window, "I fancy that I see the Honourable Mrs. George Rivers making for the Deanery. If I might suggest, madam, I will not let loose the brandy till the Honourable Mrs. George has gone. It might be just what is wanted when that event has occurred."

This zeal for her house affected Mrs. Crawley a good deal and she thanked Simnet for his suggestion. As he went away her eye caught Mrs. Morland's and she had the great comfort of knowing that her feelings were shared and felt quite brave when Simnet returned with Mrs. Rivers.

"I have had *such* an afternoon," said Mrs. Rivers, dispensing with the formalities of greeting her hostess. "Really *most* interesting. One wonders if the Liberal point of view isn't perhaps the *real* solution. Such a fine tradition. Something of real value in the present times."

To most of those present the only answer which presented itself was Don't be silly, but this one cannot say in one's hostess's drawing-room. Lord Pomfret suddenly looked more tired than ever and his Countess glanced anxiously at him.

"Do you know," said Octavia Needham, in the voice and with the manner that ran every worthy committee within her parish and a good deal further, "that in the last General Election wherever there was a three-cornered contest the Liberal vote was practically always the same as the Labour Majority. It didn't get them anywhere and it got Us out. Like pigs cutting their own throats—"

"Really, Octavia!" said her husband, though secretly we think rather as a sop to Mrs. Rivers than from any real wish to make a protest.

"—and I'll bet anyone ten to one that nine-tenths of them will forfeit their deposits this time," Octavia finished.

"I wonder," said Mrs. Morland, "who gets the deposits. I mean where are they deposited?"

The Dean begged his old friend not to be so wilfully foolish.

"Yes, but *where*?" said Mrs. Morland.

"I cannot think," said Mrs. Rivers, "that these things really matter. But if you consider the question there is but one answer."

The Dean inquired what question. Mrs. Crawley, glancing at Lord Pomfret saw with concern that he was quite grey with fatigue, but it was hardly her place to interfere when his wife was there, so she held her tongue.

"Well," said Mrs. Rivers, "look at Gladstone."

"But he was *dreadful,*" said Mrs. Morland, pushing back her hair in a very unbecoming way. "He chewed thirty-two times and jumped on his bath-sponge. I wonder when people began having sponges. One somehow doesn't imagine Queen Elizabeth or even Charles the Second having sponges. I expect one could find one in Shakespeare."

The Dean said would she kindly explain herself.

"Well, if you had the Shakespeare Concordance—Charles and Mary Cowden Clarke—" said Mrs. Morland didactically, "you would know that he used practically *every* word and lots that people don't know now. So it must be there. I expect Charles the Second just had things like dish cloths and threw them away when he had used them once. I did know a Liberal member and he joined the Labour party and I asked him if he did that because he thought the Liberals hadn't any future and he said Yes before he could think. And then he didn't stand for Parliament next time."

Mrs. Rivers said to Mrs. Crawley that the Liberals were putting up a very strong list of candidates.

"Bet you five shillings that ninety per cent of them lose their deposits," said Mr. Parkinson, most unexpectedly.

"Well, I am just the Floating Vote," said Mrs. Rivers, ignoring this remark as she got up, "and possibly I shan't vote at all. Oughtn't we to be going, Sally? I am sure Gillie is tired."

Through long habit of self-control the Pomfrets did not look at each other, nor show any sign of emotion. After a few words of thanks to Mrs. Crawley Lady Pomfret took her husband and her husband's cousin away and we are thankful to be able to say that Mrs. Rivers left Pomfret Towers next day. Not for her home in Shropshire where the Honourable George Rivers still did everything that an increasingly taxed landlord can do for his people, but for her flat in a nasty little street, formerly called Duck's Mews and, we believe, the very same mews where Charles Ravenshoe had once sat on an upturned barrow and watched the magpie pecking at Lord Ballyroundtower's coachman's wife's heels as she hung out the clothes; now renamed (for reasons best known to no one except the very silly people responsible for it) Duke's Close and all arted up, as the Vicar's wife at Southbridge had said at Mrs. Keith's working party in the happy days when England was at war under her Great Leader and at union with herself, with shrimp pink and acid green and bright orange and dead bay trees in tubs and some striped awnings and no through ventilation anywhere and a very doubtful supper club at one end: from which flat she proposed for the next few weeks to cadge invitations from her friends and harass her publisher Mr. Johns, of Johns and Fairfield, and to finish her new novel about a woman who thought she had Found Love in a young writer who had written a play which ran for one night at a kind of theatre-club all about how one must be BRAVE in Love, which included everyone being as nasty as possible to everyone else to express one's real Self.

Lady Silverbridge, having waited for her husband as long as was decent, also took her leave and could be seen from the Deanery windows driving herself away in her little car.

"When I was a boy," said the Dean, "the Duchess of Omnium drove in a closed landau in winter and an open landau in summer. For Barchester she used the brougham if she had no one with her and sometimes for the Palace Garden Party she had the victoria. I don't mean this Duchess—her mother-in-law. The Dean at that time was a Dr. Robarts, a bachelor of limited means but a connoisseur of wine. He made a translation of the first book of the Aeneid in rhyming couplets. Extremely bad they were," after which array of facts, almost worthy of Mr. F.'s aunt, the Dean said "Ha," and worked his large mouth in a kind of grim smile, which softened as Simnet came in with Mr. Wickham's brandy.

The party had by now reduced itself to the Jorams, the Millers, Mrs. Morland and Mr. Parkinson, for Octavia and her husband had gone back to Lambton to take the Girl Guides and the Boy Scouts whose respective heads had gone on a "course," to use a word that may mean anything. Mrs. Morland was looking with sympathetic interest upon Mr. Parkinson, as it was quite obvious that he was torn between one form of shyness which made him want to go back to his safe vicarage as soon as possible and a second which made him unable to say good-bye; which state of things becoming apparent to Mrs. Crawley's practised hostess-eye, she asked him if he would stay to supper, adding that everyone else was staying too.

"Well, Mrs. Crawley, I don't mind if I do," said Mr. Parkinson, which ungracious words are so common a form of thanks today that we doubt whether Mrs. Crawley particularly noticed them. "You see," he continued, addressing himself to Mrs. Miller, with whom he always felt safe, "Mavis was doing the washing today and she said if it was fine she might be able to get the ironing done too, so I thought I'd have a bit of something in Barchester to save her getting supper. There's a place in Barley Street where they stay open till nine and you can get very nice baked beans on toast. Mavis and I make our principal meal when the children have their lunch as a rule and then we have sardines or something for supper and eggs when the fowls are laying. Mavis has got four now and Mr. Welk's—that's her father's—principal assistant is a wonderful carpenter and if he ever comes to see us he always brings some nice bits of wood, so he put up a really first-class hen-house for us. Mavis is going to buy a few more hens out of the housekeeping money and lay eggs down next year. She really is a wonder, Mrs. Miller."

Mrs. Miller, who had always taken a very kind and practical interest in her successors at Pomfret Madrigal, was touched by this artless tribute and said something kind to Mr. Parkinson about his wife's good qualities, which made his thin lined face light up. Too thin, too tired, thought Mrs. Miller, and wondered whether he got enough to eat, but with her usual good sense reflected that if anyone went short in the Vicarage it would be the Vicar's wife whose children were too young to notice; and her husband much the same for that matter. And now Mrs.

Parkinson was going to keep more hens and her father's principal assistant had built a hen-house; probably of coffin boards or whatever it is they have to use for coffins now; three-ply Mrs. Miller idly thought, prefabricated at that, and soon to be plastics; when she remembered that plastics burn in a very nasty way and might not do for cremation. Luckily at that moment Mrs. Crawley came and herded her ladies away to wash their hands.

"How *do* you do it?" said Mrs. Morland, who was tidying her hair (an expression not to be taken literally in her case) in her hostess's bedroom, the others being dealt with by the housemaid.

Mrs. Crawley said do what.

"I mean having people to supper who haven't been asked," said Mrs. Morland. "Four extra and five if you count me and six if you count Mr. Parkinson."

Mrs. Crawley, herself one of a large country family and owner of uncounted children and grandchildren, said her mother had always done it and somehow always managed. Octavia, she said, for instance, had brought three rabbits with her that morning and the Dean's Australian cousins had sent a huge ham.

"I didn't know you had Australian relations," said Mrs. Morland.

"No more I have," said Mrs. Crawley. "Or ought I to say no more I haven't. They are all Josiah's. Some kind of great-uncle went out years ago—a younger brother of the Grace Crawley who married Archdeacon Grantly's son—and they seem to have done very well. Wool, I think. Laura, do you realize that we may have a Conservative Government in three weeks?" but Mrs. Morland said she didn't want to realise anything just at present and before her old friend could ask why, the booming Deanery gong was drowning all possibility of conversation.

"Benedictus benedicat," said the Dean, with authority, when his guests had finished scraping their chairs on the floor. "Did anyone listen to the six o'clock news?"

"We couldn't Dr. Crawley," said Mrs. Joram. "We were all

talking. And you know nothing ever happens if you listen. Did you expect anything? Besides nothing ever happens on Saturday afternoon."

"Excuse me, sir," said Simnet who to the mingled joy and jealousy of the Deanery servants had stayed on, unasked, to give tone to the little dinner-party, "Blackheath won; with fourteen points against Birkenhead Park with eight. It sounded a very nice game, sir."

"Ha!" said the Dean, his untidy eyebrows looking bushier than ever. "I wasn't bad as a half-back in my time," which to most of his guests, and indeed to ourselves, meant nothing at all.

"And they're fancying Tonteem at Lonchom for tomorrow, sir," Simnet continued, but the Dean, whether from a feeling that he ought not to monpolise Dr. Joram's servant, or because in England horse racing does not occur on Sundays, dismissed his Mercury with a word of thanks and turning to Mrs. Joram asked after her young people.

"Well, it depends which young," said Mrs. Joram. "Francis and Peggy and the children are very well. Peggy is canvassing, which I think is quite a good thing. She needs a mouvementé life," said Mrs. Joram, looking up under her lashes—just as Mrs. Brandon used to look—to see how the Dean took this dashing manner of speech. "Francis is on the Conservative Committee for something. He's the Treasurer which is a good thing because he understands figures. My daughter Delia and her darling little boys are staying for ten days in our old gardener Turpin's cottage. I wish they could stay for ever. But Hilary has his excavating job and Delia is going with him and the boys will fly out for their holidays, which seems peculiar somehow," said Mrs. Joram, her pretty head a little on one side, considering, as a bright-eyed bird might consider a snail or a worm.

The Dean said he could not see anything particularly peculiar in boys passing the holidays with their parents. Like Peter Piper, said Mrs. Joram, turning her lovely, deceptive eyes upon him and wondering where on earth Mrs. Crawley could get her clothes, which were obviously from a special cupboard marked "Upper Clergy Wives Only."

The Dean said he did not quite follow her drift. Peter Piper? he said, questioningly.

"Oh, that was reflex action or something," said Mrs. Joram. "I mean you said particularly peculiar—at least you said it was not particularly peculiar—to pass holidays with parents. Like Thomas a Tattamus Took Two T's, To Tie Two Tups To Two Tall Trees," and she again turned the full battery of her still lovely eyes upon him.

The Dean regretted, in a highly unregretting voice, that he did not quite follow the allusion.

"Oh yes, Dr. Crawley, you MUST know it," said Mrs. Morland from his other side. "It's in Mother Goose. It ends: To Frighten the Terrible Thomas a Tattamus. And then you say, How many T's are there in all that and everybody counts and gets it wrong, because of course you meant All That."

"What on earth are you talking about, Laura?" said the Dean, only keeping himself by the skin of his teeth from saying What the dickens, or even worse.

"Well," said Mrs. Morland, showing no sign of impatience because it is well known that men are stupid, "if you ask how many T's there are in All That, there are only two. None in All and two in That," she added with an air of lucid patience highly irritating to the Dean.

Mr. Parkinson said Mavis knew ever so many nursery rhymes and the children could say them all. Everyone, quite apart from their increasing approval of the Parkinsons, felt that gentleman ought to be thanked for having changed the subject and Mrs. Miller, next to him, said what particularly nice children Harold and Connie were.

"Let me see," said the Dean. "We first knew you when you were at the Theological College, Parkinson, I think. I remember your dining with us when Mrs. Arbuthnot, the present Mrs. Francis Brandon, and her sister were here."

"So do I, sir," said Mr. Parkinson. "And I made a frightful howler over Onesiphorus and you raised your eyebrows at me. It absolutely terrified me, sir. But I bought a dictionary, that little classical dictionary in the Everyman series, and I went right through it, a page at a time, till I felt pretty safe," at which the Dean smiled a grim approval and everyone liked Mr. Parkinson for what he had said.

"But there's quite a lot of words in English to trip one up," said Mr. Parkinson. "I did try listening to the radio, but some of them didn't seem much better than me. If I've heard them say contròversy once, I've heard it ten times, sir. Colonel Crofts gave me a dictionary by a Mr. Fowler two years ago and I often read a bit. I've often thought I'd like to write to him. He makes you feel what a fool you are. A good slap in the face but no malice. At least that's how he struck me."

Mr. Miller, quietly listening, thought indeed, indeed Parkinson was coming on.

"Contròversy?" said the Dean, who had been champing at the bit metaphorically till his uppers and unders were almost flecked with foam. "Away with such a fellow from the earth!"

"Do *you* read the Pilgrim's Progress, sir?" said Mr. Parkinson, which so flabbergasted the Dean that for the first time in human memory he was absolutely silenced. "My mother read it aloud to me again and again and we didn't have many books, because all father's had to be sold."

Mr. Miller won the gratitude of the whole company by asking what Mr. Parkinson's father was.

"He was a bookseller," said Mr. Parkinson. "At least he wanted to be one, but people wanted things like stationery and elastic bands and that sort of thing and he tried to please everyone. But some people wanted books and he got quite into the way of picking up odd books that people wanted, and I was allowed to read anything I liked. Our Pilgrim's Progress had pictures and all the good people had a kind of spotted shirt with a belt and the wicked ones had coats with tails and top hats," at which a kind of breath went up from the party, for here was Mr. Parkinson, the vicar at Pomfret Madrigal, coming from nowhere in particular, describing the very same Pilgrim's Progress that Stevenson had described. Mrs. Morland said to the company in general that it was like that story of Kipling's about the chemist with consumption who wrote Keats, but no one took any notice of her.

"And that's really how I came to marry Mavis," Mr. Parkinson continued, "because Mr. Welk, that's her father, he thought she could make a better marriage and indeed she could have married a duke if she'd wanted," by which his hearers were deeply touched though entirely incredulous, "but when she told Mr. Welk I read the Pilgrim's Progress, he said I could call every Saturday night and take Mavis to church on Sunday evening."

"And did you?" said Mrs. Crawley.

"Ackcherly not exactly," said Mr. Parkinson, "because I had to study so hard at the Theological College, so I had to give up the Saturdays. But Mavis didn't mind. She studied me and I've done my best to study her," and suddenly conscious of having opened his heart, perhaps too wide, to these people whose world, except in a Christian sense, was not his world, he plunged into his excellent treacle tart and said no more.

"May I tell you one thing, Mr. Parkinson?" said Mrs. Morland quietly. "Mr. Fowler is dead, I am sorry to say, quite some time ago. But I'm fairly good at words. I earn my living by them. And one doesn't say ackcherly; one says actually. And as a matter of fact," Mrs. Morland went on, deliberately obscuring the issue in the hope that Mr. Parkinson might not hate her for giving good advice, "one doesn't really say actually—not very much. It's a kind of habit, like children when they find a new word and drive you mad with it."

"Like Harold," said Mr. Parkinson. "He's got hold of the word complication somewhere and he uses it all the time till Mavis and I could box his ears."

"And do you?" said Mrs. Morland, enchanted by this human weakness.

"Well, not his ears, because they say it might bring on mastoid or make them deaf," said Mr. Parkinson. "But if he's cheeky to Mavis I let him feel the weight of my hand. I'll remember about actually, Mrs. Morland. Mavis will love to hear how kind you were to me. She gets all your books from the library," and even in the middle of her pleasure Mrs. Morland noticed that he did not say libery, and took it that the father with immortal longings to be a bookseller might have been an educated man. There would be a story in it for some people, she thought. But not for her.

"A penny for your thoughts, Mrs. Morland," said Mr. Miller across the table.

"Oh, I don't know," said Mrs. Morland. "Except of course one is always thinking about this General Election. But I think what They did was quite too *awful*."

Mr. Miller inquired who they were and what they had done.

"Oh, when I say They, I mean the people that call themselves the Government—at least that did call themselves the Government till they began persecuting His Majesty."

"What DO you mean, Laura?" said the Dean, his shaggy eyebrows almost coming right down over his eyes as he knitted his forehead.

"Persecuting," said Mrs. Morland firmly. "As if it wasn't bad enough for His Majesty to have to see Them every day. They had to come and bully him in bed. When They have *resigned* too!"

The Dean said that she often made him feel like St. Paul.

The other end of the table had been peaceably talking about the Barchester Film Society's production of La Courtisane Violée in which everyone was someone else's natural father and most of the women were really men, though the men were just men, and pretty nasty pieces of work at that, and how exactly like the Prebendary's wife the rich old woman was who had lived in a cheap cinema for sixty years, hoping to see the face that had won her heart in the days of silent films and when she found it all the flesh fell off it (in slow motion and Glorious Technicolor) and its toothless jaws closed in an eternal grip upon—but we will draw the curtain. It was, said Mrs. Crawley, quite extraordinary what things people thought of and so brought the very aimless talk to a close, just as Mrs. Morland, dripping hairpins, was explaining to the Dean, who was not trying to understand, exactly what she meant.

"Well, Josiah, have you read today's *Times*?" she said.

The Dean said of course he had. But he hadn't finished the Crossword because obbligato *must* be the word but it didn't fit in.

"I know what you did, Josiah," said his wife. "You spelt obbligato with one 'b' and two 'g's'. I did it myself. I suppose everyone has a blind spot for spelling somewhere," at which piece of wifely brutality the Dean frowned, but thought it better not to say anything, as it was exactly what he—usually a pedantically correct speller—had done. "Do tell us, Laura, what you really mean."

"It all began with His Majesty's illness," said Mrs. Morland, eyeing the company with an Ancient Mariner look. "Of course one couldn't be surprised, because first he had to be King when he didn't want to be and did it so Splendidly that it makes me cry whenever I think of it. And then, imagine having to have Them for one's government. And there was one of them whose name I won't mention as you would know it at once if I did, who talked about My government instead of His Majesty's government. And it wasn't even the P.M., who might have had more excuse. I don't mean because of being badly educated because I looked him up and he was at a good school, but at least the Government was more his than any other minister's though of course not his at all, as we all know," and she paused.

"Do go on, Mrs. Morland," said Dr. Joram, supported by a friendly murmur from the rest of the company.

"Like Cardinal Wolsey," said Mrs. Morland, with the air of having at last produced something from the hat. A dead silence followed.

"Ego et rex meus you mean perhaps," said Dr. Joram. "A very interesting, but if I may say so not very convincing parallel."

Mrs. Joram said she was sure the late Prime Minister, only as he wasn't dead she supposed she ought to say the ex-Prime Minister only that sounded like a revolution, didn't wear wool all the year round, at which point her hearers went mad and she sat looking very pretty and conscious of having made a good point.

"To go back to what I was saying," said Mrs. Morland, "I have *entirely* forgotten what it was. You know how one forgets, what with not enough coal and the food position and all those *dreadful* half-castes," at which point Dr. Joram asked which half-castes.

"William!" said his wife reproachfully. "Persians. And Egyptians. Not like your dear black friends. Do you know, Mrs. Crawley, the Prime Minister of Mngangaland remembered William's birthday and sent him the most beautiful leopard skin. I almost wished William were in the army."

"I would do anything for you, my love," said Dr. Joram, "but that I think is impossible. May I ask why this military outburst?"

"Well, there aren't any men except drummers who have leopard-skin aprons," said Mrs. Joram. "But one can't do anything about it, so I am having it made into a hearthrug; or a rug for the second spare bedroom which is hardly ever used. But really, William, we are interrupting Mrs. Morland."

Mrs. Morland hastened to protest that there was no interruption at all and that she now remembered what she had forgotten.

"What I have to say," said the talented authoress, "is this—if I can possibly say it before I forget it again because you know the way things that are in the front of your mind suddenly go right to the back—namely that if you read *The Times*, or any other morning paper as I believe they all get their news from the same wholesale place, you would have seen what happened. His

Majesty had to be propped up in bed it says, to sign something. Even if a person had made a will leaving one a million pounds and then couldn't sign it because he was ill, one wouldn't go into his bedroom with about a dozen people and make him sit up. It is Unkindness. And to His Majesty of all people who would never hurt a fly. There! And I wish They could hear me."

There was silence for a moment. It was clear to everyone that if a government resigned arrangements must be made for the new government to be elected and only His Majesty could sign the necessary document. But each person present thought of his or her wife or husband, in a similar position, weak from desperate illness, obliged by law and by honour to carry out a trying duty.

"One would almost rather They had stayed in," said Mrs. Morland and banged her handkerchief against her eyes.

"It is," said Mr. Miller, feeling it his duty to succour anyone in distress, "a natural feeling. But we all have to make sacrifices. And think how They would have laughed if They had stayed in," after which a very interesting discussion took place as to how far false teeth hampered freedom of laughter and the party sat talking till, quite early, they dispersed. For so much had happened in England that day that everyone felt tired and faintly unreal, with a sense of dawning hope that one hardly dared to admit and a very certain conviction that the road would be long and difficult, beset by foes within as well as by foes from without. But with His Majesty and Mr. Churchill the ship could weather the storm. And there was still the General Election to come.

CHAPTER 4

From the day of His Majesty's signing the Proclamation of the Dissolution of Parliament, there was little outward excitement in Barsetshire. The issues were too grave. Both sides had been hard at work in anticipation of an election and by the sixteenth of October the full list of nominations was published. Mr. Gresham was standing again for East Barsetshire, opposed by a Labour candidate whose name we shall not trouble to invent as he did not get in. West Barsetshire, whose Conservative member we also shall not trouble to invent, had madly produced a Liberal candidate who caused a certain amount of trouble in a three-cornered fight before he lost his deposit, giving his supporters a kind of dim satisfaction in that they nearly swung the vote against the Conservative and there had to be two recounts, thus satisfying the Liberal aspiration to be as much nuisance as possible to all parties besides finally dishing their own. In Barchester itself Lord Silverbridge was neck and neck with the Labour candidate when, at the eleventh hour, the Reverend Enoch Arden to whom Mr. Adams, formerly one of his flock, had shown kindness on more than one occasion, led his small party of what we can only describe as Independent Cranks to the poll and plumped for Labour, thus affording a living example of benefits forgot.

The County Club gave a reception at which the results were shown as they came out, but it was a quiet affair compared with the previous election at which there had been a certain amount of partisan noise and some persons introduced by a member who called himself a Communist had brought disgrace upon the Club by booing all Conservative winners, incited thereto by a gentleman not unconnected with the publishing trade in London who ought to have known better. But this time the general feeling was a kind of subdued tenseness which could hardly trust itself to betray emotion and the only incident which disturbed the surface calm was a general sigh, partaking of the nature of a groan, when a female M.P., whose behaviour in the House had been eccentric to say the least, romped in with a large and increased majority, thus throwing further doubt on the wisdom of universal suffrage including women and the very young. The Conservative gains were larger than the Labour gains, being 21 to nothing; for the 2 seats which each gained from the Liberals cancelled each other, so to speak, and the kind of people who always know everything said the Conservatives were a dead cert., but as Mr. Wickham remarked it certainly was a fairly dead one. Sixty-six out of the one hundred and nine Liberal candidates forfeited their deposits, which led to a discussion between Mr. Belton and Mr. Pilward of Pilward's Entire as to how much the deposit was, but as the discussion was based on the fact that neither disputant knew what his correct premises were it was on the whole inconclusive.

The Times, for once forsaking its customary cautious aloofness, cancelled its front page News of the Day which was to have been "URUGUAY AND U.N." and substituted the fine and simple words "Mr. Churchill Prime Minister." So once more the best loved and most fiercely hated (or shall we say feared) figure of this century came forward to take up the burden laid upon him by his countrymen; to help England to rescue herself from the depths to which her vain folly and that of her chosen servants had hurled her and—if possible—to help the vast ignorant masses of every class to recover their self-respect and assure themselves and their families of enough to eat and a little warmth during the coming winter.

Politics are not in our line and to write one word more would be to betray our rooted ignorance; so we will only report that Mrs. Sam Adams, she who was Lucy Marling, said to Sir Edmund Pridham that she had almost cried when she thought how *heavenly* it must have been for His Majesty when Mr. Churchill came to kiss hands upon becoming Prime Minister; to which Sir Edmund, hastily assuming a bluff air and voice which did not in the least mask his true emotion, replied that Gad! she was right and His Majesty must have been as pleased as Punch when the other feller went in to tender his resignation, and then blew his nose defiantly.

"Well," said Mr. Marling, who in defiance of his family's freely expressed opinions had insisted on attending the election party, "it's a good thing to see England on her feet again. Give her a chance and she'll show 'em all, eh, Macfadyen?"

Mr. Macfadyen, who through Lucy Adams and her various market-garden activities had come to know Mr. Marling pretty well, said it would be an ill day when England could no longer lead the world and he misdoubted the day had been very near.

"Decline and Fall of the British Empire, eh?" said Mr. Marling. "Come now, Macfadyen, what would our fathers and grandfathers have thought of that?"

Mr. Macfadyen, with native caution, said his grandfather had died before he was born and his father when he was but a lad, so he couldn't exactly say. It was our children and grandchildren who would have to do the thinking, he said, and not being a married man himself he wouldn't exactly say what they might think, to which Mr. Marling, flown with victory and two glasses of mild cup at the buffet supper, said give them time to get into existence and we'd see, and laughed in what his son Oliver who was at hand considered a lecherous and senile manner. But Mr. Macfadyen took it all in good part.

And so all the guests went home, confident now of victory;

but the better-informed among them feeling that the struggle would be long and bitter and alas! not always with our foes abroad, but often—far too often—with the foes within who had brought the name of England lower within six years than ever before in history, till we were Persia's wash-pot and over us Egypt had cast out its shoe; for these countries had never qualified for the feminine gender which, curiously, is reserved for those who stand highest; the others being It. Except perhaps France who has always been female, with, we must say, a good many of that respectable sex's least attractive qualities as well as its most fascinating.

So the election fever ebbed and Parliament met again and exchanged personalities and defiance and obstruction, while Barsetshire returned to its own life, hoping to goodness that there wouldn't be another election just yet. And every Sunday in public, as well as on other days in private, people gave thanks for His Majesty's recovery and prayed most heartily that their father and monarch might be spared to them. Though we may say that it did not appear to have occurred to anyone in power during the previous year that His Majesty needed care or consideration of any kind; any more than it had occurred to one of them, a good many years previously, that to speak of the rejoicings over the twenty-fifth year of his Father's reign as Jubilee Ballyhoo was in any way out of order.

Except for those successful Parliamentary candidates who had to go to London while Parliament was sitting, Barsetshire resumed the noiseless but to itself extremely satisfactory tenor of its way and the Parish Pump again became distinctly more important and interesting than St. Stephen's. The chief event of local importance that we have to chronicle was the return of Henry Grantly and his immediate plans. For the benefit of those who have of late years rather lost sight of Henry Grantly, as indeed we have ourselves, we will remind ourselves that he was the younger son of Mr. Grantly the clergyman of St. Michael's at Edgewood. When we last had the pleasure of meeting Henry he had just, to his intense satisfaction, received the calling-up papers for his military service and had been for two years in the Far East, that bourne from which few travellers return without something wrong with them. But Henry had been one of the lucky ones. He had on the whole enjoyed everything from sweating in an airless jungle surrounded by ill-disposed natives and overshadowed by ill-wishing aeroplanes to being told by the major's wife in Umbrella that she was sure he would like her elder daughter Freda who was coming out with a batch of A.T.S. in June, to which young woman he immediately and on no grounds took a great dislike which was fully justified later by her legs, her looks and her conversation, all of which were what might be called dim. And now he was at home and to his parents' surprise said he wanted to be a solicitor. His father said that if he did wish to take to the law it was just as well that he preferred the solicitoring lay as barristers had more chance if they had been to a University and if he didn't know his own mind after two years in the army he never would; an argument which appears to us to have a flaw in it, but if one wishes to convince oneself, any argument will do. Henry was accordingly articled to Keith and Keith, the old and well-established Barchester solicitors who did most of the cathedral and diocesan work and had conducted the business of the Dean and Chapter when they tried to oppose the railway coming to Barchester, now some hundred or more years ago. Since the death of old Mr. Keith, Lydia Merton's father, her elder brother Robert Keith had been head of the firm and there was an understanding that if Henry did well his father would later put down money for a partnership; for some of the Grantly wealth still survived and though there was little probability now of anyone being able to inherit what his or her parents had laboriously saved, money spent on a partnership now would be as good an investment as any. So Henry went daily to Barchester to work, and read at home even harder than he might have read at Oxford.

One of the advantages of living at home was the company of his sister Grace who was almost his twin, so near in age they were, and to whom he was much attached in a brotherly manner which combined a fatherly and protective attitude with a good deal of aimless sparring. Grace had at this time got a job at the Barchester Central Public Library where she was both giving and getting satisfaction, being mostly occupied in the section concerned with the past history of Barsetshire in general and Barchester in particular. Here she was able to make herself useful by her knowledge, inherited from her parents and fostered by them, of Barsetshire families, their intermarryings, their changes of property, their personal and political loves and hates. Her not uninteresting job at the moment was to go through and type for future reference several large boxes of the great Duke of Omnium's correspondence, consisting of a number of letters between the great Duke and the Marchioness of Hartletop of that time whose names had been much coupled in society; but apart from their allusions to interesting people of the period they had little of what is known as news value, the Duke's being mostly a few lines about a debate in the Lords or a command visit to Windsor and the Marchioness's about the trouble she had with her French cook and the Duke's kindness in recommending such an excellent valet to her husband. In only one of her letters was any warmer feeling shown when her ladyship alluded with some acerbity to a certain Madame Max Goesler whose house the Duke had long been frequenting, but as Grace had never heard of Madame Goesler she was not much interested.

It was on a November morning that Mr. Parry, the City Librarian, came into the room where she was working, a delightful room divided into compartments by high presses full of old books about Barsetshire seats and Barsetshire families, mostly bound in calf with dim gold lettering.

After asking rather vaguely how she was getting on, he stood watching her and making a few remarks about the Hartletop papers.

"Oh, they're all right," said Grace. "I mean one can read them. People seemed to write better then."

"Quill pens," said Mr. Parry. "I'd use them myself if I could get anyone to cut them properly."

"Father can," said Grace. "His grandfather taught him when he was a little boy. We've got simply *boxes* of letters, Mr. Parry. There are a lot of old ones only they're crossed. I'm rather good at reading them. But I can't do the ones that are double-crossed."

Mr. Parry asked exactly how.

"Well, first they wrote a letter in the ordinary way," said Grace, patiently but not with obtrusive patience, "and then they wrote across them and then they wrote across *that*. I say, you don't know anyone who can read double-crossed, do you," and Mr. Parry said he was sorry he didn't, and what was more he must confess he had never heard of double-crossing, except, he added, in thrillers.

"Well, these letters may be thrillers," said Grace, "but no one can read them. They were from an old aunt or something in India and it was to save postage because it was so expensive then. I wonder if anyone ever bothered to read them? Oh, I say, there's something I wanted to ask you. All those big books about the Seats of the Nobility and Gentry of Barsetshire need some hospital work. They're beginning to moulder down where you open the cover and they'll fall off if it isn't stopped. Would you mind if I brought some lanoline along and did some?"

The City Librarian looked worried. Not only was his an important and hard-working job, but he was understaffed and conducting a running fight with the City Council for one or two more good assistant librarians, and they would have to be members or associates of the Librarians' Association and have standard wages and hours, and people like Grace, however good and useful, could only be stopgaps.

"Well, Miss Grantly," he said, "I don't like to impose on you, but the lanoline certainly wouldn't hurt them. And if I hear of anyone who can read double-crossed letters, I'll let you know. And, by the way, do you know anyone who could give us a lecture at rather short notice? Adrian Coates, the publisher, has just rung up to say he has to go to America on urgent business and can't give us a talk on Tuesday week as he had promised. It's a disappointment, because he was going to have given us a practical talk about paper and binding and how much it all costs now and all that sort of thing. I have bothered our Barsetshire people so often that I hardly like to ask them again. It's got to be something not too learned and not too light. I know George Knox would, but he did stopgap last winter and I really can't ask him to do it again. I suppose your father—" and he paused.

Grace said if it was a Tuesday as usual she knew he couldn't because he was doing confirmation classes. Mr. Parry looked more worried than ever.

"Look here," said Grace. "I'm going to lunch with Henry, my brother that's in Mr. Keith's office. I'll ask him. I'm sure we can find someone," and Mr. Parry having confounded himself in thanks went back to his office to deal with the thousand and one administrative details that are a head librarian's life, while Grace went back to her typewriter and finished the letter upon which she had been engaged. It was not very interesting, being two lines from the great Duke of Omnium announcing to Madame Goesler that he would do himself the pleasure of calling at Park Lane about five o'clock on the following Saturday if convenient to her. Grace's grandparents could perhaps have filled in the gaps, her great grandparents certainly could, but it interested no one now and the present Lord Hartletop had presented the letters to the Library because Hartletop Priory was now some kind of public institution and he had nowhere to keep his masses of family papers in his present humble abode in what had been the second-best dower house when there were two dowager marchionesses living simultaneously.

As Henry Grantly was getting an allowance from his father as well as living at home he was not badly off. Whether he was getting a small salary as well we cannot say, for we know nothing at all about what happens to people who are learning to be solicitors. In any case he was an open-handed young man and liked to take his sister Grace, with whom he had always been on excellent terms varied by a kind of all-in sparring, to the White Hart for lunch, which was indeed about the only place in Barchester where one could get attention. Grace was the first to get to the White Hart and not seeing Henry in the hall she looked into the dining-room.

"Hallo, Burden," she said to the old head-waiter who knew everyone worth knowing in Barchester and for many miles around, "has my brother come yet?"

"Not yet, miss," said Burden, "but the young gentleman rang up for a table for three. You'd better come and sit there, miss. I've been keeping it for you. This way, miss," and he took her into the far corner to a table from which one could see who was going up and down the narrow street to the Close, a much coveted position. Grace asked who the other place was for.

"That I couldn't say, miss," said Burden. "Mr. Henry said a table for three, so a table for three it is and more I couldn't say, not if it was Mr. Churchill himself. Shall I get you anything, miss?" but Grace said no thank you and she would just wait. It was not at all unpleasant to sit in the warm room and watch the passers-by in the cold and the bishop's wife going home to lunch in one of the new hats that had aimless loops of stiffened material sticking out of them and didn't look like ladies' hats. But the bishop's wife, Grace charitably reflected, could make any hat look as if it had been worn in bed for three years at least. Presently her brother Henry hove in sight with a young man whom she couldn't quite place, though she thought she vaguely remembered him, and in another moment Henry was following Burden to the corner table with the partially unknown young man.

"Hullo," said Henry. "Sorry we're late. I had to wait till the senior clerk came back. You two do know each other. Hi! Burden!"

His companion, a not quite so young man with a slightly vague look, shook hands with Grace, appearing to know her quite well, but Grace still could not place him.

"That was a good game we had last summer," said the young man. "At least not last summer which really doesn't count as a summer at all. I mean the one before. You and Lufton made a very good pair," and then Grace remembered the day there had been tennis at the Priory School, the day Cecil Waring had been driven by his future wife at illegal speed to the Barchester General to have a piece of war metal removed from his inside, just in time.

"Oh, I know, you're Mr. Swan," said Grace.

"Eric, I regret to say but my mother would do it, to my friends," said the under-master from the Priory School.

Grace said it was quite a good kind of name, to which its owner replied that it was all right in its way, but it gave one a feeling that one ought to be called Bluetooth, or Longshanks. Or Littler, said Henry.

"Come, come, my lad," said Swan who though a young man as young men go was considerably older than Henry, "that's the man who owns all the theatres or finances all the shows or something. And I don't think Dean Farrar would like you to talk like that. Quite a lot of people still call me Swan, because they were at school with me, either as devilish schoolboys or beggarly ushers. However, Miss Grantly, call me anything you like and I will come," to which Grace replied not if he called her Miss Grantly and then Burden brought the drinks which Henry had dashingly ordered and stood slightly bowed over his clients to await their instructions for lunch.

"Last time I was here was with Tony Morland," said Swan (as we cannot help calling him, having known him now for so many years, since his schooldays at Southbridge), putting on at the same time a pair of large horn-rimmed (or more probably now plastic imitation horn-rimmed) spectacles, "we had some marvellously good liver. Oh my lungs and liver!" to which beautiful words Grace was inspired to responded "Goroo."

"Good *girl,* " said Swan, "if you will pardon my taking the liberty, but I'm a member of the Dickens Fellowship and your words touched a chord in the human breast—*may* I shake hands?"

"Yes, Uncle Pumblechook," said Grace, and she and Swan laughed so much that even Burden smiled before recalling them to their more pressing duties. Liver and bacon and sauté potatoes were ordered for three, also greens. Swan said, if Burden could promise that they wouldn't have been kept in a press and arrive in thin flat cubes, if he might be forgiven a mixed metaphor, at which Grace laughed so much that Madame Tomkins who was lunching there alone and had made dresses for all the best families ever since her husband deserted her directly after the '14 war, looked up, recognised an old customer and decided that cette petite Grantly was coming on nicely. There had been a time, Madame Tomkins remembered shudderingly, when la petite Grantly had modelled herself on Jennifer Gorman, a perfect produce of Miss Pettinger and the Barchester High School, and Madame Tomkins had felt obliged to tell la petite Grantly that if she wished to resemble that Génifère she had better go to Bostock and Plummer, who were Barchester's old-established drapers and got models down from London when they were just not quite up to date and were patronised by the bishop's wife. But to her family's relief, who had been very wise and had not openly tried to quench her passion for Jennifer Gorman, she had some time ago stopped wanting to go to the Barchester Odeon with Jennifer and last Christmas had not even sent her a threepenny Woolworth card and as their social paths were not likely to cross often, that chapter might be considered as closed.

"And what do you do?" said Swan. "It's a question I dislike asking because charming young women ought to sit on a cushion and pretend to sew a fine seam; but old times have changed, old manners gone. That is Scott, but I daresay you don't read him," to which Grace, not a whit daunted, said of *course* she did, again and again, only not the poems. "And I bet you," she added, "you don't know where Bonnie Dundee comes from."

Swan said it was one of Scott's best ballads, to which Grace said yes, but where from, and Swan had to confess ignorance. So then Grace, not without sinful pride, told him it came in a ghastly sort of poetic drama called The Doom of Devorgoil and confessed that she was extremely snob about knowing this, after which they simultaneously talked books and Henry sat silent, looking with an elder brother's condescension at his sister's progress, till it was time for him to go back to Keith and Keith. Grace said she must get back to the Library too, upon which Swan said he would claim an uncle's privilege and pay the bill for everyone to which Henry did not make any opposition, for nothing, he said, looked or sounded worse than squabbles about who should pay.

"And the curious thing," said Swan, tipping Burden very handsomely, "is that one never hears people squabbling about who should *not* pay: which really would be far more reasonable," He took off his large spectacles and put them in a pocket and then, under a kind of papal benediction from Burden, they left the hotel and walked with Henry to his office.

"Well, good-bye," said Grace to Swan as they turned their backs on Henry."

"But why?" said Swan. "It is a half-holiday and I am a free man and the minster clock has just struck two. And yonder is the moon," and indeed a pale decaying moon was to be seen over the cathedral roof, looking as dispirited as the November afternoon.

"I say, you do quote a lot," said Grace.

"Quite unconsciously," said Swan. "I am what is known as an omnivorous reader and it all goes right through me and out of my mouth. Where, or should I say whither may I escort you?"

"Oh, I'm working at the Central Library," said Grace, "but I needn't be back for a quarter of an hour."

"In that case we will go through the Close," said Swan, adding "and thank you for your encouragement," which words Grace wasn't quite sure if she understood. "What do you do at the Library? I know your Mr. Parry. We sometimes play chess together. So few people play chess now. They play Canasta, whatever that may be," which delighted Grace who was able to confess that she couldn't ever understand card games.

"Except screaming ones," said Swan. "I have never forgotten the way you yelled Oats when we played Pit on that day when Sir Cecil had to be taken to the Barchester General. It really made me believe in the expression brazen lungs."

"Did I?" said Grace, feeling herself go red in the face, much to her annoyance. "How awful."

"I liked it," said Swan. "That, I said to myself, is a girl of character. Can you do anything else? Besides tennis of course."

Grace said only family croquet. And she did like toy trains when Henry used to have them and allowed her to help.

"You should have known Tony Morland," said Swan. "We were at Southbridge together. He had more trains than anyone I've ever known. I stayed with him once in the holidays and we had a railway system over the whole of a big attic. Do you know him?"

Grace said she didn't, and was he any relation of the Mrs. Morland who wrote books.

"She's his mother," said Swan. "He's given up trains and has a wife and thousands of children. High hopes faint on a warm hearthstone, if you like quotations."

"Oh! do you know her too?" said Grace.

Swan said of course he did and she was very nice and never minded what she looked like and lived at High Rising, right away beyond Pomfret Madrigal; and as Grace was silent he asked whether she minded.

"Minded what?" said Grace, puzzled.

Swan said he thought she might have a conscientious objection to people living at Pomfret Madrigal or High Rising.

"Oh, no!" said Grace, to Swan's amusement almost seriously. "But Mr. Parry has been let down by Adrian Coates, who is Mrs. Morland's publisher, for one of the lectures at the library and I wondered if perhaps—if it wouldn't seem too awfully rude—I mean as you do know her—"

"What you *do* mean—let us go through the cloisters—is," said Swan, "that you want me to ask her if she will stopgap. Is that it?" he inquired, as no answer was forthcoming.

"Well, if you don't really mind, thank you most *awfully*," said Grace. "You see, Mr. Parry does get *so* worried with all the things he has to do. The one thing a Head Librarian can't *ever* do is to have time to do library sort of things. I am sure he would like to browse in books—"

"Instead of which he has to crawl onto committees and curse conferences," said Swan. "I know. But an idea has just struck me. Why shouldn't I be the stopgap? I had to lecture to my soldiers in the war and I did it rather well. I can speak on almost any subject with fluency, apparent conviction and almost total want of knowledge, skillfully masked by common-places. Would that do?"

Grace looked at him inquiringly.

"I am sorry," said Swan, more gently. "I have dazzled you by the coruscation of my genius. But, quite seriously, I know a fair amount about some out-of-the-way subjects. For instance I know the Scotch literature of the early nineteenth century like my own hand and I have read the Noctes Ambrosianae three times for the pleasure of them. How would your Mr. Parry like a talk on Minor Contemporaries of Scott? My mother was Scotch and I am familiar with the language and can be trusted not to make people feel uncomfortable by reading aloud with a phoney accent—forgive the dreadful word. Or if you don't like that, why not ask Oliver Marling to talk about the Reverend Thomas Bohun under whose monument we are at present standing. I'd love to hear Marling reading erotic religious poems aloud with a slight stammer. I am sorry, that was malicious."

Grace, indeed slightly bewildered, but keeping her feet on the ground, said he had better come and see Mr. Parry now. So they walked through the Close gate at the farther end and so to the Central Library where they found Mr. Parry in his office and for once alone and Grace was able to lay Swan as it were before Mr. Parry's altar and then sat on a chair against the wall, prepared to observe the meeting of master minds.

"Hullo, Eric," said Mr. Parry. "I've been thinking about that last game. You ought to have played your knight."

"If there weren't a lady present I'd say exactly what I think of what you have been thinking," said Swan. "But the lady has a suggestion for your missing lecturer. We did think of asking Marling to talk on Bohun, but I don't think it would do. So we thought why not me? I know it's ungrammatical, but I'm blowed if I'll say why not I. Anyway, why not myself? Scott's Younger Contemporaries—if that isn't a contradiction in terms—with quotations in the Doric?"

"Really, that is *most* kind of you," said Mr. Parry, "and I think the subject is excellent. And I must thank Miss Grantly too. What with that and lanoline you have really done a first-class day's work, Miss Grantly," at which Grace almost blushed in a becoming way but, as Swan noted with approval, remained still and quiet, looking with her very handsome eyes (as Swan again approvingly noted) upon her companions.

Then Swan said good-bye to Grace, gave a kind of salute to Mr. Parry and went away. Grace returned to her work and applied herself conscientiously to it, but somehow the Duke of

Omnium's letters seemed duller and duller and she found herself looking at the clock and then falling into a kind of waking dream from which the bell that was rung through all the building at five o'clock woke her with a jump.

CHAPTER 5

The winter lectures in the Central Library, held once a month from October to March, were a well-established institution and although free were usually well attended, with a small permanent substratum of professional cranks and a very old man with a long grey beard who looked like a mid-Victorian professor and ate crumbs out of a bag and was never seen at any other time. Philip Winter, the proprietor of the Priory Preparatory School for little boys, had a theory that he had formerly lived in London in one of the Rowton Houses founded by Lord Beaconsfield's friend and secretary and had to leave because he refused to wash, and as no one could contradict this supposition with authority it had assumed the appearance of a fact.

Local lecturers were not as a rule so good a draw as foreigners, but quite a large audience came plowtering through the nasty cold muddy streets on the Tuesday week, for apart from Swan's personal friends who were many and varied, the Headmaster of Southbridge school in whose house Swan had been in earlier days came with a party from the Upper and Lower Sixth who were "doing" the Romantic movement and some masters who were off duty. The ex-Headmaster Mr. Birkett with his wife was also there to see how his former pupil would acquit himself, and Mrs. Morland because Swan had been a friend of Tony's and these with other friends added to the usual audience made the lecture room quite crowded.

According to arrangement Swan was received in a conspiratorial way by the Library Porter and taken up the back stairs to the Librarian's office, a handsome room that Swan afterwards said reminded him of the boardroom of the Anglo-Bengalee Disinterested Loan and Life Assurance Company. Here were assembled Councillor Pilward of Pilward's Entire who was taking the chair, Mr. Parry the head librarian and one or two civic dignitaries including Councillor Budge of the Gas Works, he who during the 1945 election had done such excellent work for Mr. Adams by taking the young man from the Barchester Chronicle and the elderly man from the Barchester Free Press to the Mitre, keeping them there till closing time and seeing them both not only home but into their beds, thus suppressing Mr. Adams's heartfelt but compromising public statement that he wished Mr. Churchill would take the leadership of the Labour Party and then England would get on all right.

"Well, Mr. Swan isn't it," said Mr. Budge, "we're all looking forward to a real treat tonight. I'm not Scotch myself, but I like the Highlands. Mrs. Budge and I spent a fortnight at the Aberdeathly Hydro three summers ago and Mrs. Budge said we couldn't have had a better set of bridge-players if we'd been at Eastbourne. Mrs. Budge did some fishing with a Mr. and Mrs. Clamp from Southport and she enjoyed it thoroughly till they began to wind the fish up and then I thought she'd have passed right out. But a sip of bonnie Scotch whusky put her all right again. She couldn't come tonight because her cousin Miss Pooter, who is almost deaf, is staying for a few days and she said that is Mrs. Budge said to me Really Pops—that's just a name she has for me—Really Pops, she said, if Nellie—that's Miss Pooter's name, Nellie—if Nellie comes, she said, it will really be a case of two's company and three's none, so you go Father, she said—she calls me Father sometimes because we've had five chicks all married now and nice young families—you go, Father, she said, and I'll help Nellie to look at the television. Well, all I can say is, Mr. Swan, that Mrs. Budge is missing a real treat

I'm sure, in anticipation as they say, and I'm sure it will be an occasion we shall all appreciate."

Swan, who had won the respect of all present by listening to Mr. Budge's remarks with courteous gravity, was now rescued by Mr. Parry and penned into a corner while the other distinguished guests took their places. Mr. Parry then conducted him towards the lecture room where on the platform there was a microphone on a long leg looking rather like a tall sunflower whose petals had fallen off.

"Do I really need that?" said Swan in a whisper to Mr. Parry, backing from the machine as he spoke.

"I shouldn't think so," said Mr. Parry, also in a low voice. "Quite often it doesn't work. The electricians are always trying to get it right. But people like to see it. It makes them think they hear better."

Swan said admiringly How like science, to which Mr. Parry replied that he had always maintained that science was no pursuit for a gentleman and that, on reconsidering the matter, he thought Swan had perhaps done rightly in not playing his knight. He then delivered him to the chairman, Mr. Pilward, who introduced him with commendably few words. Swan put his large spectacles on, laid his papers before him and began.

We shall not describe Swan's lecture on The Younger Contemporaries of Walter Scott, for it can be read in the translations of the Royal Barsetshire Literary Society, whose original patron was the Sailor King, William IV, in return for the Lord Lieutenant of the day helping one of his large illegitimate family to a good marriage. We will only say that it was excellent in material and in manner and that his lowland Scotch was the authentic Doric, moving strangely many people who had read the literature of that period by eye alone; that he allowed his audience to laugh more than once; and that—perhaps most important of all—he spoke for five or six minutes less than his allotted time. And this he did by the extra sense that tells a practised speaker, or a naturally good speaker, exactly how much an audience can stand and how to compress the last fifteen minutes of a discourse into five without the hearers being conscious of it.

While he spoke he had seen several friends in the audience, but among them he did not see Grace Grantly. There was of course no reason to be annoyed by this, but hang it all! when one had offered to fill a gap at short notice it would at least have been civil of the girl to come and listen. But girls were like that. And now Mr. Pilward was asking Mr. Birkett if he would move a vote of thanks and Swan's old Headmaster who was in the front row got up, turned slightly to the audience and in a very few words expressed his pleasure in hearing a former pupil speaking so well on so noble a subject. Councillor Budge seconded him, much to the annoyance of Mr. Parry who disliked unnecessary fuss, and said he had always thought Ivanhoe a very fine book which led Miss Pemberton who had come in from Northbridge with her lodger Mr. Downing to say aloud to herself that she could only suppose he thought Ivanhoe was really Evan Dhu, which made some of her immediate neighbours have the giggles. There was more clapping and then Mr. Parry had Swan off the platform and back into the office before he knew where he was.

Evidently Mr. Parry had given some kind of secret countersign to favoured members of the audience, for all the people who came in to congratulate, to thank, or to ask a pertinent question or make a pertinent suggestion, were people that Swan knew, or had known, including several old friends from Southbridge School, among them the well-known classical scholar Mr. Hacker who now held the chair of Latin at Redbrick University and whose spectacles were as large as Swan's and very much thicker.

"I liked your thing awfully," said Hacker. "I put Kilmeny into elegiacs once. They weren't bad. But it wasn't quite the same thing."

"I say, Hack," said Swan, "do you remember the time you took your Aeschylus into the bathroom with you and couldn't find your specs and the upper dor. was flooded. I've never enjoyed anything so much. Old Carter was furious."

"And you would look at Philip Winter through your spectacles," said Hacker. "It was when he was engaged to that ghastly Rose Birkett. She's here tonight. Did you know? She came in at the back with her husband."

"Oh Lord!" said Swan and even as he spoke the lovely form and face of Mrs. Fairweather, followed by Captain Fairweather, R.N., were seen forcing their way through the crowd with a ruthless vigour which, to do their owner justice, she had employed to its fullest extent in pushing her husband up the naval ladder. Not that his own merit and perseverance would not have got him to his present position, but a beautiful and determined wife is no hindrance and though Rose was silly beyond the dreams of even sub-lieutenants, she would have lain in a puddle for her husband to walk dry shod over her, and re-made-up her face afterwards with equal composure.

"I do think you were ackcherly *too* marvellous," said Rose. "I do simply *adore* anything to do with Scott. I saw a perfectly *absorbing* film of him only it wasn't in Scotland. It simply made one *feel*."

Swan said he was so glad and what was the film called.

"Oh, I can't remember," said Rose. "But it was *too* absorbing for words and really I don't care what a film's about so long as it absorbs one. I don't know how they made the snow look so real."

"I say, Hack," said Swan to his old school friend Professor Hacker, "can you think of a Scott novel with a snowstorm in it? Rose says she saw an absorbing one."

Hacker said at the moment he could remember nothing but The Talisman and Kenilworth.

"And the dogs were *real* ones," said Rose, adding a fresh layer of purple-pink to her beautiful mouth. "I think it's *wrong* to make dogs drag sledges, poor darlings. It wouldn't be allowed now of course."

"Look here, Rose," said Swan, who although she was the wife

of a very senior Captain and mother of several children found it impossible to think of her as anything but the Rose Birkett who had for a brief summer been engaged to his present proprietor Philip Winter, then an assistant master at Southbridge School, "just pull yourself together. There aren't any sledges in Scott."

"But there are," said Rose, "because I saw them in the film."

"All right, my girl," said Professor Hacker of Redbrick University, "you *did* see them. And you saw Scott of the Antarctic."

"Wasn't that the one?" said Rose, at which point her husband said it was high time they went and not to dawdle as her parents were waiting, upon which Rose blew a kiss to the two young men and went away.

All this was very amusing and Swan did not at all dislike being congratulated by a number of people, most of whom seemed to have no very clear idea of what he had been talking about, and he had been secretly flattered that some of his old schoolmasters and friends should have come to hear him. But something was missing. If one put oneself out to give a lecture as a stopgap, at least the people who let one in for it might say thank you—just as a mere act of courtesy. However such people were simply not worth thinking about. The room was now almost empty and Swan was not thinking of Grace Grantly with considerable violence, when she came in through the other door of the big office.

"I thought you weren't there," said Swan, before he could think what he was saying. "I didn't see you in the hall and you weren't in here."

"But I *was* in the hall," said Grace, "only I was in a corner right at the side so as not to disturb you. And then I had to see the Barchester Chronicle man."

Swan asked what about.

"Well, Mr. Parry thought we ought to get your talk properly done in the Chronicle," said Grace, "but their man couldn't come till near the end, so I took down a sort of précis of it. I don't think he can do anything very stupid with it."

"*You* took it down?" said Swan.

"I did shorthand and typing when I left school," said Grace, "and it's useful to keep it up. I hope you don't mind. So I was sitting where you couldn't see me. But I simply loved it and it ought to be printed properly."

Swan felt so ashamed of himself for having mistrusted Grace Grantly that he nearly told her what he had felt. And then he realised that it could give her no pleasure to know that he had thought her forgetful—or neglectful—and that moreover it would make him cut a very poor figure in her eyes. So he wisely held his tongue about it and thanked Grace with a warmth that quite surprised her. By this time the audience had gone. Mr. Parry thanked Swan for coming to the rescue and then rather hustled them away, explaining that the porter liked to get off on lecture nights in time to listen to something on the wireless which in his, Mr. Parry's opinion was nothing but unnecessary noise and senseless laughter. So they went down, this time by the handsome near-marble stairs, and Mr. Parry thanked Swan again, said good night to him and Grace and went away to his home.

"How are you going back?" said Swan to Grace.

"Well, Henry was going to meet me and catch the last bus," said Grace.

"He's running it a bit fine, isn't he?" said Swan, at which point the porter, now in his civilian jacket and looking far less impressive, said he was sorry but he must lock up. "And there was a gentleman rung up, Miss Grantly," he said. "Your brother he said he was, miss, and I was to say he was sorry his boss had kept him late at the office and he'd be along as soon as he could. I'd say Come into my room, miss, but my wife's expecting me and I've got to lock up."

Far from fainting or turning appealing glances on Swan, Grace said it couldn't be helped and if she ran she would probably get the bus.

"You probably wouldn't I'm afraid," said Swan. "We will ring

Henry up from the telephone booth outside and tell him to come on to the White Hart, where you and I are now going, and then I'll run you both home in my disgraceful little car. Thanks," he said to the porter, pressing a nominally silver coin into his hand in a lordly way that dazzled Grace, thus causing the porter to abase himself and say if the gentleman liked to use his telephone he was welcome and it seemed a shame to have to spend threepence on a call, which invitation Swan accepted, got through to Henry, thanked the porter and had Grace into his car and to the White Hart before she knew where she was. Swan at once found Burden, said something to him and then took Grace into a dreadfully dull room marked For Residents Only. Two elderly couples looked at them with entire want of interest and went on with whatever they were doing and Burden brought them coffee and sandwiches.

"Say the word and there shall be alcohol," said Swan. "I have arranged with Burden that I am a bona-fide resident," but Grace said no thank you.

"Would you mind frightfully if I told you something?" said Grace.

Swan said it would depend what.

"It's only how *awfully* I liked your lecture," said Grace. "I always thought Scotch poems were rather awful, but when you read them aloud I didn't," to which Swan gravely replied that in that case he was awfully glad she hadn't, which made Grace look confused for a moment and then suddenly laugh.

"It's all the effect of Barchester High School," she said. "You see I never went to college."

"And if you had I shouldn't be treating you to coffee and these rather revolting sandwiches," said Swan. "It is, if you will excuse me, a certain air of arrested education about you that delights me. So much better than being education-conscious as so many nice girls are. I feel they are thinking 'You may be all very well, my boy, but I got a First in Modern Greats.'"

"Didn't you then?" said Grace.

"Greats, yes," said Swan. "Modern Greats no, not for all the wealth of Pilward and Co.'s Entire. That is why I am only an assistant master at a preparatory school instead of earning five thousand a year in Shell or I.C.I. And I may say that I like my job very much indeed and if it weren't that I am terrified of old Mrs. Allen—the mother of the delightful cook at the Priory School—all would be gas and gaiters."

As he spoke he had taken his glasses off and twirled them in his hand and Grace thought he looked very kind.

"And as I have what are known as private means," said Swan, "I am not afraid of my Headmaster. Nor he of me for that matter, though I did look at him through my spectacles when he was only a classical master at Southbridge School. But that was years and years ago, when you were a puling brat."

"I wasn't," said Grace indignantly. "I am twenty."

"And I am all of thirty," said Swan. "Rather over to be exact. And the year I was in Winter's form, before the war, you were four. I am no mathematician, but I think that is right."

"Oh, I didn't know you were so old," said Grace.

"Nor did I, till this moment," said Swan. "And here is the long-lost family solicitor," and Henry came in, pleased to find his sister being well looked after, but with the last bus on his mind.

"That's all right," said Swan. "Have some beer and then I'll take you both home in my shabby little car," so Henry gladly had some beer, as did Swan, and then they all got into the car which though modest was certainly not as shabby or as little as all that, and when they got to the Rectory Henry asked Swan to come in, which he quite willingly did.

"Oh, mother," said Grace, "this is Mr. Swan the one I told you was playing tennis at the Winters' that day when Sir Cecil had to go to the hospital. He gave us a splendid lecture this evening. He drove us back because the bus had gone."

Mrs. Grantly welcomed him and said was he any relation of her old school friend Flora Ramsay who had married a Mr.

Swan, and by great good luck Flora Ramsay turned out to be his mother which made talk ever easy and comfortable. And then Mr. Grantly, hearing voices in the drawing-room, came out of his study to see who was there and within three minutes had discovered that Swan was a scholar of Paul's, his own college and had read Greats, so that as Henry afterwards said it was all Old Jenkinson in the Common Room and what was the good of his bringing blokes home if father would nobble them, which was what always happened. Mrs. Grantly may have wondered for a moment whether her Grace was not thinking the same, but the moment passed. Presently, with an apology for outstaying his welcome which was neither meant nor taken seriously Swan said his good-byes, pressing the Grantlys to visit the Priory School when the weather was better, if ever, as his Headmaster liked him to have company and the teas were very good, an invitation which was accepted by everyone. Then the hospitable Rectory door was shut behind him and he drove back to the school, thinking what an extraordinarily nice family the Grantlys were and how nice it would be if one happened to marry into a family like that. Not of course that he was thinking of marrying. And then as happens to so many of us, the thought of his own age suddenly rose before him, a little frightening. One is a young untried creature and then one day one looks back and sees that young creature very far behind one; so distant that one can barely believe that one has journeyed so far. Grace's journey was hardly yet begun he thought: and then his inherited Scotch commonsense told him not to be a fool. The girl was doing a good and useful job and there was no sentiment about his feeling for her. None in the least. But she had a very pleasant way of confiding in one. And then he was nearly run into by a lorry with a sleepy driver and had to concentrate on his driving.

It was the custom for any master who had been off duty to report, quite unofficially, to the Head; which duty was a pleasant one as Philip Winter was as apt as not to be in his study with his wife Leslie darning his socks, or his children's socks, or some of the masses of grey stockings which the young gentlemen wore out as if they were gossamer and with which Matron could hardly keep up.

"Come in, Swan," said the Headmaster. "How did the lecture go?"

Swan said quite well, he thought, and the Birketts were there with Rose Fairweather and her husband. Rose was sillier than ever, he said, and her catchword was "absorbing."

"Do you remember the term you were engaged to her, sir?" he said to his old form-master. "We took a really intelligent interest in it."

"Young devils you were," said Philip. "You looking at me through your spectacles and Tony Morland being sententious. And now we are all old men. By the way I shouldn't be in the least surprised if Bond was starting whooping-cough. It's either that or devilry. Probably both. Thank goodness his people aren't worriers."

"But his grand-people are, sir," said Swan. "I'd never have thought that anyone so ferocious as old Lady Bond could make such a fuss over a boy, especially as there is a younger brother to carry on if necessary," at which Leslie Winter protested.

"Well, good night, Mrs. Winter," said Swan. "Good night, sir. Oh, by the way," he added, pausing at the door, "I hope the Grantlys from Edgewood are coming to tea with me sometime. May I bring them across to see you? Mr. Grantly is a classical man. I saw your book on Horace on a shelf, sir."

"And what, may I ask, do you want now?" said the Headmaster slightly suspicious of this obvious flattery.

"Oh—nothing," said Swan. "Good night. I'll see Matron about Bond first thing tomorrow."

Philip Winter waited till the door was shut and then remarked casually that Grace Grantly was a very good-looking girl and not a bad tennis-player.

"I was adored once," said Leslie, using Sir Andrew Aguecheek's touching words.

Her husband said so she was still and it was time to go to bed.

Swan was not one who let grass grow under his feet, as his schoolmasters at Southbridge had known to their cost, for in the ageless battle of Masters v. Boys, conducted with spirit on both sides though always under Queensberry rules, Swan and his confederate Tony Morland had usually been at the bottom of any trouble in the Fifth Form. Sometimes Boys had gained a point or two, as when Swan had deliberately put on his large spectacles at meals (when he did not need them) thus causing Philip Winter who was then young, intellectually red and supersensitive to show an amount of temper that he always subsequently regretted; on other occasions Masters had won hands down, especially Everard Carter the present Headmaster who could deflate any boy with a few piercing words and then ignore him in a way most disconcerting to the deflated. Tony Morland, with a wife and agreeable children, had long ago given up the world of school and might almost be called grown-up. But Swan, after going through most of the war which was in itself a form of school with the same ups and downs and likes and dislikes superimposed on backgrounds of tedium or discomfort or active danger, was, although very intelligent and a considerable amateur of life in his spare time and in the holidays, still something of the sixth-form prefect. His old Headmaster had once said of him that he was the only boy whose future he could not with any confidence predict and his present Headmaster probably thought much the same thing. However he was an excellent assistant master, as good at games as his spectacles allowed and with a temper that the most trying of the youngest fry hardly ever ruffled. The fact was, said Philip Winter to his wife, that nothing had ever jolted Swan yet, unless perhaps the war had given him a jolt that no one knew about. For delayed war shock is another of the gifts of modern civilisation and men who have seen death face to face for four or five years and then settled down to civil life may be clutched unawares by ghosts from the past and made to stand and deliver; sometimes their health, sometimes their integrity, sometimes their sanity. The science that can mend still lags very far behind the science that can mar, and cannot raze out the written troubles of the brain with any sweet oblivious antidote.

All this or something very much to the same effect Philip Winter said to his wife next day after lunch when they were talking about Swan. Leslie, firm in her deep content as a happily married woman, said it would be a good thing if Swan fell really in love, to which her husband replied that it might be good for Swan emotionally or psychologically or any pretentious nonsense one liked, but it would undoubtedly play old Harry with his work. Just, said Leslie, as Rose Birkett had upset Philip's work, if Rose's mother was to be believed.

"Yes, I must have been the world's champion pest," said Philip. "Even my red hair isn't an excuse for how silly I was. And about Rose too! I wonder that Birkett didn't sack me. I have sometimes thought that he would have if the boys hadn't protected me. I was quite impossible that term; Swan and Morland were perfect devils. What was so annoying was that they got behind my guard again and again. But never could I get behind theirs. Swan with his eternal spectacles looking at me as if I were a peculiar insect and Morland who was really quite intelligent favouring me with a vacuous stare like a white-washed wall. They never tried it on with Carter."

"Only because he had grown up a little sooner than you did," said Leslie, adding "Darling" as an afterthought.

"The army made one grow up a bit," said Philip thoughtfully. "And when you are a Colonel you really have to behave. Not but what I was pretty silly about you, my love," and he looked at his wife very affectionately.

"But not silly as I was about you," said Leslie. "Going to

Winter Overcotes on a cold winter morning just to see you at the station for one moment before you vanished."

"If it comes to silliness," said Philip, "I never took such a chance in my life as when I proposed to you all in two minutes through the window of a railway carriage. But I don't repent it."

"You *didn't* propose to me," said Leslie indignantly. "You gave that dreadful Rose Birkett's engagement ring—the one she threw at you when you got unengaged—to Lydia Merton to give to me. I don't call that proposing. I had to go to Winter Overcotes very early on a cold winter morning and ask you to marry me through the window of a railway carriage. And there wasn't even time to kiss you. Oh Philip—" and for a moment she was on that cold windy platform watching the train steam out with the man she loved, on her finger as a token of eternal loyalty the engagement ring he had given to another girl.

"Well, I must go and watch football and pretend I like it," said Philip and went away, while Leslie applied herself to repairing a pillow case which had somehow come in two while its owner was defending it against the young gentleman in the next bed. And with the whirr of the machine it is not surprising that she did not hear Mr. Swan come in and nearly jumped.

"I'm so sorry," said Swan sympathetically. "I knew a man in the army once who was going to patent a noiseless sewing-machine."

"And did he?" said Leslie.

"He did," said Swan. "At least he did the drawings for it and showed them to me and next day he and the drawings were blown up. But I don't expect they'd have worked. Have you noticed how people practically never invent *quiet* things. Railway engines, cars, aeroplanes, telephones, wireless—it's all noise. But what I really came in to say was that hundreds of Grantlys are coming to tea with me on Saturday. Will you do me the honour of pretending to be the hostess? It would give a cachet to my miserable bachelor's den."

To which Leslie replied that his room was the best in the

school quarters and the envy of all the other masters and it was useless to try flattery on her, but she would come with pleasure as a guest.

"Oh, but I can't," she said. "I am so sorry. I had quite forgotten. Ludovic Lufton is coming. And I asked Charles Belton and Clarissa. Won't you all come to tea here instead?"

To this Swan was quite agreeable and said he would show the Grantlys his quarters first and then bring them over to the Winters'.

Accordingly on the following Saturday Henry drove his parents and his younger sister over in the family car and Swan took them up to his large, comfortable bedroom-study on the first floor of the new wing—for Philip had found himself obliged to enlarge the school a year or two earlier and added some rooms where the assistant masters could be more or less on their own, though in close touch with the agreeable young devils under their care. The Grantlys were loud and sincere in their admiration of everything, including the view.

"Yes, it is lovely," said Swan, "and too, too nostalgic as that silly Clarissa Graham would say. Sometimes it looks like a Turner and sometimes like a Claude and sometimes it turns into a Bewick."

Mr. Grantly said he sometimes wondered if it was a good or a bad thing that one was so apt to think of landscapes in terms of the men who had painted them, to which Swan very sensibly as we think replied that it depended very much on who the men were. To see his view as a Turner was delightful; to see it as a Claude made him nearly ill with vague romantic feelings. But if he saw it as some moderns apparently saw things, he would rather have a railway poster.

"And one might almost say," he added, "that the railways—for British Railways I will not call them—produce some of the best art of today. And why they have the wits to do that and at the same time give us such revoltingly dirty trains and such expensive nasty meals, I don't know."

Mr. Grantly, who as a clergyman spoke with authority, said there were some things that it was not given to us to know.

"I'll tell you one, sir," said Charles Belton, who had come quietly in and made a kind of general salute to Mrs. Grantly and her belongings. "You know those lions that are painted—stencilled as a matter of fact by the look of them—on our British Railways. Well, as there are ladies present, all I can say is that they are standing in a way that shows with marked clearness that apart from a conventional mane they have no other sign of being lions."

There was a second's silence and then the three young men burst into an unrefined laugh in which Mr. Grantly and the ladies couldn't help joining and then Mrs. Grantly said if Swan meant Julian Rivers's landscapes when he was talking about moderns, she quite agreed with him, on which Charles commented by saying darkly that a man who wore a kilt when he needn't needed his face pushing in, and then felt that needn't and needed in juxtaposition darkened counsel.

"I say, you can't talk like that," said Swan. "I'm no Highlander—in fact my mother's people still look on the Highlanders as breekless, cattle-lifting loons; but, hang it all, what's wrong with the kilt? We wear them, but just of tweed, like douce, honest men. Not all stars and stripes."

"But," said Grace unexpectedly, "Julian doesn't have a tartan kilt, or even a tweed kilt. It's mustard yellow, because I saw him when I went to tea at Pomfret Towers. And he had a rather undone sports shirt and his chest all hairy like a gorilla. He said he wanted to paint me."

"If he does, I'll show him what's what," said Swan. "I was particularly addicted to unarmed combat in the war. One could travel much lighter. A part of a gun gets heavy after a bit."

"I *say*," said Henry, almost adding Sir in his excitement. "Was it fun?"

But Swan, seeing that the elder guests were not really enjoying this talk, said he would show them the boys' quarters if they cared and then they would all go over to tea with the Winters. Dormitories without their pleasing anxious inmates have very little character. Mrs. Grantly said the right thing to Matron who was hovering, inquired after Bond, and then continued her progress: rather like royalty, Swan thought. And he was not far wrong, for a good clergyman's wife (by which we mean a clergyman's good wife though put like that it seems to refer rather to her virtue in the narrow sense than her way of filling her position) is well-advised, or lucky, if she can assume Royalty's air of real interest in things which are so dull they almost make you squint. And it must have been a success, for Matron, who was really only about thirty and very nice-looking, wrote to her mother that Mrs. Grantly was a jolly good sort, and she wished Mums would get a hat like Mrs. Grantly's and described it at length. But as it was a three-year-old felt hat, bought we are almost ashamed to confess at Bostock and Plummer's, its peculiar qualities must, we feel, have been in the eye of the beholder.

Tea was in the dining-room, with excellent scones made by Nannie Allen the Warings' old hereditary nurse and excellent cakes made by her daughter Mrs. Hopkins, whose husband Sergeant Hopkins did the vegetable garden and every species of odd job known to a handy man. The Winters were already there and with them Lord Lufton, looking on the whole less harassed than he used to. As everyone was more or less acquainted the party quietly subsided into seats.

"I thought Clarissa was coming," said Mrs. Grantly.

"She has," said Leslie Winter. "Ludovic drove her over. She went over to the other house to see Cecil and Cora," and as she spoke Clarissa Graham came in; as pretty as we remember her, perhaps a little thinner, perhaps with a faint look of care, or was it boredom, or what? Mrs. Grantly, seeing her with a fresh eye for their paths did not often cross, felt glad that her Grace's good looks were untroubled and then felt very sorry for Clarissa, though on no grounds that she could specify.

"I am sorry if I am a little late," said Clarissa, taking the one empty seat which happened to be between Swan and Henry Grantly. "Too, too discourteous."

"Yes, it was rather," said Swan, putting on his large spectacles and looking at her. To his secret amusement and we may add mild surprise she looked down, then looked him straight in the face with her grandmother Lady Emily Leslie's falcon eyes and said, "Too, too right, my dear. But one just is like that, you know."

"Or one isn't," said Swan in a kind but extremely matter-of-fact voice. "One needn't be, you know. Will you have scone and honey, or bread and honey, or cake and honey? And how were Cecil and Lady Cora?"

Clarissa said very well and really, my dear, too, too baby-minded; and then checked herself. "What I mean is," she said, looking at her plate as she put honey, very neatly and without any drips, on her scone, "that they look so happy that they might burst with happiness. Do people always look like that when they are going to have babies? I never noticed."

"All the nicest women I have known looked like that," said Swan, interested in this new facet of Clarissa, "but I didn't know it worked with the husbands too. If I said Too, too couvade, would that convey anything to you?"

Clarissa looked up into his eyes and laughed, a low amused laugh with no nonsense about it.

"Serve me right," she said. "You know, I *do* need beating sometimes."

"You," said Swan, "in the decadent speech of our modern youth, are telling me. *Need* you need beating though? I am not sure if I make myself clear."

"Quite clear," said Clarissa. "After all I *am* grown-up, but no one seems to notice it. My fault perhaps. Perhaps even a little not my fault. Father is away so much with all his missions and things. Of course mother is an angel," and she put a large bit of honeyed scone into her mouth and almost gagged herself before turning to Henry Grantly on her other side. Swan felt, and was amused to feel, that he had very sweetly been given his congé and as Mrs. Grantly on his other side was talking to the Headmaster he was left to his own reflections, which were rather in the nature of Lord! what fools these mortals be. So far he had never been in love, at any rate not for more than three whole days together, and he wondered idly what it was like: the real thing. In his experience of the world, and he had had a good deal one way and another, he had quite often been a confidant, but so far had not experienced that divine frenzy and he occasionally wondered whether he was one of the born bachelors, but on the whole thought very little about it. He had sometimes compared himself with the "Charles, his friend" of patch and powder drama and was quite content to watch, to be the confidant. And here he was, being confidant for Clarissa Graham who was engaged to Charles Belton. Charles, his friend.

"And can you tell me," said the voice of Philip Winter to Mrs. Grantly, next to Swan, "why Mrs. Joram won't, or can't, give a date for the party she was going to give for Sir Edmund Pridham? We are all longing for an excuse to wear our best hat, if any."

Mrs. Grantly said she understood—and mind, Mr. Winter must clearly understand that she only said understood—that when the Bishop put off his cruise to Madeira, on the grounds of the General Election, Mrs. Joram had also put off her party sine die if that was the way to say it—

Philip said it could not be more correctly put.

—and what they all wanted to know was Why.

"As I am a schoolmaster, I must have an answer to every question," said Philip. "And as far as I can see the answer to this one is that as long as the Bishop—and particularly the Bishopess—are in Barchester Mrs. Joram feels it would be better not to give a party to which they would have to be invited."

Mrs. Grantly said all great things were so simple when once you understood them and turned to Swan, so that Philip Winter was left high and dry, for Lord Lufton and Grace Grantly were deep in conversation. The words "moth-balls," "real ermine," "insured of course," drifted towards him and he lazily wondered what on earth they meant. But it was only the robes of a baron and a baron's wife, carefully preserved with camphor and moth-ball at Framley Court, that they were talking about, for Lord Lufton had once promised that Grace should see his mother's state robes and she did not want him to forget.

"Perhaps," said Lord Lufton, with his usual gentle diffidence, "you and your people will come to tea one day. Mother would like to show you the robes. I have to wear my father's sometimes, and every time I put them on I think how much nicer it would be if he were alive."

"But then you wouldn't be Lord Lufton," said Grace. "At least I mean you wouldn't be you if time went backwards," which Lord Lufton thought very true.

"Oh, did you do anything about that flat my sister and her husband want to let?" said Grace; for there had been a suggestion that her married sister Eleanor Keith might take an eligible bachelor as tenant and occasionally feed him. Lord Lufton said he had not forgotten it, but much as he disliked boarding with his old cousin in Buckingham Gate, he was afraid Mrs. Keith's flat would be too expensive. Grace was sorry and interested all in one breath and said she knew it sounded silly, but she thought lords were still fairly well off.

"I wish *we* were," said Lord Lufton. "But what with death duties and taxation we aren't. That's why we've let most of Framley to Mr. Macfadyen, the Amalgamated Vedge man," and Grace, whose family so far were able to live on what the tax-collector left them, felt very sorry for anyone who had to let bits of his own home to strangers and said so.

"Thank you *very* much," said Lord Lufton, looking almost happy. "That's very understanding of you. I don't mind for myself, and Maria is married and Justy—that's my other sister Justinia—has a job; but I do hate it for my mother. She misses my father all the time. So do I, but one has got to go on living and father would have wanted me to do my duty," and somehow he made these words sound simple and not in the least priggish.

Grace said firmly that he was quite right. Not that doing one's duty always worked, she added, because look at His Majesty and goodness knew He always did His duty and then He had to be so frightfully ill which was *frightfully* unfair.

A good deal of noise at the other side of the table then resolved itself into Henry Grantly and Charles Belton arguing across Mr. Grantly about the Brax gun as served and loved by Charles during the last war (by which we mean the previous war, or, to make it quite clear, the war which had nominally terminated in 1945) and the Kroda gun loved and served by Henry during his military service. Short of having several thousand men on Salisbury Plain and forbidding any civilians to come within ten miles of the place there seemed no real way to end the argument, so Leslie said there was a good roaring fire in the drawing-room and took her guests away, all except Henry and Charles who had got to the point at which cups and plates and knives were needed to illustrate their theories.

Henry, who had very nice manners, did ask Charles if he didn't want to go too, but Charles had just got his guns into a position from which somebody or something could be enfiladed (which may be nonsense but sounds well) and had reached over for the last scone to represent a well-known feature of the landscape, so they stayed comfortably where they were.

In the drawing-room the grown-ups, by which we mean the Grantlys and the Winters, were having a comfortable domestic conversation, while Swan organised a game of tiddly-winks, a game which had unexpectedly become popular among the young that winter. An old-fashioned round table on one leg terminating in three claw-feet, with a thin rug over it, made an excellent battlefield and soon there was almost as much noise as when they were playing Pit on the day of Cecil Waring's sudden illness and operation. Clarissa, whose neat fingers were very skillful at the game, had all her men but one safely in the little bowl in no time.

"I wish I could flip like that," said Lord Lufton, with frank envy. "I can't get my men to budge," and he made a flip at one of his counters which sprang to the edge of the bowl and fell over backwards on to the rug.

"Bet you sixpence I'll cover it," said Swan, to which Lord Lufton said Done. Swan put his spectacles on and flipped his red over the bowl and it dropped quietly on Lord Lufton's green, who far from resenting it asked Swan in an admiring voice how on earth he did it. Swan said Just genius and Lord Lufton, recognising in Swan a kindred spirit, said Stap his vitals but he was a rare hand at a main to which nonsense Swan replied by taking a pinch of snuff from an imaginary snuff-box and flicking an imaginary jabot with his handkerchief and both men began to laugh, as did Grace, who with two nice elder brothers found young men very easy company.

"Come on, Grace," said Swan. "It's your turn," and the game went on, but Clarissa's luck was gone and everyone was home while her last man still remained on the table, at which moment Charles and Henry came in.

"Well, who won?" said Lord Lufton.

Charles said he had, but he considered Henry had the makings of a good artilleryman in him when he had been as long at the job as he, Charles, had. And how had their infantile sport gone, he inquired politely. From a triple clamour which ensued he gathered that if you allowed for the order they played in, they had all won except Clarissa whose last man was still on the table.

"Poor old girl," said Charles, rather as one might speak to a dog perhaps, but to a loved and valued dog.

Clarissa looked at him and sang, as if to herself, "Don't be so deucedly condescending," adding airily, "out of The Gondoliers, you know."

"Condescending be hanged," Charles was beginning to say when Swan slowly and deliberately took out his spectacles, put them on and looked at Charles through them. The glassy look which had defeated several masters at Southbridge School was like cold water on Charles who bent over the table and began quietly putting the tiddly-winks men away.

Lord Lufton, distressed at the little scene, distressed for Charles, distressed by Clarissa, said he ought to be getting back as Mr. Macfadyen was coming to supper.

"Can I take you home?" he said to Clarissa. "Or perhaps Charles is taking you."

"How good of you, Lufton," said Philip Winter, who had been paying attention to the little turmoil, as indeed when did he not pay attention to what happened within the bounds of his school. "It is really Charles's Sunday off, but I rather need him if it doesn't inconvenience anyone," to which Charles, almost standing to attention and saluting, said "Of course, sir," and after proper good-byes and thanks and a repeated invitation to Grace to come and see his mother, Lord Lufton put Clarissa into his car and drove towards Holdings. Clarissa, for once entirely subdued and very conscious of her own bad behaviour, sat perfectly silent and Lord Lufton did not try to make conversation.

"Will you come in and see mother?" said Clarissa when they had reached her home. "She would love to see you," she added in the neat society voice that Miss Merriman would at once have recognised as a defence against any show of feeling.

"I would love to see your mother," said Lord Lufton, "but my mother is expecting me and I'd better go on."

"Well, thank you for driving me," said Clarissa. "And I'm sorry. There!"

"Then do try not to do it again," said Lord Lufton, not at all priggishly, but as a good nurse would say it to a fractious child. Charles is far too good for it. Good-bye."

He drove home and told his mother about the party, omitting the uncomfortable scene over the tiddly-winks table, and then Mr. Macfadyen came to supper bringing, with apologies, a brace of pheasants for the larder. They had a pleasant evening and Lord Lufton thought how nice it was when his mother forgot to be a widow, and it was like old times. Except that his father was not there. But time is merciful to the young and Lord Lufton thought of his father less and less as his own duties and responsibilities filled his life. When Mr. Macfadyen had gone he talked a little with his mother whose chief subject of conversation now was her daughter Maria's expected baby and from her talk her son derived the impression that whether it was boy or girl she would be equally delighted because for them it didn't matter. Lord Lufton asked why: to which his mother replied, with gentle surprise at his denseness, because there wasn't a title.

"Then I suppose you will cut me off with sixpence if I don't have a boy, mother," he said, at which words, to his alarm, he saw his mother's speaking countenance clearly expressing the hope, the wish, nay the certainty that he was going to tell her he was engaged, so he hastily added, "but I'm not in love with anyone yet, so I can't very well ask them to marry me." And after a little more talk about the Women's Institute meeting at Pomfret Madrigal which Lady Lufton had promised to attend and at which Mrs. Morland had promised to speak, they both went to bed.

No, certainly Lord Lufton was not engaged. And even more certainly he was not in love. As he undressed he suddenly thought of the girl who had stood in the sunlight at Rushwater and looked at him, there in the gloom of the champion bull's stall, with hero-worship in her eyes. For a long time he had lived upon that unconscious betrayal of her feelings, unwilling to speak because he had so little to offer and then when he knew that she and Charles Belton were engaged, with no thought of speaking. More than once, he remembered, she had shown what seemed a deliberate want of consideration, almost a deliberate want of affection for Charles; for Charles who was his very good friend and on whose behalf he had put his own feelings towards Clarissa away for ever. But now that lovely shimmering bubble had vanished. Today's scene had shown him too clearly a Clarissa whom he was deeply sorry for, and in his compassion there was no love at all.

CHAPTER 6

The day fixed for Mrs. Morland's talk to the Women's Institute at Pomfret Madrigal was now at hand and that gifted writer found, as she was always finding, that to promise to speak was one thing and to write or even sketch a lecture was quite another.

"It is not so much that I can't think of things to say," said Mrs. Morland to Delia Grant, formerly Delia Brandon, who had come over to tea at High Rising, "as that they do so jumble each other," which Delia, who was slightly in awe of people who wrote books, begged her to explain.

"Well," said Mrs. Morland, unsettling her never very tidy hair with both hands, "it is quite extraordinary the number of things one thinks about, and quite without thinking. People do do such *extraordinary* things."

Delia asked which people.

"Oh, all sorts," said Mrs. Morland vaguely. "Madame Koska and her girls in the show-room and her old friend General Chard who has put money into the firm and the villains who I find are all Russians just now because somehow Persians and Egyptians aren't interesting enough to be villains—" at which point Delia interrupted, though very politely, to ask if Russians were interesting.

"Oh no, not a bit," said Mrs. Morland. "They *have* written some books, though books is about all you can call them. I have tried them in French and I have tried them in German and I can't find anything in them," which echo of King Charles II's words about his nephew-in-law of Denmark surprised Delia a good deal. "And as far as I know the Persians and the Egyptians haven't written any books at all."

Delia said wasn't Omar Khayyám Persian.

"One might say so," said Mrs. Morland, assuming a quite illusory air of knowledge. "But I expect FitzGerald altered it all a bit. You have to when you translate poetry, because if you don't, the lines don't fit. One must have to know Persian *frightfully* well to translate it. I mean to get the words right."

"Gosh! Yes," said Delia, in whom the old Delia Brandon was still very much alive. "There was a wonderful translation of one of Colette's things once and it said some people shared a bath at the Opera."

"How *perfect*," said Mrs. Morland, whose French was much better than most of her friends guessed, for she was a modest creature and took it for granted that if she read French without tears, everyone else must do the same.

"And anyway, wasn't Thou a man really?" said Delia, sticking to her last remark but one with admirable pertinacity.

Mrs. Morland, struck by this original view of the Rubaiyat, said she would ask Miss Hampton next time she met her; Miss Hampton was sure to know. But Delia, wise in her generation, said if Omar Khayyám or whoever he really was had been a woman and Thou had been another woman, Miss Hampton would certainly be the one; but she didn't think Miss Hampton was so good on the other way round.

"Anyway," she added, with the complete confidence of a happily married woman, "Hilary'll know. I'll ask him. He digs up bits of pottery with the most *extraordinary* pictures on them. But, I say Mrs. Morland, don't you like Anna Karenina or War and Peace?"

Mrs. Morland said she had not liked them ever since she

could remember and there was a better description of a battle in two pages of Stendhal than in all Tolstoy ever wrote.

Delia, with bull-dog persistence, said Then what about the Egyptians, to which Mrs. Morland replied that if Delia would name a book by an Egyptian, she would read it; unless, she added, it had a name like Menhopnefmepki, in which case she didn't want to hear anything about it, and what did Delia think the Pomfret Madrigal W.I. would really like. Delia said they would simply love it if Mrs. Morland would just talk about herself and say things like how she got her first book published and things of that sort, adding that as Lady Lufton was going to take the chair she would be quite safe.

"That will be delightful," said Mrs. Morland, much relieved. "The only thing is, I can't stop. When I hear myself speaking I have a delightful feeling that it is somebody else and I could go on and on for ever," to which Delia the practical said Lady Lufton would see that she didn't and Stoker, with glorious extravagance, brought in a fresh teapot of tea.

"I say, Mrs. Morland," said Delia, after a short but quite comfortable silence, "you know all about people. I wish you could tell me what's happened to Francis. He used to be such fun and now he is nearly dull. Do husbands get like that? I hope Hilary won't."

Mrs. Morland pushed her hair back unbecomingly with both hands and said her husband had always been dull.

Then, said Delia, why had she married him, to which Mrs. Morland replied that if someone asked you to marry them and you didn't love anyone else there seemed no reason not to.

"But didn't *heaps* of people want to marry you?" said Delia, who still remained in many ways rather young and couldn't understand that marriage can be a very comfortable affair even if the divine madness of falling head over ears in love has not touched one; to which Mrs. Morland replied very simply that no one had ever fallen in love with her and when the late Mr. Morland had offered his hand and heart, she had never been asked by anyone else and couldn't think of any reason for refusing.

"Henry had his good points," said Mrs. Morland, musingly. "He was quite easy to get on with and then he died," which appears to be all that anyone could say about the late Mr. Morland. And then Delia took her leave and went back to Mr. Turpin's cottage at Pomfret Madrigal, where she found her twins making toffee in the kitchen under Mrs. Turpin's supervision and her husband going through some of the material for the book, commissioned by the Oxbridge University Press, about the pre-Grombolian pottery found in the excavations near the foothills of the Chankly Bore; which was later to gain him a seat in the Académie des Inscriptions and a belated recognition of his early work on the Romantic poet Eugène Duval, better known under his nom-de-plume of Jehan le Capet. For, as M. Proust has so truly pointed out, there is practically nothing in our lives that does not come back into it by devious and unexpected ways as time goes on.

"Any news, darling?" she said, rumpling her husband's hair.

None, he said. The twins had been very good and Peggy had asked them to supper at Stories because Francis had rung up to say some business would keep him in Barchester.

"Conceited chump," said Francis's loving sister. "I say, Hilary, what *is* up with Francis? He was always an awfully good brother and he still is. And I know he adores Peggy—*really*, I mean. Why has he got to be so beastly to her. At least I don't mean beastly, but captious—if that's a word," she added.

"Yes, it's a *word* all right," said Hilary, obviously thinking of something else. "Your brother Francis is an ostrich."

Delia, anxious on her much loved brother's behalf, said he didn't eat nails and golf balls.

"Not so much that," said Hilary, "but he can't see himself at all. If he gets anywhere near seeing himself he hides his head in the sand. And his particular sand is showing off at Peggy. It makes him feel lordly. And he's a bit of a coward too. He knows she won't answer back."

Delia, much impressed, asked her husband how he knew.

"I don't," said Hilary simply. "I just *know*: which is quite different," and Delia, after a moment's consideration, saw what he meant.

"I don't know anyone who could speak to him," Hilary went on, "because from what I've seen of him he would be so rude back. Someone like Lady Cora Waring could have done it."

"I wish she would," said Delia. "But now she's married she isn't over here and I don't think she could do it when they go to dinner at the Priory."

"Or that nice Father Fewling," said Hilary, "because he is practically a missionary and having been a sailor he isn't afraid. The only other person I can think of would be somebody quite from outside and then Francis wouldn't mind so much."

Delia suggested the Bishop, but rather spoilt her point by saying what a snub he would get from Francis and having the giggles, and then they talked about other things.

On the appointed day Mrs. Morland drove over to Pomfret Madrigal and up the little drive to Stories where Peggy Brandon was to receive her and shepherd her to the little church hall where the Women's Institute meeting was to take place. Peggy was looking so pretty and so ridiculously young for her age that Mrs. Morland, who had heard rumours about Francis's offhand ways to his wife, decided people must have made mountains out of molehills, and very sensibly decided to forget all about it. Here Lady Lufton joined them and the three ladies walked down to the village.

"You won't mind if we go to tea at the Vicarage, I hope," said Peggy. "Mrs. Parkinson can't come to the meeting because of the children and she does so want to meet you, Mrs. Morland. And Lady Lufton too, if she can stay."

Lady Lufton, who in the W.I. atmosphere seemed to lose

many of her cares, was looking, so Peggy thought, very handsome; and the judgment of a really nice woman upon another woman is not to be despised. Her Ladyship said she had plenty of time and would be delighted, so picking up Delia Grant at Turpin's cottage, they went across the little green to the church hall, which was depressingly like other church halls, a kind of exalted summer-house with a resounding wooden floor, walls of something like asbestos with a sickly green wash, and at one end a large iron stove which was already almost red hot and making quite terrifying crackles and pistol shots of noise.

"Thatcher's left the damper out as usual," said Delia. "I'll tell him. I saw him outside. Hi! Turpin!"

The old Stories gardener, who was tidying the little bit of garden at the side of the church hall for the winter, very slowly stopped what he was doing and came even more slowly towards Delia.

"I say, Turpin, someone's put too much coke in the stove," said Delia, "or the damper's out too far. It's making a noise like Guy Fawkes Day and red hot."

"That Thatcher he isn't no more good than old Staylin," said Turpin. "Never done an honest day's work in his life and both his daughters no better than they should be. *I* haven't got daughters; no, nor sons neither, a plaguy lot. I'll see to the damper, Miss Delia," and he walked slowly and venomously away.

The hall was by now about three-quarters full of women from the village and near by, who whether from a hereditary respect for the gentry or to be nearer the now almost red-hot stove, were all sitting huddled together, leaving the first two rows empty. Mrs. Morland, who had gradually given in to her subconscious self and let it do most of her work for her, was already putting into phrases, almost without knowing it, the change in Lady Lufton, who now appeared to Mrs. Morland's other self to have a dual personality. Gone was the sad, stormy-eyed widow behaving almost like Queen Victoria after the death of Prince

Albert; gone was the hesitating manner, the apparent want of confidence in anything she said or did. In its place there was a woman speaking with considerable authority to the class which her ancestors had probably employed and helped and scolded for several hundred years, and evidently recognized by that class as one naturally set in authority over them, one from whom they could get help in their difficulties, good advice that they would never take, and a sympathy that took practical form. So that when Lady Lufton, standing and eying the audience, said some of them had better come up to the front as it looked so bare, at least twenty women came slowly up to the front and resettled themselves, but still leaving the front row empty.

"That is much better," said Lady Lufton, with a kind of impartial benevolence. "And now, Mrs. Grant, may we have the minutes of the last meeting," and these having been dispatched in a very businesslike way, Lady Lufton introduced Mrs. Morland who pushed her hat slightly awry and began.

As Mrs. Morland so truly said to anyone who asked her to speak, she knew nothing special about anything, but she could be utterly relied upon to fill any given time with maunderings about herself and things in general and was very good about stopping five minutes earlier than expected, a trait most endearing to any audience. About half-way through the talk Mr. and Mrs. Parkinson, accompanied by a middle-aged man who was unknown to Pomfret Madrigal, slipped quietly in and quietly took their places in the front row. It speaks volumes for the good manners of the W.I. that though every member was consumed with curiosity there was no whispering; nothing more than an exchange of glances.

The talk or lecture, whichever one likes to call it, for it cannot be accurately described as either, having come to an end and the lecturer, untidy and flushed but triumphant, having sat down to the accompaniment of a mild form of clapping, Lady Lufton rose and said she was sure some of the members would like to ask Mrs. Morland a question. Every member's eyes automatically looked out of the window, or up at the ceiling, or at nothing at all, and silence reigned.

"Mrs. Turpin, have you nothing special to ask?" said Lady Lufton. "No? Mrs. Thatcher; no? Mrs. Grant perhaps?"

But Delia, usually very ready to talk, was smitten with dumbness.

"Now, I am sure Mrs. Parkinson would like to ask Mrs. Morland something," said Lady Lufton.

"Well," said Mrs. Parkinson, getting up at the call of duty as a clergyman's wife should, "I'm not a great reader. I did used to be at home, didn't I, dad?" at which words the stranger looked up at her and nodded good-humouredly, "but I don't get much time now, but I got a book of Mrs. Morland's out of the public library and I *did* enjoy it. I think someone like Mrs. Morland that writes books that we can read and really learn something from them like about the way Madame Koska chooses her models in Paris, well reely we all ought to be very grateful," and with a very pink face she sat down.

"Thank you, Mrs. Parkinson," said Lady Lufton. "Will you answer that, Mrs. Morland?" upon which that popular writer got up and said anything—or we may say everything—that came into her head in the way of irrelevancies, put a large wisp of hair behind one ear and sat down.

"Now, I am sure there must be a great many other interesting questions that you would like to ask," said Lady Lufton, though privately convinced to the contrary. Again the faces of the audience became perfectly blank.

"Well, I'll be the mug," said the stranger, by now identified as Mrs. Parkinson's father. "There was a book of yours, madam, that I bought on a railway stall, at Liverpool Street it was of all places. I don't happen to remember the name, nor exackly what it was about, but I thoroughly enjoyed it. In fact when my girl here, Mrs. Parkinson that is, asked me to come and stay with them, I bought another copy to give to her, little thinking that I would be hearing the writer speak. A most interesting experience it has been and I am sure I heartily thank Mrs. Morland," and he sat down.

Lady Lufton, apparently quite content with this contribution, asked for more comments, but except for Miss Hamp who kept the village shop and was lame and much respected, no one came forward. Miss Hamp wished to know if publishers were honest, a question whose magnitude of scope enabled Mrs. Morland to take the whole audience into her confidence about the dreadful price of typing paper and carbons, not to speak of the difficulties with binding and distribution and the way people were buying fewer books—adding that it was all due to the Government.

Lady Lufton, impeccable in chairmanship, interrupted to say that the Women's Institutes were non-political.

"Oh, of course. I *am* so sorry," said Mrs. Morland, really blushing in a middle-aged way at her infringement of etiquette, "But of course when I said the Government, I didn't mean Mr. Churchill. I meant Them."

"I am afraid," said Lady Lufton, whose usually care-worn face looked almost amused and, Mrs. Morland thought with the working part of her mind, very handsome, "that no political allusions at all can be made here, Mrs. Morland," and Mrs. Parkinson's father was heard to say it was the same in his business and, rather irrelevantly, that it was no good flogging a dead horse.

Lady Lufton showed great presence of mind in at once calling upon Mrs. Turpin to move a vote of thanks. Mrs. Turpin accordingly did so, adding that she'd better go and see about the urn now.

Mrs. Parkinson's father looked up.

"The tea-urn, dad," said Mrs. Parkinson. "For the members' tea here."

And, said Lady Lufton, would Miss Hamp second it, which that lady did, and the meeting was over. Most of the members withdrew to a kind of pitch-pine lobby where Mrs. Turpin dispensed tea, two or three lingering to ask, diffidently, if Mrs.

Morland would autograph a book, which she did with great good will and almost with tears in her eyes owing to her romantic temperament. Some were Penguins, a few were real twelve and sixpenny copies given by old employers to a former housemaid, or by a remembering young man or woman to the old nurse of their early days. But the proudest moment went to Mrs. Thatcher from Grumper's End who had an American copy of Mrs. Morland's last but one book, sent to her by her son Jimmy, the one in the Air Force; it being part payment of a debt contracted by an American airman whom he had thrown dice with in Cologne. Mrs. Morland signed them all and Delia Grant said afterwards that she had distinctly heard her say, God bless you, my people. But nobody believed Delia and least of all herself.

The Vicarage, which some of those present had not seen since the Millers went to St. Ewold's, was certainly no more comfortable than it had been in Mr. Miller's bachelor days, being scantily furnished and the carpets almost threadbare. But there was a feeling of being lived in which even Mrs. Miller after her marriage, nice though she was, had never achieved. Perhaps some of the austerity of her father the Reverend and extremely selfish and disagreeable Justin Morris had descended to her (though none of his moral or mental defects had); perhaps her long years of being a paid companion in sparsely furnished bedrooms facing north with gas fires that gave little more than a glow; perhaps the effect of long years of privation, Gray's chill penury, had left an indelible mark. But Mrs. Morland, noticing always through her other or writing self things that she didn't know she had noticed till long afterwards, was absorbing an impression of a life which might be poor, but gave out riches; whose fires might not be very large but were lit with a generous heart. Peggy and Delia indeed, knowing the Vicarage well, were a little exercised about the large comfortable fire in the drawing-room, till Mrs. Parkinson mentioned that Sir Edmund Pridham had sent them a cartload of lovely logs.

"He's coming to tea too," said Mrs. Parkinson, as she did the honours of the vicarage. "And he sent us a bottle of brandy, because he likes it. He says it's reelly good brandy, quite medicinal, so it's all right. Excuse me just a moment while I see to the kettle, Lady Lufton," and she went away to the kitchen. We will not attempt to disguise from our readers that most of the party were longing to discuss their host and hostess and more especially their hostess's father, but this was not the moment and it was a relief to everyone when Mrs. Parkinson summoned them to the dining-room where the round table was generously spread with things which none of the guests ever ate at tea-time, but which each guest resolved to eat if he or she died in torment for it. At the same moment a noise was head outside, recognised by most of the company as Sir Edmund Pridham's rattle-trap little car, and in he came; rather more shrunk, rather more bowed, his teeth fitting rather more loosely, but still acknowledged doyen and uncrowned Lord Lieutenant of the County.

"Well, well, we're all very fine people," said Sir Edmund, looking at the company. "Nice old table you've got, Mrs. Parkinson."

"It was father gave it us," said Mrs. Parkinson. "It's ever so old. His grandfather had it. This is father. This is Sir Edmund Pridham, father."

"Your father, eh?" said Sir Edmund. "Didn't know you had one. What's his name?"

"Welk. Harold Welk," said that gentleman.

"Now, wait a minute," said Sir Edmund, letting himself down into a chair next to Mr. Welk, so do the stronger sex cling together in mixed company. "Welk, eh? There was a trooper with that name in the Barsetshire Yeomanry in the Boer War. Now wait a minute, Harold Welk, that was it. Handy man, interested in wood trade. Funny the way one remembers these things."

"My father, Sir Edmund," said Mr. Welk. "I was born while he was away, and mother called me after him. We've always had a Harold in the family. My Mavis's boy is Harold."

"And where do your people come from?" Sir Edmund asked entirely uninterested in Mrs. Parkinson's boy.

Mr. Welk said up in the north of Barsetshire. His people lived just where the woods came down by Gundric's Fossway.

"Then you're all right," said Sir Edmund, though not so much implying that Mr. Welk had up till now been suspect, as in recognition of a county name. "Welks were always round there. Before the Conquest as far as anyone knows. Rum sort of name, but the feller that's doing the Barsetshire Survey says so and *he* ought to know. Won't get to W though for ten years or so. The war held it up. Farmers, eh?"

"Woodsmen, Sir Edmund," said Mr. Welk, at which unexpected and romantic words the conversation died down as the chatter of the crowds and the splash of the fountains used to die down on Armistice Day, when it was celebrated on its true anniversary.

"Woodsmen, eh?" said Sir Edmund. "I used to go shooting up there a good bit before I got my gammy leg. Bodgers they used to call 'em."

"That's right, Sir Edmund," said Mr. Welk. "But my father he set up in the funeral business, because my mother's old dad said he wouldn't have his daughter marry a gipsy. Not that we ever had any doings with the gipsies. Horse-copers they were mostly and a bit of rough basket-making and not above taking an egg when the hens were out of the hen-house; or in for that matter. They can take an egg without the hen knowing it. There's one of them going about selling ponies still. He sold one to Lord Pomfret for one of the young gentlemen."

"And what's *your* business?" said Sir Edmund. "This is a good cake, Mrs. Parkinson. Wish my old housekeeper could make one like it," at which Mr. Welk looked gratified and Mr. Parkinson looked at his wife with a pride that nearly made that amiable sentimentalist Mrs. Morland cry.

"Undertaking, Sir Edmund," said Mr. Welk. "My dad he married into the family and as there wasn't a son he went into the business and made a good thing of it."

"Pretty close business too, isn't it?" said Sir Edmund, deeply interested in everything human. "Make you swear an oath or something, eh? Like the Freemasons. You must find wood a bit of a problem now, don't you? Mustn't talk business at Mrs. Parkinson's table, but if you like to come over I'll drive you round my place. Plenty of wood about if I had the men, but it's all I can do to pay the wages of one when I can get him. Those damned fools in the Government don't give *you* a permit, I suppose. Last funeral I went to, the coffin was a shocking affair. I wouldn't have been buried in a thing like that if they paid me. When my old governor was buried it took eight men to carry him. Rode to hounds sixteen stone and never a day's illness in his life. You ring me up tomorrow morning," and having dispatched Mr. Welk he turned to his hostess, renewing his compliments on the cake.

"Oh, I am *ever* so pleased you like it," said Mrs. Parkinson, her pretty thin face flushed with the excitement of a party. "We've been saving the marge for it and Mrs. Brandon gave me some currant and she's going to give me some young cockerels too. We'll fatten them a bit for the table and keep one for the hen run. You know father got one of his men to build us a lovely hen-house and it makes all the difference for the kiddies to have fresh eggs."

"Damned fools in the Government," said Sir Edmund. "I'd like to see *them* on one stale egg a week."

"And Mr. Francis Brandon is going to let us have a bit of his pig when he kills it," said Mrs. Parkinson, pursuing her artless tale. "It *will* be nice to give Teddy and the kids a taste of reel bacon."

"And nice for you too," said Sir Edmund, looking piercingly

but benevolently upon his hostess. "Must look after yourself you know; eat for two, eh? If some of those damned fellers in the Government had children of their own—no names, no pack drill—we'd get decent rations."

Here the gentle voice of Peggy Brandon from the other side of him said, "Sir Edmund."

"Well, young woman," said Sir Edmund. "How's everything with you? Needn't ask. You look as blooming as a rose."

"Oh, I'm always well," said Peggy. "But Sir Edmund, forgive me for interfering, but you've said 'those damned fools in the Government' three times."

"Do you mean to tell me they aren't?" said Sir Edmund.

"Well," said Peggy Brandon, her eyes alight with amusement, "you know Mr. Churchill is the head of His Majesty's Government now. The Election was more than a month ago."

"Good Gad!" said Sir Edmund loudly, which expletive gave intense pleasure to his hearers. "Putting my foot in it, what? Thanks, Peggy. I'll keep a look out on myself. But it's hard to get rid of an old habit. And it did me a lot of good to curse the Government. Well, God help this one, and worse I can't say. All right, Parkinson: you know what I mean. If God doesn't help us, then nobody can, except ourselves."

"But we can help him to help us, Sir Edmund," said Mr. Parkinson, "by asking him to," and so simply were the words said that no one felt uncomfortable.

"But how much *ought* one to ask?" said Delia Grant, ever ready for fresh explorations. "I mean what I'd *like* to ask—I mean what I'd like to have asked before the election—was Please kill *all* the Government. Perhaps that isn't a real prayer?" but there was not one of the company present who felt in a position to criticise this cri de cœur.

"One great comfort about Mr. Churchill," said Mrs. Morland who, in the strange incommunicable way of writers of fiction lived a good deal inside herself (if we make ourselves at all clear) in the company of people who, at any rate while they engaged her pen, were almost as real to her as her old friends; people to whose conversation she listened intently, whose daily paths she followed, whose motives she attempted to understand, whose turns of speech she tried to reproduce, whose fleeting thoughts she tried to crystallise; often sorely thwarted by her own roving ungovernable mind which would stray when its attention was most needed, or suddenly like an obstinate horse pull up on its haunches and refuse to budge, or taking the bit between its teeth dash away from the pastures where it was peacefully cropping the grass for its owner's benefit and carry her so far that only with considerable difficulty could she find her way back to the point at which this divagation had begun, "is that now I needn't bother so much about half penny stamps," and she looked round for her audience's approval.

Delia Grant, a practical woman, asked why halfpenny stamps, because you couldn't post anything for a halfpenny.

"Well," said Mrs. Morland, pushing a loose end of hair behind her ear in a very unbecoming way, "when They put all the postage up, I was so angry that I decided to use nothing but halfpenny stamps," and she paused, awaiting comments.

Lady Lufton said she must have needed a great many, with all the writing she did; a remark in which there was more kind interest than clear thinking, for—so far at any rate—writers are not expected to pay a stamp duty on their manuscripts as if they were cheques or receipts, though doubtless this would have been an item in the next Budget had They returned to power.

"I thought of it for myself," said Mrs. Morland, collecting the attention of the whole table by her impressive manner. The irrepressible Delia was heard to say, "'It's all my own invention.'"

"You know," Mrs. Morland continued, "how *very* nice it is when the Post Office sometimes doesn't cancel a stamp by mistake, because then you can use it again; though one has to hold it in one's mouth for quite some time for it to come off properly. So when They put up the postage to twopence halfpenny for letters, which was so un-English, because twopence halfpenny is only for *abroad*, I had an idea. If you put five halfpenny stamps on a letter there is always a chance that *one* may escape being postmarked and then whoever you wrote the letter to can lick that one off and use it again. And as for fourpence for France, said the well-known authoress, concluding her diatribe against the late Government, "it is *most* un-English and very un-French too. But now we have Mr. Churchill I shan't bother to do it any more."

There was a short silence while her audience attempted to assimilate and digest this peculiar financial and political statement.

"You'll pardon my saying so," said Mr. Welk, "and I'd like to say I'm going to read all your books and I daresay I could give you an idea or two, for you'd be surprised the things I come across from time to time in my Profession, but to return to what I was about to remark, there's a bit of a mix-up, isn't there?"

"There usually is," said Mrs. Morland, with the air of one resigned to Fate's buffets. "In one of my books, do you mean?"

"I'm sure," said Mr. Welk, with the whole suavity of his well-trained profession, "that *you* don't make mistakes, Mrs. Morland."

"But I *do*," said Mrs. Morland, eager to exculpate herself from so untrue a statement. "I am *always* getting muddled about who married who—or whom—and what relation people are to one another—just *exactly* like real life. And I get simply hundreds of letters telling me about them and I am *most* grateful because then I can correct them if Adrian Coates—that's my publisher—has enough paper to reprint which he usually has which is the *great* advantage of having an old publisher. I don't mean an old man because he might be my son, or at any rate my nephew, though nephews can of course be older than uncles, and than aunts too I suppose in spite of being different sexes, but established quite a long time, as time goes now. But," continued the well-know authoress, putting her hat a little less straight, "what was exactly the mix-up you *meant*?"

Seldom in Mr. Welk's professional career had the patience and courtesy which is part of the training stood him in such good stead.

"The mix-up, and reelly I am ashamed of having used such a word about a lady," said Mr. Welk, "was about the stamps. I'm all for making an odd halfpenny on the side, as you might say, but it's the man who cancels the stamps at the post office you're penalising, Mrs. Morland; not any of the Government. It makes him work five times as hard."

"I take you up there, Welk," said Sir Edmund. "He'll knock off at the same time whether he's sorted a hundred letters or a thousand," to which Mr. Welk, secretly flattered, we think, by Sir Edmund's form of address, generously admitted that he was wrong, adding that it was the public who would have to wait for their letters and they were so used to waiting for everything now that one more wouldn't count.

There was a silence, while Mrs. Parkinson looked at her father with a mixture of admiration for his argument and a fearful pleasure at his courage in brow-beating a reel lady writer (her words, not ours), while Mr. Parkinson's thin, tired face was lighted by an amused smile.

"Thank you, *very* much," said Mrs. Morland earnestly. "Now I can stop doing it with a clear conscience. And I'm glad on the whole, because my tongue has been getting quite *sore* with all the licking."

At this point Lady Lufton, seeing that their kind hostess was quite incapable of dealing with her tea-party, said she must be going but might they see the children first. Mrs. Parkinson went very pink and looked appealingly at her husband.

"They are playing in the kitchen," said Mr. Parkinson, "because it's warmer. Will you come and see them Lady Lufton? They are quite safe."

No one felt quite sure whether Mr. Parkinson meant they

were safe from putting their heads in the gas oven, or could be trusted not to assault the visitors, but as the host was showing them the way to the kitchen the party followed him, with the exception of Sir Edmund and Mr. Welk who were already deep in conversation about different kinds of wood in its relation to the undertaking profession.

In the large Vicarage kitchen the old-fashioned kitchener was shedding delicious warmth over the whole room, protected by a stout fender fastened to each side of the range. The big kitchen table, scrubbed spotlessly clean, was pushed back against the wall and on the shabby oilcloth which partly covered the scrubbed floor Harold Parkinson and Connie Parkinson were playing with a cheap toy railway train which at the moment was waiting in a station made of cardboard boxes.

"They play in here because it saves a fire," said Mrs. Parkinson, apologetically, "and the other rooms do need such a lot of coal to heat them. Teddy found the fender at a sale for four and sixpence and it's padlocked to the wall so as the children can't move it. Teddy made the station too. And we're going to give them some more rails for Christmas. We'd love to give them a reel Meccano, but we can't afford it. And they're very useful. If the fire needs making up and I'm not there, like today, Harold comes and tells me. I'll make it up a bit now, if you'll excuse me," and she moved towards the big coal-hod at the far side of the hearth.

"I say, Mrs. Parkinson, you can't do that," said Delia Grant, and laying hands on a poker she rattled the cinders between the bottom bars, lifted the round iron lid above the fire with the same useful implement, picked up the hod with apparently no effort and let a cascade of coal fall on to the glowing coal.

"There," she said, when she had replaced the iron lid, dusting her hands one against the other.

At this point Harold Parkinson suddenly flung himself upon her saying "That's daddy's job" which words were repeated by Connie Parkinson, but in an imperfect way and obviously without attaching any meaning to them. Mrs. Parkinson looked distressed.

"I like it," said Delia, thinking of her own twins in their youth. "Aren't they ripping, Lady Lufton?"

Lady Lufton who had been looking at them with far-away eyes suddenly came to, and if her son had been there he would undoubtedly have said "Thinking of the old 'un," for so he and his sister Justinia unfilially described their mother's attitude to all children of the age of potential grandchildren.

"Yes, they are darlings," she said, in a voice that entirely reassured their mother. "Would you mind," she continued, turning to Mr. Parkinson, "if I sent them a bigger train? It's only clockwork, but Ludovic—my son—had it when he was a little boy. I've kept it ever since and no one uses it. I did think—" and then she checked herself, for to confess in public that her son had disappointed her by not marrying and producing granny-fodder was against her canon. "I could send it over by the carrier," for there was still a carrier in those parts who lived at Hatch End, and though he was called Hamp's Motor Haulage Limited he was very obliging and would do anything for any-body let alone the gentry.

If Mr. Parkinson felt for a moment that his pride did not wish to accept alms, the feeling vanished at once before his wife's joy and Lady Lufton's evidently sincere pleasure in giving, and he added his thanks.

"You really are spoiling my grandchildren, Lady Lufton," said Mr. Welk who with Sir Edmund had now followed the others into the kitchen.

"I *couldn't*," said Lady Lufton. "You can't spoil nice children. Only nasty ones. And these are darlings. I really must go now. Good-bye Mrs. Parkinson and thank you for a most delightful party."

Mrs. Morland said she must go too and Mr. Parkinson escorted them to the Vicarage gate, while Delia and Peggy helped Mrs. Parkinson to take the tea-things into the scullery, for by dint of ignoring her efforts to stop her guests working their passage they had got their own way for some time.

"A very nice couple," said Sir Edmund, looking benevolently at the children who had quietly returned to their battered little tin train. "You're a lucky man, Welk. What are you doing for them, eh? You must be pretty warm. Always plenty of work in your line, eh? People dyin' that never died before. Wonder I'm not dead myself, but I'd like to see England on her feet again before I give up. It's worth making over some of your capital now, you know. Can't take it with you and our lot will need capital. They tell me at the County Club that old Winnie cried like a child when he saw the Treasury figures after the election. Well?"

Mr. Welk, quite unaccustomed to such filibustering methods, would have liked to resent this intromission into his affairs, but the eye that had frightened the toughest troopers in the Barsetshire Yeomanry out of their wits and made the Bishop, who was saying the Russians were our brothers, wilt uneasily into a mumbling explanation which Sir Edmund ignored, was too much for him, and he said, far more apologetically than he meant to, that he had to work hard himself when he was young and so did his wife and it didn't do young people any harm.

"All very well, Welk," said Sir Edmund, sitting against the kitchen table to take the weight off his leg, "but you came into a business."

Mr. Welk said things was different then and then realising that he had talked common—his own phrase for any manner of speech natural to him as a boy but not in strict accordance with the high standards of his profession—entirely lost his head and mumbled something about rising costs.

"Now, let me tell you," said Sir Edmund from his vantage point of the table, unfairly as Mr. Welk felt, "that things may have been different then, but they're damned different now. Your daughter's a fine young woman and a good-looker and a good mother"—and so overcome was Mr. Welk by these words about his only daughter that he quite forgot to take exception to the word woman "—and she's well on in the family way again. Can't feed and clothe three children on what Parkinson gets. *I* know the stipend. Managed to get it increased a bit just before the war, but it's not much. With your girl behind him, that young man will go far, you can take it from me. Every time we've had a good parson here he's had a good preferment. Look at Miller; a good feller, did his job well, married the right sort of wife—a bit long in the tooth but a first-class wife for a parson—he's at St. Ewold's now, and every man from St. Ewold's goes up the ladder. Now, what you've got to do is to get together with your lawyer—got a lawyer, eh? *That's* all right then—and make over a good bit of capital to your daughter. Put it in trust for the kids if you like so that she can only touch the interest, and by Gad! You'll see that son-in-law of yours a Bishop."

It is probable that almost any one of us, so bullied and flummoxed by an old baronet with a fine war and county record and a gammy leg, would have been hopelessly outclassed. Mr. Welk felt, for perhaps the first time in his well-ordered, hard-working, competent life, that here was a man who understood things better than he did. But he could find no words to say this.

"That's all right, then," said Sir Edmund, getting heavily down from his perch against the table. "Look here. I'll come for you in my car—she's twenty-eight years old but she gets along—about ten o'clock tomorrow. We'll go and look at that timber and if you are prepared to do something handsome for your daughter, I'll give you the bargain of your life. Bring your man—coffin-maker or whatever they call themselves now—never can see why they say shell when they mean a coffin. If they'd seen some shells in Flanders in the '14 war they'd sing another tune. Well, now, that's settled. Tomorrow at ten," and he went heavily away to say good-bye to his hostess, leaving Mr. Welk to contemplate his innocent grandchildren who were certainly a fine pair and it was a pity Mavis's mother was dead who would have loved to spoil them.

* * *

Just as Sir Edmund got to the sitting-room, where Mrs. Parkinson with Delia and Peggy who had finished the washing-up were now tidying the furniture, helped by Mr. Parkinson, in came Francis Brandon, who greeted the Parkinsons very pleasantly, kissed her sister rather carelessly and asked his wife if she was ready to come home yet. Peggy said she had been helping to wash up. Francis did not exactly shrug his shoulders, but managed to hint a good deal with those unexpressive parts of the human frame. Peggy gave no sign of seeing or understanding what he did and after good-byes and thanks they went out into the nasty, cold, dark evening.

"Come on, Silly Dilly," said Francis to his sister. "I'll drop you at Turpin's," to which Delia replied it wasn't worth while as it was only two minutes' walk. Francis insisted and his sister, calling him a silly old chump, got into the car by her sister-in-law.

Francis started the car, saying over his shoulder that they were very unkind to leave him alone in the front seat, to which Delia replied by some piece of nursery impertinence. Outside the cottage Francis hooted and Delia was met at the gate by her husband who had been expecting her, heard the noise and come out. By the headlights Peggy saw her kiss Hilary, saw Hilary's arm go round her fur coat.

"I'll come in front now, shall I?" she said to her husband.

"Oh, I thought you didn't want to," said Francis as he started the car. It was a matter of two minutes to go round to Stories and up the drive. To Peggy it seemed like two hours, so strong was her anxiety to explain to Francis that it was not because she didn't want to sit by him that she had gone behind with Delia; it also seemed like two seconds to the sick fear she had that Francis might go on being offended by what was never meant to offend. The time passed at its usual speed in the great scheme of things, however slowly however fast it might have seemed to one individual out of teeming millions, and they were at Stories.

"You didn't think I sat beside Delia because I didn't want to sit by *you*, Francis?" said Peggy, trying to laugh, as she got out.

"Oh, I didn't think at all," said Francis and drove the car round the house to the garage.

Peggy went upstairs and tidied herself as quickly as she could, for Francis did not like to be kept waiting, but it was not always easy to see quite clearly what one was doing. She went to the night nursery to look at her babies, all asleep in different attitudes of warm, baby-scented abandonment, and then into the day-nursery where Nurse was sewing.

"Well Nurse, have they been good?" she asked. "We had a very nice time at the Women's Institute and tea with Mr. and Mrs. Parkinson. Their children are such dears. And then Mrs. Hilary and I helped Mrs. Parkinson to wash up the tea-things."

"Oh yes, madam," said Nurse, deeply disapproving her employer's demeaning herself in the Vicarage though, to do Nurse justice, had she been there she would certainly have helped to wash up and probably not have allowed Mrs. Parkinson to help. But Peggy was already feeling low and Nurse's chill attitude did not do anything to restore her spirits. Nor did Francis's two or three allusions during dinner to her having preferred Delia's society to his. After their meal he went to his room to work and Peggy sat mending his socks, on the very sofa where she had been sitting after the Red Cross Fête when Mrs. Brandon had brought her back for the night and Francis had gone on one knee and proposed to her. It all made it rather difficult to see the black socks that she was darning with black wool.

CHAPTER 7

It had not all escaped Philip Winter's eye that one of his assistant masters, namely Charles Belton, was behaving very well under difficult circumstances, and he had talked about it with his wife more than once. The Christmas holidays were near and he said to Leslie that he really would like to know what Charles and that blasted girl—for in those terms, we regret to say, he alluded to Clarissa Graham—were thinking of.

"If Charles's head weren't screwed on uncommon tight, he'd have knocked her on the head long ago, or gone to Australia," he continued. "It was bad enough being in France while you were in England, my love, but here are Charles and Clarissa both in England and both in Barsetshire and apparently both engaged and not doing a damned thing about it. He must have the patience of the devil," at which comparison his wife couldn't help laughing.

"I know," she said. "But I can't help feeling sorry for Clarissa. She looks like a dainty rogue in porcelain, but I think she's as tough as nails inside. Much tougher than we are, but when you get inside *that* toughness, she is afraid, I don't know of what. She had all the dullness of the war without being old enough to do anything and when Lady Graham gave her a season she didn't apparently enjoy it," to which Philip's comment was that Clarissa was a conceited moppet and he couldn't make them marry any more than his wife could, but Clarissa might show a little more consideration.

"For Charles, darling, or for the Priory School?" said his wife and Philip laughed and thought for the millionth time what fun it was to have a wife that understood one. And then they forgot about Charles Belton and talked, as indeed they mostly did now, about their move.

It was now more than a year since Philip Winter had begun negotiations with Mr. Belton and the Hosiers' Company for a long lease of Harefield House. The fine Palladian mansion would never be lived in by Beltons again, as far as anyone could see. During the war the Hosiers' Girls' School had taken it. Since the war the Hosiers' Company had bought from Mr. Belton the large piece of land on the Southbridge Road which had been saved from the Barsetshire Agricultural trying to put it under wheat; it being notoriously the worst piece of corn-land in the county and very little use for anything else. In these negotiations Mr. Samuel Adams, not ungrateful for Mrs. Belton's kindness to his motherless daughter Heather, now Mrs. Edward Pilward, had played no inconsiderable part. By what miracle, or what sleight of hand the Hosiers' Company had obtained the necessary permits from Them was never made plain, but there were those who darkly said that Mr. Adams Knew a Thing or Two which he did not scruple to use as a lever, and now the new school, designed by the same architect who had built the new City Hall in Barchester (and a very good one too with everything handsome about it and not too near the old part of the city) was ready and the Hosiers' Girls were all to move in during the next summer holidays. And at the same time Philip Winter was to move the Priory School into Harefield House, while Sir Cecil Waring would resume possession of the wing of Beliers Priory which had housed the Priory School, where he hoped to carry out his plan for helping the boys of naval men who had been killed in the war, or incapacitated from serving, and were badly off.

Sir Cecil's plan would naturally hardly be self-supporting, except that the house and the land were his own property, but he was well off, as those things go now, and under his care the estate was beginning to earn money from wood and fruit and vegetables, not to speak of the very large sum for which he had sold some acres away over the hill beyond Golden Valley, to the Barsetshire Golf Club.

For Philip Winter things would not be quite so easy, but he had some private means, as had his wife, and owing to the great passion of the English for not having their darling children at home, at whatever cost to themselves, it was probable that the school would go on making a handsome profit and, what is more, remain a good realisable asset.

It was just before the Christmas holidays that Philip asked Charles Belton to dine with him and his wife and another assistant master, Eric Swan, to discuss future plans. Their dinner was slightly impeded by Marigold, the village ex-problem-girl, now properly engaged to Geoff Coxon whose father kept the garridge, for Marigold, spurred thereto by a dress parade at Bostock and Plummer, which old-established shop could always be relied upon to have the worst style, material and colour in the whole West, had appeared in the newest wasp-waisted crinoline-skirted creation in an unattractive sham tartan design.

Leslie Winter, coming in to see whether the table was properly laid, as she had done ever since the dreadful day when Marigold, sodden with Glamora Tudor and her new leading man Croke Scumper in "Legs round your Neck," had filled the salt cellars with sugar and the sugar sifter (horrible expression but we cannot think of a better at the moment and it was Georgian silver, exquisitely polished by Selina Hopkins the cook, who would not allow the heavy-handed Marigold to touch it) with salt, and Marigold had cried till all the cheap mascara ran down her face, striping the cheap rouge, Leslie Winter we repeat (that we and our readers may find their bearings again), coming in, was so horrified by Marigold's appearance in her New Look outfit that she had been obliged to tell her to run up quickly and put on that nice grey woollen dress Lady Cora had given her. Which Marigold obediently did, for though she had not an idea in her head beyond cheap finery and Geoff Coxon, she had a nice disposition and accepted her employers as an Act of God: our expression, not hers.

So five minutes later Marigold, looking really very nice in Lady Cora's grey dress, put her head into the study, said "Mrs. Winter says it's ready, Mr. Winter," and fled. Charles Belton and Eric Swan who were having sherry with the Headmaster exchanged looks of amusement and followed their employer to the dining-room where Leslie was waiting.

As mostly happens at school there was plenty of conversation, because there is always the school to talk about. In a few days all those fiends angelical would be fetched by their parents or guardians. Matron was going to Bournemouth where a friend who was at Knight's with her had a cosy little house for one or two old ladies who needed mild nursing but not bed cases or mental cases of course and there was an ever so nice nurse, partly trained, who could always come in as sitter while Matron and her friend went to the cinema, or had morning coffee in a shop, or went in a motor bus to Christchurch and came back by another one. The senior master who had just got his second pip by the skin of his teeth before peace broke out and the junior master who like Charles had been a captain, were going to Switzerland with a jolly party and a general intention of spending every franc they had, even if they had nothing to eat between Grässlichboden and Dover on the way home; and the two or three masters whom we do not know and have no intention of inventing as they are not of any use to us were going to their various homes. Charles of course was going home to Harefield for Christmas and Swan was going with him, which both young men looked forward to a good deal. And when we say young men, we are apt to forget the passage of time and those six timeless years that were to be so many years of lost youth, for Charles and Swan were now all of thirty, so time does pass.

The talk at dinner was, as always, about school affairs, and when they had finished an excellent meal (pheasant by courtesy of Sir Cecil Waring Bart. and Jasper the half-gipsy keeper) Philip carried the men away to his study while Leslie went by invitation to take her coffee with Matron and see the snaps of Matron's elder niece's bonnie kids.

Not only was there coffee in the Headmaster's study, but brandy too, from a bottle whose appearance and label made Swan almost fall on his knees and forcibly reminded Charles of a lunch with a Belgian patriot, not long after D-Day, who had kept the best of his cellar hidden all through the war, an of how ill he and his friends had felt for the next twenty-four hours, not being used to good living.

"I'd like to drink to our new home," said the Headmaster, "but we haven't decided the name yet. Have you any ideas?"

Neither man spoke, for the matter required thought.

"Did you think of keeping the name, sir?" said Charles, on his formal under-master's behaviour. "It's a jolly good one."

"I did," said Philip Winter. "And in a way I do. A lot of parents know it and have passed the name on. But if Cecil really gets his school, or home, or whatever it is to be going, he may like to keep it. After all Beliers Priory, revolting though it is, does belong to him. It's been in the family quite a hundred years now."

"What does Sir Cecil say, sir?" said Swan.

"Just what you'd think," said Philip. "'Call it what you like and good luck to it.' They are far more interested in what the baby is to be called. When I last heard from them it was to be Harry after Cecil's uncle or Louise after Cora's mother. I never knew her name till then. She was a godchild of a royal princess I believe. But that is a side issue. Have you any views?"

"With all due deference to you, sir, and your position," Swan began, putting on his large glasses as he spoke—

"Don't look at me through those foul spectacles, boy!" said Philip, with so good an imitation of his own irritable temper when he was an under-master at Southbridge and miserably engaged to the dreadful Rose Birkett that Swan laughed with quite unseemly loudness and clasping his hands round his knees rocked himself backwards and forwards, a favourite trick of his when amused.

"Charles?" said the Headmaster.

"Well, sir," said Charles, "I don't mind a bit one way or the other. None of us will be able to afford to live there again and I think father is jolly lucky to get it off his hands. I'm what I believe is called an interested party, so I won't go in for this competition."

"You are both singularly unhelpful," said Philip, refilling their glasses with the precious brandy as he spoke and looking at them with a kind of amused liking. "And as you refuse to collaborate I will now tell you what Leslie and I have decided, subject of course, Charles, to your father's approval. We think Harefield House School."

The two masters were silent. Not from want of interest on Swan's part or any family feeling on Charles's, but because they had nothing particular to say.

"No objections then, may I take it?" said Philip.

"Quite a good vintage, sir," said Swan. "What about you, young Belton?"

"Young yourself," said Charles, throwing a heavy cushion at him. "Sorry sir, but these jumped-up men with commissions are apt to get above themselves. It is Harefield House; and it is—it will be—a school. As a matter of fact father will love it. He'll be pottering about all the time telling you what it was like at Winchester when he was a boy and how these youngsters are mollycoddled. And, honestly sir, the better the school does the better he'll be pleased. He'll feel it is partly his doing. Good luck to Harefield House School, sir. I warrant it will prove an excuse for the glass," and with great presence of mind he refilled his and Swan's glasses to the brim and the toast was drunk.

"Thank you both," said Philip. "Here's good luck to the beggarly ushers," and he raised his glass to them.

Philip then took them a good deal into his confidence about the details of the new school, the number of boys it would hold at once and the possibilities for enlarging if and as the school grew.

"Those two wings with the pavilions at the end rather worried me at first," he said, addressing himself rather to Charles who knew the place, "but I have planned with Leslie and I'd like to hear your views."

Charles said he'd like awfully to know. Swan, realising perfectly well that the Headmaster was bringing Charles into it because the house was his childhood and boyhood home, sat back and listened, well hidden behind his spectacles.

"I'll put it as briefly as I can," said Philip, "and of course our plans will be modified by events. Leslie and I are going to live in that more modern house near the gates, so that we can get away from you all. All right?" Charles said a very good idea. It was built by his grandfather, he said, as a kind of dower house for his bullying old mother and his father used to be frightened of going to tea with her because she had such big eyes that he thought she was the Wolf in Little Red Riding Hood.

All the kitchen staff, Philip went on, would be in the big basement which on one side was ground floor owing to the rapid slope of the ground before the house. Boys and masters would sleep in the upper floors where some rooms would be thrown together for dormitories. Matron was to have her sanatorium in a house they had bought just outside the gates. The whole ground floor and first floor would be classrooms, dining-hall and recreation rooms. Gymnasium in the old stables and that was about all they could afford for the present. Swimming in the lake subject to Mr. Belton's permission and the school sergeant's.

Charles said it all sounded very nice. And he truly meant it, but it was still a little confusing. He had always vaguely hoped that there would be a miracle. Now the miracle had come and, like the old man in the story with the black pudding at the end of his nose, he wished it hadn't. But travellers must be content and he reflected that whenever he had a night or a weekend off his parents' house in the village would be open to him and then he suddenly laughed out loud.

"Hysterica passio I take it," said Swan.

"It's not, you fool," said Charles. "Sorry sir, I was only thinking you don't know what you're taking on. My father will be poking into everything unless you get a special clause in the lease and drive you mad. He's as pleased as Punch about it and there won't be a brick laid or a chimney swept that he won't come up and inspect."

"I hope he will," said Philip kindly and Charles felt slightly abashed.

"And one more thing," said Philip. "Leslie and I didn't quite know how to use those pavilions on the wings, but Mrs. Carton, you know she was the Headmistress there when it was the Hosiers' Girls' School in the war, said she used one as her private house. Leslie and I thought that an excellent plan. So there will be two houses for married masters, one at each end. Not that we have any at present, but you never know. They will be converted to self-contained lodgings of course, with bathroom and kitchen and so on. First come, first served it will have to be. After that it will mean they'll have to find lodgings in the village. But we needn't cross that bridge till we come to it. I think that's all," and he got up and stretched himself, for he had been working harder than anyone but Leslie knew over his plans.

"Thanks awfully, sir," said Charles, taking this as a dismissal. "Good night."

Swan also said good night and the two assistant masters went back to Swan's room where that gentleman usually had, by favour of his mother's Scotch relations, a bottle of real whisky.

"Well, Benedick," said Swan, pouring generously into Charles's glass and his own, "what about it?"

"Why Benedick" said Charles. "Here's to more and better married quarters. Lord! the Old man does think of everything."

"Ignoramus," said Swan kindly. "It's Shakespeare. But I daresay you didn't do Much Ado for your School Certificate. Benedick; the married man."

Charles did not answer.

"Sulk if you like" said Swain. "I'm an older brave lad in khaki than you are. But look here, Charles, you'd better talk to your Clarissa about this. It's a chance in a million to get a house thrown at your head. Most of us have to live with one of the parents, or in lodgings. Your bread is buttered on both sides, my boy."

Although Swan spoke lightly he was looking very intently at Charles. He liked the young man, as from his superior two or three years longer in the world he liked to call him: and indeed Swan would always be older in every way than Charles. His old Headmaster at Southbridge School, who by a sixth sense knew more about every boy than the boy's housemaster or form-master, had always noticed a very mature mind in his spectacled pupil and wondered what he would do with it. Obviously, from Mr. Birkett's point of view, a University Fellowship was the thing for Swan and possibly that might have been except for the war in which he had acquitted himself extremely well, emerged as a Major covered with ribbons, and almost directly gone back to the world of school. What ambitions he might have even Philip had never discovered, though he was sure they were there. He knew that Swan worked a great deal at night and that Mr. Birkett, the ex-Headmaster of Southbridge School, thought very highly of him and had been glad of his help in the book he had been writing since he retired on the Analects of Procrastinator. Swan also had money and would have more, but apparently no particular desire to spend it, though very generous. When Mr. Birkett had once questioned him directly about his future, Swan had put on his glasses, looked through them at his old Headmaster and said A Grown-up

Son at Home, sir, for which impertinence Mr. Birkett would willingly have given him five hundred lines.

"I don't want to drag a woman's fair name in the mud, but do you mean to marry the girl?" said Swan.

"Does she mean to marry me?" said Charles, looking intently at the fire, for wood was plentiful and Sergeant Hopkins would bring up all that was wanted.

"My dear fellow, don't ask *me*," said Swan. "I'm not a marrying man. I merely take a kindly interest in young women—in a highly respectable way of course. But we'll talk about something else. Let's go and look at the new school while I'm staying with you. If it's anything like that article in Country Life before the war it must be one of the prettiest bits of domestic Palladian in the county."

Charles said Palladian be damned: adding "Sorry."

"Granted," said Swan, graciously. "Tell me, what is the best attitude for me to take vis-à-vis your male parent? Does he like to be treated as an old codger or one of the boys?" to which Charles, grateful to Swan for this change of subject, said if Swan would say Sir to his father now and then, it would give great satisfaction.

"I see. I'll tip the Aged P. a nod," said Swan, but Charles who was uneducated merely took this as part of Swan's peculiar brand of humour and then, being at the bottom as sweet-tempered a creature as one would wish, he described to Swan the joys of Harefield, all on the small or domestic scale but dear to him from childhood, to which Swan listened sympathetically. A dance, so Swan gathered, was not possible at Arcot House where the Beltons lived, but there might be a dance shared by the Beltons, Dr. Perry and his wife, and the Updikes who were the Harefield lawyers, to be held at the Nabob's Arms which had quite a decent room. Like Emma, said Swan, but Charles, who had never been much of a reader of fiction, let the allusion pass.

"Let's see what we can do," said Charles, pulling himself

together. "Have you any paper? Let's make a list. You and me," at which Swan shrugged his shoulders and turned up his eyes in mute mock despair, "three Perrys—no, Bob is too starchy to come now he's Harley Street—two Updikes, that's six; we might get a couple of Clarissa's brothers, that's eight, my father if we have a polka nine—"

"And what about a few girls?" said Swan, already enchanted at the thought of a polka-ing father.

"It's a funny thing," said Charles after scribbling a couple of names, "that girls are harder to get than men. There are those two Updike girls, awfully nice only I've known them all my life, and Clarissa—Lady Graham might let Edith come for a treat too—and—Lord! There must be some more somewhere."

Swan suggested Grace Grantly, which Charles approved, adding however that it wouldn't make any difference because then they'd have to ask Henry Grantly too. Lord Lufton was also passed because he could bring his sister Justinia, but there they were again, overmanned.

"Give it up," said Charles, throwing the paper in the fire. "After all Mrs. Perry and Mrs. Updike are doing it, so why worry. And if there are too many men we can play darts. The barman at the Nabob is rather a dab at darts. Thanks awfully for the drinks," and he went away to finish his packing and so to bed to consider houses for married masters, and feel, as he had felt far too often, a kind of gnawing fear to which he didn't care to give a name. For if a girl has promised to marry you and you don't get any forrarder—then what? Which inelegant turn of thought is poor Charles's. Not ours.

The school broke up as usual, with a great deal of agreeable little-boy noise and chattering. The Winters went to stay with friends for a fortnight, Selina with Marigold and various village helpers, attracted not so much by the one and sixpence an hour (for that was still the current rate round Lambton) as by the hospitable warmth of the School kitchen and endless cups of tea, cleaned everything ferociously from top to bottom. Charles went back to the bosom of his family with Swan, who made an excellent impression on Mr. and Mrs. Belton.

"Well, my boy," said Mr. Belton to Swan after breakfast next morning, "what are you going to do today, eh? Sorry there's no shooting."

Swan said it was just as well, as the only shooting he knew was his guns in the war, but if Mr. Belton would be so kind as to take him round the place he would very much enjoy it, simultaneously exchanging with Mrs. Belton looks which implied that she thought Swan was an excellent guest and he was pleased that she thought it. Charles, who had more dashing thoughts in his mind, such as seeing if Gus Perry was going to do any ratting, sulked for a moment. But his naturally nice disposition could not sulk long and when his mother asked him to go down the street with her on her morning rounds, he accepted with a deliberate cheerfulness that soon became real.

Mr. Belton and Eric Swan—whom we go on calling Swan by habit because we have known him since he was a boy at Southbridge School—set out at the same time for their tour of the estate, up the garden, through the door in the wall, and so into the parklands. As they went Mr. Belton pointed out spots of interest, such as the place where he had shot his first rabbit and the exact spot where his father had thrashed him for leaving a gate open so that two of the deer got out, to all of which Swan listened attentively, and asked, with just the right shade of deference, if any deer were left, and was sorry to hear, with exactly the right amount of sorriness, that the last of the herd had to be killed owing to general manginess and decay.

"Pretty creatures they were," said Mr. Belton. "Used to feed out of my hand. But it's like that now. Thank God, Churchill is alive still. He'll pull us out if anyone can."

"And if we pull too, sir," said Swan.

"You're right, my boy," said Mr. Belton and they talked very comfortably with question and answer till it became known that

Swan, through his mother who was a Ramsay, was distantly connected with Lady Ellangowan who was a cousin of Admiral Sir Christopher Hornby R.N., who had married Mr. Belton's daughter; from which point Swan felt he was one of the family.

Although Swan had heard a good deal about Harefield and had seen the *Country Life* illustrated article on it, he was not quite prepared for what he saw as he and his host topped a little slope in the parkland. Before him, framed by the rise of wooded hills behind, given added dignity by the gently downward slope in front of it to the stream that made the lake in the grounds, was a finely proportioned crescent; a central block with a pillared portico and on each side a curved wing with a pavilion at its end.

"The half was not told me," said Swan aloud to himself, which comment gave Mr. Belton great pleasure, and when Swan added, quite deliberately we regret to say, "I think it is better in Kings than in Chronicles, sir. Do you agree?" Mr. Belton nearly fell on his neck and embraced him. For he was accustomed to read his Bible every day, even what his children called the Begot parts, and had read it almost every Sunday in church since his father's death many years ago, and to find a young man who had been brought up in the way he should go pleased him deeply.

After so auspicious a beginning there was not one inch of the house that Mr. Belton spared his guest, taking Swan down to the spacious kitchens and other offices, up to the top floor and even onto the roof, from behind whose elegant parapet they overlooked a vast view of the countryside. Below them on the far side of the valley lay the slopes of the downs, lovely in their winter bareness, with a clump of leafless trees here and there, by some called Druidical, by others (better informed) known to have been planted by an eccentric landowner in George IV's reign. From the left to the right the stream meandered through the valley, feeding the lake and then continuing its course to join the river. The High Street of Harefield was visible and the church. On the other side of the house the ground rose gently to a grassy plateau where cows grazed. And far away, out of sight the ground dipped again towards the Southbridge road, to the place where the new Hosiers' Girls' School was waiting for its chattering flock of girls and mistresses.

"Used to hope I'd die here," said Mr. Belton wistfully. "Have to die in Arcot House now. Well, one's got to die somewhere I suppose. My old father died here, in the big mahogany bed, and so did his father, and his father before him. All born in that bed too. Born there myself. I like the idea of dying where you were born. Seems to round things off nicely, eh?"

"A kind of universal dovetailedness, sir," said Swan, respectfully, and enjoying himself immensely.

"So you know your Dickens, young feller," said Mr. Belton good-humouredly and Swan, probably for the first time in his life, was completely silenced and slightly ashamed. His host added, "Quite right too. Know your Dickens—and your Bible of course—and you won't be far wrong. We'd better go down now. You go first and I'll lock the door," and so down they went and Swan, humbled by Mr. Belton's having seen through him when least expected, took special pains to be respectful; which did not pass unnoticed by his host.

"We needn't look at the pavilions," said Mr. Belton when they got back to the hall with its black and white marble floor. "Used to be servants' quarters. Men one end, girls the other. Made no difference though. I remember my father telling me that in his father's time Harefield held the county record for marriages the day before the baby was born. None of that now," he ended with a kind of sigh which Swan took to be a lament for the carefree immorality of a more golden age, but when his host added, "it's a month after the child's born now and often not even that," he was glad he had not made any comment.

"The Headmaster is thinking of making those two wings into quarters for married masters, sir," he said, hoping this would not offend Mr. Belton, who however seemed to think it an excellent plan and would have dragged Swan back to look at the rooms had not the mellow sound of the church clock floated across to them twelve times, causing Mr. Belton to say they must be getting along. So they went down the drive, out of the gates, past the house which was to be the Sanatorium, past the parsonage, past the house of Mr. Carton who had married the Headmistress of the Hosiers' Girls' Foundation School, past the Nabob's Arms and so along the wide part of the High Street where several handsome old houses remained and luckily neither Gaiters, nor Lukes and Huxley, nor even Sheepskins had yet thought it worth while to invade so small a territory; and so to Arcot House and lunch, after which Charles said Swan had better come along to tea at the Perrys and get the low-down on the dance.

So to Plassey House they betook themselves, where in her comfortable, rather overfurnished drawing-room, with a large fire and all the electric lights on, they found Mrs. Perry the doctor's wife, busily tying up Christmas presents for her family. Charles had secretly been a little anxious about this meeting, for Mrs. Perry was apt to ask any newcomer the most searching questions till she had, to her own satisfaction, established him or her as All Right, but he was at once reassured by Swan asking Mrs. Perry whether an extremely kind and intelligent consultant called Perry, who had stopped a hospital cutting all his inside out during the war, was any relation of hers.

"That must be Bob," said Mrs. Perry, who obviously found Swan a most charming and valuable new acquaintance. "He's down here for Christmas with his wife. Here they are. Bob dear, this is Mr. Swan who is staying at Arcot House. He thinks he knows you. You haven't met Mrs. Bob yet Charles, have you?"

Mrs. Bob, or to give her her lawful due, the Honourable Mrs. Bob, was a good-looking young woman dressed with expensive simplicity, her hair, hands, legs, stockings and shoes all of striking correctness, and a manner which her father, a well-known consultant with a title, said was worth at least a thousand a year to any husband: though in fairness we must say that he allowed her the thousand a year himself, saying that she was his only child and sooner she than the Government. And though England had now rung out the False and rung in the True, he still stuck to his bargain. Charles was introduced and then Swan who, with an ease that Charles admired but did not envy, at once said he was sure he had had the pleasure of meeting her at his cousin's, Catriona Ellangowan, and so plunged into a delightful talk about families, talking a language that Charles did not quite know. The two other young Perrys followed, Jim who was a rising surgeon and to be distinguished by his long nose and Gus who was the one with bushy eyebrows, a passionate student of skin diseases and at present in partnership with his father.

Owing to the number of guests tea was in the dining-room at the large table with its leaf in (a description that all house-wives will recognise) and when to the party were added Dr. Perry and the four young Updikes from Clive's Corner the uproar was terrific. The Honourable Mrs. Bob looked at Swan with a smile of friendly toleration for the barbarians and though Swan thought the barbarians a nice lot and distinctly more amusing than Mrs. Bob, he so far humoured her as to smile back with a freemasonic look, thus winning her entire approval.

"Isn't it a *priceless* old house?" said Mrs. Bob under cover of the noise. "Absolutely period, I tell the Madre. And I *adore* Ruth; too fantastically rude."

Swan, enchanted by her conversation, asked who Ruth was.

"Oh; the really *too* faithful maid," said Mrs. Bob, looking at the domestic in question who with disapproval of everything gleamng sullenly behind her hideous steel-rimmed spectacles had just brought in a large plate of meltingly, crumblingly delicious scones. "I do love Christmas in the country. And we are to have a dance, you know, at the Nabob. Their room will hold fifteen couples or even twenty easily. We are having a quite good little pianist from Barchester and a man with every kind of percussion, *such* a silly word, and really I think we shall have a quite amusing time. I believe there are to be reels. All the young people do reels now. I hope you do, Mr. Swan," to which Swan, enchanted (as was Gunner Heppinstall when a guest at Faith and Works) to find that Mrs. Elton though dead was yet very much alive and kicking, said that unfortunately his poor sight made reels impossible, and languished at Mrs. Bob through his spectacles to that extent that Charles, observing them from the far end, nearly had the giggles.

Swan, a welcome guest but not yet quite sure who everyone was and not of the Harefield group, gradually sat back as it were, listening and observing, well protected by his spectacles, feeling that he was older than most of them; though if we go by dates he was probably wrong. But he had always walked by himself even in his schooldays and though he had been in close company at that time with Tony Morland and Hacker, the one was now a heavily married man, the other a distinguished Professor of Classics at Redbrick University: and there was he, being a schoolmaster, and as the surge of talk roared round him he wondered idly whether, with his quite comfortable means and his expectations, he ought to have done better than being an assistant master at a preparatory school.

By this time some of the younger members were suggesting that if one cleared the tea-things away and shoved the table to the end of the room, one could put the gramophone on and dance. Mrs. Perry and Mrs. Belton went back to the drawing-room and Swan was wondering if it would be considered presuming to join them when Dr. Perry, winking at him, took him by the arm and led him away to the surgery, which was gloriously stuffy and comfortable.

"I remembered you the minute I saw you," said Dr. Perry. "You're a master at the Priory School. Remembered you by those glasses. Do you need them?" which may have appeared a silly question, but Swan did not think it so.

"Partly yes," he remarked, taking them off, "and partly no," with which he put them on again. "It's rather like putting one's coat collar up when the shells come over. Moral support. I suppose a psychologist would say it was a mother-complex or worse," at which Dr. Perry gave a kind of snorting laugh and offered Swan some whisky.

"We had enough of that here in the war," he said. "A female called Dr. Morgan was wished on us. *What* a woman. The cottages couldn't stand her. Said she put ideas into their girls' heads. So you're moving into Harefield House, eh? You've got an excellent man, Winter I mean. I'll be up at the Priory off and on all next term I expect. Mumps and measles and whooping-cough and 'flu and the rest of it. You're staying at Arcot House aren't you?"

Swan, amused by Dr. Perry's talk, said he was, over Christmas, and enjoying it very much.

"And what about Charles?" said Dr. Perry. "I'm very fond of Charles. He's not got that war out of his system yet. Lots of 'em won't. Perhaps not for years. Perhaps never. My boys have been lucky. The doctoring is so strong in them that nothing can hurt it. But I don't see where Charles is going. He's a good boy and a good son and he'll make a good husband. What's his young woman up to? She'll lose him if she isn't careful."

Part of Swan rose in revolt against this unexpected and as he considered slightly treacherous attack by Dr. Perry, but the other part—the cool-headed part which had for years observed, drawn conclusions and kept its own counsel—had to admit that Dr. Perry as an old friend and family doctor had a right to inquire. Charles was also keeping his own counsel and one of the bonds between the two masters was that Swan never asked what Charles did not volunteer to tell. And what he had told Swan during the last year about Clarissa was just nothing. He was silent for a moment, thinking as quickly as he could and as steadily as he always did.

"Du mal qu'un amour ignoré, Nous fait souffrir . . ." said Dr. Perry suddenly and most surprisingly. "Don't jump. I did a year in Paris when I was a young man and read my romantics on Sunday mornings—the only time off medicine I allowed myself. Is that it?"

"Not exactly ignoré," said Swan, taking his glasses off and holding them in one hand, "considering that he has been engaged to that blasted china shepherdess openly and officially for a year. And if I know my Charles he will *not* allow himself the luxury of having an âme déchiré, Jusqu'à mourir. But he will die before he will complain. What she needs is a Petruchio. Blast the girl!" and he put his spectacles on again.

"Well, thanks for confirming my diagnosis," said Dr. Perry. "Take it from me—and if you like to pass it on to Charles I haven't the least objection—that the sooner he marries that girl out of hand, the better. A spoilt piece of goods if you ask me, keeping one of the best young men in the county on the doorstep. Now, I don't see you letting yourself be kept on the doorstep, Swan."

Swan was silent. Then he looked at Dr. Perry through his glasses and said, apparently choosing his words carefully, "No, I don't see it either. But you see I haven't even rung the bell yet, Dr. Perry. What a charming woman your daughter-in-law is. We got on *so* well."

"All right; you win," said Dr. Perry, no whit put out. "Yes, the Honourable Mrs. Bob is a perfect wife and a perfect daughter-in-law and she'll have Bob a knight and quite likely the highest-paid consultant in England and a lord before she's done. But we've lost Bob for good. That's that, and that's how the world goes. Doctors see lots of family skeletons and even have some themselves."

"Don't we all," said Swan. "Shall we join the ladies?" a line which it was certainly not his place to say, but Dr. Perry took it in perfectly good part and the two men went back to the company, each having acquired a considerable respect for the other, although Dr. Perry had known Swan as a schoolboy when Swan had thought Dr. Perry was at least eighty or ninety. But we all come to be the same age as time goes on.

In the drawing-room most of the company were discussing the arrangements for the dance at the Nabob's Arms with a good deal of noise, all except the Honourable Mrs. Bob who was saying the right things to Mrs. Belton and listening in the right way to what Mrs. Belton said with a tact that made Charles, who happened to be near them and overhear part of it, wink at Swan, thus much reassuring that gentleman who had been more depressed than he would have liked to admit by his talk with Dr. Perry.

The discussion was getting noisier and noisier till Gus Perry who had a fine bellowing voice outnoised (if we may be permitted the expression) all the others, with a suggestion that they should go to the Nabob for a drink and look at the room which was still called the Assembly Room. What good this would do was not apparent, but it was not to further their plans for the dance that the young people really wished to go (and not so young either, thought Swan, looking at them with a dispassionate avuncular eye), but to satisfy their perpetual wish for change, for movement, for any mild excitement.

"Schoolboys! schoolboys!" said Swan sententiously to Mrs. Belton, who laughed and told him to see that he and Charles were back by half past seven as her husband hated to wait for his dinner. Swan said he hated it too, sketched a kind of salute to Mrs. Belton and Mrs. Perry and joined the younger people. It was a horrid night of cold damp that clung to one's coat, one's hair and one's whiskers, or so Gus Perry said, though as no one had any whiskers it couldn't be proved, and it was therefore necessary to make a good deal of noise going up the street, though what warming effect the noise really had, we cannot say. Inside the Nabob all was warm and almost snug. Sid Wheeler the landlord, cousin of Mrs. Belton's old nurse now housekeeper at Arcot House and of Bill Wheeler the chimney sweep and the only man who really understood the chimneys at Pomfret Towers, was in the bar with Mr. Pratt of the fish shop and Mr. Pilchard of the rival and even smellier fish shop and Potter the chemist, which somehow led to beer all round under the chairmanship of Gus Perry and almost as much noise as there had been at tea.

"We'll never get anything done at this rate," said the elder Updike, he who after being a Lieutenant-Colonel in the war was now in partnership with his father the lawyer. "Let's go and look at the Assembly Room, Charles. We might as well decide if we ought to ask any more. It wouldn't do to look empty," and he led the two other men through a passage and up a dark flight of stairs. At the top he opened a door and turned on an electric switch.

"No," said Swan firmly. "It is NOT true."

"True enough," said Charles, flattered by the effect made on his senior. "The Nabob—you know, my great-great-grandfather or whatever he was who built Harefield House—had a French lady, if you can call her that, living with him and his sister was furious, so he built this house for her, for the French lady I mean, and she added a little ballroom so that she could give balls which she didn't, because nobody would come, at least not any respectable people. The French Madam people called her. And a bit of a madam she was too. The Nabob built the Garden House for her—I'll show it you, or do I mean I'll show you it, hang it they both sound wrong, some time. And she then ran away with the Frenchman who built the Garden House and all the Nabob's jewels too. It's a pretty piece, isn't it?"

"Pretty piece!" said Swan bitterly. "Pearls before swine, my Charles. I've seen nothing in England to touch it except the Rooms at Bath after they had been redecorated and then those blasted Germans had to drop bombs on them. But they were on the grand scale. My aunt! My aunt! Look at those mouldings and those arabesques. And properly lighted too."

"That was the Barsetshire Archaeological," said Charles. "About two years ago. That man Adams put up a good bit of money for it because his daughter had been at school here—when there was a girls' school at Harefield House. And Oliver

Marling found a man from London who dug out some old plans and—well look."

"I do," said Swan, reverently, while the elegant crystal chandeliers sparkled with rainbows in their cut-glass ornaments and every curve of the plaster arabesques was more elegant than its neighbour and the golden curtains—at least they gave an illusion of gold—reflected the light and the parquet floor shone. "And how *beautifully* kept."

"Local patriotism," said Charles. "And the Women's Institute, which is much the same thing. They keep it clean and polish the floor and make their husbands do any small repairs that are needed. Father still has an estate carpenter, but the younger men don't like to work with him much. They say he looks at them in a queer way; like you looking at Philip Winter through your glasses at school. Well, how many people?"

After a little discussion it was agreed that they could safely ask forty because some were sure to drop out. Charles said fifty, because as a rule some accepted and didn't come. If he wanted to be accurate, said young Updike, they had better ask twenty to allow for people coming who weren't invited. So back to forty they came.

"Eric ought to come in on this," said Charles. "Have you any names?"

Swan said all their friends were his friends and they went back to the bar.

"And leaves the world to darkness and to me," said Swan nostalgically as young Updike snapped off the last light. "Pity we can't have candles."

"By Jove!" said Charles, suddenly stopping short in the narrow passage so that his friends all banged up against him. "Jim Perry knows all about electric things; ever since he ran my electric train off the lights at Harefield House and fused the lot. Look here. We'll ask him if he can stick in a transformer or something so that we can dim the lights and then un-dim them again," which proposal was unanimously carried, the self-constituted committee vowing silence so that it would be a surprise to the others; just like William Tell and his ghastly friends said Swan sententiously.

"I know them," said young Updike. "I saw them in Switzerland painted somewhere. Caspar, Melchior and Balthasar."

Or words to the same effect, said Swan graciously, and there was a short free fight, considerably hampered by the narrowness of the passage.

By the time they got back the rest of the company were peacefully drinking what in these degenerate days is practically non-alcoholic beer and playing darts with the other members of the public, young Humble, son of Mr. Belton's old general factotum, winning easily every time.

"He's darts champion of West Barsetshire," said Charles to Swan, "and probably going up to London for the Inter-Allied Darts Clubs finals at Harringay. He was proxime accessit last year."

"Runner-up, I suppose you mean. Talk English!" said Swan, to which Charles replied that Swan would show off once too often and be sorry for it, and they both had another pint and then left the party, because of not keeping Mr. Belton waiting for his dinner. And a very good dinner it was, of a bit of pork sent by Lady Pomfret that had some real crackling on it, and the proper adjuncts of stuffing and apple sauce. Florrie Wheeler, niece of Mr. Wheeler at the Nabob, or possibly second cousin twice removed, for the Wheeler relationships were beyond anyone's power of reckoning, had been forcibly co-opted during the war by her aunt Miss Wheeler, ex-nurse to the Beltons and now housekeeper, as a kind of general under-study and so had indistinctly acquired over a long period the rudiments of waiting at table. She was a nice young woman and zealous to an extent that made her bang the dishes down on the table with a hearty good-will that terrified Swan, for the china was old and good. Her employers, having got used to it during the last seven or eight years, appeared to take it as an Act of God and very sensibly ignored it. Mr. Belton talked families with Swan whose Scotch mother had brought him up in the way he should go to know cousinships and the families with which he could call kin to the *n*th relationship and he was even able to correct Mr. Belton on one point, subsequently with great tact allowing Mr. Belton to win an argument about the beautiful Lady Ellangowan who was carried off in a decline at twenty-five and whose portrait by Raeburn hung in the drawing-room, so that dinner passed very pleasantly. While they were having dessert—real Ribstons from the old orchard and crystallised fruits sent by benefactors in U.S.A. who never tired of being kind—the telephone was heard and Wheeler came in to say Mrs. Carton said could she and her husband look in for a few minutes on their way to a party at the Updikes'.

Swan asked if that was Carton of Paul's. Mrs. Belton said it was, and his quite delightful wife who used to be Headmistress of the Hosiers' Girls' Foundation School, and would Wheeler keep the coffee back till Mr. and Mrs. Carton came. While they waited Swan asked if he might have a good look at the Raeburn and Mrs. Belton came with him.

"I am in love with her," said Swan. "Quite deeply in love. It is partly the high light on her nose, I think, bless her. *Not* a Watteau, Mrs. Belton?" he added, passing on to a picture with a deeply carved frame in the middle of a white panel.

Mrs. Belton, turning on another light that Swan might the better see it, said she was afraid not. Not even a Pater or a Lancret, or at any rate the man from the Wallace collection had said so.

"But it is even better than a Watteau," she said. "I would like to show you something."

From a lovely little French writing-table with gilded ornaments she produced a small key which she put into a tiny hole in the frame and the picture swung outwards on a hinge, showing a small secret cupboard with a little safe in it.

"By Jove!" said Swan.

"Nothing much there, I'm afraid," said Mrs. Belton. "A few odds and ends that I have left from my mother and my old aunt Thorne. This is the only good thing," and she took out a green leather case in which lay a diamond spray of small roses. "It is very lovely, but very cold," said Mrs. Belton. "I offered it to Elsa—my daughter that married Christopher Hornby—but she felt the same and I gave her some pearls instead. One of the major pleasures of old age is to give trinkets you have loved to the younger generation whom you love."

Swan, respectfully but firmly, said Mrs. Belton ought to wear them herself implying, in a way she could not help recognising, that she was not old and in any case more worthy of them than a younger woman, and thinking of a Latin tag about a beautiful mother with a more beautiful daughter, words which he felt, though never having seen Elsa Hornby, might probably be reversed in this case. In which he was right, for Elsa's very handsome face had a certain hardness while her mother's, though marked by time and anxieties, had a beauty of spirit as well as of bone and a kind of light which Swan, a stickler for words, could only describe as mother-of-pearl.

Charles, who had joined them, though not having spoken or even made a noise of beginning to speak, gave his mother and his friend an impression that he had thought of saying something and then thought better of it. But it was evidently a mistake, for he remained silent and Mrs. Belton put the case away and closed the picture-door, which shut with a spring.

"If I knew the Snow Queen I should give her that cold, cold spray," said Swan, but in his mind there was a girl to whom he would not give that chill beauty; no Snow-Queen.

Soon afterwards Mr. and Mrs. Carton came in and Wheeler brought the coffee.

"This is Eric Swan," said Mrs. Belton, introducing her guest. "He is with us for Christmas."

"So *that* is what you are like," said Mr. Carton unexpectedly in his precise, donnish voice. "One never knows. Mr. Swan and I have been corresponding for some time about Fluvius Minucius, whose works Madeleine's grandfather did so much to elucidate," and he looked at his wife very affectionately. "I liked your suggestion of a possible influence from Scriptor Ignotus of Aterra very much. In fact I have done my best to demolish your arguments, but find myself confuted at every turn. We must have a talk about this. I still have some little influence at Paul's. As for Lazarus—but have you heard?"

Swan, enchanted by this meeting, looked at Mrs. Belton as if to inquire whether she minded her drawing-room being turned into a classical bear-garden. Mrs. Belton said please say whatever they liked.

"The Master, some industrial fool having given a large sum of money to Lazarus for a Professorship of Culture," said Mr. Carton, speaking with quiet venom and giving the impression that he was ejecting every word because of its horrid taste, "has appointed that dreadful boy of Mrs. Rivers' to the job. Eight hundred a year it is."

"Not *Julian* Rivers," said Mrs. Belton, incredulous.

Swan said, rather affectedly, The Same, to which Mrs. Belton, well trained in academic hates by Mr. Carton, said Serve Lazarus right.

"I'm all with you there," said Mr. Carton. "But I don't think they'll notice it. They all read Modern Greats or P.P.E. Pah! They'll have an Artistic Appreciation Degree next."

Charles, who was not often witty, said he hoped all the Lazarus men would get a D.Ph., adding proudly Damned Fools.

"I am here, by Mrs. Belton's kindness, for part of the Christmas holidays, sir," said Swan to Mr. Carton, thinking this a good moment to change the subject, "and if you would allow me to come and see you—?"

"We shall like it very much," said Mrs. Carton, with the air of authority, though very pleasantly exercised, which her years of Headmistressing had stamped upon her. "Sidney; if Mrs. Belton can spare him, perhaps Mr. Swan would come to dinner one evening and you can talk shop," to which Mrs. Belton of course asserted, glad that her Charles's friend should have a treat in what she felt might be a dull Christmas, for she was one of the people who imagine that guests might like grouse and champagne and houris, while they are probably quite happy with rabbit pie (especially if Wheeler made the pastry) and beer and the local society, which was exactly the case with Swan. And particularly the case in this instance, for he had plans of his own in which Mr. Carton's advice and help might be very useful. Not yet, for there seemed to him to be two paths just ahead of him. But one had Apollyon straddling right across the way; well there would be the other perhaps.

Then the Cartons, having settled an evening for Swan to dine with them, went away to the Updikes' and the elder people went to bed. Charles and Swan stayed by the comfortable drawing-room fire, replenishing it from time to time, talking about life in general. But not very much about life in particular, for Swan had a strong impression that Charles did not wish to discuss himself and Clarissa, while Charles felt vaguely that old Swan had something up his sleeve and he, Charles, did not want to appear curious. But they did not enjoy themselves, quietly, any the less.

CHAPTER 8

Charles and Swan might have spared themselves the trouble of worrying about the guests, for the Honourable Mrs. Bob, to everyone's amusement, had taken the whole thing in hand. And very well she had done it, inquiring everyone's taste, and when there seemed to be not quite enough girls (though many more than Charles in his pessimistic mood had allowed), had imported some from East Barsetshire who were pretty, nicely dressed, well-mannered and altogether most satisfactory. The catering was arranged by Mrs. Belton, Mrs. Perry and Mrs. Updike with help from Pomfret Towers (pheasants beautifully cooked and glazed), Holdings (a large American ham), Beliers Priory (two large rabbit pies so beautifully cooked by Selina that even the most prejudiced did not know what they were eating), Sir Edmund Pridham (a large home-reared turkey) and six dozen champagne and an enormous amount of ice cream (Mr. and Mrs. Samuel Adams, who were unfortunately in London doing intensive Christmas shopping and could not come). The glasses, cutlery and china were supplied by the Nabob, who also had one or two respectable old waiters in their pockets.

Opinion was divided about the weather, some hoping it would stay mild, others that it would snow and sleet and freeze so that they would all have to spend the night on sofas and shakedowns in other people's houses. But we are glad to say that though very cold the weather offered no apparent hindrance to getting home again, for which the older guests were thankful. For you have to be very young to enjoy going to sleep on a sofa in someone else's pyjamas, or having to share a bed in someone else's nightgown and use someone else's Liquescent Removing Balm and Exquisita Face Cream, not to speak of the wrong shade of Foundation and Powder next morning.

By eight o'clock the young Perrys, the young male Updikes (not so very young now, but young as opposed to their parents), Charles and Swan were at the Nabob, each faintly surprised to see how well the others looked in tails which there had been far too little opportunity of wearing. Taking them all round Bob Perry's suit was the newest, his figure and manner the most perfect, as became a rapidly rising consultant. But a dispassionate and invisible looker-on (not ourselves who have always had our favourites, Charles being one) would, if his or her audience were discreet and safe, have said that Swan was in a way the pick of the lot; perhaps because of his Scotch blood, perhaps because his mind was keener in its own way than even Bob Perry's though without Bob's steadfast ambition for visible place and power, perhaps because he was a good classical man; though this last does not always affect the outside, as witness the old tutor at Lazarus who had a flat bath in cold water twice a week and wore trousers falling into concertina wrinkles with age and an old coat white at the seams and shiny at the elbows and green all over.

Proxime accessit our observer might have placed Charles who, though his figure was not quite so good as Swan's, was so upright and easy in his bearing and had such a pleasant expression that Mrs. Wheeler, the wife of the Nabob, said he reminded her of Pill Kreelson, the new film actor starring at the Barchester Odeon with Glamora Tudor in "One night in the Vatican." The elder Perrys and Updikes as co-hosts and hostesses also looked well and as the other guests began to come in the ballroom was on the whole pleased with its occupants. For they were at least ladies and gentlemen which, said the ballroom, yawning after a long sleep, was more than the French Madam's friends had been even if their clothes were prettier.

Lady Graham, a preposterous and charming travesty of herself as a dowager in rose-coloured lace and a black lace scarf, had brought her two younger boys and Clarissa, also Edith who really had no business there at all, but it was Christmas and she had a white chiffon dress of skilled simplicity whose price every girl in the room guessed at once. Charles came to greet them and was kissed by Lady Graham very affectionately. Edith jumped up and down with delight and hugged him with both arms, while Clarissa pretended a cool cheek to be kissed. Then came Oliver with the Honourable Mrs. Marling, a majestic rather mobled figure but looking very handsome; Henry Grantly and his sister Grace; Captain Freddy Belton with his wife Susan; Lord Lufton with the Honourable Justinia Lufton who surprised most of the company (for the Luftons were not known in Harefield) by being rather small and very elegant, unlike her tall brother and sister, being considered in the family to take after the Lady Lufton who had been the parson's sister at Framley. And it was the opinion of several people that Justinia was on the whole the best-looking girl or perhaps woman in the room and certainly the best dancer where all were good.

"How very pleasant to meet you again," said Swan to Grace Grantly. "I have been hoping against hope that we should have programmes and you would let me fill yours," to which Grace replied by holding up a programme as yet virgin.

"I shall now be too, too Edwardian," said Swan, with a rapid glance to make sure that Clarissa could not hear him, though even if she had it was doubtful whether she would have noticed anything, "and fill your programme. Or at least as much as you will give me."

Grace said no one had asked her yet, but she expected they would because she saw lots of friends.

"Then may I have one and two, and five and six, and supper, and two more afterwards, and perhaps some more?" said Swan.

Grace laughed and said they would go as far as supper and then see. Besides, she said, if he had looked at the programme, he would have seen that there were to be the lancers after supper. Swan said he was sorry there weren't to be reels.

"Well, I'm not. Not really," said Grace, "because I'm no good at them. And there aren't enough people with kilts really, or anyone who can really play the bagpipes. And some people do look so funny in kilts."

"I don't, really," said Swan, "so long as you don't really look at my face," at which parody of her previous word Grace laughed very charmingly. "I have a neat leg and a swaggering walk, but my spectacles spoil the fun. I did think of contact lenses, but they make me sick to think of."

"I did know a girl," said Grace, "who tried for six months and she cried every time she put them in and took them out."

Swan asked what happened then.

"Oh, she sold them to a friend," said Grace, "and luckily they suited the friend fairly well, at least one eye did," and Swan marvelled, as he had often done, at the things other people did and inquired after the Barchester Central Library which, it appeared, had given Grace a fortnight's holiday and proposed to clean the room where she worked. And when she said clean, Grace added, it would only be the floor and a feather broom round the cornice because Mr. Parry didn't let anyone touch the old books unless he were there himself.

Mrs. Belton, as one of the hostesses, asked the Luftons if she could do some introducing. Lord Lufton was stricken with dumb shyness and did not answer, but his sister Justinia, who seemed to have all her wits about her in a very pretty neat head, said yes please, because they didn't know many people over here.

"I hoped your mother was coming," said Mrs. Belton kindly. "She did accept. And so did your tenant Mr. Macfadyen."

"Oh, she said to say she would be here later," said Justinia. "Mr. Macfadyen's bringing her. He's got a *real* car. Ludovic's is more like a meat safe on wheels—the draught get in everywhere. What a *heavenly* room, Mrs. Belton," which admiration, whether feigned or real (and as far as we know it was completely unfeigned) gave Mrs. Belton great pleasure, for she always felt it was in a way a Belton preserve, having been built by the Nabob.

The Honourable Mrs. Bob then came up and asked Mrs. Belton if she should tell the little band to begin, with such graciousness and so obviously being Courteous to Old Age, that Mrs. Belton nearly had the giggles. But she pulled herself together almost at once, thinking it must all seem rather provincial to the Harley Street chatelaine, and said it would be a good idea.

"Of course I have asked the Madre," said Mrs. Bob, which title she had bestowed on her mother-in-law from—and indeed before—the moment of their first meeting, "and Mrs. Updike," thus somehow conveying to Mrs. Belton that though the three elder ladies were the hostesses and paying (in the persons of their husbands) for the dance, nothing was likely to happen until the Honourable Mrs. Robert Perry, in her very smart not-too-evening crinoline dress swirling well off the ground, her sheer nylons, her silver shoes, her pearls and her exquisite sleek windswept hair, had waved her magic wand. So Mrs. Bob went off to the musicians.

The three hostesses with Lady Graham were very comfortably off on sofas at the end of the room away from the band, of which secretly they were glad, as the noise was to them far too loud and far too hideous. We need hardly say that several of the younger men had nervously approached Lady Graham in the hope of gaining immortality by partnering her ladyship, but Agnes only laughed—very kindly—and said they must find younger partners, which words came from the heart for she did not in the least wish to tire herself or spoil her charming pose of dowager and had brought with her an old diamond-set face-à-main to that end.

"May I sit on the arm of your sofa for a moment, Lady

Graham?" said Swan, perching beside her with an elegant swish of his coat tails so that they might not be crushed.

"How *sensible*," said Agnes approvingly. "My husband was always *most* particular about not sitting on his tails and he always had them properly pressed, by his tailor of course, after a ball or a dinner-party. But I daresay you have never been to a dinner-party," she added, not in the least meaning that Swan was not what the Germans (when they still spoke a language almost suitable for Society) called Salonfähig, but realising that her companion, though a very well-bred and personable young man, could not have known the 'twenties, when Society had its Last Days, or even the feverish 'thirties.

Swan, perfectly enchanted by her ladyship, said it was his greatest grief that he had been born too late and would she tell him what it used to be like. Nothing could have been more agreeable to her ladyship than to expatiate upon the society of her young days, when her father Mr. Leslie still used to take a house in Cadogan Square every summer for the season and her mother, Lady Emily Leslie, presented her and took her to balls.

"And *proper* dinner-parties at the Good Houses still," said Lady Graham. "An engraved invitation card and one wore one's long white gloves and went in arm-in-arm which was quite awkward in some houses where the staircase was narrow, and at least six or seven courses and sometimes a sorbet in the middle, which always annoyed Papa. And my uncle, old Lord Pomfret, was *most* particular about people talking on the right side—I mean the *right* side of course, not the right side—and if everyone didn't turn to the other side in the middle of dinner and talk to the other person he used to shout down the table at them. It was all so nice and *easy* then," said her ladyship with a sigh.

"May I say," said Swan, who was enjoying himself enormously, "how *deeply* I sympathise with you about all the life you have lost, the life I never saw. I hardly know how to express my feelings, Lady Graham. At least there is one way, but you might not like it."

"I cannot possibly say till you tell me what it is," said her ladyship, raising her beautiful dark eyes to Swan's face.

"Then, may I show you?" said Swan, and slipping his hand, palm downwards, below her gloved hand, he raised it slowly and tenderly, brushed it with his lips and restored it with great care to its owner.

"How charming of you," said Agnes, entirely unimpressed. "Robert—my husband—had some charming Austrian friends before the war who kissed one's hand just like that. And what are you plans?"

"Which plans?" said Swan, for the moment out of his depth.

"I mean your plans for life," said Agnes, opening her black lace fan which she held idly as a kind of screen.

"Schoolmastering at present," said Swan, by now ready to tell this siren almost every secret of his heart. "Then perhaps a college fellowship. That depends on several things."

Lady Graham, suddenly bringing up from a corner of her mind something she thought she had once heard, said But Fellows couldn't be married, could they.

Not, said Swan, when the Universities *were* Universities, but now it was far, far too common and he understood that at Lazarus, a college of which he and many other people had the lowest opinion, the quad outside the Master's Lodgings was popularly known as Pram Quad, at which Lady Graham laughed quite charmingly, much to Swan's delight who was certain that she had not understood him.

"And you? Are you thinking of being a married fellow?" said Agnes.

Swan paused before he answered.

"No, I won't ask," said Agnes. "You are troubled," to which Swan made no reply.

"I am sorry," said Agnes. "Does she know?"

"I haven't tried," said Swan. "I have the next dance with your daughter Clarissa. I must go."

"If it goes well, do tell me," said Agnes, thinking of her eldest, her James, in Swan's place. "And if by any chance it doesn't, come to me if I can help you, dear boy. And now enjoy yourself," and she turned to Mrs. Belton while Swan went off to find Clarissa, slightly dazzled and not a little moved by what Lady Graham had said.

Had Swan been a native of Barsetshire, he might have drawn a comparison between Clarissa and that Griselda Grantly who—perhaps a hundred years ago now—kept her breath for dancing which she enjoyed rather than waste it on words. Except for the tennis party at the Priory School when Cecil Waring had to be taken to the Barsetshire General, he had very seldom met her. Whether it was that she did not want to dance and talk, or for some other reason, she was very silent, answering when spoken to but not carrying on the conversation or making any remarks on her own initiative. But she was a sufficiently good dancer and several of the older people noticed them, including Charles, who was industriously taking the elder Updike girl round the room and was pleased to see Clarissa so well partnered.

Sitting-out room was not the strong point of the Nabob. Some chairs and rather decayed sofas had been put in the passages, and in the refreshment room were a few hired chairs that couldn't be fitted into the ballroom, so they sat on two chairs in the passage side by side and Swan said what fun it was to stay with the Beltons. Clarissa said Cousin Lucy was always so nice. And so, said Swan, were Mr. Belton, and Freddy Belton. He hadn't met Elsa Hornby, Charles's sister. And Charles was the very best kind of fellow. Charles's betrothed, putting back with her elegant fingers a piece of hair which the dance had ruffled, said ye-es? in a kind of questioning drawl. It would have given Swan great and unchivalrous pleasure to smack her, but prudence forbade this, so he spoke of an episode during the war when he and Charles, not then properly acquainted, had come up against one another somewhere in France and how coolly and bravely Charles had carried out a difficult and dangerous operation.

"Oh, Charles isn't a dastard in war," said Clarissa. The words meant something, Swan was certain; what exactly he did not know, though he felt he ought to. But he was determined not to let Clarissa feel she had won that move—whatever she may have meant by it—and made conversation in a way that forced her to take her part, for she had a social conscience. On the whole he was relieved when the next dance began and he could feel easy with Grace Grantly who was enjoying everything from the beauty of the room to the coldness of the ices with wholehearted pleasure. Their conversation was not so deep as a well, nor so wide as a church-door, but it was enough, it served. And just as her tennis had been first-class amateur, so was her dancing. No showing-off, but a head for rhythm, feet that moved with her partner's, a body (if we may be allowed the expression) that swayed like an intelligent reed to each of his movements; and Swan with a lightness of foot inherited from his Scotch mother was no mean ballroom dancer. Their talk was not about anything in particular but it fitted as comfortably as did their steps.

Grace told Swan what fun she had had lanolineing some of the old books in the Barchester Central Library and how Percy Thatcher, better known as Purse, the very intelligent child of shame of her parents' cook, had got a scholarship to the County Technical School (and if there is not such a thing it must be taken as existing) where he proposed to concentrate on Woyreless (for so he spoke of it in pure Barsetshire) and would doubtless make a name and a fortune. And Swan told Grace how he had meant to go home for Christmas but his mother had been invited to go to Rome so he was at the Beltons'; and altogether it was extremely comfortable. Then they talked about some of the guests and Swan said what a pretty little creature Justinia Lufton was and how he would never have guessed that she was older than Lord Lufton and who was the woman with the large sad eyes who had just come in with the good-looking middle-aged man and Grace said Oh that was Lady Lufton and the man was Mr. Macfadyen, the Head of Amalgamated Vedge who had taken part of Framley Court and was very nice. And though Swan had enjoyed his dance with Clarissa and admired her, he felt that with Grace one could, as it were, put on one's bedroom slippers and sit back, for which condition there was something to be said.

Meanwhile the dance had been going on with much pleasure to everyone. Lady Lufton having once forced herself to accept the invitation found in the room a good many old acquaintances and rather enjoyed the talk while Mr. Macfadyen, having seen her well established, had got into a comfortable corner with Mr. Belton to talk about the varieties of West Barsetshire soil and to them had been added Dr. Perry with a fresh load of Barsetshire gossip and Mr. Updike to contradict Dr. Perry when his gossip was too outrageously wrong; and Mr. Macfadyen told them a story against the late Government that made them all laugh and so each gentleman had been—or at any rate felt, which is almost as good—rather a wit in his own line, though not without a certain solidness and dependability. Owing to lack of room and difficulties of serving there was no regular sit-down supper, but everyone had large plates of cold food and Mr. Adams's champagne flowed and the younger dancers ate ices till the elders thought their insides would be frozen. The coffee was of course odious, but it was hot, and there was a pleasant amount of noise and laughter.

After supper the ball was re-opened by what we can only describe as an exhibition set of the Lancers, in which the older people had consented to take part. Two Beltons, two Updikes, the two elder Perrys, Mr. and the Honourable Mrs. Robert Perry, two Grantlys, Lady Lufton (persuaded thereto by her son), Mr. Macfadyen, Lady Graham, Mr. Carton (whose wife did not dance), Oliver Marling (under considerable pressure from his wife who was like Becky Sharp: of the ball, yes; of the dancing, no) with a nice well-bred woman from East Barsetshire supplied by Mrs. Bob. How enchanting the Lancers seriously danced can be, only those who remember know. There was always a faction who descended at once to what were called "Kitchen Lancers," ruinous to everyone's hair and train, especially if there were any spurs about; but the real thing was a fine piece of ordered pageantry. Ladies could swirl round then, somehow never touching their trains which spread behind them like comets' tails, and the square or the circle or the wheel moved with the graceful precision of a Musical Ride at what we shall continue to call The Royal Military Tournament as performed when we were young at the Royal Agricultural Hall, Islington. On this evening in this year there were not any long trains, but the elder ladies, especially Mrs. Belton and Mrs. Grantly, gave the onlookers a complete illusion of them. The younger guests who had crowded the walls and the doorways, rather hoping to be amused, found themselves frankly envious and in several young breasts a stern resolve was formed to chuck those reels and do a spot of Lancers: we hope we have reported them correctly.

Swan, watching with every sense (an expression we refuse to modify), felt perfectly intoxicated by the stately ordered rhythms, the marchings and counter-marchings, the Grand Chain in linked sweetness all drawn out; and Edith Graham was so excited that she jigged up and down the whole time to the great annoyance of her neighbours.

There had been talk of a tango, but none of the younger people knew enough about it, so the dancing continued on ordinary lines, with the added excitement of the lights (thanks to the electrical gifts of Jim Perry) being dimmed and turned slowly up again.

Edith by this time was quite above herself, showing off in a most dashing way and already deeply in love (or what she took for such) with both the unmarried Perrys and Mr. Macfadyen; who received her advances very seriously, amused by her artless fancy for him. All through the evening Lord Lufton had been doing his duty as a peer and a landowner should; dancing with older ladies who all approved of him and with one or two girls who were a little out of it (as someone always is even at the best-organised party) and presently with Clarissa, who said what fun it was when Lady Lufton let her sit in the old basket-work pony carriage and hold the parasol whip.

"You must come again," said Lord Lufton, who felt quite kindly about her though nothing more. "Grace Grantly is coming over next week. If you will come too we can look at the Coronation Robes. You said you would like to see them," at which Clarissa had the internal sulks, for one did not wish to be asked to a party just because Grace Grantly was coming, but said it would be too, too amusing. "I'll ask Charles too," said Lord Lufton. "What a very good fellow he is. Perhaps he would bring you over and we'll get mother to play. She used to play a lot and somehow after my father died she didn't, but she has begun again and Justy sings. I don't mean like opera, but just songs. Do you sing at all? You look as if you ought to."

Clarissa, from whose gifts music had been omitted, said she didn't care much for music; and then feeling that this was not very polite to Lady Lufton, nor indeed to Lady Lufton's son, became confused and angry with herself and missed her step, so that Lord Lufton nearly trod on her foot.

"Stupid of me, it was all my fault," said Clarissa. "Let's sit down for a minute."

Lord Lufton good-naturedly said the dance was nearly over so they might go and have ices in the refreshment room where Mrs. Carton's excellent servants Wickens (an ex-scout of Paul's College) and his rather deaf wife, and the Vicar's cook Mrs. Powlett were enjoying themselves immensely, with a rabble of village women washing up all the time behind a curtain and having cups of tea. There were no other dancers in the room except Dr. Perry and Edith Graham who with some forty years between them were getting on like a house on fire, discussing life, while Edith ate ices of which she said she had never had enough. And then Charles with Justinia Lufton came in. The ladies, if Edith may be counted as one, were left together while their cavaliers went foraging. Charles was back very quickly with three large ices which he offered on one knee.

"I'll eat mine quickly," said Edith, "because dear, dear Dr. Perry is getting me one too.

> I'll dance and be merry
> With dear Doctor Perry,
> And go on the ferry
> With dear Doctor Perry,
> And drink up my sherry
> With dear Doctor Perry.

I could do a lot more," she added, "but I must finish this ice quickly before he comes back and put the saucer under the chair. Then I can eat his."

"You'll have a frozen stomach, my girl," said Charles, who (to Lady Graham's amusement and pleasure) treated Edith as a younger sister, to be teased for her good. "Justinia?"

"Oh thank you," said Justinia, taking it with a smile.

"And Clarissa," said Charles, still kneeling. "Last, loneliest, loveliest, exquisite, apart—and God send no one will come down on me for royalties as it's Kipling—will you accept an ice, as cold as your heart, as pink as—" at which point Clarissa got up with brimming eyes, looked round for help, saw none, and went quickly out of the room. Swan, who had looked in to see if his next partner was there, saw her face and quickly went away, unnoticed by the others.

"Silly Clarissa,

Why don't you kiss her?

No one will miss her" said Edith, not meaning anything in particular and even the greatest poets—as witness John Keats—have had their lapses on trivial subjects.

Charles got up and dusted his knees. Lord Lufton, doing the

first best thing that came into his mind, said to Justinia "Our dance I think" and took her away, carrying Edith with him.

Charles also turned to go.

"Sit down, you young fool," said Dr. Perry, who had not had three sons of his own and known Charles since he was a boy for nothing. "If *that*'s all the army does for a man, we'd better all be pacifists. Where's that brandy, Wickens? Updike and I brought some," he said to Charles. "Not for the youngsters, but you'll do with a spot. Put it down."

Charles put it down obediently and felt better.

"Sorry, sir," he said.

"Don't be a fool," said Dr. Perry. "Come outside," and he took Charles by a side door into the Nabob's yard where it was extremely cold. "How long have you been engaged to that girl?"

Charles said he didn't know. As far as he was concerned he had always been engaged to her and he didn't think he could discuss it.

"Rubbish!" said Dr. Perry. "I saw you when you were five minutes old and a silly sight you were. But not half as silly as you are now. What do you think your girl's thinking of?"

"I don't know," said Charles, sitting down on the running board of a car and letting his clasped hands fall between his knees.

"Well, I do," said Dr. Perry. "It's you, my boy."

Charles looked up.

"Damned young fool," said Dr. Perry crossly. "Hanging about, keeping the girl waiting."

"But I didn't want to hurry her," said Charles. "I mean she didn't know what she wanted and I didn't like to bother her and Cousin Agnes and mother didn't say anything. And I haven't got much to give her. I've a bit of my own and my salary and when my old aunt dies I come in for a bit—all of us do. And when father and mother are both dead there'll be a little more and——"

"It's not your money the girl wants, it's you, you fool," said Dr.

Perry. "Marry her and damn the consequences. *I* know when a girl's in love. It's oozing out of her everywhere. She'll probably murder someone or go mad," said Dr. Perry, driving his argument home by fair means or foul. "Marry her and do the worrying afterwards. And don't say I told you. And thank your God that you're marrying a girl your parents will love. Bob's wife is a fine girl and her father is one of the top consultants and there'll be money for everything and she'll push Bob for all he's worth. And he'll like it. But *we* shan't see much of the grandchildren. They will go to expensive seaside lodgings, or to grandfather Bronson-Hewbury with his place in Berkshire. I—and my wife—have done what we could for Bob: they will dispose of him and very well too, I admit. Now come in, or you'll get pneumonia," and he pushed Charles, not unkindly, back into the Nabob.

"Thanks awfully, Dr. Perry," said Charles. "I'll—I don't know what I'll do. I feel such a brute. But there's one thing: we can have a home at Harefield. Philip Winter is turning the west pavilion into a resident master's house and I'll have that house if I have to kill someone for it. I say sir, I'm sorry."

"Damned young fool," said Dr. Perry again. "And now go and dance. You've probably broken someone's heart by cutting the last one. Here, Wickens, another brandy please. It will be by the mercy of Providence if I don't get pneumonia. It's freezing all right."

"You didn't had ought to go outside, sir," said Mrs. Powlett, reproachfully yet soothingly. "Cold on the stomach, that's what Powlett had and the doctor said when a man's over sixty there's no saying where it'll go next. Strikes inwards, that's what it does, and that's what it done to Powlett. But I gave him a lovely funeral, sir, and I put flowers on his grave every year on his birthday," and doubtless Mrs. Powlett would have continued her gentle Crabbe-like moralisings indefinitely had not a fresh irruption of between-dancing young people burst in for more ices.

By this time, we regret to say, Edith Graham, quite above herself, was established with a group of admirers for whose benefit she improvised on any given subject.

"Now do one for Dr. Perry," said one of her admirers.

"Our honoured Doctor Perry
Is kind and thoughtful very,
He is most good at healing
And always stops ill-feeling,"

said Edith promptly. "I don't mean he stops one feeling ill. I mean when Clarissa was cross to Charles when we were having ices and Clarissa went out with a Flounce, he showed great tact. I shall marry someone very tactful."

"You will need to," said Dr. Perry who had come up while she was speaking. "Your mother is looking for you, Edith. Can anyone dance the polka? That's the last dance except for a galop. It's snowing outside."

Edith, feeling like all poets that her bread was bitter and other people's stairs inhospitable, nevertheless got up and went to find Lady Graham whom she ran to earth on the sofa in the passage with Mrs. Belton and Lady Lufton, all rather enjoying being middle-aged together.

"Oh, here you are, darling Edith," said her mother. "We must go soon. Mr. Belton told me it was snowing and it is so disagreeable if the roads are too snowy. I remember once my uncle had a ball at Pomfret Towers and it snowed so hard that quite a lot of people had to stay the night. It was really quite difficult to find enough beds and Lord Hartletop—he was Lord Dumbello then—made quite a horrid burn on the sofa in the Green Room by pulling it too near the fire."

"Oh *can't* I have the galop, mother?" said Edith, which was a skilful move for Lady Graham rashly said yes, forgetting that the polka came before it, which was exactly what her youngest daughter had hoped; and having given her word did not go back on it. But it was a Pyrrhic victory, for Edith did not dance the polka with the necessary élan, so incurring the freely expressed censure of Swan who had kindly volunteered to partner her. Luckily he was old enough not to feel the disgrace of an incompetent partner and when Edith had got the hang of it she enjoyed herself vastly, as indeed did Swan.

By this time the nicely dressed, well-mannered girl from East Barsetshire had gone home in the car reft from her parents for the occasion, as had Lady Lufton, escorted by Mr. Macfadyen, and several more people who lived at a good distance, so there would be plenty of room for the galop. Charles was in the ballroom putting up a very good show of nonchalance which made those who loved him best wonder what on earth had happened and, with his usual kindness, had offered to partner the nice rather dull elder Updike girl. Swan had hoped to dance with Grace Grantly but she was already bespoken by Dr. Perry (rather lecherously as Swan considered), so he fell back upon Justinia Lufton and had his reward, for she was a perfect dancer, with a light mouth and easy to handle. Agnes was besieged by three Perry boys at once and chose Gus because he was the least good-looking of the three, finding herself rewarded by his skill and courage as a steersman and a fascinating account of an elderly woman in the Barchester General who was having a piece of skin from her thigh grafted on to her left arm and, as far as she could understand Gus's description, had to stay for three weeks in a position not unlike that of the Quangle-Wangle with his head in his slipper.

"I always hope," said Agnes, who could have danced even so violent a dance as the final galop without turning a hairpin or for one moment losing her composure, "that no one will fall down in a galop. I remember at Malta once, when my husband was stationed there, a man in his regiment whose mother I am sure you must have known—she used to drug quite dreadfully and was arrested in Piccadilly wearing black tights and a coronet trying to break into Fortnum's—catching his spurs in someone's dress and falling down. I could not help feeling sorry for him."

So overcome was Gus by the beauty of her ladyship's compassion that he nearly bumped into the younger Updike's partner and had to apologise to Agnes.

"But we *always* used to bump into people in the galop," said Agnes. "It was considered quite fast then. No one says fast now. Suppose we stopped for a while. You must feel quite tired," which invitation, far from being as Gus imagined given in compassion for him, was rather that her ladyship's silver shoes, seldom worn now, were just on the tight side and Gus had trodden on them twice.

But of course the hero of the evening was Mr. Belton. Gallantly partnered by the ex-Headmistress, Mrs. Sidney Carton, he volleyed and thundered, charged 'em home again, seized his own again, rammed and sank the Carthaginian galleys, and in general charged the company like Prince Rupert, putting all the younger men to shame. Mrs. Carton, quite unmoved, a black-coated arm well round her, with every confidence in her steersman, enjoyed it vastly and thought how much her grandfather would have liked to see it. Mrs. Belton, looking at her husband with detached affection as she went round in Mr. Updike's reliable legal arms, thought what a dear he was and how thankful she was that what with the Hosiers' Girls' Foundation School buying that bit of land over by the Southbridge Road and now the Priory School coming to Harefield House, there would be quite a reasonable sum of money in hand. There had been a moment when her courage almost failed; namely when her husband after the sale of his land to the Hosiers' Company, had decided to make over a good deal of capital to his sons; for she very sensibly felt that to do so meant that he would die at once, or that both boys would die before their father, so bringing all his plans to nought and crippling him in his old age. There had been a certain amount of difficulty at the time, for both Freddy Belton and Elsa Belton had made what are called good marriages; the one having married a daughter of the wealthy engineer Mr. Dean who had generously dowered all his children, the other Christopher Hornby, now Sir Christopher and an Admiral, with lands in Scotland and large holdings in various northern industrial concerns: both of whom had generously insisted on something being added from each of their shares to Charles's, to which their father had finally agreed, saying rather grumpily that Charles had better not know or he might get above himself: which was perhaps only his way of expressing his affection for his latest-born. His elder children had laughed at him quite kindly behind his back and kept his secret. So whatever blows fate might have for Charles there would probably be enough and a little more—a very little more since They had squandered all They could lay hands on, but well worth having.

Perhaps the person who enjoyed it all most was Edith who so bewitched and led astray the good-looking Bob Perry that he galoped and tally-ho'd with the loudest and as soon as the music stopped gave at the very top of his voice Three cheers for old Winston, greeted with a terrific outburst of noise and people imitating various musical instruments, thus incurring later the well-bred remonstrances of his Honourable wife whom he hugged very affectionately and told not to be a silly idiot like her father. Which words, when followed by whole-hearted congratulations on the way she had helped to run the dance, did the Honourable Mrs. Bob a lot of good, and we think that Dr. Perry's gloomier prognostications will not be fulfilled.

"Good-bye, dear Charles," said Lady Graham, looking up rather anxiously at him as she took his hand. "Come and see us soon. I can't talk to you now, dear boy. I feel for you so much. I can't say any more," to which Charles replied by kissing her hand and casting towards Clarissa a look that her mother could not understand. Edith, quite intoxicated by the homage of all the older men, was collected as were also her brothers whom we have not particularly mentioned because they were delightful boys about whom we do not at present know much else. The

Marlings had gone, Oliver making what his wife called an old maidish fuss about getting her home and she wasn't Mrs. Wittitterly and would *not* remember her medical man. Just then Henry Grantly came up with his sister, Grace, the two Luftons and Swan following hard upon them and Lady Graham wafted herself and her party away.

Profuse and heartfelt thanks were given to Mrs. Belton and the two other hostesses and Swan asked each of them to thank her husband on his behalf.

"I say," said Grace to Swan, "I wish I'd thought of that. It's always the hostesses that get thanked. Like at our garden party at the Rectory when no one bothers about Father. Do come and see us soon, Mr. Swan."

Swan said he would like it of all things, but considering the length of his friendship with Charles and several of their common acquaintance, and that he had mentioned the matter before, wouldn't she call him Eric.

"Of course I will," said Grace. "I did mean to only it takes a bit of getting used to."

Swan agreed. It was, he said, the one thoughtless action of an otherwise perfect female parent. Eric, he said, appeared to him to have no value at all except possibly as Anag. in the *Times* Cross Word puzzle, at which Grace laughed and Swan felt flattered by her quick apprehension.

"Could I just say Swan?" she said. "That nice Mrs. Morland always says Swan when she talks about you."

"And what *does* she talk about me?" said Swan, amused.

"Well, I don't quite know," said Grace. "It's mostly about things you did at Southbridge when you and Tony were there."

"My rôle in life," said Swan with mock resignation. "Only to be the Pylades, the Pythias, the—" and he paused, hoping to recollect another couple of names. Grace with a serious face said try Guildenstern, which made them both laugh.

"Let me say Swan," she said. "I always think of you as Swan," which words, though he knew they meant nothing in particular, suddenly fell upon him like a blow. But even if a thousand little shafts of flame Are shivered in one's not at all narrow frame, one is a gentleman saying good-bye after a cheerful Christmas Dance and must behave as such.

"Pray let it be Swan," he said and then she went away with her brother. The two younger Perrys (Bob having been removed by the Honourable Mrs. Bob), the two Updikes with Charles and Swan then gave Mr. Wheeler and his staff a hand with the clearing up. Dr. Perry (or Mr. Updike, but we suspect the former) had removed what was left of the brandy, but there were still four bottles of champagne, two of which they gave to Mr. Wheeler. The other two they took back to the ballroom where they drank each others' healths and felt sentimental.

"Dim them once more, Jim, there's a good fellow," said Charles, and Jim Perry went up to the gallery and once more the lovely sparkling lights went slowly down. Swan who was near one of the windows pulled the gold-coloured curtains aside. The snow had stopped. There had been just enough to whiten the roofs and the fences of the Nabob's back premises and sprinkle the hill beyond where Harefield House stood like an enchanted palace of marble. The unreal, unloving light of the low moon caught the lustres of the chandeliers and made the young men look ghostly white against their black clothes. Swan felt afraid, for no reason. He drew the curtains again, Jim Perry turned off all the lights and they went back to the bar to say good night to Wheeler and the other helpers who were having beer (the men) and small ports (the ladies), as is the proper etiquette.

With a good deal of talk and laughing, though not enough to constitute a brawl, the young men went down the wide High Street. At Arcot House they said good night with vows of eternal friendship. Charles and Swan went quietly in, the Perrys were engulfed by Plassey House and the Updikes by Clive's Corner. Arcot House was dark, but not cold for Mr. Belton by his own methods had lain in a good store of fuel for the central heating which, though not in every room, at least mollified (and we do not mean modified) the temperature of the hall and the staircase. They went very quietly upstairs and to their rooms. Neither young man slept well. It was not a night of memories and of sighs; rather a night of hopes, doubts and in Charles's case of a firm resolution. Much had to be considered and he was going to talk to his elder brother Freddy about various things in the morning.

Swan lay awake for some time in pleasant drowsiness, thinking how perfectly bred Grace Grantly was, how quick in the uptake and, with a sudden pang of joy in his heart, how she had said she always thought of him as Swan. A college fellowship was perhaps not an inheritance but if one had some money of one's own it was a not unpleasant life. Whether a girl whose whole background was country would take to university life one could not tell. Probably a girl with beauty and brains and kindness would take to any life if her heart were in it and his own beat faster at the thought. From one girl his mind went to another, to that spoilt little bitch (we regret the word but are not responsible) Clarissa for whom Charles was far too good. Remembering her sudden outburst of temper that evening he was seriously concerned for Charles his friend. And his mind went back to the earlier talk with Clarissa when, trying to fire in her some spark of enthusiasm for her betrothed, he had told her of Charles's gallant behaviour in a tight place; how Clarissa had said "Oh, Charles isn't a dastard in war," with some implication he could not understand. What on earth was it? And then, just as the answer fleeted past him, he caught it. Of course: A laggard in love and a dastard in war Was to wed the fair Ellen of young Lochinvar. What did she mean? And it dawned upon him, to his fury, that the little jade thought Charles was not, in modern jargon, frightfully keen.

"Damn that pink-faced conceited piece," he said aloud to himself, which did him good. But so many thoughts were crowding on him that he could not catch them all. *Quick*, thy tablets, Memory, he implored aloud. And he remembered her stricken face as Charles knelt to her with the ices, and her swift flight. From Charles he had thought: and so Charles had thought. But it was not from Charles, it was from herself, from her love for Charles, a love that could no longer bear to wait, that was too proud, too fine (for by now he was alight with compassion for the pretty creature) to ask. What a star-crossed business it was. Compassion for her rose so strongly in him that he began to blame Charles for the trouble. Well, the only thing at the moment was to try to go to sleep. The morning would bring counsel—*not* as the French said the night which was already feverish enough—and he had better go to sleep. After an hour of industriously going to sleep he gave it up, turned the light on, and began to read one of Mrs. Morland's thrillers which he had found in his room, and so fell asleep with the light on, to wake cold and unrested at six o'clock when, finding sleep impossible to regain, he got up and did two hours' serious reading, not one word of which he could understand or remember. But doubtless some of it soaked through.

CHAPTER 9

What with the General Election and one thing and another the Bishop's cruise to Maderia had been put off several times. Mrs. Joram said it was a deliberate attempt to stop her having her party, and the celebration of Sir Edmund Pridham's birthday, but neither she nor anyone else believed it, and Sir Edmund said any birthday would do for an old fellow like him so long as Mrs. Joram was happy. However before Christmas the news went round that the Bishop and his wife would really be going early in the New Year, when they would get the full benefit of a warmer climate to prepare them for the rigours of an English spring. Mrs. Joram, through the medium of Simnet her butler, was able to discover the exact date when the Palace would sail to Madeira's Isle and began to issue her invitations accordingly.

Christmas had come and gone with its accustomed fuss and fever. All the shops in Barchester burst into cheap (or as cheap as the times will allow) window displays and considering the financial depression and the mountains of debt with which They had saddled this country, a good deal of shopping was done. Bostock and Plummer had a number of new-look dresses and it was rumoured that the Bishop's wife had bought a crinoline evening model with a velvet coatee to wear with it on less formal occasions, but it was not proven. A competition was held at Southbridge School among such of the staff as had not gone away for the Christmas holidays to find quotations from the English poets suitable to members of His Majesty's late Government, the first prize being awarded to the Senior Housemaster's wife, Mrs. Robin Dale, she who was Anne Fielding, for a reference to Tennyson's *Maud*, Part I, Section II, line six, with proxime accessit to a junior master, Mr. Traill of Maria Cottage, who said he was all for the classics and Pope was the man for him, and on being challenged remarked that The rest to some faint meaning made pretence But Sh.nw.ll never deviated into sense; and, he added, if anyone cared to look at *Maud*, Part II, Section V, verse 3, lines 5 and 6, he would find something to his advantage, but he wasn't giving anything away.

All well-thinking people went about saying that everything would be *much* worse now, for ever and ever, but so long as we had Mr. Churchill we could stand *anything*: both of which statements were, we think, fair comment: and then Christmas had swallowed everything. For three or four days life was dead except for eating too much, which was still possible if one could do without meat and could digest quantities of farinaceous food, or had a rabbit, or could afford a turkey. Charles and Swan took an enormous amount of exercise with the young Perrys and young Updikes, even managing to hire and borrow enough horses for a long ride over the downs; a great success except that they all got home hungrier than ever. Swan, quite deliberately, laid himself out to become the family friend of Mr. and Mrs. Belton and of Captain Freddy Belton, R.N. and his wife who had been Susan Dean, succeeding so well that the whole family one after another confided in him.

Mr. Belton, being alone before dinner with Swan in what he still called the estate room while the others had gone to a Bring and Buy at the Updikes', said Well what about Charles and his young woman. In *his* young days, he said, there wasn't all this shilly-shallying; to which Swan replied that Charles didn't talk about it, at which Mr. Belton looked pleased and said something about a lady's name in the mess which nearly made Swan have the giggles, but he recovered himself and said he expected Charles felt he ought to be earning a bit more before he could support Clarissa properly. To which Mr. Belton replied Rubbish, and if Charles couldn't keep a wife on his salary and the bit of money his old aunt who wasn't expected to last out the week had left him and what he, Mr. Belton, had made over to his children just in time to escape the last extension of the years one had to live, he must be backing horses. Swan, putting on his spectacles, said that threw an entirely new light on things and so impressed was Mr. Belton by this that he was at some pains to get out his papers and show Swan exactly what Charles's present income and safe expectations were. If *anything* was safe, said Mr. Belton cautiously: and if Charles was fool enough to shilly-shally much longer he'd lose the girl altogether. Swan asked, in as casual a way as he could command, whether Charles had ever seen the figures, at which Mr. Belton said *he* never asked his old father what his affairs were and Charles had never asked *him*. Swan, the spectacled young scholar sitting at the feet of an older man of vast experience, said of course he knew nothing about it, but if Sir Robert Graham could see those figures he would surely be interested and let his daughter marry as soon as reasonable.

"Well, well, young man, you've got a head on your shoulders," said Mr. Belton. "Tell you what I'll do. I'll get Updike to write to Graham's solicitors. Tell 'em exactly how we stand, eh?" which Swan applauded as an original and most intelligent suggestion.

Later in the evening when Charles had gone over to the Perrys about the ratting and Mr. Belton was fast asleep with the Times, looking very distinguished, Mrs. Belton also opened her heart to Swan who said he had noticed that Charles was getting rather worried about his future and though it wasn't his business he was fond of Charles and wondered if he could help in any way. Mrs. Belton, thankful to talk to an outsider whom she could trust, said that she and Lady Graham were really at their wits' end about the young people and wished they would make up their minds: even, she added anxiously, if it was only to break everything off. Did she know, Swan asked, that Philip Winter was turning the pavilions into married quarters and it would probably be first come, first served, so Charles had better hurry up or he, Swan, would get in first.

"Oh, are you engaged?" said Mrs. Belton, at once losing interest in her younger son. Swan said not in the least, but one never knew.

Next day he nobbled, to use his own expression, Captain Freddy Belton, R.N., in the Nabob and elicited from him that he thought his young brother was a sight too patient and if he were Charles he'd get a licence and marry the girl out of hand. Charles, he added, could perfectly well afford it and there were lots of fellows much worse off and would Swan come in for a drink about six, which Swan did and was rewarded by being allowed to see the Freddy Beltons' gifted son and their equally gifted daughter both splashing in the bath. And very nicely they splashed too. And Swan thought that Mrs. Freddy was one of the nicest and most sensible women he had met, so that the conspiracy for Charles, or against Charles if you prefer, seemed to be making headway.

That same evening Swan was dining with the Cartons at Assaye House. There was a fourth guest, a very pleasant not young woman. Swan thought he had never seen a face with so many reserves behind it and such quiet competence.

"I don't think you know Mr. Swan," said Mrs. Carton to the guest. "He is with Mr. Winter at the Priory School. This is Miss Merriman, Mr. Swan."

Swan and Miss Merriman had not met before, but it was one of those lucky meetings when an Elective Affinity if we may use those alarming words, though not so alarming as Wahlverwandtschaft, is immediately apparent.

"Miss Merriman lives at Pomfret Towers now and used to be at Holdings," said Mrs. Carton and Swan was able to say at once, and truthfully, how much he had admired Lady Graham at the dance; a genuine tribute to a charming woman which—or so it had appeared to Swan then—she had taken as her due. Not with conceit, not with smugness or self-satisfaction, but as one who knew her own worth and her own place and would never underestimate the one or overstep the other.

Miss Merriman said, in her quiet pleasant voice, that Lady Graham had much enjoyed her talk with Mr. Swan and—if Mr. Swan did not mind her saying so—had said how unusual it was to meet a young man with such delightful manners. Swan had a faint feeling that his reaction to this praise was being closely watched by Miss Merriman, but as he didn't know what she wanted him to say he did the next best thing; namely to speak the truth, that he had been captivated by Lady Graham and had much admired Clarissa. As for Edith, he said, he was reserving for himself the honour of falling in love with her in a few years, to all of which nonsense Miss Merriman listened with a kind of composure that made him feel about ten years younger than he really was.

To them were shortly added Mr. and Mrs. Samuel Adams from Edgewood. Swan had often heard of the wealthy ironmaster who had married the Marlings' younger daughter and had formed—as we all do unconsciously—his own idea of him. What exactly it was we are not sure—probably a nice vulgarian with a wife rather above him—but it was (as our preconceived ideas nearly always are) shattered for ever, and past remembering, by the very handsome woman and the large, capable-looking man who came into the room.

Mrs. Adams on hearing that Swan was a friend of Charles Belton at once took him in tow, so to speak, for there was a kinship between the Beltons and her own family the Marlings, and then put him through a searching inquiry about himself from which, he gathered, he had emerged with at least two credits.

"And what are you doing now?" asked Mrs. Adams. "I mean you aren't going to be a schoolmaster always, are you?" to which

Swan replied that if she could tell him what he was going to do next he would be grateful, for it was more than he knew himself. He liked schoolmastering, he said, but it wasn't exactly an inheritance.

Mrs. Adams, putting both her elbows on the table, said was he going to leave the Priory School then.

"Oh not now," said Swan, properly shocked. "My old school tie wouldn't let me. No, I shall stick to the ship till she is launched and making fairway, or headway, or whatever the right word is, with a favouring wind. I have other plans, but I daresay they can wait. I had the most delightful experience this afternoon. I went to the Freddy Beltons for a drink and saw their children having their bath. My bachelor heart was completely melted."

"I'll tell you what," said Mrs. Adams, much impressed by his most proper attitude," "you'd better come over to Edgewood and see Amabel Rose. She is perfectly *divine* in her bath. Isn't she, Sam?" she called across the table to her husband, who said that Amabel Rose was the best job the Works ever turned out and returned to his talk with Mrs. Carton.

Swan said he would love to and he hoped Amabel Rose would let him be an uncle, which appeared to puzzle Mrs. Adams. Swan was quick enough to realise that joking, whether fantasy or persiflage, was not Mrs. Adams's strong point and inquired with a serious face about Amabel Rose's eyes and hair and whether she could talk, which amused Mrs. Adams vastly.

"Could you come over next week and bring Charles?" she said. "Perhaps Friday. We are having some people for drinks. My brother Oliver and his wife and the Rector and Mrs. Grantly and some of their family and one or two more. Not a party."

Swan said he would love it, for he was much taken by Mrs. Adams. And if the Grantlys were coming, possibly their daughter would be coming too he said, but Mrs. Adams said she was pretty sure Colin and Eleanor weren't coming down.

"I don't know them," said Swan, a little uncertain as to who

Colin and Eleanor might be—whether son and daughter-in-law, or daughter and son-in-law. "I meant one called Grace. She has a brother called Henry."

"Oh, *that*," said Mrs. Adams. "Of course they'll come. Do come too," and she turned to Mr. Carton leaving Swan to Mr. Carton who had taken to him at sight.

Any profession or trade must establish some kind of bond between people engaged in it, even if it is the bond of feeling that if Wilkinson will say "Top o' the morning" as he comes into the room every morning one will poison his beer, or that if Miss Crowther mentions her uncle who was a Rural Dean once more one will say something unkind about deans. So were Mrs. Carton and Swan drawn together, though the one was a past mistress of her profession and the other a fairly new hand. Swan greatly admired in Mrs. Carton her distinction of looks and her extremely intelligent talk, as also her pleasant manner, for intelligence does not always live with kindness; while she observed in him a man who, whatever excursions he might make, would in her opinion always be a scholar in mind. And although they did not particularly discuss professional subjects their minds agreed very well.

"Sidney tells me," said Mrs. Carton, with an affectionate look towards her husband, "that you are thinking of an Oxford Fellowship."

Swan said Mr. Carton had been kind enough to give him some excellent advice and that the pleasure of knowing him—and his wife, he added with a slight deliberately pedantic bow—would, he hoped, be taken as an excuse if he did not succeed.

Mrs. Carton said she did not see any special reason why he should not succeed and the more soldier-scholars the better and added, with a quite pleasant touch of the headmistress, that she and her husband would follow his career with great interest.

"You do comfort me," said Swan, taking off his spectacles and laying them on the table, and Mrs. Carton seeing him for the first time without their owl-like barrier thought very well of his face, possibly as well as her husband thought of his brains, and we may add that both were very good judges.

"May I tell you something now, Mr. Swan," said Mrs. Carton, looking round the table where everyone was talking or being talked to by his or her neighbour, making just enough noise to cover her voice. "Miss Merriman is here particularly to meet you."

Swan put his spectacles on again and looked at her as though he could question better from behind this barrier.

"You know she was Lady Emily Leslie's secretary—companion—friend—whatever one likes to call it," said Mrs. Carton, "and lives with Lady Pomfret now. I need not tell you," and Swan felt quite unreasonably flattered by her emphasis on the word you, "that they are all a good deal worried about Clarissa. Just as," she added, "his friends are about Charles. This dinner is really a plot. Will you be so kind as to be a conspirator? I will see that you and Miss Merriman have a chance to talk quietly. You will not mind?"

Swan thought he might mind, but could not well refuse a hostess who was also a classical scholar and what was more a delightful and still handsome woman. A small surge of annoyance rose in him against Charles his friend who was really becoming a public nuisance. Then he blamed himself, for poor Charles did not go about showing his wounds, nor was it his fault that his lovable nature made so many people want to meddle in his affairs. All of which thoughts ran through his mind in the brief interval before he answered his hostess, saying that he would of course do whatever she wished and then he changed the subject to Fluvius Minucius who was really of far greater permanent interest than that couple of shilly-shallying young fools. The rest of the dinner passed very pleasantly and when Mrs. Carton had removed her ladies there was some really good port upon which Mr. Adams remarked, for it was one of the many surprises in that self-made ironmaster that he had a considerable knowledge of wines and enjoyed them.

"Part of a parcel the Bursar of Lazarus wanted to get rid of just after the war," said Mr. Carton, smiling his grim, tight-lipped smile. "He tried to buy it back later. Lazarus!" and the amount of scholarly venom he managed to put into that one word filled Swan with admiration.

"You are a friend of young Belton's," said Mr. Adams addressing Swan. "It was his mother that started me on wine, what's good and what's bad. I have a great respect for her. The old gentleman's a fine old fellow, too. And what are you doing now?"

Swan, looking at Mr. Adams through his spectacles, said he was spending the Christmas holidays at Arcot House, adding that as the Priory School where he taught was shortly moving to Harefield House, it was an advantage to know the terrain. He had, he said, already earmarked the room which he proposed to have as his bedroom-study.

"Sensible thing to do," said Mr. Adams approvingly. "Always look a step ahead. That's the way to get on."

"So they say, sir," said Swan. "But one sometimes can't quite see the next step. It might be a wrong one."

"Like the boy in *Kidnapped*," said Mr. Adams unexpectedly. "I got a secondhand copy off a stall for fourpence when I was a kid and I used to read it to my mother. Dad was usually pretty late coming in and usually pretty drunk when he did come. I'll never forget the first time I read that book. If Barchester had been near the coast I'd have run away to sea," at which sidelight on the successful iron-master's life both the other men were surprised. But it was not one of Mr. Adams's least endearing qualities that he could be relied upon to surprise on pretty well every occasion.

The port having been respectfully drunk, Mr. Carton took the men into the large library-sitting-room, formerly a barn, where the ladies were comfortably talking and though pleased (as we always are) to see the gentlemen, had been getting on very well without them.

"I should like you to see the edition of Fluvius Minucius by my wife's grandfather, Canon Horbury," he said to Swan, taking a calf-bound volume from a shelf. "Have a look at it here," and he laid the book on a table with two comfortable chairs by it. "Don't hurry."

Swan was divided between a genuine interest in the book and a slight though not unnatural resentment at being forced into the position of Common Informer on the matter of Charles; and then his sense of humour got the better of him and he decided that as he had been gently conspiring himself for some time it was probably only jealousy of the other conspirators, and when Mr. Carton brought Miss Merriman to the table he got up and said it would be a privilege to show her his fine edition, though from a scholarly standpoint its views were now largely superseded by the discovery of MSS. to which the editor could not at the time have access.

"It had somehow got to Sweden," said Mr. Carton, "and those Germans in human form wouldn't let my wife see it. But one of the big men at that University wanted the Oxbridge Press to publish a little book of his on Frederika Bremer's visits to England. I was then one of the Press Delegates. I put pressure on him. I am sure it will interest you, Miss Merriman," and he went back to his wife and the Adamses.

Swan put his spectacles on and waited for Miss Merriman to begin. If that admirable woman felt any embarrassment at his silence she did not show it; nor do we really think she had any to show, for her sense of duty to the class whom she had helped and protected for all her working life was very strong in her.

"Mr. Swan," she said, "I won't apologise for what I am going to say, for it has to be said. Sir Robert and Lady Graham wish me to say it."

"If it's about Charles, I do too," said Swan. "What is wrong, Miss Merriman?"

"Her father doesn't know; her mother doesn't know. And even I don't know," said Miss Merriman, thus plainly betraying that her party was helpless. "They are young, but not so young as they were. Charles is a good, honest man, for whom Sir Robert has a high regard," which tribute would have surprised Charles, who owing to his own absence first at the war and then at the school and his possible future father-in-law's long and frequent absences on missions, or on important work in London with a brief visit to his home on an occasional weekend, had only once seen Sir Robert since he came back, "and both he and Lady Graham are distressed and I may say puzzled by Clarissa's behaviour. It was all very well for her to miss Lady Emily Leslie—her grandmother—but that is quite a long time ago. There is no reason why they should not get married, but Clarissa puts it off every time and we sometimes think she finds she does not really care for him, but does not like to say so."

There was a silence, in which Mr. Adams could be heard telling Mrs. Carton that Amabel Rose on being shown a watch had quite distinctly said Ga.

Swan took his spectacles off and passed his hand across his eyes as if to clear cobwebs away.

"She loves him even more than he loves her," he said. "Even I can see that. But I am only a looker-on."

And probably see most of the game, Miss Merriman thought, but did not say anything for every belief and every value were being rapidly turned over, examined, accepted or rejected, and at last reclassified in her intelligent and in a quiet way worldly mind.

"You are quite sure of that?" she said, not questioning his veracity, but rather imploring him to say again that it was true.

"As sure as I am of Mr. Churchill," said Swan, remembering Clarissa's stricken face as she had—in her sister Edith's words—gone out of the room in a Flounce.

"I don't think she would die for love," said Miss Merriman thoughtfully. "The Pomfrets and the Leslies wouldn't let her," and Swan felt certain that it was no flesh and blood that Miss Merriman meant, but the mind and heart of her mother's people; and had he known anything about metallurgy he would have said she was—as Mrs. Adams had said years ago and not about his wife—the finest stainless steel and then some.

"Poor child," said Swan. "Can you help, Miss Merriman? Can I help?"

Miss Merriman made no answer. She thought of Lady Emily Leslie, that iridescent, opal-changing, diamond-sparkling fountain, that wind-blown spirit, whose looks, whose dark hawk's eyes Clarissa had inherited but not, or not as yet, her unquenchable acceptance of everything that life brought her, even of her death.

"You know," said Swan, again covering his eyes with his hand for a moment, "Charles isn't so badly off. I believe Mr. Belton is getting his lawyer to write to Sir Robert's. Settlements, I suppose, and that sort of thing. I did read a little law once, but it was all quite unpractical. If you could encourage her to elope, Miss Merriman, it would be rather a help. Or even to have hysterics and say she would sooner marry a coal heaver. Anything to get them both out of this glue-pot where they seem likely to stick for ever. Couple of blasted nuisances I say."

"So do I," said Miss Merriman, at which point said Swan, when telling Charles all about it long afterwards, he began to see light.

"Miss Merriman," he said, sitting forward and letting his spectacles swing in one hand. "I have a suggestion."

Miss Merriman looked interested.

"You know the Priory School is moving to Harefield House next autumn," said Swan. "And there will be married quarters for two masters."

"That," said Miss Merriman, "is excellent. But where could they live till the end of the summer term? Two more terms to come, you know."

"During which time they will both go mad and Charles will probably be sacked," said Swan. There was a silence, again broken by Swan who said Did Miss Merriman know there was a furnished cottage in the Priory grounds, which was only let to favoured people. The late tenant, an old cousin of the Warings, had died of rage as the result of the General Election under the mistaken impression that Mr. Gladstone had beaten Lord Salisbury and Cecil Waring had just had it done up. One didn't like to be too sure of anything—and he left what he had to say unfinished.

"Well, thank you very much, Mr. Swan," said Miss Merriman. "I shall tell Lady Graham what you have said. I am very grateful to you for your help," and she got up, or as Swan said afterwards Rose, in a way that clearly showed the interview was terminated and they joined the rest of the party.

No one felt like keeping late hours and Miss Merriman had to drive back to Pomfret Towers, so the party soon came to an end. Mrs. Adams earnestly repeated her invitation to Swan and said he could come up and see Amabel Rose in bed if he liked, an invitation which Swan at once accepted because, as he said in an aside to Miss Merriman, one might as well try everything once. As he walked down the High Street he wondered whether he would tell Charles's parents about his talk with Miss Merriman, but decided not to, feeling we think that they were much younger and simpler than Miss Merriman and himself. In which he may have been right: or possibly may not.

The infinite void, the state of suspended animation, the thrice daily super-repletion (even in these hard times), the good English habit of shutting oneself and perhaps some favoured friends and relations up in one's house with all the food one can lay hands on and not letting anyone out till the larder was bare, at last came to an end, leaving a great many people feeling rather fat and cross: fatter than the year before because the unwholesome starchy diet by which They had done their best to break us to Their will (and the bounds of whose consequences appeared to be limitless owing to the state They had got us into) had as one might say bloated us considerably while leaving us far more easily tired. But now, like the Tiber as so well described by Lord

Macaulay, Charles and Swan burst their curb and bounded, rejoicing to be free, and whirling down in wild career anyone who wanted to put forward other plans, rushed headlong not to the sea but over to Edgewood where Mr. and Mrs. Adams were giving what they called a small cocktail party, but as it consisted of their personal friends it had become pretty big.

We have so often described the quiet beauties of The Old Bank House that we will not do so again, merely stating that Mrs. Adams, distrusting her own powers as an interior decorator, had asked Clarissa Graham to come in the morning and put holly and ivy and mistletoe in all the right places with her own untaught art, with excellent results. Mrs. Grantly had kindly lent the Palafox Borealis, old Miss Sowerby's most beloved and rarest plant, cherished by Purse Thatcher to its flowering in the Rectory kitchen where it had thriven on loud laughter, perpetual cups of tea and snacks and above all—or so Purse Thatcher maintained and who are we to contradict him—by the woyreless which was turned on at full blast before it began (a statement which all wireless addicts will understand) and very often not turned off at all, thus increasing the revenue of the Barchester Electricity Board to an appreciable effect. How hideous Palafox was, no words can describe; a clump of ugly serrated leaves, fleshly and covered with a kind of whitish bristles as if they had forgotten to shave, among which rose a short grey-green stalk crowned by a sticky knob from which depended, apparently, three strips of housemaid's flannel; but to all gardeners a triumph of Man over Nature and to be worshipped as such. The central heating—oil, and thermostatically controlled, though no one but Mr. Adams could have brought it off—was exactly right except for the people who complained that it was too hot and of them we have no opinion at all; and a delightful kind of hum of well-bred people enjoying themselves pervaded the well-proportioned hall with its handsome square staircase and the two big ground floor rooms.

"*How* nice it all is," said Lady Graham who with Clarissa and one of her younger boys was the first to arrive. "So lovely to have the curtains drawn and not see the darkness. It reminds one of the War," and all the older people present agreed with her, remembering nostalgically the happy days when our greatest statesman had offered us blood, tears and sweat, with such minor adjuncts as the black-out; all—since Darkness had covered the land—a half-believed dream. But now to have our Pilot at the helm and to know that behind the curtains no danger lurked was, forgetting the heritage of degradation and want bequeathed to us by Them, almost a luxury. "May I go and see Amabel Rose?" she added, for which we need not say Lucy willingly gave permission and it was only with difficulty that several other baby-worshippers were headed off, for nurse, though very tolerant of the gentry, had said One at a time, and Lucy was too wise and too grateful for her devotion to Amabel Rose to contravene her instructions.

As was proper for a small Christmas gathering a good many of the guests were young. Lady Graham, gravitating by nature to the beautiful Chinese-Chippendale sofa which stood at right angles to the noble fireplace where a brilliant fire illumined the austere delicacy of the golden marble mantelpiece, established herself upon the pale gold brocade cushions and received homage. There was another court at the far end of the room where the younger people were gathered round Clarissa, and Edith was showing off and getting as usual a good deal above herself; but it might have been noticed that Lady Graham, by merely remaining in one place and being herself, was still the greater attraction.

"She reminds me," said Mr. Grantly to the Dean's wife who had brought some granddaughters (for she had married very young and so gained an unfair advantage in the third generation), "of my favourite Bible character."

"And who is she?" said Mrs. Crawley, wondering who Lady Graham could be like, and rejecting the Queen of Sheba, Judith, Jezebel and Athaliah out of hand.

"The Tachmonite who sat in the seat," said Mr. Grantly, as if that explained everything.

Mrs. Crawley said she thought she knew her Bible, but had to admit that she was totally stumped.

"There was a great Master of Balliol," said Mr. Grantly, "my old college, you know——"

"Not Jowett?" said Mrs. Crawley, who was very good at dates and hoped to catch Mr. Grantly out.

"He *was* a great Master," said Mr. Grantly, realising that a part of time which is real to us may mean nothing to others—not even our near-contemporaries. "But I wasn't thinking of him. This was Strachan-Davidson. My father was a pupil of his and he told me Strachan-Davidson maintained that the Tachmonite was the character he liked best."

"That is *most* interesting," said Mrs. Crawley. "I wonder if the Bishop has ever heard of him."

Mr. Grantly, showing a sad want of broad-mindedness towards his spiritual lord, said he didn't think so for a moment, and asked about as many of Mrs. Crawley's grandchildren as he could remember, making but a poor hand of it.

"And how are your young people?" said Mrs. Crawley, alluding not to Grace and Henry, but to the married Grantly daughter, now Mrs. Colin Keith.

Very well, said Mr. Grantly, and a second due in April, at which he tried not to look puffed up, with no success at all. Mrs. Crawley said approvingly that it was a very good thing. And, he added, Colin had done so well in the last year that they weren't going to let the upper part of their house, as they had thought of doing; for Colin Keith had by now an established place among the few lawyers who really knew about railways and was getting briefed right and left.

"But, to go back for a moment to what we were saying," said Mrs. Crawley, "who *was* the Tachmonite?"

"He was just that," said Mr. Grantly. "One of David's lords—or servants, much the same thing—it's in Samuel somewhere," and then one of the younger guests came up with a tray of drinks. Mrs. Crawley took some orange juice and Mr. Grantly a glass of sherry.

"Why not something stronger?" said Mr. Grantly, laying a detaining hand on the tray. "All our host's drink is first-rate. I wouldn't dream of taking sherry in most houses; pure reinforced rotgut, if I may use the expression," and Mrs. Crawley took his advice and was none the worse for it, though she wisely confined herself to orange for the rest of the evening: for drinks on an empty stomach do us little good in our present low condition, though red wine with our meals, when we can afford it, cheers the heart of woman (and man).

The arrival of Charles Belton with Swan his friend, as that gentleman had called himself, parodying the Charles his friend of the older drama, gave a distinct fillip to the younger members of the party and when to them were added Lord Lufton and his sister Justinia the noise became deafening (though not rowdy), every guest, like canaries in a cage, trying to outshriek the other.

"Dear boy," said Lady Graham to Lord Lufton, who had come to pay homage. "I am so glad to see you. And do tell me, how did *you* come to know Mr. Adams?" for the effortless infiltration of that gentleman into good society had, before his marriage, vastly interested the county and still continued to interest it.

It was, Lord Lufton explained, partly things like the bench and partly the Marlings and a good deal, of late, his tenant Mr. Macfadyen who had professional dealings on a large scale with Mrs. Adams in the market-gardening line. Indeed there was now hardly a house to which his position and his wife's vast tangle of relationship had not carried him. Gatherum Castle had fallen some time ago owing to Mr. Adams's firm dealing with a leaky tap in the Duke's stable-yard and the strong bond of cows between the Duke's bailiff and Mrs. Adams. Pomfret Towers had dined and been dined. Sir Edmund Pridham had spoken his mind to Mr. Adams about the proposed town-planning over Hogglestock way and Mr. Adams had expressed his entire agreement with Sir Edmund's point of view, coupled with a promise to put a spoke in the Ministry's wheel, appealing in proper form from the Ministry badly informed (by Them we need not say) to the Ministry better informed under Us, thus unintentionally adding another link to history, and a promise of support in the County Council from his co-grandfather. Mr. Pilward of Pilward's Entire. Lady Cora Waring said she adored him. Sir Robert Fielding, the Chancellor of the Diocese, had said he wished he had the brains of that man Adams. Only Hartletop Priory stood out: or to be truthful it had not stood out so much as been completely ignorant of and uninterested in what was happening, for the Hartletop interests had always been for London rather than the county.

To the young people were now added Henry Grantly and his sister Grace, rather late because of following the hounds on foot and having to clean up, but in excellent and untired spirits after spending half the day running faster than they could run or trying to keep warm while they stood still in squelching mud. Swan, always the friend, saw that Clarissa's sparkle had dimmed when he and Charles came in and now gently inserted himself between people's bodies till he was next to her and asked her if she had been to any more dances. She said Oh yes, two; but they were rather dull ones. One was at Hartletop Priory, a stuck-up kind of affair but mother thought they ought to do the civil, at which breath of another age Swan couldn't help laughing; another had been in East Barsetshire, quite amusing.

"And have *you* been dancing, Mr. Swan?" said Clarissa. Swan, though sorely tempted, did not say Come off it, my girl. But, perhaps with a little deliberate unkindness, he said he hoped he was Eric, though a ghastly name he must admit.

"Of course Eric," said Clarissa, and Swan had an unaccountable feeling that she wanted to placate him, to woo him; not for himself, of that he felt certain. "Oh, did Charles come over with you? I didn't notice."

Swan, feeling that if she thought he would believe that she had managed to not notice Charles she must have singular powers of self-deception, said Charles was probably in the dining-room whence the drinks and the eats emanated. Clarissa, looking with great interest at one of her own pretty hands with its tip-tilted fingers, said they might go and look at the eats which they accordingly did. Here the noise, unchecked by the presence of elders, though gentlemanly was terrific, the centre of the noise being Charles Belton and Henry Grantly who were arguing about the new Kronk gun; the one from his war experience now six years behind him of the older type, the other from his more recent experiences as a conscript, and as neither had met the gun upheld by the other, honours were fairly even. Two small drinks consisting largely of orange or lime were all the disputants had had; but the company, the lights, the warmth and in Henry's case the pleasant fatigue of a day in the open air, made them argue almost noisily. Clarissa had imperceptibly wormed her way to the middle of the guests and touching Charles's sleeve, said his name.

"Oh, hullo Clarissa," said Charles, quite kindly. "Look here, Henry," he continued, as though no interruption had occurred, "let's get this right. You said forty-five millimeters and an angle of thirty degrees with the Kronk-Babbitt Mutilator" (or if these were not the exact words, our intelligent reader will at once know what we mean). "That's impossible. Look here. You see the Mutilator at six point three——"

"No, you don't, you great ass," said Henry. "You *can't.* It's been proved again and again. You'll only blow your own arm off if you do that. But with the Klopstock torsion-retractor you can do the whole thing with one hand. I'll show you," and forcing his way to the table, followed by Charles, he rapidly collected various articles of cutlery and glass and some biscuits, the better to demonstrate his theory to his unbelieving friend.

"It's rather a crowd, isn't it?" said Clarissa to Swan, in a voice just too natural to deceive him. "And too, too hot. Let's go back to the drawing-room."

So back they went and found Lord Lufton with Grace Grantly and Edith Graham and a few other young people playing a very good game, which was to take a glacé cherry spiked on a toothpick and see if you could get it into your mouth holding the toothpick between your teeth and chewing or mumbling it up till with a kind of tapir-like elongation of the lips you got the whole thing in, after which you extricated the toothpick from your mouth and ate the cherry.

"Can you do this?" said Clarissa, burning (or so Swan felt) to make herself considered, somewhere, in some way, and she spiked a preserved cherry on the end of a fork with her right hand, twisted it round behind her back, up past her left ear, and turning her head as far to the left as possible just managed to mouth the cherry from the fork, which feat her young friends at once began to emulate, but signally failed to get anywhere near, including (rather to Clarissa's pleasure) Grace Grantly; with the exception of Lord Lufton, to whom it appeared to offer no difficulty at all.

"I'll tell you what," said Lord Lufton to Clarissa (possibly influenced without his knowledge by the atmosphere of the Old Bank House's mistress), "I bet you sixpence you can't do it left-handed," with which words he skewered a cherry, wound his long left arm behind his back, turned his head and swallowed it; all with no apparent effort. Clarissa, with a little air of doing something that was too, too easy, just to amuse the children, picked up her cherry left-handed, tried, tried again in vain and at the third try dropped the cherry. Lord Lufton, who had an orderly mind, stooped and picked it up, and as he rose saw that Clarissa's eyes were misty.

"Oh, I say Clarissa," he said, quickly getting between her and the others, "could you come over to tea at Framley tomorrow? Grace Grantly is coming and mother is going to get out her peeress's robes. Do come. It will be such fun. Justy will be there, but not a party; come too." So broken was Clarissa's spirit that she thanked him and said she would love to, and did not even think Earl Percy (in the person of Grace Grantly) sees my fall.

As Miss Amabel Rose was now washed and just going to bed, nurse graciously sent down word that if any of the young ladies would like to see Baby, they could come two at a time as Baby would soon be asleep, and there was quite a rush to the nursery, not including Clarissa or Grace; for Grace could see the Paragon any day and Clarissa felt, we think, that if she went up to the nursery some of the party, or perhaps one in especial of the party, might have gone by the time she got back. So she stayed in the drawing-room and watched her brother Robert and a nice boy, Frank Gresham, whose mother was the daughter of old Admiral Palliser at Hallbury, in keen and disgusting emulation as to who could cram the largest number of small biscuits into his mouth.

Swan went back to the dining-room. The guests had nearly all gone now, but Charles and Henry Grantly were still at it hammer and tongs and as neither of them listened to what his adversary said, or was ever going to listen, there seemed to be no reason why they should ever stop. But he had not reckoned with the power of the faithful servant who knows her place. Miss Hoggett, her mind bent on getting everything nice and tidy so she could lay the table for dinner (her construction, not ours) laid sacrilegious hands on the cutlery and crockery which represented the Kronk gun, piled them and everything else on a trolley and had wheeled it away to the kitchen quarters before the disputants could say a word, reminding Henry Grantly forcibly of his battery sergeant-major, though without that gentleman's command of language.

The remaining guests were now saying good-byes in the drawing-room, and Lady Graham was gathering her little flock, Charles standing near her.

"Oh, Lady Graham," said Lord Lufton. "Clarissa is coming to tea tomorrow to look at mother's robes and things. Would you come too?" but Lady Graham said she had to stay in because the secretary of the Women's Institute was coming to tea to talk business. Clarissa, she said, could have the little car and she felt sure they would have a delightful visit and so enveloped her children in her maternal ambience and took them away. Charles, who had been listening idly to this talk, walked to the other end of the room and stood by the window that overlooked the street; the window near which Oliver Marling had heard the news of Jessica Dean's marriage to Aubrey Clover and known that life was now a desert: notwithstanding which he was now most suitably and comfortably married and, as we already know, about to be a happy father made. To Charles his own hopes seemed pale, dying creatures now. But he was of finer metal than Oliver (not that he would for a moment wish to disparage that imminent father-to-be) and had determined within himself to fight to the last ditch, to go down fighting if necessary, and then to try as hard as he could not to let his wounds be seen. The last shot had not yet been fired and he did not propose to let anyone know how his knees trembled, though he was nailing the flag to the mast: and then he began to laugh at himself and with a gleam of sense told himself that nothing was as bad as one imagined and put the subject resolutely away for the moment.

"Oh, *must* you go?" said Grace Grantly to Swan. "It is so horrid when parties are over. Why don't you and Charles come back to supper at the Rectory. I'll ask him," she said, not giving Swan time to speak. Charles was willing and quite nice about it, though not particularly interested, till he remembered that given another hour or so he could totally disprove Henry Grantly's heretical ideas about the Kronk gun. Lady Graham had gone while they were talking, so no more good-byes had to be said; one did not have to see a pretty, proud head turned from one—or really in need of one perhaps? Oh, blast it all. Supper at the Grantly's and a further argument with young Henry were the jobs ahead: not to stand about feeling sorry for oneself.

As he and Swan with the young Grantlys walked up the street to the Rectory Charles was suddenly overtaken by a feeling of apology to Mr. and Mrs. Grantly who had not been consulted about his being invited, but then he thought of Arcot House and its ever hospitable doors and stopped worrying. In which he was perfectly right. Mrs. Grantly made the young men welcome and asked Grace to tell Edna there would be two more.

"Come and see the kitchen," said Grace to the guests, but Charles was answering the Rector's questions about his old college and paid no attention, so Grace opened a door in the hall and took Swan down a rather dark passage to a swing door and so to the kitchen quarters.

"It's all rather large and inconvenient," she said, "but it's rather nice because we have lots of room," and she pushed open a green baize door, much worn at the bottom by the thousands of feet that had kicked it open since it was first put in, and took Swan into the large, very clean, very hot, deliciously-smelling Rectory kitchen. Two good-looking women were busy getting the dining-room supper while Purse Thatcher and his slightly younger cousins of shame Glad, Sid, Stan and Glamora Thatcher (for both mothers used their maiden name, having indeed no other) were making a hearty high tea of sausages and chips and pickles, and doing their diet the greatest credit.

"Oh Edna——" said Grace.

"Now shut up you kids," said Edna, not that the children were doing anything but eat steadily and ferociously, but a little bustle is always agreeable.

"Mr. Swan is staying to supper and so's Charles Belton," Grace continued, "and mother said to do the best you can."

"That's all right," said Edna. "I'd two strangers in my tea this morning so I got four pounds of sausages and there's that nice rabbit pie I made with that American lard out of the tin. Tell your mother not to worry. Stand up, you kids, and behave properly when a gentleman comes in the kitchen!" at which words, with a terrific screech and scrape of wooden chairs on the stone floor, all five stood up.

"Are they all yours?" said Swan to Edna, who seemed to be in command.

At this she and her sister laughed very loudly though most good-humouredly.

"Mine?" said Edna. "One's enough for me. One man, that's to say. I never had but the one but Doris here had four. One for each of them. Doris always was a caution. I'm one of the quiet ones. I'll have supper ready by half-past, tell your mother not to worry. Say good-bye, you kids."

The five children at once said Good-boy, grinned and went back to their steady, purposeful stoking. Grace took Swan away.

"A very interesting kitchen," said Swan, "and," he added as he held the swing-door for Grace to go through, "probably an excellent base for our future world."

"Oh, do you think so?" said Grace, stopping short in the dark passage, the better to conduct an argument. "I thought you might think it a bit funny. Some people do. Old Lady Norton does, but Edna told her she'd be ashamed only to have the one son if she was a lady."

"But I thought Edna *had* only one child, you said," Swan replied, feeling the argument beyond him.

"Yes, she's got Purse, but Doris has four," said Grace. "Edna only meant it seemed funny to be *properly* married to a lord and not have a lot of children," and she led the way back, Swan following, a little confused by her argument. The handle of the door between the passage and the hall was rather stiff.

"Shall I try?" said Swan, when Grace had turned it vainly. He put out his hand, touching hers in the dark. For a moment he was quite unable to speak, hardly able to breathe, making but a poor show of dealing with the handle.

"All right," said Henry Grantly's voice from the hall and the door was opened. "I must get Purse to put a new handle on. One day somebody will be mistletoe boughed in that passage."

"'A skeleton form was mouldering there In the bridal wreath of a lady fair,'" said Swan sententiously; but one must say something, if it is only to show that one isn't stricken dumb, blasted with excess of light; and they went back to the study which had a larger fireplace in proportion to its size than the drawing-room, and was therefore mostly used in the winter.

The sausages and the rabbit pie, not to speak of a belated plum pudding from cousins in Australia, were extremely well cooked and made to look pretty silly. Swan, an only child at home, or used to the communal meals of university, army and the Priory School, basked gratefully in the family life, taking part as required or listening with pleasure and amusement to the talk. Quite one of the nicest and easiest-to-get-on-with families he had met, was his opinion. Charles was sparring right and left with Henry and Grace. Swan might have liked to join them, but Mrs. Grantly was asking about the move to Harefield so he told her all he knew, at considerable length, finding her very pleasant and intelligent. After supper they went back to the study where the Rector got Swan, whom he looked upon with reason as far more his equal mentally than that nice Charles Belton could ever be, to himself in a corner to ask about Oxford and his old college.

"I'm afraid I've been down a long time, sir," said Swan. "I was at Paul's till I was old enough for the army and then did the last three years of the war and a year after it and then I went back and read with Mr. Fanshawe."

"Fanshawe of Paul's?" said the Rector. "You couldn't do better. We were contemporaries though I think he is my junior," and he told Swan a good many amusing stories about Paul's, or Swan would have found them amusing if he had not felt a hand and a door-knob in his own. A door-knob is hardly a peg for romance one would say: but if two hands have met on it, even for a moment, it may become a symbol of everything.

"I'm so sorry, sir," he said, coming to with a start. "I think it's your good dinner and the fire on top of Mr. Adams's drinks. Yes, I have been thinking seriously about the possibility of a fellowship at Paul's. Mr. Carton was very helpful about it. Of course I can't leave the Priory School while my Headmaster is moving and settling. That becomes a duty—and I'm all for doing one's duty even if it's in the state of life to which God has been pleased to call one," and as he spoke the Rector thought he looked dejected, or something like it to which he couldn't give a name, but he soon forgot this in talking of Oxford and of Swan's plans for life, which he said he might be able to do something to further, for he had many friends there.

"I wonder," said Swan to Grace when the good-byes were being said, "if you would care to come and see the Priory School some time."

"Oh, I'd love to," said Grace, who had a pleasantly unspoilt interest in almost everything. "I've always wondered how they work. I mean who has meals with whom and whether there are really rags in the dormitories and conspiracies against horrid masters," to which Swan replied gravely that he would see that a conspiracy was got up for her especial benefit and after quantities of good-byes to everyone they got into Charles's little ramshackle car and drove back to Harefield. The Beltons had gone to bed. Charles said he would go round to the Perrys where they were always late and see Gus about the ratting, so Swan went upstairs alone. As he had done after the dance, Swan lay awake—or rather could not go to sleep. But not for Charles's troubles; nor for Clarissa's. He had seen his one true goal and to that lodestone his heart must now forever turn. He did not fear his fate too much and his deserts—if a good mind and a not despicable income and expectations count—were not particularly small. But one cannot tell till one has put it to the touch. There were to be two sets of married quarters at Harefield House. Charles would be having one—and then he told himself to think no more of this sudden and hourly more violent feeling that had taken possession of him and read paper-covered thrillers till he dropped asleep with the light on, not knowing what he had read, only to awake early with an unreasoning sense of unhappiness to come. By the time breakfast was over he had laughed himself out of the mood—or thought he had. Mrs. Belton, who had seen her own elder son smitten to the heart, wondered what had happened to her guest, but kept her own counsel.

CHAPTER 10

Next day according to plan Grace Grantly went over by the bus to Framley Court where she found Lady Lufton in her upstairs sitting-room, who greeted her kindly and said Ludovic was somewhere about and would be in soon. Not a party, she said, with her usual air of trying to placate everyone, though no one needed to be placated; just Clarissa Graham and the tenant Mr. Macfadyen who presently came in from his part of the house—out of his front door, across the bit of garden, through the iron gate in the wall and so onto the gravel sweep at Lady Lufton's front door—and Grace talked to him very comfortably about Aubrey Clover's new play, He pulled out a Plum, which neither of them had seen. Nor had Lady Lufton, but they had all read about it in the Sunday papers.

"I hear," said Mr. Macfadyen, addressing Grace, "that your parents have a fine specimen of the Palafox Borealis. Yon flower, if flower it is, must be a queer creature, if what I hear is true."

"It's *ghastly*," said Grace, though not without pride. "It's perfectly *hideous* and no use at all, but the Royal Horticultural seem to think a lot of it. It's got a long stalk and a hideous kind of knob on the top of it and the leaves are a sort of grey fur. I'm sure mother would let you have some seeds."

Mr. Macfadyen with characteristic caution said he would like to see the plant first. Had it been a vegetable he would have said Yes at once, but not even the most revolting prize orchid could tempt him from the straight path and he had been known to say, after a dinner with other vegetable-minded friends, that a sybo, or a good white neep, or a fine ingan were worth all the roses of Sharon.

"But, Mr. Macfadyen," said Grace, "you really ought to see it. We grew it in the kitchen—at least Percy, that's our cook's boy, grew it and it seeded with him when it wouldn't ever seed at the Old Bank House when Miss Sowerby had it. Percy says it's the wireless. They have it on all the time in the kitchen and he says the electricity brings it on. I don't understand it quite, but it might happen, mightn't it?"

Mr. Macfadyen, who took a strong interest in the scientific approach to vegiculture (if this is a word) appeared to be impressed by what Grace said and pressed her for details; but so little had Purse's experiment interested her that she was unable to supply more than the broad fact that Palafox lived in a sunny kitchen on the window-sill above the sink and that the wireless was on from 6.30 a.m. to the hour at which the kitchen went to bed and Purse—Percy she meant—said the wireless made it grow.

Mr. Macfadyen said he would not just say that it didn't, but he would like to see it for himself, upon which Grace invited him to come over any day to look and, much to the admiration of Lady Lufton, pinned him down to next market day. Then Lord Lufton with his sister Justinia came in hot, in spite of the dull day, from trying to follow the hounds on foot for a couple of miles.

"I'm sorry we're late, mother," said Justinia, kissing Lady Lufton, "and you are Grace Grantly and we are going to try mother's robes on. What fun. Hullo, Mr. Macfadyen. I say, mother, couldn't we have father's things out as well and Ludovic put them on, or Mr. Macfadyen? It would be rather fun to see peer and peeress," and Grace wondered if Lady Lufton would mind.

It is probable that a year earlier, or even six months earlier,

Lady Lufton might have minded, though we think she would have tried to conceal it for she was tender of other people's feelings—owing perhaps to having too many of her own—but now she said quite easily that Ludovic should get them out after tea and wear them.

"For which I thank your ladyship," said Mr. Macfadyen, "for it would ill become me to wear, even in jest, robes that I have no title to," and Lady Lufton smiled her thanks to him. Mr. Macfadyen felt how much younger Lady Lufton was looking of late and Lady Lufton thought that Mr. Macfadyen, who had done so much for Framley, was becoming more and more like one of its real inmates.

Swan, also coming by bus, now joined them and was made welcome.

"We won't wait for the others," said Lady Lufton and, much to Grace's interest, rang the bell, a thing unfamiliar to most of our young and possibly never again to be known to us. One of the many Podgenses, most of whom preferred to remain in what the Reverend Enoch Arden called Babylonian captivity, coming daily to work with good wages and returning to their homes after a large tea or supper, brought up the tea, put it with hearty good will on the table, set a kettle on the hob of the old-fashioned fire and said was that all. Lady Lufton said they wouldn't wait for Miss Graham and the Podgens went away. Just as they were sitting down the door was opened and in came Oliver Marling with his wife and Clarissa who, Maria explained, had been having lunch with them so they had brought her on. The round table took them all comfortably and when Maria Marling had told everyone (at far too great length so Clarissa considered for one in her position and of her size) about her golden cocker's new litter who all looked like future champions, the talk was pretty general and if there were private words they never lasted long and the speakers plunged back into the fray.

"It's about the noisiest tea since father died," said Lord

Lufton to Clarissa, for whom his kind nature felt a vague compassion. "Tea used to be such fun when he was here. Mother wants me to get father's robes out as well as hers. She thought it would amuse you."

Clarissa said How nice; adding How kind, but not as if she cared what the words meant and rather in her prim young lady voice which was amusing when she was a very young lady, but somehow now sounded almost condescending. Lord Lufton, too good-natured to take offence, asked after her three brothers. Oh, very well said Clarissa. James still adored the Guards and John was longing to be in them and Robert had got a scholarship and had a poem printed in the school magazine, too, too clever. Had Lord Lufton been Charles he would quite probably have told Clarissa to come off it; had he been Swan he would at once have diagnosed a mind ill at ease, hiding behind words; but Lord Lufton was, we are glad to say, and would there were more like him, his own self: gathering a kind of world-sense or shrewdness as he went, not particularly clever about other people's feelings except with the insight that a truly kind nature gives, though it hardly ever sees the worst. If it does, it is less easy to placate than a more complex nature, for it sees good and bad with fewer lights and shades. Swan—to his great joy—was asked by Lady Lufton to ring the bell and had the satisfaction of pulling down the painted china knob of the handle, of holding it down a moment while he admired the painted china front (or whatever one calls the main piece of an old-fashioned bell) and then of letting the handle go, almost feeling the quiver of the bell wire and following it in his mind through the wall down to the ground floor and so, from one three-angled thing to another (for though we have seen them since we could notice anything we have never known what they are called) till it reached its bell and set it quivering over the words Blue Boudoir, or Her Ladyship's Dressing-Room.

"What was this room, Lady Lufton," he said, "when you first came here? It can't have been a sitting-room then."

"My mother-in-law was the first person to call it a sitting-room," said Lady Lufton. "Before her time it had always been called 'Lady Lufton's dressing-room,' but I think dressing-room meant more a sitting-room then."

"Of course," said Swan, delighted. "In the Heir of Redclyffe Mrs. Edmonston's dressing-room is the place where everyone comes. She writes her letters and the children have lessons and the invalid boy lies on the sofa—if I remember rightly."

"We had the edition with the Kate Greenaway illustrations," said Lady Lufton, "and Guy looked such a bounder in his bowler hat and his coat buttoned nearly up to his neck and his stove-pipe trousers that I *couldn't* feel romantic about him. I think it is somewhere in the old nurseries if it hasn't been given away," and then she had to devote herself to the teapot and Swan turned to Grace, with a sudden sense of looking homeward.

"And how have you been since the Adams's party?" he said, for one must say something at a tea-party.

Grace said she had been quite well, thank you, and had had great fun with Mr. Parry at the library. The Duchess of Omnium had found some letters of the Great Duke in the library at Gatherum behind twelve volumes of *Curiosities and Rarities of Literature* on a top shelf when she was helping the Duke to dust the books and turn some out to be sold, and the Duke had most kindly given them to the Central Library, to add to their collection.

Anything amusing in them, Swan asked.

Grace said absolutely nothing at all, and that was what made them so fascinating.

"You mean they make the Duke seem more real?" said Swan.

Grace said she would have liked to be able to say that herself and wished she had, but she couldn't.

"Anything I can say for you I shall always say with the greatest pleasure," said Swan.

"Oh," said Grace, not quite sure if she understood him. "And some of them are about a man called Finn, a member of

Parliament, but nothing interesting. I think he murdered somebody, or something of the sort," for so does fame or even notoriety perish. "Oh, and there were one or two letters from the Duchess Lady Cora is called after. And we couldn't make out at first who they were from, because she didn't put her name, only G. Omnium."

"That is quite right," said Swan. "A well-bred peeress—I'm not sure about the lower orders of the peerage, but a duchess certainly—signed her initial. To sign her full name wasn't done; unless to very intimate friends."

"That is quite true," said Lady Lufton, overhearing from the other side. "My grandmother always told me the same thing. How did you come to know, Mr. Swan?"

Swan said he really didn't know. One knew such extraordinary things without knowing why that sometimes one almost believed in transportation, or transmogrification or whatever it was.

"Now, you really know quite well," said Lady Lufton in a motherly way that tickled Swan, "that you mean transmigration. Or don't I mean that?" she added, suddenly overcome, as we all so often are, by the realisation that we have said something quite silly and then she was recalled to her teapot for Mr. Macfadyen who wanted a third cup and Swan was able to continue his talk with Grace, seeing in her a steadfast light of which he had often dreamed, whose dwelling-place he had never found. But one must behave in an ordinary way at a tea-party so Swan dutifully resigned Grace to Oliver Marling and turned to his hostess and a three-cornered conversation with her and Mr. Macfadyen, who on discovering that Swan's mother was a Ramsay at once accepted him as the right sort of person. The talk was chiefly about the estate and various possible improvements and necessary repairs in which Mr. Macfadyen appeared to take just as much interest as his hostess, while Justinia joined their talk across the table. The general opinion was that this year which had nearly run its course had been in a way the worst we had known and that our journey up from Hades to the light of day would be long and hard, assailed by foes without and poverty within.

"But we have Mr. Churchill," said Lady Lufton.

"And we are pledged to repay the generous help of the United States at last," said Mr. Macfayden. "I sometimes just wonder how they have borne with us so long. Money will be harder to come by and harder to keep, but our word must be kept above all. I hear a good deal as I go about on business. One or two firms in Barchester are pretty near a crash," at which words a chill touched the hearts of his hearers; or, if we are to be perfectly correct, it was more the stomach or the solar plexus, whatever it may be, which, when we hear bad news that might however remotely touch ourselves, suddenly gathers itself into a small hard ball full of brimstone and fire-works.

"Not friends of yours, I hope," said Lady Lufton.

"I would not say friends, nor unfriends," said Mr. Macfadyen cautiously. "They are firms connected with finance in London. I hope they may pull through, but it's an anxious time."

Grace, with the unaccountable sympathy that makes us hear what may affect us, even if the words are not addressed to us, said she hoped it wasn't Keith and Keith because Henry was there and was reassured when Mr. Macfadyen said the firms he had in mind were nothing to do with legal matters. Then the other end of the table, who had been talking dogs (Maria Marling) and Hospital Libraries (Justinia Lufton) to whoever would listen, pulled itself together and said what about the dressing up.

The tea-things were removed and with some mock ceremony and a good deal of laughter Justinia took Clarissa and Grace into a spare bedroom while Lord Lufton, accompanied by Oliver as a kind of sponge-holder, went to his own room.

"I *say*!" said Oliver, who had never seen the paraphernalia of a baron at close quarters.

"Not much when you think of marquises and dukes," said

Lord Lufton, "but barons are the oldest. We look on all other titles as very parvenu," and he showed Oliver how everything was worn. "Would you like to try them on?" he said. "We're much the same height, but you're a bit bonier," and the child that lives in us all made Oliver, after a faint and perfunctory protest, accept the handsome offer and allow Lord Lufton to be his valet.

"Do I look an *awful* guy?" he said, when he was dressed. "Help! the coronet's going to fall off!"

"No it isn't," said Lord Lufton. "You just have to put it on right. It must have been much easier when people had wigs because then you could pin things on to them. I believe in the full-bottomed wig period men skewered their hats on with hat-pins, just like ladies," to which Oliver countered with a rememberance from Dumas that Henry III and his mignons pinned their toques onto their own frizzed hair and then Lord Lufton said he must come and show himself, at which Oliver felt he would have an attack of nerves and began to tremble like an Italian greyhound, being in figure not unlike that bone-slim animal, though without its quivering charm. Finally with a protest, though secretly we believe rather admiring himself, Oliver allowed his host to precede him to the sitting-room and open the door. He was on the whole very well received by the audience. He could have wished that Lady Lufton and Mr. Macfadyen would have done more than turn their heads from where they were comfortably on a little sofa near the fire and say the one that in his opinion The Lyon King at Arms had a finer dress, the other that Ludovic *must* get that bit of fur seen to; and that his cherished wife, mother-to-be of whatever kind of baby it happened to turn out, had not said in an audible aside that he hadn't the right calves for silk stockings. But attention was now removed from him (not that this pleased him either) when Clarissa came in dressed by Justinia in the robes of a baron's wife and looking very charming but not, so Swan the onlooker thought, her best. Too self-conscious perhaps, a little to anxious

too

to please, and as she turned to show off the robes he saw, with kindly interest but no emotion, that she was tired and not in looks. However the rest of the audience were nicely uncritical and when Mr. Macfadyen said Was that the first syllable, his pleasantry was quite well received.

How well do we all know when our darling children and grandchildren act charades how unwillingly we stop talking about whatever it is we are talking about and pretend to be interested, how sycophantically we clap, with what relief we see them go away to dress up again for the next uninteresting syllable. So, we fear, were Oliver and Clarissa received, but very luckily neither of them knew it.

"Now it's my turn," said Lord Lufton, quite like an eager child at a tea-party. "I must say it's rather fun wearing them," and he arrayed himself with a deftness unsuspected by Oliver, who admired without envy.

"You know, it's a funny thing," said Lord Lufton, taking a rapid survey of himself in the old-fashioned cheval glass, "how so many people look like their ancestors in their robes."

Oliver said lots of people looked like their ancestors anyway. Look at the Pomfrets, he said, whose faces hardly varied from the earliest portraits at the Towers and Lady Cora Waring who was exactly like the American duchess of three or four generations ago, which led to a most interesting argument as to whether bishops could derive by the laying on of hands from their predecessors, and how this bishop was exactly like the effigy of Galfridus de Malacord, the twelfth-century bishop of Barchester, in the cathedral; the same nasty, hard, tight mouth and the same kind of dewlap under his chin and the same pinched-looking nose, which naturally led to the expression of a pious wish that the bishop might follow his predecessor's example and be smitten by a fell disease in which he would languish until his early death. Lord Lufton wondered what the disease was. Better not inquire said Oliver darkly, for his researches into the life of Thos. Bohun D.D., sometime Canon of

Barchester, had left him with no very high opinion of clerical life in the seventeenth century and hence even less opinion of life in the twelfth century. Perhaps, said Lord Lufton hopefully, he might get yellow fever or something in Madeira and have to stay there and be a hermit, but Oliver said the bishop's wife wouldn't allow it, at which point Justinia banged on the door and said to hurry up.

So Lord Lufton, wearing the heavy robes with a natural easy dignity which the historical part of Oliver's mind could not help admiring, walked into his mother's sitting-room and obligingly turned and postured so that everyone could see the dress to the best advantage, all the while observing his mother out of the corner of his eye, for he had a not ungrounded fear that it might make her think of the old 'un, and though he had been kind and dutiful in every way about his mother's prolonged grief, he did not wish to see the old wounds bleed anew. But she looked at him with a love that was now purely maternal and though Lord Lufton secretly wished that she wouldn't, he was on the whole relieved. He was at the far end of the room, standing against the curtained window while his sister Maria fingered and examined and admired, when the door was opened by Justinia holding one of those hideous but most practical lights which are rather like the skeleton of a giraffe except that they can be bent in any direction and have a very strong reading light with a movable shade. This light she now turned full onto Grace who—perhaps going back to her father's clerical ancestors who believed in a Presence in the reading-desk or pulpit—stood quite still, looking almost like a waxwork as the white light made the coronet and jewels gleam and threw the heavy folds of the robes into sharp relief

"Hold it!" said Swan, partly with a recollection of Mr. Earl P. Neck and Seth Starkadder; partly because the emotion he felt must have some outlet. Beauty and brains and goodness; the words rang through his head, and his heart echoed them. All that heart could desire. And if one was blinded, battered, breathless, it did not matter at all. Lord Lufton, with what we can only consider to have been inherited skill, bowed to her without letting his coronet fall off. Grace with equal skill made a deep curtsey without getting her feet entangled in her robes, which reflects the greatest credit upon Miss Pinkie Parradine whose dancing class at the Barchester High School she had attended; neither with like nor dislike but as a matter of routine, except for the one term when she and the now discarded Jennifer Gorman had exchanged confidences on the burning passion inspired in their young breasts by Miss Parradine's extensive and peculiar wardrobe.

"Exit," said Justinia. "I mean exeunt," and she put out the light. The figures of baron and baroness went through the door preceded by Justinia who was going to help Grace to disrobe. Outside the door the baron looked down at his baroness. She looked up at him and found herself in his arms, but so quietly that it hardly disturbed her. Cheek touched cheek and she was free again and followed Justinia to the bedroom to be helped out of her borrowed plumes.

It did not take Lord Lufton long to change, for his sister Justinia, quite rightly distrusting his capability to put the robes away tidily, had ordered him just to leave them on his bed and then come back to the drawing-room. When he got there he found a pleasant Babel of voices because Mr. Macfadyen had asked Lady Lufton if she would play to them. She had at first refused, then protested because it was only an upright piano in her room, and the drawing-room which was rarely used except in summer was too cold. (And if anyone thinks that the beautiful grand piano was neglected, let us tell them that they should think before they speak, for it was tenderly covered with a thick quilted material and lived by the wall farthest from the window, near but not too near the only radiator in the room: and now perhaps they will be quiet and not trouble us again.)

"Besides," she said, "I really can't play alone now. I don't practise. I would accompany anyone if they would sing," but alas, so has the practice of singing in the home faded with the wars and the growth of artificial music, that not one of the guests sang for pleasure, unless in concerted music: at which point we would like to state that though singing in parts is one of the nicest things in the world to do, we don't particularly want to listen to other people doing it.

"Aweel," said Mr. Macfadyen, "they say there's no fool like an auld fool. If you would play some Schubert, Lady Lufton, I would do my best, were it but to amuse the weans," he added, looking round at the company in a way that made them all feel younger than they were. Lady Lufton, very much surprised by this unexpected accomplishment in her tenant, said she would like nothing better as all her children—and here she turned a tolerant but withering look on them—were too self-conscious to sing alone, though Justinia (who almost stopped loving her mother for the moment) had a charming light soprano.

"And where did you learn your Schubert?" she asked her tenant, who replied that he had spent a year in Holland near the German border, learning about bulbs at one time and heard a good deal of lieder-singing there. No man, he said, disliked the Germans more than he did now and always would, but he must in justice admit that they had a corpus of minor lyrics set by great composers which, it appeared to him, would soon be lost altogether by English singers, thus making some of his audience feel guilty, for such of the great songs as they knew were mostly in highbrow translations which are far more offensive than ordinary bad ones.

With great cunning Mr. Macfadyen began with Who is Sylvia, because it was in English, and followed it with Hark! Hark! the Lark for the same reason, and then suggested to Lady Lufton a song or two from the Schöne Müllerin. It was a pleasant surprise to the company to discover that the wealthy head of Amalgamated Vedge could, like Mr. Frank Churchill, take if not a second the song itself, slightly but correctly. Most of the younger members of the party liked the songs as noises, without understanding the words, except for Swan, who had been in Germany for some time after the war and had there vastly improved his knowledge of the language and heard a good deal of music and fallen under its spell: though never for a moment wavering in his views upon the German nation.

When Mr. Macfadyen had sung very pleasantly and unaffectedly a couple of songs, Swan went over to the piano and asked if he could oblige with something from the greater cycle, the Winterreise. After a short consultation and a turning over of leaves, Lady Lufton kept the book open at Rückblick and Mr. Macfadyen sang with the touch of feeling that we are now almost too self-conscious to use, a song of love spurned remembering young love. Swan's eyes as he stood against the wall by the piano turned towards Grace, who sat with her eyes upon the other side of the room where Lord Lufton was stretching his long legs before the fire, looking into its glow. "Und ach, zwei Mädchenaugen glühten, Da war's gescheh'n um dich, Gesell," sang Mr. Macfadyen in his pleasant baritone and Swan knew what had happened. If Grace Grantly could love him all would be well. His mother would love her: she would be a perfect wife whether at Harefield House School (as he must now remember to call it) or in Oxford if he got a fellowship. He was like the singer of those songs. Love had shot his arrow to the mark: all was up with him. For a moment he was drowned in pure bliss. He looked again towards Grace Grantly. Her eyes were still steadfastly upon Lord Lufton. A log fell with a scattering of sparks. Lord Lufton took the tongs and put it back upon the fire. As he replaced the tongs he looked up at Grace. Their eyes met. Swan knew all that he need know. Far, far more than he had ever thought to know. This was the end. It did not hurt him much now but his nature told him that the hurt would go deep; it was not so deep as a well, nor so wide as a church door; but it was enough, it would serve.

"Thank you very much, Mr. Macfadyen," said Lady Lufton as she got up. "Perhaps you will let me play for you again some time" and she went over to the fire to remind her son about drinks.

The question of the cocktail hour was becoming very difficult on account of the price of all drinks and many people who didn't particularly care for them themselves wished they had the courage to stop giving them, but hadn't, and we must say for the young that they do not expect them as a right though pleased to have them. And so has the common standard of living fallen that un-Spanish sherry (to give it no harsher name) is all most of us can afford: and damn liverish it is, as Mr. Wickham, the Noel Mertons' agent, so truly remarked.

The Oliver Marlings said they would drop Clarissa at Holdings as the buses were so full and so the party dispersed having enjoyed itself very much. Mr. Macfadyen went back to his own quarters. Lord Lufton and Justinia put the robes back in their wrappings while Lady Lufton shut the piano and put away the music.

Earlier in the afternoon, though it was already nearly dark then, Charles Belton had come over to Holdings by special appointment to see Lady Graham, who was in the little sitting-room where her mother used to rest so often at the end of her life. We will not say that her ladyship was nervous, for seldom has so exquisite and apparently fragile a creature been so essentially calm and practical; but she had been increasingly exercised about her daughter Clarissa, the strange bird among her large normal brood, with all her grandmother Lady Emily Leslie's gifts and charm, but without as far as could yet be seen her underlying stability. If anyone really understood Clarissa it was Miss Merriman, Lady Emily's quietly efficiently devoted secretary who after her employer's death had gone to the Pomfrets to carry on her work of protecting the upper classes. She was often at Holdings and, as we know, Lady Graham had no secrets from her and Sir Robert Graham had the greatest opinion of her; or so his wife said and as they were an extremely devoted couple we expect she knew. Lady Graham and Miss Merriman had more than once discussed the question of Clarissa and even Miss Merriman had to admit that she had not the key to the child. Both ladies were agreed that things couldn't go on like this. In more peaceful days there would have been announcements in *The Times*, general fuss and excitement and a wedding. Now one's unmarried daughter went her own way (without prejudice to living in comfort at home and having a generous allowance where means still permitted it) and one did not like to ask questions, for to accept a rebuff or a deliberate change of subject (which is really the same) from one's own child is not easy.

"I do wonder what Charles wants to see me about," said Lady Graham, not for the first time that day, to Miss Merriman who had come over from Pomfret Towers for the night. "Do stay with me, Merry. If Robert were here I am sure he would know what to do, but of course when he is in Paris he can't be at Holdings. It is really *very* difficult."

Miss Merriman quite agreed and there was a silence during which both ladies thought of Lady Emily, the one person who could understand and control the granddaughter who was so like her, but so star-crossed by a girlhood in the uncertain post-war years. Many of her contemporaries had taken to it as a matter of course, but poor Clarissa looked longingly to the past, useless for us all, most useless for her.

"Either Charles must marry her soon, or I shall wash my hands of the whole thing," said Lady Graham suddenly, which was rather as if a dove had suddenly flown at one's face and begun to peck one's eyes out.

"I don't think you can, Lady Graham," said Miss Merriman quietly.

"No, I can't," said Lady Graham, subsiding into her usual self. "Oh dear, there's the bell. It must be Charles."

And Charles it was, looking just like Charles in a quiet reassuring way.

"How cold your face is, dear Charles," said Lady Graham

when he had kissed her. "Sit down and we will have a real talk, and Merry will help us. What *is* the matter, Charles?"

Charles made as if to speak but did not.

"I think, Lady Graham," said the calm, efficient voice of Miss Merriman, "that Charles might find it difficult to explain, because he might sound conceited. Clarissa has been very difficult, as we all know. The times are difficult and she has never felt quite at home in them. She loves Charles," at which words Charles looked at her with a kind of grateful surprise but said nothing. "And when I say love," said Miss Merriman with her usual calm dispassionate manner, "I mean it. But she is too proud to say what she feels. If Charles thinks he ought to wait till he has more to offer he is being chivalrous, but I think silly. My advice, Lady Graham, as you have allowed me to be here this evening, is that Charles should marry her out of hand—and if necessary beat her."

Never, in all her long experience of being trusted yet impersonal friend and adviser to her employers had anyone heard Miss Merriman speak out with such authority and there was complete and surprised silence which Agnes was the first to break.

"I think you are quite right, Merry," she said. "And when Robert was here last weekend, before he went abroad, he said much the same thing, only of course rather differently," her ladyship added, with a lively remembrance of her husband's words which were that he did not see the sense of this shilly-shallying and Clarissa was behaving extremely badly and being very troublesome; that Charles had put his position and his present income and his prospects before him through their lawyers, and that if Clarissa didn't make up her mind she would lose a very good husband; at the same time mentioning that he had told his lawyers exactly what he could do now and in the future for Clarissa—provided there were any future, he added, but that trouble was common to us all. He had then kissed his wife very affectionately and been driven to Barchester Central to get the London express and the train-ferry to France.

"I had a very good letter from Cousin Robert," said Charles. "We both think Clarissa has behaved very badly. But I happen to love her. I hoped she loved me and then it seemed as if she didn't, but I have made up my mind. I want to tell you exactly what I've done."

"Tell me, dear boy," said Agnes, for once laying her work aside and giving her whole attention.

"I am going to marry her," said Charles, "whether she makes up her mind or not. As soon as the School moves there will be a home for us in the east pavilion of Harefield House. Till then Cecil Waring will let us have a little kind of dower house in the Priory grounds. It is furnished, quite bearably. I have also got a special licence, just to make sure. If you and Cousin Robert would like us to be married at Little Misfit, that's all right. I think that is all," and he fell silent, looking into the fire, with his loosely clasped hands swinging between his legs and Agnes thought as she looked at his face that she had for a long time been taking him for a boy. But it was a man who had been speaking.

"May I ask Charles," said Miss Merriman, "whether he has thought of any other place for his wedding?"

Agnes looked at Charles.

"Yes," he said. "Rushwater. But that is for you to say, Cousin Agnes."

There were very, very few people who had ever seen Miss Merriman outwardly moved, but possibly fewer who had seen Lady Graham under strong emotion. She, like her mother before her, was quick in sympathy and her feelings would fleet across her face like shadows over the downlands so beloved by all her people. In matters of real import her Pomfret mind let her stand aside and help others rather than expect to be helped. Now, suddenly, the hand of lost time passed over her face and Miss Merriman saw—though Charles did not, perhaps could not—what Agnes would be like fifteen, twenty years hence; a beauty ravaged perhaps but with added nobility from its ever growing kindness and thought for others. The shadow quivered, melted and was gone.

"Dearest Charles," said Lady Graham, taking his hand. "How darling mamma would have loved it. When is it to be?"

Not perhaps the question that the bride's mother usually puts, but—or Miss Merriman thought so and we trust her judgment—a question which, so both ladies felt, Charles had a right, after his many trials, to decide.

They had not heard the front door being shut and Clarissa was among them, looking tired her mother thought. At the sight of Charles she stopped dead, the firelight shining on her proud, pretty face.

"Oh, Charles," she said.

"Yes, Charles," said he, looking up but not moving. "How soon will you marry me? It can be anywhere and at any time."

"Do you want me to?" said Clarissa, conscious only of Charles.

"I do," said Charles, "though really I say that later. At Rushwater Church, this week, tomorrow if you like. I can't wait any longer. Your mother says yes. So does your father."

"Do you really *want* me to?" said Clarissa, coming nearer.

"I always have," said Charles. "I oughtn't to have let you wait. I was silly. I didn't know."

"You *weren't*," said Clarissa. "Forgive me, Charles," and she knelt, with her peculiar quickness and grace, before Charles.

Lady Graham looked above her daughter's head, laid against Charles's rather shabby tweed jacket, and looked at Miss Merriman. Both ladies quietly went away to the Saloon, where there was a good wood fire and some central heating.

"Do you think Tuesday?" said Lady Graham.

"That is the day after tomorrow," said Miss Merriman. "And New Year's Day. Why not?" which calm way of taking it did Lady Graham all the good in the world and, like her enchanting and quite maddening mother, she began to plan everything. A great deal because she wanted to help her lovers; and a good deal from her inherited love of meddling, though her intromissions, as old Mr. Macpherson used to say, were less devastating than her beloved mother's.

"I was wondering," she said, sitting down by the telephone, whether I would ask the Dean, but I think it would be kinder to ask Mr. Bostock. After all he *is* our Vicar at Rushwater and I daresay he has never seen a special licence," and from the soft radiance of Lady Graham's eyes as she thought of a treat for Mr. Bostock, Miss Merriman gathered that the Dean would have no chance at all. "And I think Martin had better give her away. Gillie was so kind about Emmy, but I don't like to trouble him again. It is so annoying that Robert can't be here, but he almost always isn't. I remember when James was confirmed Robert had to go to Cairo, and why Cairo, I cannot imagine," at which moment the telephone rang, almost startling her ladyship, and announced itself as Lieutenant James Graham to speak to his mother about forty-eight hours' unexpected leave.

"Then you can give Clarissa away, " said his mother. "She and Charles are to be married at Rushwater on New Year's Day."

The voice of Lieutenant Graham said that would be fine and why hadn't they got married before and he'd bring Clarissa a ripping present from Fortnum's like what Bobby Bingham had given his niece when she was married, but Cousin Dodo went off the deep end about it. Why? said Agnes, deeply interested in the views of her very strong-minded elderly cousin Lady Dorothy Bingham. It was, said Robert, a kind of super-corkscrew that played Drink to me only on a little musical box while you were pulling the cork out and all the fellows were green with envy, to which his mother, with great presence of mind, replied that Charles wouldn't be able to afford much drink she expected and it might be a little unkind; and Lieutenant Graham said O.K. then, he'd give them a lot of drink instead and would his mother leave the front door unlocked as he would probably be driving down after midnight on Monday, which her ladyship took very calmly, merely asking him not to have an accident as the wedding was on Tuesday, and after a few family inquiries the talk came to an end and her ladyship said she must look at Clarissa's clothes next day. In the hall they met Charles and Clarissa, both with a kind of peaceful radiance that made Miss Merriman (who had secretly felt a little anxious but did not show it) quite at ease about them. They had found themselves, she thought, and that was more than a great many people ever did.

"Good night, cousin Agnes," said Charles embracing his future mother-in-law. "Take care of this girl for me. I may not be able to get over tomorrow. I've got to tell father and mother and I ought to let the Winters know. And don't worry. She won't do it again," with which he kissed her almost like a husband. "Oh, Cousin Agnes, would you like to see the licence? It's the most expensive sort. It cost over twenty-five pounds with some odd tips," but Agnes said Another day and Charles felt as if he were in the nursery. Then he went away and Miss Merriman tidied the cushions.

"And now we really must think about things," said Lady Graham. "Cook will be quite annoyed if we keep supper waiting any longer. Do shout down the passage darling that we are ready and Charles isn't staying," and Clarissa, in a kind of quiet dream went away to do as she was told. "I have often thought that when Clarissa was married things might be easier," said her ladyship to Miss Merriman. "Darling Clarissa; but she *has* been troublesome," all of which Mr. Meredith had already said, in words that will last while our language lasts, in *Love in a Valley*; but we do not think that either of the ladies knew that poem well.

As Charles drove homewards his courage sank a little: but not much, for he drove quickly and sang, very badly, as he went. When he got to Arcot House the dining-room was empty and from the light in the estate room he knew that his father was there, so he looked into the drawing-room where his mother was trying to read Mrs. Morland's latest thriller with one hand and mend her husband's pyjamas with the other, if we make ourselves clear. She looked up as he came in, and asked if he had had a nice time at which point he began fiddling with his mother's knitting till she could willingly have killed him.

Charles said very nice. "Oh, and Cousin Agnes sent you her love," he added. Mrs. Belton said she really must go over and see Agnes, perhaps on Tuesday.

"Well, I'm going to be married on Tuesday, mother," said Charles. "I didn't mean to bother you about it, but—" and his voice trailed away before his mother's eye.

When Charles had gone to the wars, almost without a farewell, and his mother had been to his empty bedroom where his civilian clothes lay scattered, she thought she had felt all she could ever feel. But she was eight or nine years older now.

"Married, darling!" she said, almost adding To whom? so long had Charles been waiting.

"Well, mother," said Charles, very patiently we think, considering that he had already been through a distinctly emotional scene at Holdings, "I thought Clarissa had had enough rope, so I bought a special licence. It cost more than twenty-five pounds," and he paused, gratified by his mother's look of surprise. "I can get married with it anywhere," he continued, "and Cousin Agnes says on Tuesday at Rushwater. I did think secretly would be rather fun, but I expect Cousin Agnes is right. You will come, mother, won't you?" he added, suddenly wondering, much as Mr. Swiveller did, if the old lady (not that anyone, as she once said of herself indignantly, could call her either) was friendly.

"Of course I'll come, darling," said Mrs. Belton, forcing herself to speak calmly and knowing that she would have a sleepless night for her pains. "Who is to marry you?"

Charles said he thought Mr. Bostock.

"Well, darling, I hope you will be very, very happy," said his mother; not that she felt any doubt, but if she did feel any she wanted to squash it thoroughly. "I shall give Clarissa the diamond spray. It will suit her. Darling, is it *really* all right?"

"Absolutely all right," said Charles. "I'd had enough of her silliness, bless her, and that's that. Cecil Waring will let us have the dower cottage till we go to Harefield."

"Of course," said Mrs. Belton, her mind somewhere else. "Then your children will be born at Harefield!" which, slightly to Charles's mortification, seemed to interest and please her even more than his marriage.

"Well, you'll have to wait a little, mother," he said apologetically. "We really can't have any for about nine months you know. But as soon as we do we'll call the boy Fred after father," which touched his mother more than she would have liked to say. So she asked him if he had had anything to eat.

"Lord! I'd forgotten clean about it," said Charles. "Never mind. Where's Eric?"

His mother said at Dowlah Cottage, so Charles said in that case he would go and rout something out of Wheeler. On his way to the kitchen quarters he looked into the estate room to tell his father the news, who appeared to be under the impression that Charles's sudden marriage was a kind of Fleet wedding and not quite legal, but when Charles offered to show him the special licence he was as interested as a child with a toy and exercised his ingenuity in suggesting various possible cases in which such a marriage might not be valid, all of which Charles countered with admirable good temper and allowed his father to show him a number of old letters written by the Nabob's son from the Continent, being mostly demands for money and almost illegible at that. He then went to the kitchen and wheedled a hearty supper out of Wheeler the cook and formerly his nurse, who very properly cried on hearing the news, by which time it was fairly late and he decided to go to bed. He had only got as far as taking his coat and tie off when Swan came in, after a pleasant family evening with Captain Belton R.N. and his wife.

"Well, what's the news?" said Swan, and when Charles said that he would tell him what, as Lucy Adams said, which was that he was going to marry Clarissa by special licence on New Year's Day and beat her with a stick not thicker than his thumb, Swan most annoyingly said For thumb, read pigtail, which led to an argument followed by a fruitless hunt for some old volumes of Marryat that Mrs. Belton had sent to the Red Cross Hospital Library some years previously.

"Who is going to be best man?" said Swan.

"Lord! I never thought of that," said Charles. "I thought with a special licence you didn't have to have one. Would you be?" to which Swan replied that he was flattered, but felt there were a good many other people Charles ought to ask first if he did have one at all and owing to ignorance on both sides the matter dropped.

"What a world it is," said Swan, yawning. "Your brother was full of ancestral voices prophesying woe. People going bankrupt all over the place if they aren't careful. Well, good luck, Charles. I wish I were you, only not with Clarissa," which wish Charles took very kindly as no reflection on Clarissa, rather indeed as an indication that Swan would like to be married to a nice girl the day after tomorrow by special licence himself and then they both yawned and Swan went away to his room, there to think of a girl who, he was now quite sure, would never look at him as she had looked that day on another and perhaps worthier man. So better to bury that short-lived hope and let the earth lie heavy on it: as heavily as his short-lived hope was lying on his heart.

CHAPTER II

Clarissa's wedding was so quiet and so entirely for the immediate families that we shall not intrude upon it, except to say that as time goes on we believe she will be as happy as it is given to anyone to be and that Lady Emily, if in the words of a bard of lost Ireland spirits can steal from the region of air, will know that her beloved, difficult grandchild has found the husband to whom her increasing devotion will be given. Charles will always love her and cherish her; Beltons will be born in the home of their forbears. But all this is to come.

Swan not unnaturally offered to cut his visit to Harefield short, but Mrs. Belton said they would like him to stay and as Charles and his wife (a word to which his parents were not yet quite accustomed) had gone for a fortnight to the villa at Cap Ferrat, lent to them by the Pomfrets, he slipped quite easily into being a son of the house. At Arcot House he was able to combine business with pleasure, seeing about a number of odd jobs connected with the Priory School and the move, for much had to be planned before the change was made and Philip Winter and his wife had taken a week with friends in another county. For his own ends he saw a good deal of the Cartons and tried to make up his mind about the rival claims of the school and a possible fellowship, strongly pressed to the latter by Mr. Carton who was of opinion that Swan's brains would be wasted at a prep. school, while Swan rather wondered whether such brains as he had would not be as usefully and less selfishly employed with little boys. But at any rate he would be at the Priory School for at least another year.

The rumours of business troubles, first heard through Mr. Macfadyen, were not unfounded and a good many people were in considerable anxiety and cross at breakfast without giving a reason. But Peggy Brandon had, alas, been quite used to a rather spiky Francis for some time and perhaps did not notice any change. What was almost worse was the ridiculous friction between Francis and Nurse and really we cannot blame either—or to be more truthful we heartily blame both. As we are completely ignorant of business and finance and have not the faintest idea what Francis did in business hours, we cannot give any details. We can only say, as everyone in the Barchester financial world said, that if several houses of good standing had to give up business it would not be by any lack of help in the way of galling restrictions, senseless and weathercock changes of plan and crippling (or, as the Barchester Exchange wits, a little behind the times, said, Crippsling) taxation on the part of the late Them. Among those involved was certainly Francis Brandon and though as events proved his brains and cool business head were going to get him safely out of the difficulties, there is no doubt that he had been increasingly anxious during the last year. Unfortunately, or fortunately, we cannot say which, as it depends on what way you look at it, he made up for his cool and competent work in the office by being increasingly difficult at home. And we must admit that he had one very valid reason in Nurse, for this estimable and devoted woman after the custom of nannies still saw in the not so young successful man of business the yellow-haired little boy in a green linen suit, while the man who controlled several important interests not unnaturally resented being as good as told to run along and wash his hands for lunch.

As we already know and I hope our readers remember, for we cannot at the moment lay our hands on the passage, there had been some talk of Nurse being transferred to Lady Cora. Her ladyship had indeed begun negotiations to that effect but there were two difficulties. The first and least important was that Nurse, while fully alive to the social status she would acquire in the Nanny World by taking charge of a duke's grandchild, had a very real devotion for Francis's babies and though she sometimes admitted to Cook that she found three a bit of a handful now and wasn't so young as she used to be, she was jealous of her position as their supreme judge and ruler. The second and more difficult objection was Nanny Allen, who though long past work herself said she didn't fancy That Woman looking after Master George's little nephew, though the baby's sex was as yet perfectly undecided and he or she would in any case be, as far as we can work out the relationship, a second cousin once removed of the George Waring who was killed in the 1914 war just before the Armistice. As Nannie Allen had a home in the village, No. I, Ladysmith Cottages, and spent most of the time in the Priory School kitchen, it was not likely that she and Nurse would often have to meet, but both ladies were so ready the one to resent the other that even Lady Cora's dauntless spirit quailed slightly at the thought of trains of gunpowder from the Priory nursery to the Priory School kitchen with a highly inflammable fuse at each end. It is true that when the School moved to Harefield in the following autumn, a plan was maturing for Nannie Allen to live with her daughter Selina Hopkins who cooked for the school and her son-in-law ex-Sergeant Hopkins, who would have their own quarters, and in her more optimistic moments Lady Cora thought that for a few months she could bear it.

With this end in view she had driven herself over to Pomfret Madrigal to see Peggy Brandon after Christmas. Her husband had tried to stop her solitary journeys in what used to be known as an interesting condition, but she said she was told far too often by too many people that she must eat for two so why not drive for two, and as she was one of the best drivers known to the county police, who all respectfully adored her, Cecil gave in and very sensibly almost stopped worrying.

"Well, my lamb?" said Lady Cora to her hostess, "and how is everything? I am longing to have a word with Nurse."

"So am I," said Peggy. "I mean I am longing for you to have her. She and Francis are not on speaking terms this week."

"What you need is a man to look after you," said Lady Cora, very kindly, when to her horror Peggy turned her face away and blew her nose.

"My *lamb*, I didn't mean that," said Lady Cora, truly shocked by the effect of her words. "Is it so bad?"

Peggy, her voice considerably impeded by trying not to cry, said she didn't know what Cora meant.

"Yes you do," said her ladyship. "Does Francis beat you? No? Good. At least Bad. It would be much better than picking on you in public; and if he picks on you in public don't ask me what he does in private. Sit down."

"He *doesn't* pick on me," said Peggy indignantly, but she sat down.

"Very well, he doesn't," said her ladyship. "But you look as if he did," at which Peggy said, rather indistinctly, that she thought Francis was worried about business perhaps, though he hadn't said so.

Her ladyship, suppressing a natural inclination to say that Peggy, of whom she was really fond, was as silly as they make them, said Francis was fascinating but as selfish as they made them. Peggy, speaking in a voice muffled by immediate tears said not *half* so selfish as her first husband, at which Lady Cora didn't know whether to laugh or to cry.

"May I tell you something?" she said. "I have seen quite a lot of men one way and another and they're all much alike," at which point Peggy interrupted to say that Francis wasn't.

"Then why don't you tell him so?" said Lady Cora.

"But why?" said Peggy.

"Now listen, my sweet," said Lady Cora. "You needn't take my advice but I'm going to give it to you. Have you ever heard of buttering a cat's paws when you take it to a new house, to make it settle down and purr? That goes for men. Butter their paws and make them purr. Yes—I know that Francis is quite, quite different from anyone else, but he is just like them all the same. Just tell him how wonderful he is sometimes," and then tea coming in stopped any further private conversation for the moment. And with tea came Mrs. Parkinson, so bubbling with news that she forgot to be shy with the duke's daughter.

"What *do* you think, Mrs. Brandon?" she said. "I felt I must come over and tell you and Mrs. Turpin kindly asked Harold and Connie to tea, so I thought I'd run over. Oh I *am* so excited."

"Then you'd better drink some tea first, Mrs. Parkinson," said Lady Cora assuming, as she usually did, the leading part. "And when is the baby? We only need Maria Marling here to make it perfect. What sights we all are."

"Teddy says," said Mrs. Parkinson, with an affection in her voice at her husband's name that touched Peggy to the quick, "he thinks ladies look beautiful, sort of, beforehand. Of course I just laugh at him, but it does help," at which her hearers were divided between thinking how incredibly simple she was and a slightly choking feeling combined with prickling behind the eyes.

"Quite right," said Lady Cora, "and apart from feeling—and looking—as if one were pushing a perambulator in front of one all the time, I'm all for it. Now do tell us what has happened."

"It's father," said Mrs. Parkinson. "What *do* you think, Mrs. Brandon? He has given us I really couldn't tell you what a wonderful present. We didn't hardly believe it, but it's true."

"That," said Lady Cora, "is excellent. And now, do tell us what it is. Just drink up your tea first and Peggy will give you a fresh cup."

Mrs. Parkinson obeyed, as anyone who came within Lady Cora's orbit usually did, and then embarked upon a statement so confused by her expressions of gratitude and of how wonderful it all was that her hearers had some difficulty in making out what had really happened, which was that Mr. Welk, after a day profitably spent with Sir Edmund Pridham and some serious consideration of that gentleman's advice, was making over to his daughter a most respectable sum of money, which if he lived long enough or the laws about death duties weren't made even more unfair than they are, would put the Parkinsons in a much better position not only now but later.

"And now," said Mrs. Parkinson, her eyes wet with grateful emotion, "I can have a new kitchen sink and a gas heater for the washing up and get some new sheets in the sales."

Both the other ladies felt they would like to cry, but didn't, and confounded themselves in expressions of joy and Mrs. Parkinson, all her shyness drowned in excitement and thoughts of what she could do for her husband and children, spoke of her husband's kindness and how hard he worked and how the village people liked him and even the half-gipsy families at Grumper's End were sending their young to the children's service.

"You see, it *is* so nice for them to get the kids off their hands for a bit," said Mrs. Parkinson, "and Teddy's making a lovely Children's Corner and he's starting the Wolf Cubs," and whatever her hearers' feelings were about Children's Corners (and they were, as ours are, in entire agreement with the gifted authors of *Babylon Bruised and Mount Moriah Mended*), they felt that Mr. Parkinson was being a real parish priest and assuming responsibility for the young of his flock and respected him very much for it.

"There's only the one thing," said Mrs. Parkinson. "Father's got to live for however many years it is because of the death duties. But if father says a thing, he means it," from which rather addled statement her hearers gathered that Mr. Welk was not the man to draw back when he had put his hand to the plough and would consider it a serious dereliction of his duties to die before the years necessary to make his gift duty free had expired.

As the atmosphere was now highly charged with emotion, Peggy suggested that Mrs. Parkinson should come up and see the children, while Nurse should be sent down to see Lady Cora, which was done.

"Well, Nurse," said Lady Cora, "I've been meaning to come over and see you. Do sit down. Mrs. Brandon said you were thinking of a change."

"Well really, your ladyship, I couldn't think of it," said Nurse, speaking not of the change but of sitting down with a Duke's daughter; and having made her protest she sat down.

"It's my first baby," said Lady Cora, "and it won't be my last. I want someone who thoroughly understands babies, as I am sure you do. The Priory is extremely inconvenient, but the nurseries are large and sunny and Sir Cecil is having a bathroom and a little kitchen put in. I shall come into the nursery whenever I like, that must be clearly understood. The bus service to Barchester passes the bottom of the drive. When Sir Cecil and I go away you will have complete responsibility. I don't know the first thing about babies but the baby will be mine, not yours. And when we go to Gatherum you will allow the Duke and the Duchess to see the baby as often as they want. What wages are you asking?"

Nurse, fascinated by this peculiar new employer, named the sum she was getting.

"That will suit me perfectly," said Lady Cora. "And of course I shall pay you more when there are two," at which Nurse, slightly bewildered by her future employer's summary methods, nearly asked when the second was expected.

"And one other thing," said Lady Cora. "What are you doing about finding someone for Mrs. Brandon if you come to me?" But if her ladyship thought she had given Nurse a poser, she was agreeably undeceived, for Nurse said there was a very nice girl at Grumper's End, a cousin of Mrs. Grantly's maids over at Edgewood, who had been nurse with Mrs. Gresham at Hallbury and wanted to be nearer home, at which point Francis Brandon came in.

"Don't go, Nurse," said Lady Cora. "Well, Francis, I haven't seen you for ages. Nurse and I have been making all sorts of plans and she is coming to the Priory to look after the future Bart. I expect Peggy has told you."

"She did say something," said Francis, "but I'd rather forgotten. You're looking marvellous, Cora," to which her ladyship replied that he had said a mouthful and marvellous wasn't the word and Siamese twins was more like it. "Well, Nurse," she added, "thank you very much. You had better come over to Beliers one day when Mrs. Brandon can spare you and look at the nurseries," and Nurse, who was not used to being given her congé, went away like a lamb and boasted quite unbearably to Cook when she went down for her supper about the life she was going to lead, to which Cook replied darkly that handsome was as handsome did.

"And now, my sweet," said Lady Cora to Francis, "tell me all about yourself. I hear the most *terrible* rumours going about. You aren't bankrupt, are you? I've never known a bankrupt. Gerry owed money right and left and he put it in his will before D-day that all his creditors were to have first cut, poor lamb, but he didn't get as far as being bankrupt. And some of them wouldn't even take their cut. People loved him."

Francis, partly annoyed at her question, partly flattered by her interest or what he chose to take as such, said it had been a difficult time for the last two years, what with taxes and licences and permits and the dollar situation and the direction of industry and one thing and another, and he and his partners had really been worried.

"Of course this is rather private," he said, going back to the almost familiar terms on which he had acted and danced with Lady Cora two summers ago for the Conservative Fête at Gatherum. "Don't say anything to Peggy. It would only upset her."

"Not half so much as you do," said Lady Cora. "The whole county has been noticing it."

"They couldn't," said Francis. "We have kept everything under our hats. There has been quite enough wrong in the office without bringing it home."

"I wasn't thinking of your worries, I was thinking of your temper," said Lady Cora, with all the spirit of the self-willed heiress Glencora MacCluskie and the wealthy American Isabel Boncassen, the duchesses of the last century, one of whom she so closely resembled in her fine bones and elegant hands and feet; and we think that she also had more than a touch of Lady Glencora's spirit. "It's the talk of the county. How Peggy puts up with it I don't know, except that she's an angel. I expect it's on account of the children. If I were married to you I'd have a few words to say."

Francis, with a not very successful attempt at dignity, said she had in his opinion said quite enough.

That, said her ladyship, was as maybe, but at least she had said it in his drawing-room. All the others were saying it all over the place and she instanced the Deanery, Southbridge Vicarage, Mrs. Freddy Belton at Harefield and various other more or less intimate friends.

And Peggy at the bottom of it all he supposed, said Francis sulkily.

"Really too, too silly; that's what you are," said Lady Cora, for Clarissa's little affectation had infected a good many people and whether they said it deliberately or by force of hearing it elsewhere we do not know. Probably both.

Francis said Damn in a mumbling way and then said Sorry. Lady Cora said that was nothing to what her great-uncle Algy Palliser, the one who married old Mr. Marling's sister and was drowned with her in the Titanic, used to say, if her parents were to be believed.

"I'll tell you what, as that remarkable woman Mrs. Adams says," Lady Cora continued, not troubling to raise her attractive husky voice. "If I were married to you and you were troublesome in the house I'd take the children to Gatherum and stay there till you begged my pardon. I shouldn't be in the least surprised if Peggy went over to her sister at Southbridge for a bit. You couldn't stop her, you know," and Francis, though furious, had to admit inside himself that to object to his wife taking the children for a visit to their aunt-in-law at the Vicarage would only make people laugh.

The conversation was not getting anywhere in particular. Lady Cora had on the whole the upper hand though Francis, and she had to admit it to herself, was behaving with considerable self-restraint. But she was still as far from convincing him of his own trying ways as ever and began to feel tired and wonder if she had made a bad mistake in having it out with Francis, when Nurse, who in virtue of her position had a kind of squatter's right to come into any room at any time, opened the door and stood in the doorway.

"Excuse me, my lady," she said, talking right through and over Francis as Lady Cora said later when describing the scene to her husband, "but Number One has just done one of her nightgown buttons up herself, at the back of her neck, and Madam thought you'd like to come and see."

Francis, conscious that Nurse was deliberately not seeing him, said Hell! and in the same breath began to repeat it. Nurse retreated, shutting the door after her in an ominous silence far more alarming than the loudest slam.

"Look here, Cora," said Francis, "do you wonder it gets on my nerves a bit? That woman gets me down. If I had a revolver I'd shoot her."

"If I shoot her for you, will you swear to be extremely nice to Peggy for ever and ever amen?" said Lady Cora.

"Of *course* I'll be nice to her," said Francis indignantly. "I've never *looked* at another woman since I saw her."

"You even threw *me* over at the Conservative Do the summer before last," said Lady Cora. "Do you remember how you made her do Aubrey Clover's Argentina Tango with you, instead of me? You were so right. I have never seen such a performance. Yours especially. Peggy followed your steps quite wonderfully, but you made it." And she added to herself that if the heir was born with LIAR tattooed on his chest she would be pained but not surprised.

"I didn't think you remembered that, Cora," said Francis, at which words, or rather at the Auld Lang Syne voice in which they were said, Lady Cora nearly had the giggles.

"That's a bargain then," she said. "I'll shoot Nurse and you will be your own charming self again," and if you can swallow that, she added to herself, you'll swallow the whole muddle the Labour Government have left behind them. "And to show you that I'm a man of my word, Nurse is coming to me to take the heir from the month, which is I believe the correct expression. Now it's your turn," and she held out her elegant fine-boned hand to Francis who bowed over it and just touched it with his lips.

After a suitable interval Lady Cora came back, with Peggy, full of admiration for the good looks and intelligence of the three children and managing very cleverly to convey to Francis that all their gifts came from him. Francis took her to the door and saw her into her car.

"Ought you to be driving about alone?" he said with what Lady Cora considered quite unnecessary chivalry, at which she smiled, waved her hand, drove away at a very reasonable speed and at dinner gave her husband a very amusing account of her afternoon's work, on which his comment was that Brandon needed taking down a peg and Cora was the woman to do it.

"But don't forget he has about the best business head in Barchester," he added. "Everything he has done for me has been done extremely well and I am quite sure he will come out of this trouble all right. I was talking to the Duke's lawyers and they said the same," which pleased Lady Cora, but almost entirely on his wife's account.

* * *

When Lady Cora had gone Francis went up to the nursery to say good night to his children. Number One was in her tall chair having milk and biscuits, while the twins were already in bed looking uncommonly snug. Francis kissed them both, thinking how remarkably nice they were, and then sat down near Number One.

"Bolygocks," said Number One.

"Now, that's not the way to ask Daddy for Goldilocks," said Nurse and Francis was just going to feel annoyed by her interference when it occurred to him that he had not, till Nurse interpreted, the faintest idea what Bolygocks meant and had to admit that her interruption was not altogether ill-judged. The story of the Three Bears had its usual success and while he was telling it his wife came in and sat by the fire.

"I wish I could do the Three Bears' voices like you," said Peggy. "I can growl for the Big Bear and squeak for the Little Bear, but I can't find a proper voice for the Middle Sized Bear."

"Oh, I don't know," said Francis carelessly, but flattered underneath. "Sometimes I think of old Pilward, you know, the one whose son married Adams's daughter. He's a perfect Middle-Sized Bear. I expect the theatricals I used to do are a help. I always liked character parts."

"You did them awfully well," said Peggy. "But I think you were best in the dancing parts. Do you remember Aubrey's Argentina Tango at the Red Cross Fête in Barchester?"

"Lord! yes. How long ago it seems," said Francis. "And we did it at Gatherum too."

"Oh that was Lady Cora," said Peggy, her kind heart seeing an opportunity to repay her adviser. "She said you ought to do it with me instead of with her," to which Francis replied in rather a smug way that Lady Cora had the wits to see that she wasn't up to his style, which Peggy did not contradict but said, rather wistfully, that she wished there were some dancing now.

"But why not?" said Francis. Peggy said she thought he hadn't been very keen so she hadn't bothered.

"Well, I suppose I wasn't," said Francis. "Things have been pretty worrying at the office, but I didn't like to bother you about it."

"But you *couldn't* bother me," said Peggy. "Is it all right now?"

Pretty all right, said Francis. Nothing really to worry about now except the appalling muddle the late Government had made of everything, deliberately hampering and restricting all freedom.

"There's only one grudge I've got against old Churchill," said Francis, "that he waited so long before he told us what a ghastly mess the Labour lot have left behind. A Treasury practically bankrupt and the lowest stocks of food we have ever had. I suppose he feels a kind of loyalty to the men who were with him in the Coalition Government and doesn't want to uncover their nakedness. By jove, I'd uncover them! He's too great a gentleman sometimes. What is it, Nurse?" for Nurse was hovering in a very disturbing way.

Nurse was heard to say something to the effect that her babies couldn't go to sleep if there was a noise. Peggy caught her husband's eye.

"I'll be down in a minute, darling," she said. Francis went away and did not hear his wife say very quietly that if Nurse spoke like that at the Priory Sir Cecil Waring certainly would not tolerate it and it must be understood that Mr. Brandon was master in his own nursery; most of which was special pleading or half truth but frightened Nurse, for a dove that suddenly flies at your face and pecks you is much more alarming than a bird of prey who probably wouldn't pay any attention to you.

When Peggy came into the sitting-room Francis looked up from the Barchester Evening Star (owned by the Barchester Chronicle) and asked, almost anxiously, if everything was all right.

"Nurse wasn't and I had to Speak to her," said Peggy. "As long as she is here I *cannot* have her be rude to you."

"And I'd hate her to be rude to you, old thing," said Francis, with real admiration for his wife.

Peggy said nothing for a moment. Then she looked at Francis and said, "She wouldn't." And Francis felt that she was perfectly right and reflected upon the rather stupid fuss there had been with Lady Cora.

"I was thinkng it would be rather nice to take the children over to Southbridge for a few days," said Peggy, and Francis nearly dropped his newspaper. Could it be that Lady Cora—meddling woman—was right? And if she was right about that she was also quite right in saying that he would only look silly if he made a fuss. "When Nurse goes," his wife continued. "Then the nurseries could have a good cleaning and we could start fresh. Of course I won't have the new nurse in the house with Nurse at all. It would only mean trouble."

Francis's sigh of relief had it been expressed might have been heard in the Close, but he managed to make it inside himself. After dinner Francis said he was damned if he was going to let the office get the upper hand of him; he had brought some papers back that he ought to look at and they could jolly well wait and what about a spot of gramophone. Peggy was of course delighted. Those who knew Stories when Lavinia Brandon, now Mrs. Joram, lived there will remember how often Francis and his sister Delia turned back the rugs in the large drawing-room and danced there and may remember, like an echo of the happier and easier days now for ever reft from us by the united forces of the Germans and Them, how in that comfortable flower-scented room Mrs. Brandon flirted happily and outrageously with Noel Merton, then an attractive bachelor. The room was not much used now except in warm summer which appears to have died with many other delightful civilised things, but owing to Francis's firmness in making his mother have central heating installed just before the war, it was possible to keep it warm enough for a party (which quickly generates its own heat) and for occasional family use. The gramophone was turned on. Again owing to Francis's prevision and we may add his gift for making money, it was no longer the machine whose records had to be changed but the almost newest kind of machine that does everything for itself except put the records back in their proper place afterwards. Just as they were taking the floor the telephone rang in the sitting-room next door. Peggy went to answer it.

"It was your mother," she said when she came back. "Just to ask after the children and sent you her love and says everyone has accepted for her party. Oh, and the Precentor told her that the Palace servants are to be put on board wages while the Bishop and Mrs. Bishop are in Madeira and his housekeeper—I mean the Precentor's—says they are all going to give notice the day they come back. Now let's dance."

So the seductive strains of Aubrey Clover's Argentina Tango floated lusciously and slightly lasciviously on the air and the dancers enjoyed themselves vastly. Francis was still feeling a little sore from Lady Cora's handling (though not altogether displeased by the interest taken in him by a Duke's daughter) and found the rhythmic ordered music very soothing: so much so that when it came to an end he said they would have it again. So they began to dance again till half-way through Nurse came in. Francis said DAMN, softly enough for Nurse not to hear it, though her dark suspicions were well founded.

"It's Mr. Parkinson, madam," she said. "I just happened to be near the front door when the bell rang and I thought I'd open the door as I was there. He says can he see you, madam. Something very important."

"Blast the fellow," said Francis to Peggy, which words Nurse sensed though she could not hear them and became rigid with disapproval. "Ask Mr. Parkinson to come in, Nurse," which she did, taking back to the kitchen the good news that Mr. Parkinson looked shocking and she shouldn't wonder if Mrs. Parkinson had been taken bad.

Prophets are without honour in their own employers' kitchens and Cook openly derided Nurse's words. But Nurse was perfectly right (for which Cook could never quite forgive her).

"It's Mavis, Mrs. Brandon," said Mr. Parkinson. "She was to go to the Barchester General for the baby and the kids were going to Mr. Welk for a fortnight. I've rung up the doctor and he's on the way, but we're afraid—I mean—" and he crimsoned and stammered wretchedly, unable to find suitable words for the elementary facts of life, "—so I thought perhaps—"

Even Mrs. Joram could not have been prompter and more helpful than Peggy.

"Call Nurse, darling," she said to Francis. "Now be calm, Mr. Parkinson. You *can't* kill babies—they are frightfully tough and——"

"It's Mavis I'm worried about," said Mr. Parkinson.

"Now don't," said Peggy. "Oh Nurse," she went on as that lady, her sleeves metaphorically rolled up for battle, came hurrying in, the joy of a crisis in her eye, "Mrs. Parkinson's baby is a little sooner than they expected. The doctor will be there soon. You had better go back with Mr. Parkinson and see what you can do. Mr. Brandon will run you both over. And bring the children here for a night or two till things are straight. Is the car there, darling?" she said to Francis.

The car was there. Within two minutes Nurse was ready and Francis drove her and the distracted Mr. Parkinson to the Vicarage. Meanwhile Peggy went to the kitchen and broke the news to Cook and Mrs. Turpin who had come in for a kind of rere-supper of strong cups of tea. We need not say that Cook had clearly seen from the tea-leaves at the bottom of her cup that an Unexpected Event was Imminent (as expounded in "What the Tea-Pot Tells us," a booklet issued free with every half pound of Rajah Tasty Tips) and took it calmly; much sustained by the hope that the baby would (a) be born dead, (b) be so deformed that it would have to be Put in a Home (though what precise meaning she attached to these words we do not know) and (c) that Mother and Child would both die and be buried in one grave. But when she heard that the older children were to come to Stories for a few days her kindly nature got the upper hand and she began to talk about a nice hot cup of Bovril for the poor little things, at which point Peggy retired, for she was certain that Nurse would have her own views about what other people's children ought to have before being put to bed in a strange house and did not wish to be involved.

Within a very short time Francis came back with Nurse and an excited and rather frightened Harold and Connie wrapped in blankets, whom she immediately took upstairs.

"Everything's in hand," said Francis. "Doctor arrived with a nurse and ambulance from the Barchester General and everything's all right. I think Parkinson will go mad, but that can't be helped. I saw Mrs. Turpin coming out of the kitchen when I put the car away and she's going over first thing tomorrow morning to do for Mr. Parkinson—at least that's what she said. Lord! it's only a quarter past ten. I thought it must be at least three in the morning. I must just look at a few papers. You go up, darling. I'll put the drawing-room tidy." So Peggy went up to the nursery where Nurse had laid a mattress out of the spare room on the floor and Harold and Connie were already asleep.

"A nice pair of children, madam," said Nurse, whose disapproval of "those Vicarage children" had hitherto been freely shown. "It'll be quite a treat for our Number One to find her little friends here in the morning. I'll just run over first thing tomorrow if you can keep an eye on them all, madam, and get some clothes for them. Beautifully tidy their room was, quite a picture."

We are certain that our readers are not really anxious about Mrs. Parkinson, so we will only say that the neighbourhood rallied as one man (Sir Edmund Pridham) and any number of women. In fact during the next few days the Vicar's progress through the village was rather like that of Mr. Baptiste through Bleeding Heart Yard, with housewives lying in wait at every door to say they had a shocking time with little Gary, but just look at him now; or how the whole medical faculty had given them up when Myrna was born and next week they were doing the week's wash just as usual; the prize being unanimously awarded to Miss Hamp at The Shop whose auntie had twins when she was forty-four and buried them both. All of which would appear to prove little or nothing but made a good excuse for having cups of tea at all hours. Perhaps the truest sympathy was shown by Mr. Miller, who hearing that his successor was in trouble put off a visit to an old college friend and took the whole of one Sunday's services, losing his own holiday but gaining his own soul, except that he was so genuinely and unfeignedly good that it hardly seemed fair. Sir Edmund Pridham offered to drive Mr. Parkinson into Barchester in his own rattling little car whenever he liked and though Mr. Parkinson would far rather have gone on his bicycle he could not refuse such kindness and had to wait in the hall of the hospital for nearly an hour afterwards because Sir Edmund's car had to be taken to a garage for a minor repair: which was its normal state. The Close rallied like anything. Gifts of woolly garments, mostly of a small nature, poured in from the Deanery, from the Precentor's mother, from Lady Fielding the Chancellor's wife, from Mrs. Joram, from old Miss Thorne (the sister of the late Canon Thorne) who sent a pair of long surgical stockings under the impression that someone was going to have an operation, and even from the old gardener at the Palace who contributed six new-laid eggs from the Palace hens whose houses he was supposed to clean. And what with the joy of a new baby and the peace of being in a private room at the Barchester General (paid for by Francis Brandon with a generosity that was none the less real for his being well able to afford it) Mrs. Parkinson looked very well and much younger, and thoroughly enjoyed (her phrase not ours) the latest books of Mrs. Morland and Miss Hampton, both sent to her by the writers who had heard her story and been moved by it. As for Mr. Welk when he came over really, as Matron said, you would have thought he was the father, he was so proud of the baby.

There was a good deal of discussion among people who had nothing to do with it about the baby's name. The Dean was assuming the office of godfather and Mr. Miller was to be second godfather though, as he said to his wife, Indeed, indeed, he had done nothing to deserve being made a guardian of so young a baby. Peggy Brandon was asked, rather timidly, to be godmother and please to help Mrs. Parkinson choose the baby's names.

"Teddy and I were thinking," said Mrs. Parkinson, who was now sitting up in bed in an elegant pink jacket knitted by Mrs. Joram, "we'd like to call him something after you, because you *were* so kind, Mrs. Brandon. Only you being a lady makes it difficult. We've named Harold after father and Connie after Teddy's mother. I wondered perhaps if Edmund would be nice as Sir Edmund has been so kind to us and father says he's a fine old gentleman, but it seems asking a bit much. Besides Edmund would be Eddie and we've got Teddy in the family already. I did want to call him after father too, but we've used Harold."

This difficult question was then put to Mrs. Joram who had just looked in to see mother and child, bringing a small hot-water bottle in a pink plush coat with a rabbit's head. It was then that Mrs. Joram had what Mr. Parkinson afterwards said was just as if it was Meant, and what exactly he meant himself we are not quite sure: we see a glimmering of light from time to time and then it eludes us.

"Well then," said Mrs. Joram, putting on her large horn-rimmed spectacles the better to think, "why not Josiah Parkinson?"

"It's a bit short, isn't it?" said Peggy Brandon.

"Then Josiah Welk Parkinson?" said Mrs. Joram. "It will sound very well when he grows up. It would do for *any* profession. Doctor, Professor, General—they'd all sound well."

"There's only the one thing," said Mrs. Parkinson. "Would it do for a bishop?" at which her visitors were silent, overcome by her long-term plans for her younger son.

"But, dear Mrs. Parkinson," said Mrs. Joram, "if he's a bishop he won't have any names. At least only one. We must think. How would Josiah Bath et Wells sound?"

"Or," said her daughter-in-law, carried away by the idea, "How about Welk first. Welk Cantuar, do you think?"

"Oh, I don't think father would like that," said Mrs. Parkinson. "He's never one to put himself forward. Hullo father," and in came Mr. Welk himself, who had taken advantage of a visit to the Cathedral tailors-in-chief to look in on his daughter. When the question of names was put to him he laughed good-humouredly and said he'd be pushing up the daisies by then and whatever Mavis liked would suit him. "And the expense of our suits for professional work, Mrs. Joram, you'd hardly believe," he added, more interested (as we all are) in his own affairs than other people's, even his daughter's. "It's the shoulders."

Mrs. Joram said she didn't quite understand.

"Well, let alone the cost of a decent coat for Carrying," said Mr. Welk, "it's the shoulder that's the trouble. Some people are born right shouldered and some left. I'm left myself, always was. I couldn't do justice to a funeral if I was Bearing with the right shoulder. And the way the material wears out you'd hardly credit. If it's a busy season you'll be down to the lining with the material we get now. Some say, why not a piece of leather on the shoulder, like patches on gentlemen's shooting jackets. Well, it's practical, but does it give Tone? No, you give him the old gentleman's name," said Mr. Welk, alluding to the Dean who would not at all have liked this description of himself. "Josiah Parkinson. How's that? Well, I must be off."

"Then," said his daughter firmly, "we'll call him Josiah Welk Parkinson," at which Mr. Welk was sincerely moved and after kissing the downy top of Master Josiah Welk Parkinson's head he went away.

The ladies also said good bye to Mrs. Parkinson, and Peggy went back with her mother-in-law to wait for Francis who was to fetch her by arrangement. Mrs. Joram had for long been exercised about her young couple as she called them, even going so far as to have a completely inconclusive talk with Mrs. Crofts about it, who was the elder sister of Peggy's first husband and very fond of her much younger sister-in-law. But both ladies had sadly come to the conclusion that you cannot interfere between husband and wife without risking the loss of one or both of them or of precipitating an even more difficult position.

"And how is Francis?" said Mrs. Joram, when they were in her handsome drawing-room overlooking the Close.

"Very well," said Peggy. "Darling Mrs. Joram, please don't worry. It's all right now. I can't explain, but it is. I really think it was partly Nurse and now she's going to Lady Cora Waring quite soon everything has calmed down. She really was *awful* to Francis and I don't wonder he was cross. And I've got a girl from Grumper's End instead and it will be MY nursery, not hers."

"Poor Nurse," said Mrs. Joram, thinking how good, how devoted Nurse had been to Francis and Delia when they were little; how helpful, though trying, as they grew older; how reliable and utterly maddening in the war years. "Old servants are a mistake. But what can you do? You can't turn them away, or if you do you must pension them and most people can't afford that. Well, my darling, I'm glad it's all right."

And then Francis came in and kissed his mother's hand with pleasant affectation and took his wife away. Mrs. Joram sat thinking about them, blaming herself as we all do for what she could not have foreseen or prevented and finally deciding that time and patience were the only remedies. But she did not know about Lady Cora and it must be said to her ladyship's eternal credit that so far as we know, no one ever suspected that she had taken the first step to freeing Peggy from the incubus and so helping her life to be almost as happy as she had once believed it would be.

CHAPTER 12

The nine days' wonder of the Clandestine Marriage, as various people rather boringly called Clarissa's wedding, had quietly simmered down and the county was busy getting over Christmas and, in the case of the younger married members, feeling that with all love and devotion towards their offspring, the school holidays would never end. At Beliers Priory Lady Cora was preparing for her baby in a kind of placid waiting dream which included a state visit from Nurse, who came over from Pomfret Madrigal for the day to inspect the nurseries which, we are glad to say, met with her approval; and just as well, for Lady Cora had no intention of giving in to her now or ever. Nannie Allen, rather to the alarm of Sir Cecil, had insisted on his bringing Nurse to the School quarters to visit her and he said afterwards that he felt like a new boy shut up with the Headmaster and the Head Prefect and could distinctly feel his collar turning into an Eton collar while the ladies talked over his head. But to everyone's relief the tea-party had gone off well. Nurse had reported to Peggy Brandon that her Ladyship had really got everything quite nice and the old nurse at Mr. Winter's school had a lovely collection of photos and her ladyship had got a nice Kiddicomfort pram all in cream. Nannie Allen had said to her daughter Selina Hopkins that her ladyship's new nurse seemed quite a nice person who knew her place, and it was just as well that Nurse never heard this tempered praise or she would have burst. As it was, she devoted herself to telling Bessie Thatcher, the nice girl from Grumper's End who was to take her place, every detail of her young charges' daily life, to all of which Bessie paid no attention at all with a very good pretence of listening and told her mother afterwards that the kids were ever so sweet and she was taking her orders from Mrs. Brandon not from that old fusspot.

Preparations were also going on in the rival nursery at The Cedars. There had been a moment of tension when Lady Cora and the Honourable Mrs. Oliver Marling might have come almost to blows over Sister Chiffinch as monthly nurse, but most luckily that lady had long ago arranged to take a fortnight's holiday with an ex-patient Lady Tadpole (sister of Mrs. David Leslie) down in Shropshire and, quite rightly we think, never altered her holiday plans for, as she so truly said, It was quite important for we nurses to keep fresh. However by great good luck her pals Wardy and Heathy that she shared the flat with were both free and were at once engaged; though we do not know which lady had which nurse, for we have never been able to distinguish those good and capable women the one from the other.

Maria Marling was having a family tea-party of her mother, her sister Justinia, her brother Lord Lufton and her husband's parents from Marling Hall, to whom she was a perfect daughter-in-law. As she took no interest in the inside of a house so long as it was warm and comfortable, she had wisely left it all to her husband who had excellent taste and liked things to be exactly as he liked them and the result was so good that most people didn't realise how good it was. It will hardly surprise our readers to hear that Maria's chief preoccupation had been not so much the preparations for her baby, which she appeared to regard as a two-legged and possibly more troublesome kind of puppy, as for the comfort and care of her cocker spaniels when she was reft from them. If no one suitable could have been found she would have had to send the dogs to a high-class Dog Boarding

Establishment where, she was quite certain, they would have mange, hydrophobia and every unpleasant disease of the canine race. But by great good luck Miss Hampton over at Southbridge knew a highly skilled ex-kennelmaid who would like a temporary job and Miss Hobb had come over to Marling, seen eye to eye with Maria in everything concerning dogs, and was already in Mrs. Cox's lodgings in the village. The dogs, those friends of man whose fidelity to their owners is a byword, had of course at once turned their backs upon their mistress and fawned round Miss Hobb's legs; rather unfawnable specimens, being permanently encased in a kind of chauffeur's black hard leggings, but cockers have no sense at all.

"Dogs all Worship me," said Miss Hobb, who believed in Seeing Things Straight and Speaking Out. "D'know why, but they do. Don't you give them a thought, Mrs. Marling. No Nonsense about me. Give me a job and I'll See it Through. Like Old Winnie, God bless him," from which moment Maria, most sensibly, took her mind right off her spaniels who fawned happily upon Miss Hobb, apparently taking her for their old mistress.

"Where is Oliver?" said Lady Lufton presently. Maria said he had been into Barchester to a meeting of the Friends of Barchester Cathedral and would be back any moment. And very shortly he came in, accompanied by Henry and Grace Grantly whom he had found, he said, miles from anywhere.

"We were following the hounds," said Henry, "and they got right away from us and we took a short cut," which to all those present seemed a reasonable explanation of the young people being miles from their home and muddy from head to foot. "We meant to get the bus back but we just missed it. It's awfully good of you to have us, Mrs. Marling," from which moment he hardly spoke again, devoting himself to tea, for in spite of having done his army time and being bound apprentice to the eminent legal firm of Keith and Keith, he remained a schoolboy in many ways.

After tea Maria Marling took her mother and Mrs. Marling

upstairs to see the nursery arrangements, followed by her brother and sister. Less interested in nurseries than their mother they remained on the wide landing while the grandmothers-to-be and Maria talked about cot blankets and Lady Lufton's offer of a number of Walter Crane's fairy story pictures which used to hang in the old nurseries at Framley Court: and how good those original coloured pictures were those who have only seen them in debased cabbage-hued modern reproductions can never know.

"I say, Ludovic," said Justinia, who was so often staying at the Deanery doing odd secretarial work for Dr. Crawley in her off-time that she seemed almost like a married daughter, "you didn't really mind about Clarissa, did you?" which might have been a rash question for a sister to ask a brother, but as Lord Lufton was the youngest his sisters were rather apt to treat him as a nephew, except in public when they very nicely acknowledged his place as Head of the Family.

"Not a bit," said Lord Lufton, quite truthfully. "Sooner Charles than I. He'll beat her. I would have been too frightened of public opinion. And why on earth the French call it human respect I shall never know. No, it's all right, Justy. I stopped thinking about her ages ago. Do you mind?"

"Of course I don't," said Justinia. "I only asked because I think we ought to go over the Old Parsonage. You'll have to marry some time and we ought to be prepared. And don't say you don't like the idea of turning your mother out, Ludo, because that's silly. She wouldn't like to stay on any more than you would. And if she wants me to live with her I'm going to. It'll be a bit of a strain, but there it is. I can always stay at the Deanery for two or three nights in the week."

"What a good girl you are, Justy," said Lord Lufton, looking down from his great height upon his nearest sister in point of age; not tall like Maria and himself; of middle height with elegantly finished hands and feet and a head beautifully set upon her pretty neck and shoulders. "That old Lady Lufton that was the parson's sister must have been just like you by those old photographs. But she was a little silly and tried to turn great-grandpapa down because she wasn't his equal or something," to which Justinia replied that she wouldn't be so silly as that, but so far the only people who had proposed to her were a budding missionary who came to stay two nights at the Deanery and Lord Dumbello who had just gone to his pre-prep. school and said he would marry her when he was ten. "But I agree about the old Parsonage," he went on, "and I'll see what mother really feels like," and though Justinia could not have accurately described her feelings, she had an impression that Ludo was older than she was, now.

"Well, good luck to you and I hope mother won't cry," she said, "and after all you are the Head. Good old Ludo."

By this time the nursery explorers had finished and they all went downstairs, where they found Mr. Marling and Oliver talking families and the two Grantlys almost falling off their chairs with drowsiness owing to a large tea in a warm room on top of a day's hard going.

Lady Lufton said they must be getting home and one of those very boring conversations took place about who should go with whom, as both Lord Lufton and his sister Justinia had a car, and little to choose between them in the way of shabbiness.

"One moment," said Oliver to his brother-in-law. "I nearly forgot what I wanted to say to you. I shan't be going up to town more than two days a week at present. Maria needs me here and I can do pretty well everything in two days. If you would like to use the flat while the House is sitting we'd like you to have it. There's a woman who comes in every day. And no nonsense about paying token rent. It's a present from Maria and me, so stop thinking about it. I shall be with you for bed and breakfast on Wednesday and Thursday as a rule. It's a more or less permanent offer. Now, give me the pleasure of having you as un-paying guest."

Lord Lufton, hardly able to believe his luck, thanked Oliver warmly.

"I can't tell you how *ghastly* it was with old Cousin Juliana in Buckingham Gate," he said. "Colin Keith did ask me to P.G. but he wanted more than I could afford. Thank you more than I can say."

"That's all right," said Oliver with the glow that being Lord Bountiful gives us. "We'd honestly like you to have it. There are three bedrooms. I'll keep mine and the other two are yours. Sitting-room, dining-room, kitchen and usual offices. Two baths, but I must break it to you that one of them is mine and can only be got at through my bedroom," but even with these conditions the plan seemed quite perfect to Lord Lufton. Not to have to board with Cousin Juliana and have to meet her horrible friends; not to have one's ration book taken and then be starved; not to have it rubbed in that one was being taken cheap because one was a distant relation. Never, never to be forced to eat Kornog for breakfast again. In fact, so delightful was the whole affair that Lord Lufton wondered, with the touch of superstition that we all have somewhere or other deep in us, what piece of ill-luck would immediately befall him. However for the moment his obvious job was to take the Grantlys home.

"I say, what a marvellous car!" said Henry Grantly, looking at Lord Lufton's battered old car by the light of his sister Justinia's headlamps. "Could I drive it?"

Lord Lufton was willing to oblige, but said he ought to warn Henry that when once you got her into bottom it was a bit tricky to get her out, so Henry who was by now yawning himself to pieces said perhaps better not, but he would sit in front and watch Lord Lufton drive. Grace sat behind and after her long open-air day and the warm rooms at The Cedars fell into a kind of doze, not waking till the car stopped. It was very dark and she asked if they were there.

"Well, we are there in so far as we are here," said Lord Lufton, "but something seems to have gone wrong. Henry is going to look. He understands cars much better than I do."

"Where are we then?" said Grace, still confused from her sleep.

"Don't be a goose," said her unsympathetic brother. "We're in Edgewood all right, but the wrong end of the High Street. I'll knock up the Post Office. If young Goble is in he'll see what's wrong," which he did. Young Goble was in and he and Henry, who had been united during their military training by their adoring service of the Kronk gun, got out young Goble's little car and by the light of its headlamps began a delightful piece of research on Lord Lufton's car.

"Well, I'll go home, I think," said Grace. "Thank you so much Lord Lufton.

"I'll walk up with you," said Lord Lufton, taking no notice of the hand she put out. "There might be a ghost or a cat burglar. You never know," to which Grace raised no objection and they walked, rather slowly, up the High Street. All was quiet and people safely behind their curtains in the mid-winter darkness.

There were two ways to the Rectory. One was by the front gate and the short gravel drive, or what had once been gravel and was now just dirt: the other by the lych-gate, cutting across the churchyard and so into the Rectory garden by a wooden door in the wall. This way Grace took and they stopped for a moment to look at the church by moonlight. The silence grew (as Mr. Browning so truly said) and neither of them felt equal to breaking it till Grace, on whom as a woman the feeling of responsibility for conversation weighed more heavily, said the Marlings' flat sounded very nice and it must rather fun to sit in the House of Lords. Lord Lufton said he didn't know. A lot of them were dreadfully old, he said, and a lot were very peculiar and had names like Lord Pandle of Boilerworks, at which they both laughed rather aimlessly.

"I do try to attend to what they are saying," said Lord Lufton, "but there are such a lot of them now and mostly so dull. And going back to Cousin Juliana afterwards is pretty grim."

Grace reminded him that he would now be able to go to Oliver's flat.

"So I shall," said Lord Lufton. "It'll be a bit lonely, but anything will be better than Cousin Juliana's ghastly friends."

Grace, her hand still on the latch of the wooden door, said he could always have someone to stay with him and then found herself unable to say any more. The silence grew and anyone with the faintest sense would have more than half believed it must get rid of what it knew, its bosom did so heave. She lifted the latch and the little click restored Lord Lufton's power of speech.

"You did look at me at Framley—the day we put the robes on—" he said. "Look at me now. Could I ask *anyone* but you?"

Grace took her hand from the latch and lifted her face to Lord Lufton who held her as if he could never let her go.

"Oh my darling!" he said as soon as he had regained some control of his speech, at which point their conversation became so silly that they had to walk up and down under the yews in the very cold January night, each surprised by his or her own fluency and freedom in terms of the most passionate endearment.

Meanwhile Lord Lufton's car was repaired (and what was wrong we have not the faintest idea as we cannot drive a car and would not understand the machinery if we did) and Henry left it at the gate and went into the Rectory where he found his father and mother peacefully in the study.

"Where have Grace and Lord Lufton gone?" he said.

His father, raising his eyebrows but not his eyes from Mrs. Morland's new thriller, said he had not seen them so could not tell.

"But they came up to the Rectory ages ago," said Henry. "His car had something wrong with it so I got Goble to have a look. It's all right now."

Mrs. Grantly suggested that they had looked in at the Old Bank House.

"They might have looked *at* it, my dear, but they could hardly have looked in," said the Rector. "The Adamses went to the Riviera with the young Pilwards yesterday."

Mrs. Grantly said How stupid, she quite forgot, and she expected they had gone to look at the church by moonlight. And even as she said the words Grace came in with Lord Lufton.

"Oh, how do you do, Mrs. Grantly," said Lord Lufton. "Grace and I were just looking at the church by moonlight," at which Henry laughed, much to Lord Lufton's discomfiture.

"But you didn't say it *all*, Ludovic," said Grace, who was hanging in a most unmaidenly way on his arm. "We got engaged. We simply *had* to. Oh *mother*!"

Apart from the slight shock and on Mrs. Grantly's part a feeling of annoyance with herself—not with either of the lovers—for not having seen what was up, the parents took it extremely well. It was what Miss Dolly Foster's grandfather had called a most suitable alliance. The Luftons were of good family and had been barons for a very reputable length of time. Framley Court was the right sort of place. Both Mr. and Mrs. Grantly had liked what little they had seen of Lord Lufton and Lady Lufton was well known as an indefatigable worker in the county.

"I'll do absolutely everything I can for Grace," said Lord Lufton. "She's much too good for me and she's an angel, and when I saw her in mother's robes, the day we dressed up, I knew she was the only person in the world who was fit to wear them."

"But that is *most* interesting," said Mrs. Grantly, whose mind was forever inquiring into things. "Do a peeress's robes go to her daughter-in-law by right if she is a widow?" and so obviously unfeigned was her interest that Lord Lufton could not have taken offence even if he was of an offendable nature, which he certainly was not. He had to confess that he did not know the rules about a peeress's robes, but he could easily find out.

"How soon can we be married?" said Grace, in a most unmaidenly way.

"That, my dear, the lawyers will have to decide," said her father, who though pleased by his daughter's choice was all for things being done in an orderly way.

"Why lawyers?" said Grace indignantly.

"Because Lord Lufton is marrying a young woman with money," said her father.

"He *isn't*," said Grace indignantly.

Lord Lufton, quite bewildered, said he was sorry and then wondered if he had said what he meant.

"Look here, Lufton," said the Rector getting up. "I am delighted to have you for a son-in-law: and that's more than I would say to most people. But Grace's interests have got to be looked after. I'd like you to come and see me when this young woman isn't here. Or better still, have lunch with me at the Club any day you like and have a talk. Then you can get your lawyers to communicate with mine—Keith and Keith."

"Oh, but father, is that fair?" said Grace. "Henry's there," at which everyone laughed and in the laughter Lord Lufton was kindly driven out of the house and told to go straight home and not wake his mother, which he would in any case not have done for he was, as we know, a very kind and considerate son. How he did get home we do not know, but the car was put away and he did go to sleep.

After the excitement of that evening Lord Lufton and his future wife felt very happy but a little flat. They both had what Dr. Johnson called a sound bottom of common sense and realised that a peer with estates and a young woman who owing to great-aunts and other relations on both sides would have as good a dowry as the confiscations of the late They allowed, cannot rush off and be married like ordinary people: just as Lord Silverbridge and Isabel Dale had realised it. Also there was the question of telling Lady Lufton. Mr. and Mrs. Grantly—

speaking by the mouth of their daughter Grace on the telephone—said her son ought to tell her as soon as possible, with which he agreed. This conversation had taken place soon after breakfast to which Lady Lufton did not usually come down with the excellent excuse that it was not worth getting up if you only had tea and an apple. So Lord Lufton presently went up to his mother's sitting-room where she was, as always, busy with one of her good works each of which entailed a good deal of correspondence.

"Good morning, Ludovic," said his mother, putting down her pen and lifting her head.

Her son stooped and kissed her.

"I've got something very nice to tell you, mother," he said, pulling a chair near her writing-table and sitting down.

Now, Lady Lufton felt, it was coming. She had been wanting Ludovic to marry for some time. She had had hopes of Clarissa whose family and background were so suitable; but Clarissa had preferred Charles Belton—a nice boy (for so Lady Lufton still thought of him, as we all thing of our sons and their contemporaries, now well past their youth) but not of course for one moment to be compared with her own son. Looking round among the children of her friends and acquaintance there seemed to be a sad dearth of suitable girls, and the nice ones were not marrying, as witness her own Justinia and several others she could name. That good-looking Grantly girl too, who had looked so well when the young people dressed up in the Ceremonial robes.

"Well, what is it, darling?" she said. "Maria hasn't had the baby, has she? She was talking to me on the telephone last night and sounded all right," under which words she concealed her conviction that Maria, or the baby, or to make it all perfect both, were dead and probably Oliver had tried to commit suicide.

"Well, not exactly," said Lord Lufton, suddenly feeling though on no particular grounds except nervousness that he must put off his news as long as possible. "But she and Oliver are letting me use their flat when the House is sitting, so to hell with Cousin Juliana. Sorry, mother."

"I could not," said Lady Lufton, who from time to time amused or outraged her children by using the slang of the day just as it was going out of fashion, "agree more. But it was about all we could afford," and her son reproached himself for his dislike of the Honourable Juliana Starter, thinking how simply his mother lived so that she might help his heritage for him as far as the late They allowed. However that was all over now. "Two bedrooms. How *very* nice of them," she went on. "Then Justy or I can come up to you sometimes. Dear Oliver," for like many mothers-in-law she liked her daughter's husband almost more than her daughter; though in fairness we must say that if Oliver had beaten or neglected Maria she would have scratched his eyes out with calm and ladylike precision.

"That will be lovely, mother," said Lord Lufton, feeling that his mother had now made it even more difficult for him to break the news. "But I've got someone to share the flat with me."

"Oh, who?" said Lady Lufton. "Is it one of your political friends? That would be rather nice when the House sits late," said her ladyship, apparently under the impression that Bill Sykes and his friends, or Corinthian Bloods, were roaming the streets nightly, knocking down watchmen's boxes and wrenching off knockers.

"Well, not exactly," said Lord Lufton. "Actually" (and even as he used this misused word his mother gave thanks for a fleeting second that he did not say ackcherly), "I mean really, mother it's Grace Grantly."

Lady Lufton looked at her son, her fine sad eyes expressing quite clearly that she could not believe her ears.

"It only happened last night," said Lord Lufton. "I'm awfully sorry, mother, and I hope you're pleased because she's much too good for me."

"Too good for you, darling?" said his mother. "No one is good enough for you. But you couldn't have made a better choice," said her ladyship, falling unconsciously into the speech of a bygone generation. "When I saw her wearing the robes I thought how well she carried them. So handsome and so dignified in her own way. Wait a moment, darling. It is all such a surprise. Oh, *how* pleased I am. And now there will be someone to wear the emeralds. I shall never wear them again. My *darling*," and she looked up with tears on her face, but tears of pure joy. Her tall son got up and bent over her, hugging her very tightly by way of expressing his feelings and feeling very like crying himself.

"Now, about the wedding," said Lady Lufton, her organising instincts at once rising in her. "I don't suppose the lawyers will have anything settled for a couple of months. And it is Leap Year which of course makes everything a day late. But when Parliament rises for Easter would be quite suitable. I must see if dear Grace likes the emeralds as they are. Resetting would be rather expensive, except that I could, of course, sell that really hideous diamond rivière that my great-aunt Maria left to me. No one wears that kind of thing now and the stones are really good. I must get it out of the bank and have it valued."

Lord Lufton, a little alarmed by his mother's swift flight into Time Shall Be, said wouldn't it be rather nice if she went to see Mrs. Grantly, a suggestion which her ladyship thoroughly approved. And when we say that she accepted it without apparently the least sadness that her husband was not there to do the heavy parent, we have clearly shown how deep was her satisfaction; and Lord Lufton, when telling his friend Charles Belton all about it later, said he was sure he had heard his mother say And now we can have the nurseries done up.

Lady Lufton then wrote to Mrs. Grantly, for telephoning would have been in her opinion highly improper, asking if she might come to tea at the Rectory and to that end got her daughter Justinia to take a day off from her Hospital Library duties and drive her over, telling her the good news with strict instructions not to let Mrs. Crawley know, as the engagement was not yet formally announced. Had Justinia been left to her very sensible self she probably would have kept her own counsel, but her mother's wish at once worked the wrong way round and when next she went to the Deanery she burst into the study with the words, "Oh, Dr. Crawley, isn't it *lovely*! Ludovic's engaged to Grace Grantly!" and as Mrs. Crawley came into the room almost as she was speaking and the Dean at once repeated the happy tidings, it was now going to be a pretty open secret. But as no engagement can really be a secret, we do not think that it mattered. There were no dragons, no previous entanglements, and no delays would be necessary except those that the lawyers of the contracting parties might make.

To their children both Lady Lufton and Mrs. Grantly appeared as elderly grown-ups, full of course of the wrong ideas and rather silly in a nice way, but in full command of their respective selves and on the whole immune to emotion, though this last was probably wishful thinking, for nothing makes children more ashamed of their parents than to see them freely expressing their feelings.

Mrs. Grantly was in the drawing-room when Doris Thatcher, with Glad, Sid, Stan and Glamora in the background to see The Lady, entirely against their mother's orders, announced "Lady Lufton, Mrs. Grantly, and the young lady" and retreated without shutting the door to cuff her offspring back into the kitchen quarters.

"I don't know what to say, Mrs. Grantly," said Lady Lufton, advancing with both hands outstretched and almost crying. "We do *love* your Grace," upon which Mrs. Grantly said something incoherent about dear Ludovic and Lady Lufton knocked her hat crooked against Mrs. Grantly's face and for a moment both ladies were too full of happy emotion to speak. "And this is Justinia," said Lady Lufton. "She is working at the Red Cross Hospital Libraries. Your *dear* Grace! I admired her so much when she wore the peeress's robes the day they all dressed up. Just as if she had been born in a coronet. I remember how it nearly fell off the first time I wore it, not long after the end of the war. I mean the Real war not this last one," and muddled though her speech was we think we see what she meant, for the First World War to End War did come to an end with maroons and mad rejoicings, while the end of the Second World War to Ensure Further Wars slipped in sideways as it were, remote, unfriended, melancholy, slow, ushering in the re-birth of the fourth century A.D. and the gradual encroachment of barbarians from all sides upon the civilised world; except that the Romans in Gaul did manage to keep a fair amount of civilisation going in the country while ours, so-called, would appear to be gone.

Mrs. Grantly, also slightly damaged by her embrace, said Grace was leaving the Central Library early and should be back at any moment, as indeed she was almost at once, and greeting her future mother-in-law with a very pretty mixture of confidence and deference. Justinia she knew, though not well, and suggested that she should come to the kitchen and see the Palofox Borealis which Purse Thatcher had brought to its flowering by means of the woyreless. Left together the two elder ladies found there was nothing to say except how kind and reliable and steadfast Mrs. Grantly found Lord Lufton, if Lady Lufton did not think that too dull a description.

"But he *is* all those things," said Lady Lufton. "Just like my husband," and it might have been noticed by anyone who knew her ladyship well that there was no regret or self-pity in her voice; only a comparison of a perfect son with a perfect father. "And your Grace, with beauty and brains and goodness. She will look *superb* as a peeress with that neat head and her lovely figure," which words, from the heart, made her mother want to laugh and cry at once.

"And Oliver—you know Oliver Marling who married my elder daughter," said Lady Lufton, "is lending Ludovic his flat while Parliament is sitting which is a blessing, for we really couldn't afford a nice flat for him. But I think we had better leave the money part to the lawyers, don't you?" with which Mrs. Grantly heartily agreed and at the same time felt a kind of protective affection for her co-mother-in-law, who was obviously born to be protected and sheltered and should never have been a widow with a place to keep up and heavy responsibilities. At the same time Mrs. Grantly experienced, as other people had, a curious kind of shock at finding that a woman who on the platform at Women's Institute Meetings or any other county activities was so competent and practical could be quite helpless and indeed almost foolish about private matters; and perhaps liked her all the better for it. We often love our friends like a Bridge hand, to strength from weakness.

"Now, we must be business-like," said Lady Lufton, taking the chair at a meeting of the Mother-in-laws' Union, with Mrs. Grantly as an audience that must be suitably dealt with. "Those dear children will of course live at Framley Court. Part of it, as you know, is let to Mr. Macfadyen, a very good tenant and a good man. Justinia and I shall move into the Old Parsonage which is a kind of dower house. The vicar has a *hideous* little house, very comfortable and practical, but you know as well as I do that when one has lived in proper houses one *cannot* live in practical ones," and when Mrs. Grantly, later, came to consider this statement she found herself in complete agreement with it. For people who have lived in spacious houses—they need not necessarily be palaces or castles—can never be really happy in a cosy little villa. Not from any snobbishness, for any place they live in will automatically become a suitable setting for them, but from the curious fact that if you have spent your childhood and youth with plenty of elbow-room, you will find that the small compact dwelling without cupboards and shelves, or empty rooms or even attics, will be far harder to organise than the more spacious home; just as an old-fashioned kitchen with a built-in dresser and cupboards is easier to keep tidy than an eight by ten with kitchen units (dreadful things of steel or more often painted tin, made to dazzle the rash beholder's eye, but prone to rust that travels as fast as dry rot, not to speak of the drawers being very heavy to pull out or push in and a capacity for condensation under the lightest steam from the washing-up water which makes it necessary to keep all the dry stores somewhere else). "Would you come over to lunch one day, Mrs. Grantly? I should so much like to show you the Old Parsonage."

Mrs. Grantly accepted the invitation with pleasure. It might have occurred to some people that if one lunched at Framley Court one might wish to see that pleasant but not very interesting house rather than the house where the clergyman and his family used to live in earlier days. But Mrs. Grantly, like so many of us (and when we say us, we wish to be taken in the feminine sense), enjoyed seeing an empty house with possibilities even more than a house with a tradition, settled in its ways where each piece of furniture has finally come to anchor in its appropriate place.

Meanwhile Grace and Justinia were getting on very well in the kitchen where Edna Thatcher said she had seen it in her tea-cup no later than Sunday, as her sister Doris would bear witness, only it was to be a Misunderstanding followed by True Love. Grace said she was very sorry, but she didn't think she and Lord Lufton had ever had a misunderstanding, adding very simply that they hadn't known each other long enough.

"That's like me and Purse's dad," said Edna. "Really I didn't hardly have time to know him, as you might say, till he was gone."

"I am so sorry," said Justinia. "It must be dreadful if your husband dies so soon."

"Ow, he may be alive and kicking for all I know," said Edna. "Went off with his company he did—the Army Service Corps it was and he looked lovely in uniform—and that's the last I heard of him."

"Was he killed?" said Justinia.

"I dessay," said Edna. "There was plenty of them as was, and married men too. But Purse is a good boy and does anything with his fingers. Mend the wireless, or my sewing-machine or the lawn mower; it's all one to him. It's a pity you aren't stopping to supper, miss. There's a lovely bit of liver—all fresh and doesn't need no thoring out. You'd better go back to the drawing-room. Doris is just going to take the tea in. Get up, you kids, when a lady says good-bye. She's got a Lord for a brother, the one that's going to marry Miss Grace."

"We didn't ought to have no lords, teacher says," said Glad, the eldest of Doris Thatcher's children of shame.

"Well, you tell teacher from me to wait till she sees one," said her aunt Edna. "The electrician's young man from Barchester's about all she's seen and she'll see *him* once too often if she doesn't look out and you can tell her I said so. And I *know*," which indeed seemed so extremely probable that the visitors left the kitchen so that they could have the giggles in the passage.

"I say, it *will* be fun to have you for a sister-in-law," said Justinia, which Grace took, and rightly, as a high compliment. "Mother and I shall go to the Old Parsonage. Let's all go and see it. Ludovic's going to do it up, or anyway the estate is," and Grace, who like most of us loved going over other people's houses, accepted with enthusiasm. The ladies then had tea and Mr. Grantly came back before they had finished and fell metaphorically into Lady Lufton's arms over county relationships, till Justinia firmly told her mother it was time to go. A date for the Grantlys to visit Framley was settled and everyone said good-bye with a very friendly feeling of waiting to meet again.

CHAPTER 13

On the appointed day which was a Saturday Mr. and Mrs. Grantly and their daughter came over to Framley Court for lunch. It was a family party, the only outsider, if one can call him so, being Mr. Macfadyen to make the numbers even; a statement which any hostess will understand and wish she had a reliable bachelor handy. Mr. Grantly had met Mr. Macfadyen once or twice at the County Club and liked him, while Grace said openly to her affianced that if she had met Mr. Macfadyen first, he, Lord Lufton, would never have had a look in.

"After lunch," said Lady Lufton, "we will go and look at the Parsonage and then I should like to show you the rest of Framley Court. Mr. Macfadyen, you will be kind enough, I am sure, to let us see your part," but she must have been very sure of his answer, for she did not wait for it.

Those who have read about Framley Parsonage, so well, so enchantingly described by one Mr. Trollope nearly a hundred years ago (though it is difficult to believe that any place and any people a century old can be so real, so alive, as they are today) will remember that the Parsonage had all the details requisite for the house of a gentleman of moderate means, with gardens and paddocks exactly suited to it, with accommodation for the parson, his wife and children and four servants, one being a manservant, besides stabling for at least two horses, a gig and a pony-carriage. But during the last hundred years many changes had come. The present incumbent lived not in the Parsonage, not even in the big staring brick house which the curate of that time inhabited, but in the neat cottage residence where, in those bygone days which yet seem so real, so alive, the widow of a former curate had lived. The Parsonage itself had for many years been a drain upon the Lufton property, having been turned more or less into a dower house and let on not very remunerative terms during the non-dowager periods. During the war it had been let to a firm that wanted space for furniture storage, who had at least kept it in good repair, but among the many less obvious blessings of peace was the return of this firm to London, followed by the impossibility of letting a house too small for offices and needing a considerable amount of reconditioning (a horrid word for which we have no excuse except Modern Usage). Since his father's death Lord Lufton had done, bit by bit, what he could for it, very wisely beginning with the kitchen quarters and the ground floor, but a good deal would still have to be done to the two upper floors and the old-fashioned bathroom arrangements. Had Maria still been at home she would have used the stables for her dogs, but now they would probably have to be let.

We must say that Lady Lufton's handling of the whole affair of the engagement had been impeccable and showed all her excellent qualities to the best advantage. The retirement of the Queen Dowager is not always easy. Sometimes she resents her dethronement and can make the new Queen wish she had never been born or had married a blacksmith; equally she can resign with a flourish of muted trumpets and muffled drums calculated to make her successor wish she were dead or in the Falkland Islands. But it was so obvious that Lady Lufton stepped down to her parsonage in pure love and willingness that no one could feel uncomfortable for a moment.

Lunch, with Mr. Macfadyen as a disinterested party, went very easily, and far from being shy or embarrassed the young couple behaved as if they had been married for at least a year, filling their respective parents with pride. Mr. Macfadyen also helped by inquiring about Palafox Borealis, though in an academic manner as he thought on the whole but poorly of any member of the vegetable kingdom that was not edible. The conversation not unnaturally touched on Clarissa Graham, now Clarissa Belton and it was just as well that the pretty creature, already calmer and sweeter in her long-cherished, lately fulfilled devotion to her Charles than she had ever been, did not hear all that was said of her, for her behaviour when she visited Framley Court had undoubtedly been quite abominable, Lady Lufton, usually the most charitably minded of creatures, going so far as to call her a heartless little flibbertigibbet.

The meal had been so agreeable that they had sat on talking till Lord Lufton said he didn't want to be a nuisance but if they were to look at the Parsonage before it was dusk they had better go now and accordingly they walked down, admiring as they went the way that Mr. Macfadyen kept the lawn and the drive. Each one of the party was intelligently interested in property as such, which is perhaps one of the deep differences between the born town-dweller and the born country-dweller. All their forebears, whether county aristocracy, county landed gentry, or in Mr. Macfadyen's case an honourable line of farmers with a minister in each generation, had lived on the land and by the land, in which expression we include the roof that sheltered them and what Mr. Macfadyen still called the policies; and each of them whether consciously or unconsciously appraised such property with an intelligent eye and also its potentialities, so that the visit to the Parsonage was not lightly undertaken. And if the Grantlys may have felt any faint discomfort at the thought of their daughter ousting her mother-in-law from the Court, that discomfort died at once in the light of Lady Lufton's keen and intelligent views on what was to be her home. To the younger people, even to Lord Lufton, it may have seemed rather a bore though our young are quite kind in concealing, not too ostentatiously, their opinion of the things that we find interesting, but somehow Lord Lufton and Grace managed to get left behind in the stableyard while Lady Lufton with the elder Grantlys and Mr. Macfadyen made a thorough tour of the kitchen and living-rooms, Mr. Macfadyen particularly distinguishing himself by his suggestion of a hatch between kitchen and dining-room and the removal of a couple of bricks in the larder wall for its better ventilation. The rooms upstairs were light and of good proportion, especially the best bedroom which Lady Lufton declared was far too large for her, when Mr. Macfadyen suggested that it would make a good music room.

"What a very good idea," said Lady Lufton. "I could have my own piano from the drawing-room up here and practise as much as I liked. Unless of course dear Grace would like to keep it," but Mrs. Grantly said that Grace was not particularly musical and Lady Lufton certainly ought to keep her piano. A further inspection showed an excellent bedroom for Lady Lufton, two other good bedrooms and one of those rooms that are useful for nothing but to keep the sewing-machine and an ironing-board in, where an extra bath could easily be put. As for the top floor it would be easy to shut some of the rooms up and they could be aired from time to time and might of course be needed later said Lady Lufton, with grandchild-lust in her eye. And such is the joy of going over houses, whether one's own or anyone else's, that anyone might have thought that Lord Lufton's wedding had been arranged for the sole purpose of giving his lady mother some really interesting occupation—as if she had not enough already. It was decided to get the agent to look at the proposed alterations and Lord Lufton said he would ask him about letting the stables at which point Mr. Macfadyen made as if to speak, or it may have only been that Lady Lufton thought he did, for no more was said. The depressing twilight of a nasty cold wet January was now falling and the party went back to Framley Court.

"There is time to look at some of the house before we have tea," said Lady Lufton, "if you are sure it won't tire you," but it takes more than one domiciliary visit to tire county stock and the Grantlys expressed entire willingness to do the tour at once.

Such of us as are by birth and upbringing town dwellers would probably have felt a certain depression at the dust-sheeted drawing-room, and the big dining-room now used by Lord Lufton as a kind of combined gun-room, office and general depot for things that weren't wanted at the moment but might come in handy, such as various mahogany baize-lined cases of silver which no one had time to clean, two very fine Chinese folding screens at least seven feet high and the big Persian carpet from the drawing-room together with the beautiful Italian brocade curtains, these last all wrapped carefully with layers of newspaper and mothballs. But this has been for many years common usage among the owners of large houses and the not so large too, and called for no comment. They then went upstairs and had a halt for tea in Lady Lufton's sitting-room. Lord Lufton and Grace, though not ignoring the grown-ups and certainly not forgetting to pass the excellent home-made scones and cakes, were able to compare notes as to exactly how they had felt on the occasion of the dressing-up and Lord Lufton apologised, in a most unshamefaced and unconvincing way, for having put his arms round Grace as she came out of the sitting-room into the passage.

"But I *liked* it," said Grace. "Really I was wondering if you would, only I didn't want you to know. I wish you could wear your robes at breakfast, Ludovic," to which her betrothed replied that they were a great nuisance to put away and his sister Justinia was the only person that could do it properly, but it certainly would have been fun to be married in them, "because," he added, "you looked like I don't know *what* in them, Grace," which appeared to her the most beautiful and romantic words that had ever been said. Presently Justinia came in full of welcoming affection to her new sister, and everyone felt a pleasant tickling at the backs of their eyes and Mrs. Grantly had to blow her nose quite violently for so quiet and self-controlled a woman.

"Mrs. Crawley sent heaps of love," said Justinia to her brother, "and she and the Dean were going to give you an old mahogany wine cooler with silver gilt claws and things so that it doesn't need cleaning" (a remark which will be perfectly clear to all housewives) "but I said they'd better make it a cheque," and though Lord Lufton felt that Justinia had perhaps exceeded the bounds of propriety he could not but be grateful: for what, he said, was the use of a wine cooler when you hadn't anything to put in it.

Mr. Grantly, speaking to an unseen audience on the cornice, said that the beautiful old wine cooler in the Palace had ferns in it now. "And by the way," he added, "his lordship and the bishopess must be well down the Channel by now. I see in today's *Times* that heavy gales are expected all along the Atlantic seaboard," and though Lord Lufton did say afterwards when telling Charles Belton about it that he had distinctly heard Mr. Grantly add the words Deo Gratias, no one need believe him.

"And where are you going to be married, Ludo?" said Justinia. "The Dean wondered about the cathedral."

Lady Lufton and Mrs. Grantly looked at each other, putting as much meaning into the glance as if it were Lord Burleigh's nod. Mrs. Grantly's said, "I am the bride's mother. I know that the place of her marriage is for my husband and myself to decide, but if you wish it to be the Cathedral we shall certainly consider your wishes." Lady Lufton's, as far as we can see into the mind of the widow still mourning her loss but now beginning to look eagerly to the future, said, "She is your daughter and will be as dear as a daughter to me: but I shall not dream of interfering with what you wish. It is yours by custom and by right and by my loving free-will."

But all this silent interchange was made useless (though we think it had added to the mother-in-law-ly liking between the two elder ladies) by Mr. Grantly saying, simply as a matter of common knowledge, that Grace would be married in St. Michael and All Angels at Edgewood and the wedding reception, for all friends who were at the church, would be at the Rectory.

"I *am* so glad," said Lady Lufton. "I was married in the little church at home and it was a fine day in July and we all walked from the church to my father's house with the sun shining and a little breeze and the village children scattered the most dreadful paper flowers in front of us and the village idiot held all the traffic up at the cross-roads and Lord Hartletop who was going to Goodwood was *furious*."

"I say, mother, you never told me that," said Lord Lufton, at which his mother smiled most affectionately and said he wasn't old enough.

"Well, hang it, mother, I'm getting on," said Lord Lufton indignantly.

"Yes, darling," said his mother, "but you are still really quite young and if I had told you about Lord Hartletop before the war you would have said it was mother going on about old times again," at which Lord Lufton was inwardly abashed and at the same time made the great discovery that we all have to make for ourselves, namely that the gap between ourselves and our parents, years and a hundred leagues apart when we are little, gradually grows less with the years till the day comes—as it will one day come to Lord Lufton and to so many of us—when we are older than the very old parents we remember. So that it appears possible that in another world we may all be the same age and meet as equals, for our elders will perhaps not forget their youth in which we can hardly believe and we will no longer feel that even if we were ninety we could not be so old as our parents used to be. One does not know.

So the question of the wedding was settled and then came the matter of bridesmaids and best man. Grace at once said Justinia and then suggested a Grantly cousin who was rather younger and that would be enough for a country wedding she said firmly. "And what about you?" she said to Lord Lufton.

"If only old Charles hadn't gone and got married," said Lord Lufton, "he'd have been just the right person. We might even have dressed in tight trousers and stocks and done it properly. Selfish beast. I really don't know, darling. There are several fellows that were in my regiment, but one has lost touch a bit. And really I've been so busy with the place and with the Lords that I never seem to see anyone now. But I'll think of someone. There's a quite decent Robarts cousin somewhere about and some older fellows. Come on, mother, let's show Mr. and Mrs. Grantly the rest of the house."

"There isn't really very much," said Lady Lufton, apologetically, "because Mr. Macfadyen has the other half where the servants' bedrooms were and some of the spare rooms, but I would like to show you what we still have," and she opened two or three doors of rooms empty now but beautifully kept and aired and dusted, and showed Grace the marks on the brass rail of the school-room fender made by Ludovic with a red-hot poker while Nurse was out of the room, and the indelible ink stain on the table where Maria had thrown the ink at Mademoiselle because she didn't want to learn Le Chêne et le Roseau and was punished by having to learn Le Savetier et le Financier as well, and other relics of bygone days really interesting to no one except herself but, so Grace felt and very nicely showed, the gifts of most value that she could give to a daughter-in-law. Then they came down again to the first floor and Lady Lufton took the Grantlys into her bedroom. Here she opened a drawer, took a key from it, opened another drawer and took out a large jeweller's leather case, rather the worse for wear.

"These are yours, dear Grace," she said and opened it, showing the emeralds, set in heavy Indian gold, that had come to her on her marriage. Necklace, coronet, bracelets, earrings, a rivière and a ring of one stone in an open setting.

"I wish we could have them reset for you," said Lady Lufton and she did not add the words "We cannot afford it," for none of us can afford it now and we can only make the best of our worst and accept with gratitude what is given. But Grace had no doubts about the beauty of the stones and was almost confused with pleasure.

"The ring does not belong to the set," said Lady Lufton, speaking more to herself than to those present. "Ludovic's father gave it to me when we were engaged. The rest of the set came to me from my mother-in-law. Ludovic—" and she held out to him the emerald ring. He took it, looked at his mother and then raising Grace's left hand he put the ring on her third finger and kissed the hand. Everyone wanted to cry and Mr. Grantly coughed quite horribly. Grace looked up to Lord Lufton's eyes with such serious deep love in hers as almost deprived him of speech and then turned to his mother and the two women held each other tightly for a moment. Justinia was the first to ease the tension by saying to her mother that she bagged the little diamond earrings if no one else wanted them and Lady Lufton, laughing in a way that her son hardly recognised, took the earrings from another case and handed them to Justinia.

"Oh, I didn't mean now, mother," said Justinia, suddenly much abashed, "I meant—" and then stopped short.

"Well, Justinia," said her mother, very sensibly, "if you want to have them some day you might as well have them now. Put them on," and Justinia took out her own little second-class pearl earrings and put the diamonds in their place. As the two girls stood together time seemed to Mrs. Grantly and to Lady Lufton to flow backwards, and they saw Grace Crawley—she who married Major Grantly—as she looked when Mr. Watts had painted her, only this Grace's hair was not parted in the middle and knotted behind, but prettily waved by nature with a little assistance from art and just not touching her shoulders, while Justinia Lufton with the soft brown hair, the exquisite dark tint of the cheek, and the small regular teeth that made Lucy Robarts the parson's sister who married the Lord Lufton of the time so much admired, was just like the George Richmond drawing of her in Lady Lufton's sitting-room except for the high light upon the tip of the nose which is almost a signature of that delightful artist. And we may say that while each mother knew her own daughter to be the more beautiful and perfect of the two, each also fully recognised the different beauty of the other woman's child and each was drawn to the other by it. What Mr. Grantly felt we do not know and he was in a poor position, for men are always at a disadvantage in these prenuptial scenes and Mr. Grantly had no co-father-in-law to keep him in countenance.

Lady Lufton then showed them the other rooms on that floor, quickly, for time was passing and the unused rooms were chill. The last room was a large one looking into her little south garden where Lady Lufton loved to work among her flowers.

"This room was always the nursery," she said, "and if you like to use it some day I shall be very happy. But of course, any room you like, dearest Grace—" and then she closed the door and they went back to her sitting-room. As Lady Lufton opened the door a man who was sitting by the fire got up and came forward.

"Will you excuse me, Lady Lufton," said Eric Swan. "I was over this way and came in to pay my compliments. One of your admirable Podgenses said the ladies and gentlemen were looking at the house and she was sure her Ladyship wouldn't mind if I waited in her sitting-room, so I took the liberty. I hope I am forgiven."

"But how *nice*," said Lady Lufton, who would have liked Swan in any case for his pleasant ways and good manners and of course liked him doubly because Ludovic seemed to think him a good substitute for Charles Belton, now temporarily swallowed up in matrimony. "I wish you had come earlier. We have been looking at the house and now we are just going to see the servants' hall—we still call it that—and Mr. Macfadyen's wing. You will come too, won't you? Ludovic, have we any sherry?"

Lord Lufton, though not quite approving his mother's manner of asking, for they did still buy their sherry by the dozen, set bottles and glasses from a cupboard upon a table and became a useful and thoughtful host, though his eyes did so follow Grace that he filled more than one glass too full.

"Stap my vitals, my lord," said Swan, "but your hand is deuced shaky, damme. I would lay twenty guineas that you were playing late at the Cocoa Tree last night and fairly foxed. Have I hit you?"

"Nay, Horace," said Lord Lufton, "—sorry, but it's a better name than Eric—'twas but Clorinda's eyes that, blister me, have lighted such a fire as a hogshed of claret will not quench. Will you have one?" he continued, dropping into English, and he offered a glass to Swan, who said "Thanks. All the best" and drank it, secretly mocking himself for his deliberate use of this banal phrase. Various healths were drunk, quietly, and Swan congratulated Grace in well-chosen words.

"I have taken the liberty of bringing you a present," he said, giving her a little packet beautifully done up in what the people of the period that Lord Lufton and Charles patronised called silver paper, a term so much prettier than tissue paper, but now degraded to chocolate wrapping—except that the tinfoil of chocolate has gone the way of this morning's rose. Grace, young enough to feel proper excitement at a parcel, exclaimed, "My first wedding present! Oh *thank* you," and then added, thinking that she might have hurt Lady Lufton, "except yours of course, Lady Lufton, but that was different," with which explanation her ladyship, never really to suspect a slight, seemed perfectly content; as indeed we think she always will be with whatever her successor says or does. "What is it?" and she tore open the paper.

"Tut, tut," said Swan. "Not the way to treat books."

"Oh, it is a book!" said Grace. "Oh, by *you*. How lovely. And all in Latin so that I can't understand one word. Oh thank you *so* much," and she looked with almost a savage's awe upon the little book.

"It is about a minor Latin poet called Fluvius Minucius," said Swan. "I am sorry. I couldn't think of anything better. It is really all I have to give and I wish it were more," and damn you, why have you got to talk Swinburne he said to himself, very crossly. Leave the girl alone.

"But a *real* book," said Grace. "Oh, please will you write my name in it?"

"That might," said Swan sententiously, "present a little difficulty, but I think we can overcome it. Have you a pen, Lufton? I cannot abide those Byronic things with ball points."

Lord Lufton produced his fountain pen and Swan, in his neat scholar's hand, wrote Gratiae Gratias Cycnus Haud Immemor, with the date in Latin (which we shall not attempt as we can never remember whether it is the Nones or the Ides that fall respectively on the seventh and fifteenth days or any other day).

"May I come to the wedding?" said Swan. "I will guarantee to kiss the bridesmaids and drink everyone under the table."

"Of course you must come," said Grace, delighted with a real wedding present of a real book written by a real person. "You are the first person to be invited."

"And what's more," said Lord Lufton, "could you bear to be my best man? Charles ought to have been, but the foolish youth has contracted a clandestine marriage. I call it thoroughly hole and corner to be married by special licence and no one there. I am having a church and everything handsome about me."

His mother, hearing him, wondered at what seemed to her a new manner of speech in her son, for so had her sad and rather self-centred widowhood weighed upon Lord Lufton that in her presence his manner had been as it were muted. Of his silly talk with Charles Belton and his few other young friends his mother heard little and perhaps had gently discouraged it by her mere sad existence. Suddenly she laughed, a laugh so young in its frank enjoyment of her son's silliness that Mr. Macfadyen looked up in surprise.

"Now, Mr. Macfadyen," said Lady Lufton, "may we see your part of the house and we will go through the kitchen passage so that Grace can meet Mrs. Podgens." So she led her party downstairs to the hall and so to the old-fashioned kitchen quarters where various Podgenses and hangers-on were having one of their frequent tea-drinkings and all stood up as the party came in.

Lady Lufton said a few words about her great pleasure in bringing Miss Grantly, whose engagement to Lord Lufton they all knew about, to meet them and that she was sure they would all welcome Miss Grantly as she did. The audience listened with a kind of respectful lack of understanding and when Lady Lufton had finished there was a dead silence. Mrs. Podgens, giving a wifely look at her husband said, "Well, Podgens, can't you say something?" to which Podgens said aloud to himself that Mrs. Podgens wasn't behind the door when tongues were given out and he wasn't one to interfere. Mrs. Podgens, giving Podgens a look that boded him little good, said she was sure they were all very pleased to see Miss Grantly and she was sure they all wished her the very best of luck and his lordship too and she was sure it wouldn't be long before his lordship and the young lady had a nice young family, and from everyone in the kitchen rose a joyful murmur of assent. Grace took it very well, quite unembarrassed and smiling very nicely at everyone.

"May I shake hands with all these new friends, Lady Lufton?" said Grace, which her future mother-in-law approved highly and Grace went round the table saying a word to everyone till she came to Podgens who had been rubbing one hand up and down his corduroys nervously.

"I'm very glad to meet you, Podgens," said Grace, holding out her hand.

Podgens muttered something that might have been Thank you, miss, or just as well mightn't.

"Don't be a fool, Podgens," said his wife. "Don't you see the young lady's waiting?"

Thus adjured Podgens reluctantly took his other hand out of his trousers pocket, rubbed it up and down his trousers leg and extended it nervously to Grace, who took it quickly before he could again resume it and shook it with a heartiness that surprised its owner.

"Sit down now, Podgens, and don't look a bigger fool than you are," said his wife, "and I'm sure, miss, we all wish you the very best and lots *of* them."

Lady Lufton then withdrew her party, several of whom were on the verge of having giggles, and took them through the hall into Mr. Macfadyen's part of the house, where their host was now waiting for them.

"I am sorry we are so late," said Lady Lufton, "but I had to let dear Grace meet Mrs. Podgens. How beautifully warm your rooms are, Mr. Macfadyen. It must be the central heating," at which her son and Swan exchanged glances expressing gratification at her ladyship's unerring instinct.

"It would be the easiest thing in the world," said Mr. Macfadyen, "to extend the central heating to your ladyship's wing. The contractors are good friends of mine and you would only have to say the word."

"How kind of you," said Lady Lufton. "I shall be at the Old Parsonage next winter of course, but I would like Ludovic and Grace to have the heating. The old nursery does look south, but it has never been a very warm house. I really cannot tell you how many extra woollies I wore when we had that cold spell before Christmas."

"If you will pardon my intromission," said Mr. Macfadyen, "I should like to have my contractors to look at the Old Parsonage. With a small furnace in the kitchen, Lady Lufton, you could keep the house warm at a comparatively small cost. In fact," he continued, with the remote expression of someone who is thinking very hard about another place, "if your son would consider letting the Parsonage stables to me—and fine I need them, Lady Lufton, for my own purposes—I could easily have the heating put in and heat your house from it as well."

"But, Mr. Macfadyen, I couldn't take all that from you," said Lady Lufton. "I don't want to be ungracious—you are *most* kind and always have been—but I really couldn't. I should feel I was presuming upon your charity."

"And now abideth faith, hope and charity," said Mr. Macfadyen, looking at something that seemed to Lady Lufton very far away, "but the greatest of these is charity. You would not deny me the privilege of charity, Lady Lufton?"

"I don't quite understand," she said.

"A bachelor like myself does not often have the opportunity to put those words into practice," said Mr. Macfadyen. "Charity on a large scale, yes. I can write cheques now for deserving societies and little did my father's son ever think that he would be able to exercise that power that comes with money. I have tried to exercise it not only in public but in private. Whether I have succeeded or not my Maker knows and doubtless I shall have to account for it at my latter end. But, Lady Lufton, could you have it upon your mind that you had refused to help a fellow-creature who has aye striven to follow those words, though with more backsliding than he likes to think on?"

"I don't think I understand yet," said Lady Lufton.

"Women are but the weaker vessel," said her tenant, "and one must deal with them accordingly. I am going to ask the young lord to let me have a lease of those stables for my own purposes. I am always needing storehouses for one thing or another in my trade. If I am to use those buildings they must be heated. If they are heated I shall ask him if he will not use the heat for his mother's comfort. And whatna son would he be if he refused. I think the position is clear, Lady Lufton?"

Lady Lufton felt that far from being clear the whole world appeared to be whirling like a kaleidoscope. Mr. Macfadyen's arguments seemed to her irrefutable, but that there was a flaw somewhere she was certain. On the other hand central heating would be a great comfort and she knew Ludovic would like her to have it, and on yet another hand, which made her think vaguely of Manx cats (a chain of reasoning which our readers will readily follow), it did not seem kind to interfere with Mr. Macfadyen's projects for what was really his own convenience.

But before she could puzzle herself any further the Grantlys came up to say good-bye, full of apologies for having stayed so long and promising to write about the date of the wedding, and other plans. Her son took them back to his part of the house and put them into their car and after a most satisfactory embrace of his own true love the car drove away. He went back into the house and nearly banged into Swan who was putting his coat on.

"Oh, I say, don't go," said Lord Lufton, shutting the front door. "Lord! what cold. Stop to supper. Mother's over with old Macfadyen still. We'll go and fetch her," and the young men went back to Mr. Macfadyen's warm quarters.

"Now Ludovic," said Mr. Macfadyen, who had of late fallen into Christian-naming his young landlord, though there was no disrespect in his use of it, "come and make your lady-mother see sense. Women are kittle cattle. And you will have some real Scotch whisky," to which Lord Lufton and Swan said Yes as one man.

"Now," said Mr. Macfadyen, "judge of this. It would be very convenient for me to have the old stabling at the Parsonage. If you will let it to me, I shall get a permit—and do not ask me any questions for that is a thing I cannot thole—to install heating in those buildings; and that same heating will, at very little extra expense, be able to heat your mother's home. Can you see any reason against something that will benefit us both?"

Lord Lufton said he supposed there was a catch, but he couldn't see it though he supposed he would have to ask his lawyers.

Swan said it was no business of his, but if anyone offered him central heating he wouldn't even stop to think.

"If you are going to see your lawyers, that is enough for me," said Mr. Macfadyen, and turning to Lady Lufton he continued, "the heating will be installed well before Easter, Lady Lufton, if I know what I am about, for English weather can be terribly cold after Easter which falls in the middle of April this year but that is no guarantee of decent weather. And then you will be able to move into a warm house," and as this seemed very reasonable to Lord Lufton and to Swan, her ladyship felt she was making a nuisance of herself by objecting and accepted Mr. Macfadyen's suggestion very gratefully. Then they said good-bye and went back to their own rooms.

Talk during the simple dinner was partly about Lord Lufton's wedding and partly, for Lady Lufton liked the young men, about Swan's future plans.

"But I thought you were going to Harefield with the school," said Lady Lufton.

Swan said he probably would, but there had been a chance of an Oxford Fellowship and he was undecided. Lady Lufton asked about the Priory School and he told her how it was moving to Harefield and what a big step it was, but his Headmaster had some money behind him and was obviously one of those men who were bound to get on. And a first-class wife and children, he added. And then, as the dining-room was not very warm, they went back to Lady Lufton's sitting-room where it was nice and stuffy with the curtains drawn and the fire made up. Lady Lufton was deeply interested in the running of a little boys' prep. school and asked Swan a great many questions, most of which were intelligent. The telephone rang. Lord Lufton went to it.

"If it's Grace, darling," said his mother, "do take it in my bedroom. I know you'll go on all night," and of course it was Grace, so Lord Lufton went off to his mother's room, put the electric fire on and settled down to an exchange of delightful nothings.

"You can't think, Mr. Swan," said Lady Lufton, "how comforting it is to feel that Ludovic is settled. I did think he might be caring for Clarissa Graham, or Belton I suppose one must say now, but it would not have done at all."

"It wasn't altogether her fault," said Swan. "What she wanted was to be with Charles all the time; i.e. marriage. And no one had the wits to recognise the symptoms. There might have been a crash if Charles hadn't practically eloped with her. Now they are settled. And pray, Lady Lufton, do not say how nice it would be if I were settled, for there isn't a woman I could bear to be settled with, much as I love The Sex. Not but what I am all for matrimony as a general principle," and he took his spectacles off again and stared into the fire.

"I do hope you can be best man for Ludovic," she said, to change the subject. "He lost touch with so many of his friends. Some were killed and some stayed in the army, and then he isn't very well off and has to go to London to sit in the House of Lords and somehow doesn't meet many men of his own age. And he gets absolutely buried here when Parliament isn't sitting. It was a great disappointment when Charles got married as he had counted on him. I do hope you will, Mr. Swan."

"To give you pleasure, Lady Lufton, I will," said Swan, "and do my very best not to lose the wedding ring and to make Ludovic thoroughly drunk the night before: which is, I believe, the whole duty of a best man. And I have my respectable blacks, miraculously untouched by moth during the war owing to my mother's care. What an unusually good fellow Mr. Macfadyen is," to which Lady Lufton warmly agreed and then she began to talk of her own plans and how she looked forward to living in the Old Parsonage with Justinia and had determined to visit Framley Court only when she was asked and not be a mother-in-law.

"That, if you will forgive my saying so, is what I am sure you can never be," said Swan. "Any more than my mother would."

"I should very much like to meet your mother," said Lady Lufton, who had taken a great liking to her son's friend, though she was by nature a reserved woman, steadfast in her friendships but not given to quick likings. "Does she never come to these parts?" but Swan said she had gone back to her own people in Scotland after his father's death during the war and settled there for good which, he added, meant very nice holidays for him.

"But you didn't go this Christmas," said Lady Lufton.

"No," said Swan, looking into the fire. "I was kept down here."

Lady Lufton said of course the School moving must keep them all pretty busy.

"Indeed it does," said Swan. "We are supposed to move in as a whole next autumn term and as you can imagine there is an enormous amount of planning and rearranging to be done."

Lady Lufton said hadn't there been some talk of an Oxford Fellowship too, to which Swan, still looking into the warm cavern of the wood and coal fire, said he thought his first duty was to Philip Winter, who was an excellent Headmaster and a man it was good to work under.

"Then, I suppose you haven't much ambition," said Lady Lufton, with such real and kindly interest that Swan could not take her words amiss.

"None," he said, looking at the glowing hollow of the fire till he had to put his hand before his eyes.

"Mr. Swan!" said Lady Lufton, anxious, she knew not why.

"I am being Ludovic's best man. I can't say any more," said Swan, still shading his eyes from the glowing heat.

There was a silence, only stirred by the shifting of a log on the fire and a little rain of sparks.

"My poor boy," said Lady Lufton, with such heartfelt kindness that it could not be taken amiss.

"I hardly knew till it was too late," said Swan, still shading his eyes from the hot glow of the fire. "Things are better as they are. No one will ever know. I shall never do, or say, or look, anything that could make Ludovic wonder. Or her either. You will forget, or pretend to forget, Lady Lufton. I can ask this of your kindness. For you really are extraordinarily kind, you know," he said in his usual gently mocking voice, getting up as he spoke. "And now we will forget everything for ever and ever."

Lady Lufton would willingly have tried to comfort him, but she respected his wish to bury a dead and useless sorrow and said, trying to speak as if nothing had happened, that she hoped he would come and stay with her for a weekend when she was in the Old Parsonage, and Swan made most sympathetic inquiries about her arrangements and by the time Lord Lufton came back they had turned the big bedroom on the first floor into a music-room, constructed a bathroom on the most up-to-date lines, installed a very good elderly cook that Lady Pomfret knew about, arranged for relays of daily women from the village and got radiators from Mr. Macfadyen's proposed heating plant all over the house.

"There is only one thing I shall miss," Lady Lufton was saying as her son came back looking, we have to own, as silly as people who are head over ears in love can look.

"Not if I can help it, mother," said her son, sitting down. "What is it?"

Lady Lufton said the little south garden which she had so carefully tended; but when Swan pointed out that her grand-children would probably pull the heads off her flowers as soon as they were old enough and leave their toys all over the grass, she saw that he was right.

"But—if I may make a suggestion—" said Swan, "there is that piece of the garden on the south side of the Old Parsonage, the bit that has that nice high wall on the north side. You could have a border on three sides of it and perhaps some sweet-scented things like lavender along under the drawing-room windows," which suggestion seemed very good to Lady Lufton and though everything except Miss Grace Grantly appeared dull to Lord Lufton at the moment, he was so fond of his mother that he managed to put up a good pretence of being interested.

"It is all settled about Mr. Swan being your best man, darling," said Lady Lufton, "and I am sure he will do it very well!"

"Need I be Mr. Swan?" said that gentleman. "I admit that Eric is not a name that I would have chosen myself, but——"

Lady Lufton said she rather agreed with him, but as it was his name she liked it. Or, she said, if he would prefer it she would simply say Swan, for she was used to hearing of him by that name, which relieved the slight emotional tension and then Swan said he really must be getting back to Harefield. Lord Lufton went down to the front door with him.

"Sink me if th'art not the prince of fellows," said Lord Lufton, "and thanks most awfully. Grace will be so glad. She likes you awfully."

"I am Miss's most humble obedient sarvant," said Swan. "A pox on these horses," he added, as he pressed the little knob that people press, without producing the proper throb of the machinery, "they are farcy—if that's a word—they have the bots, odd's life," at which words the engine suddenly roared into being.

"Odd's fish, no sir," said Lord Lufton, "they are nags of mettle. She'll go all right now", he added, falling back into the twentieth century. "Thank you more than I can say. We'll see you again soon," and as the car sped away into the night he went back into the hall and shut the door.

CHAPTER 14

Our readers may have forgotten that Mrs. Joram had for some time been trying to give a party, but we have not. Owing to the arbitrary and uncooperative attitude of the Palace she had been forced twice to alter her arrangements, but when at last the date of the Palace's departure was known she breathed a part of the great sigh of relief that went up from the Close and sent out her invitations.

"People are accepting very nicely," she said to her husband at breakfast a few days after the events described in the last chapter. "It's a pity about the Warings and the Marlings, but there it is. It would be so awkward if anything happened to either of them before they could get home and last time I saw Lady Cora she looked as if she were boiling over. I did think their husbands might look in. I remember Francis's father went to a party the day before he was born—I mean the day before Francis was born. You know, William, something *most* peculiar must have happened to Francis. He is being so much nicer to Peggy again. William, I should *die* if you stopped being nice to me," to which Dr. Joram replied that in that case she would *never* die and these foolish very middle-aged people looked at each other in a way that quite upset Simnet coming in to clear away, or so he afterwards said to his wife, who was quite sharp with him about it for no one, she said, knew what Madam's feelings were; an unfortunate remark as Rose, Mrs. Joram's faithful and slightly tyrannising maid who had come with her mistress to the Close, happened to come into the kitchen and overhear it and took offence. For anyone, she said, who had been with Madam as long as she had, knew Madam like a glove as the saying was and if Mr. Simnet happened to know where that piece of green baize was she would be glad, as she didn't like to trouble Madam about it not with the party to be thought of and all. Mr. Simnet, without a word, took from the kitchen table the piece of green baize (which had been an apple of discord for the last fortnight though the origin of the discord had been entirely forgotten), folded it very neatly and handed it to Rose.

"Thanks, Mr. Simnet," said Rose sweetly. "I'll take it upstairs and press it," and shaking it ostentatiously from its neat folds went out of the kitchen.

"Now, you've no call to say nothing, Mrs. Simnet," said the butler to his wife in whom wrath was swiftly boiling up. "One of you is bad enough without two. What was the weather on the eight o'clock news?"

Mrs. Simnet, in whom Rose's successful exit still rankled, said she didn't rightly remember. Something about gale warnings in the Channel and there was a ship in distress.

"It wasn't the motor ship Anubis was it?" said Simnet. "That's the one his lordship is in—and the old cat too," he added, with great want of respect to the lawful spouse of a dignitary of the church. "Well this time tomorrow I dessay we'll know more," and he went away to clean his silver in preparation for the party next day.

Last time the Vinery had given a party was as a kind of rere-feast to the Garden Party at the Palace, when Dr. Joram was still a bachelor. Since his marriage he and his wife had given a number of very pleasant dinner-parties, not more than the Muses nor less than the Graces which showed, as the Precentor so amusingly said, how silly the ancients were: for two wouldn't be a party at all and three wouldn't either, while at the other end nine would be extremely awkward and except the Deanery he didn't know anyone whose table held ten. But they had not yet had the kind of rout or assembly that this party would be, and Barsetshire looked forward to it very much.

Society is a curious affair. There are no fixed rules for it. It makes its own as it goes along, never put into words but somehow recognised by all well-thinking people. Let us give an example of its curious workings. Mrs. Brandon, who was nobody in particular, her parents having been quiet well-to-do people in another county, had married, many years ago now, Mr. Brandon who was also nobody in particular, but well-off and the owner of that charming place Stories at Pomfret Madrigal. Here his wife had settled down quite happily, for if you do not notice quite how dull your husband is and he is kind to you and provides you with a charming house, money for plenty of pretty clothes, a good well-trained staff, a very rich aunt from whom he has expectations and two very nice children, you can lead a very pleasant contented life, as Lavinia Oliver when she became Mrs. Brandon undoubtedly did. And if, just as your wife is beginning gently to realise how uninteresting you are, you very obligingly die of a chill on the Riviera and are buried there so that no one has to visit your grave, leaving her very comfortably off, it seems to us that no one can say a word against you. His widow mourned him very properly and though old Miss Brandon left most of her money to charity she did not forget Mrs. Brandon's son and daughter, Francis and Delia. She had also given her niece by marriage a valuable diamond ring which looked its very best on Mrs. Brandon's lovely hand. Neither as wife nor as widow had she tried to get into any other society than the small circle of her friends and even when Lady Cora Palliser as she was then had taken up her son Francis and his wife a couple of years earlier, she had been pleased for them but entirely unambitious for herself. Now as a middle-aged woman but ageless in her own charm and the becoming touches of silver in her hair, she was the wife of Dr. Joram, a Canon of Barchester, a Doctor of

Divinity by favour of His Grace the Archbishop of Canterbury, sometime Bishop of Mngangaland in sub-equitorial Africa, who was himself no one in very particular as far as family went. And, much to the interest of the Muse or Goddess who presides over the vagaries of Society, Dr. Joram had undoubtedly become Someone and his pretty wife had taken precedence accordingly. Not that she minded in the least about her social position and would have talked just as charmingly and with an equal lack of real interest to a brand-new curate from a Theological College or an archbishop, but the Close and the County had, in their own slow-moving, traditionally thinking, impartial way accepted her husband and much to her own amusement she found that she was Somebody in his right, and that people liked to come to her house and had even been heard to say with deliberate carelessness, "When I was dining at the Vinery last week," or "Oh, the Jorams; *such* delightful people. Oh, but you *must* know them. I shall ask you some evening when they are here." So when it was known that Mrs. Joram was having a sherry-party in the New Year there was a good deal of feeling about invitations and the A's and B's went about rather puffed up while the W's and Y's (for there were not any X's or Z's) pretended that they did not care if they were invited or not till the invitations came, when they said they supposed they must go.

Lady Cora Waring, owing to the presence of the future Bart who had slightly antedated his appearance, could not come and though she dearly loved a party she was very much better off at home with warmth and the heavenly smell of Baby; and her husband, who she indignantly said had transferred his whole affection to Master Harry Waring, absolutely refused to go to the party alone. The Adamses were still in the south of France and the Pomfrets in the villa at Cap Ferrat, but otherwise most of the invitations had been accepted. Oliver Marling had tried to persuade his wife not to go, but she was so scornful of his prognostications that he lost his temper for almost the only time in his life and gave so fine an impersonation of Old English County Gentleman, exactly like his father as his admiring wife admiringly said, that she stayed at home. But as the baby was three weeks later than anyone's calculations she was considered to have won on points and old Mr. Marling who had always kept up the classics of his school and Oxford days, insisted that her second name should be Mora; as it finally was.

Owing to the size of the party Dr. Joram's butler had co-opted his brother, formerly Apparitor of Worship to the Hosiers' Company and very knowing when it came to pulling corks and making each bottle of sherry give its full number of glasses, and his brother's rather half-witted but adoring wife Dorothy, sometime slave of Mrs. Powlett, housekeeper to Mr. Oriel the Vicar of Harefield. Imposing as were the preparations above stairs, with real fires in the fine living-rooms and lights and bottles and glasses, they were as nothing to the preparations downstairs where the Simnets were entertaining such of the élite of the Close as could get rid of their employers for the evening and also Mr. Tozer of the well-known catering firm of Scatcherd and Tozer, who was said to be the best hand at carving a turkey for at least forty miles round Barchester, and the better to show his skill had got a fine turkey cheap through his catering connections and had delivered it to Mrs. Simnet on the previous day for the kitchen supper.

"We *have* got a nice house, William," said Mrs. Joram as they went through their rooms before the guests came, from the stone-flagged hall with its fine square staircase and painted walls and ceiling, and the dignified dining-room with its mahogany and silver, to the beautiful double-drawing-room on the first floor through which the guests could circulate freely, for it had two doors on the wide landing. And indeed they had a nice house: and in spite of the unspoken rivalry between the Vinery and the house belonging to Sir Robert Fielding the Chancellor of the Diocese we are still not sure which was the more beautiful. On the hall and staircase the Vinery scored heavily, but the

Fieldings' house, always known as Number Seventeen, had the advantage of a drawing-room with five windows overlooking the Close, and for this it seemed almost worth having a less handsome staircase.

The Deanery, staunch allies of the Vinery, were the first to arrive, full of the enchanting possibilities of shipwrecks off the coasts of Spain and North Africa; not wishing to appear too hopeful, for hope so often tells a flattering tale, but prepared to hear and bear the worst with truly Christian resignation.

"I am afraid there was nothing on the six o'clock news," said Mrs. Crawley. "We just waited to hear it before we came. Perhaps at nine. We look forward to seeing you," for it had been arranged that the Jorams should go over to the Crawleys after the party for a cold collation; not that Mrs. Crawley was the woman to give her husband a meal cold from start to finish, but a large turkey as yet unprofaned by the knife was to be what is called in some circles the Main Dish.

Sir Robert and Lady Fielding were the next to arrive with their daughter Anne and her husband Robin Dale, a housemaster at Southbridge School, bringing with them a story, wholly unauthenticated, via Matron's nephew, wireless operator in one of our largest liners who always spent his leave with his auntie, or rather in tinkering with his own wireless in his auntie's sitting-room.

"Her nephew—I can't ever remember his name but everyone calls him Sparks—" said Robin Dale.

"It is Empson, darling," said his wife. "I always remember it because Matron's name is Dudley."

The Dean said it was one of those things that it was not given to us to understand, implying on the whole that if the Creator of Matron's nephew had seen fit to have him born into a family called Brown, or Smith, he would have made things less confusing.

"Well," said Robin Dale, "Empson gets all sorts of things that ordinary sets can't get and he said there were several S.O.S.

messages mucking about—his words not mine—somewhere round latitude thirty-eight. I looked it up in the atlas and it seemed about right."

"Well, we will have a nice comfortable talk about it after supper," said Mrs. Crawley to Mrs. Joram and then the Deanery party moved on to make room for more and the rooms began to fill quickly, for Mrs. Joram had cast her net fairly wide and everyone liked coming to the Vinery. The Precentor and the Canon in Residence (whose names we shall not invent for there are, as our friends and well-wishers so often and so truly tell us, far far too many people in Barsetshire already, but there they are and what can we do about it) were having an animated but entirely academic discussion as to what exactly happened in the case of a high dignitary of the church being suddenly Taken From Us in absentia as it were. The Precentor instanced the case of Bishop Aelthwithric (whose existence depended on the very doubtful testimony of a fragment of MS. attributed to Brother Diothermic of St. Ælla, now Hallbury) who went on a pilgrimage to the Holy Land with most of the ready cash and such plate as the embryo cathedral possessed and was never heard of again, but as his throne was not filled for some fifteen years (the revenues and estates being looked after by Earl Toothbane much to that gentleman's advantage) they did not get anywhere in particular. Nor were they helped by that eminent scholar Mr. Carton from Harefield, who said that it was better to go abroad with the cathedral plate than to go abroad and preach communism. He then added Ha! and moved on to talk to friends elsewhere.

At about this time, when people were getting comfortably jammed together and the noise of well-bred people talking about the weather and the winter sales was absolutely deafening, Mrs. Joram became conscious through her hostess's sixth sense that something was happening downstairs. Whether Simnet had dropped a tray with six bottles on it, or old Miss Thorne had had another of her attacks, or the Bishop and his wife had chartered a helicopter and flown back to the Palace, she could not guess: though none were really at all probable. But whatever it was Simnet would be dealing with it and as she had every confidence in him she went on talking to Lady Fielding about the dreadful price of postage stamps and how they would change the colours till one never knew which was which.

"For twopence halfpenny was *always* for abroad, and *blue*," said Lady Fielding indignantly, "and now every time I go to the Post Office something is a different colour and all I can say is twopenny stamps are unnatural and being brown makes them worse; it is so un-English. Besides what *is* the good of postcards if they only cost a halfpenny less than letters?"

"I quite agree it is all most confusing," said Mrs. Joram. "But if Mr. Churchill can bear it, we can," which patriotic words led to an interesting and wholly inconclusive discussion as to whether Mr. Churchill had to pay for his own stamps and if so, who licked them on for him. Mrs. Robin Dale, who as usual was close in attendance on her mother, was saying she wondered if Mr. Churchill had a private post office and if not he ought to, when Simnet, in a voice formed on the towing path objurgations of the rowing coach when Lazarus for one brief day of glory got into the Second Division in Eights Week, said, "Lady Graham. Mr. and Mrs. Charles Belton," and in came Agnes, looking as proudly maternal as a hen who has hatched a duckling, accompanied by her second daughter and her son-in-law. The cathedral organist who was there said afterwards that it had reminded him most vividly of the irruption of Don Ottavio with Donna Anna and Donna Elvira all dressed like the Inquisition at Don Juan's supper party, but this was a foolish comparison, for far from shrieking and running away—or in the case of comic characters getting under the table—the company pressed forward as one man and Mrs. Joram, her pretty silver hair waving wildly round her face with excitement, came forward with both hands outstretched and with a word of welcome kissed Lady Graham and Clarissa, neither of whom she had ever dreamed of kissing before and would probably never kiss again. Murmurs as from the Honourable Mr. Slumkey's supporters at Eatanswill rose from the admiring crowd when Dr. Joram, taking the tray from Simnet's brother, offered it to the newcomers with his own hands.

"I cannot tell you," said Lady Graham to her hostess, "how sorry I am Robert is not to be here. He got back the night before last and my young people came to dinner and he liked Charles so much. And he did hope to be free today, but the War Office rang him up and he had to go to town. So I thought you wouldn't mind if I brought Clarissa and her husband instead," said her ladyship, with her mother's own smile as of an angel who has thought of a highly satisfactory piece of meddling and is certain that it will be a success.

"But of *course*," said Mrs. Joram. "And *what* a good-looking pair they are. I want them to know my son and his wife," and catching Francis and Peggy who were near by she threw them at each other and retired. For a moment Clarissa's pretty face clouded, for she saw several old friends and wished to do a little peacocking before them. Then she remembered who she was and behaved as charmingly as Lady Emily's granddaughter could hardly help behaving and was rewarded by Peggy's frank admiration of her general appearance, while Charles and Francis, finding that they had during the war been each in a different Belgian village at a different time in different years, at once became temporary blood brothers.

And now Simnet was clearing the way on the staircase for Sir Edmund Pridham, in whose honour the party was nominally being given. Owing to his bad leg his progress was slow and he was stopped again and again on his way upstairs with congratulations and good wishes.

"*Dear* Sir Edmund, how good you are to come," said Mrs. Joram, swimming forward (for only this Victorian phrase expresses how she was manifest in her walk) to greet him. "And on your eightieth birthday!" and she embraced him with charming effrontery.

"That's all right, Lavinia," said Sir Edmund. "Now you've done it you needn't do it again. Nice to see so many old friends, my dear. Lots of 'em gone now and if we have a hard winter lots more of 'em will go. It's not the cold that kills us old fellers, it's going to other fellers' funerals. Old Lord Pomfret—you wouldn't any of you remember him," said Sir Edmund, looking round with an air of defying anyone to remember anything unless they were at least ninety—"not this Pomfret's old cousin, *his* father—wouldn't ever go into a church in winter. Sensible feller. He used to sit outside in his brougham with a fur rug and a foot warmer and follow the service in his prayer-book, and always raised his hat for the Creed. But he *was* an earl," which comparison with the hard-working, unselfish present Earl who was doing his best to kill himself in the service of the public seemed to some of his hearers distinctly unfair.

"Well, I shan't be here much longer," said Sir Edmund, who had now got into his stride as for an after-dinner speech at the annual dinner of the Barsetshire Club.

"Nonsense, Sir Edmund," said Mrs. Joram. "Look at Mr. Churchill."

"Fine man, Churchill," said Sir Edmund. "Good English stock."

"But his mother was American," said Mrs. Joram, to which Sir Edmund, who was apt in ordinary conversation to take a rather unnecessarily patronising view of our transatlantic cousins, said it was all one now, adding De mortuis you know and all that, which left his hearers in complete bewilderment as to the meaning of his words, if any.

"Well, here's to your health, Sir Edmund, anyway," said Mrs. Francis Brandon and after drinking with a very dashing air she put both arms round his neck, stood on tip-toe and kissed him.

Mrs. Joram looked at her son Francis with a moment's sick anxiety as to how he would take it, for too often when she was still living at Stories and afterwards had she seen him give his wife a rather scornful look, or say a cutting word that made it difficult for Peggy to conceal her wound.

"I don't see why I shouldn't have my fun too," said Francis and taking from Simnet's brother the last glass on the tray, much to the annoyance of the cathedral organist who had marked it as his own, he said, "To your bright eyes, Mrs. Joram," emptied his glass and, as he used to do in fun, took his mother's still lovely hand and kissed it, saying softly as he restored it to her, "Peggy is an angel," which words, though to what they referred she had not the faintest idea, comforted her immensely and she was able to enjoy the rest of her party without the old gnawing fear that Francis might deliberately wound someone whom he loved.

"Well, Mrs. Joram, I must be going," said the Precentor. "What a delightful party. And I must congratulate you on your son. He has a longer head than any of us," and he went away.

"Sir Robert," said Mrs. Joram to the Chancellor, who, being a lawyer, must obviously know everything. "What *has* Francis done? Everyone says he is so wonderful."

Sir Robert said he did not know any details, but from what he had heard, he thought that Francis had been a very cool and competent judge of the difficulties of the money market under the present fluctuating conditions and—from what his friends who were cognisant of such matters had told him—that Francis had got through a difficult time with great skill and far from leaving bits of his fleece in the hedges had done well for himself and he must congratulate him, and then he went away, leaving his hostess no wiser than she was, but with a mind at last fairly free from anxiety about her loved son and her loved daughter-in-law.

Do not let any reader think that we have forgotten Clarissa Belton, for we have not. But Clarissa for the present has quite forgotten herself. Every lovely image evoked by Mrs. Robin Dale's favourite poet Lord Tennyson is now her living world, and in the words of a poet from beyond the Atlantic ocean who in his short ill-starred life wrote some of the rare lines of authentic magic that a few poets have been allowed to give us, all her days were trances and all her nights were dreams. But Kilmeny will come home again: not late in the gloaming but to the full sunshine of home and children and every happy care and sweetest sorrow that life can give, and in her much of her beloved grandmother will live again and be handed on to future generations. She had enjoyed the party, loving to see Charles greeted by smiles and goodwill. Now they were going home to the little furnished house in the Priory grounds and there we shall leave them.

There were of course the guests who will outstay their welcome, saying how nice it is to get a few quiet moments with you, dear, and they must tell you about the wonderful film they went to last Thursday, no Friday it must have been because that's the day I always get the meat ration and what *do* you think Mrs. Gorman said when I met her in the chemist's; but even these were at last disposed of and the beautiful rooms empty.

"Don't trouble about tidying, Simnet," said Mrs. Joram as that useful servant came in. "We are going over to the Deanery now and when we come in we can use Dr. Joram's study. But I expect we shall go straight to bed."

Simnet said Very good, madam, in a voice which clearly indicated that consideration for employees was not what he approved and that by the time his employers came back, everything would be as if a party had never been. There is no armour against Fate, so the Jorams tidied themselves and went across the Close to the Deanery.

We will here interrupt the thread of our narrative for a moment (if anything can interrupt it more than we consistently have ourselves) to say that the party in the Vinery kitchen and servants' sitting-room was perhaps the greatest success of the evening. Mrs. Simnet produced a slap-up meal which Mr. Tozer said Scatcherd and Tozer wouldn't have been ashamed to set before the Lord Lieutenant himself if he was entertaining Royalty. Mr. Tozer had provided four bottles of what is known in catering circles as Christening champagne (implying that you can give people pretty well anything at three in the afternoon and get away with it) and a number of very sentimental and witty toasts were drunk. The only incident that marred the complete harmony of the evening was when Dorothy, the gently half-witted wife of Simnet's brother, said she did feel sorry for the Bishop if it was rough, because Mrs. Powlett had taken her to the sea for the day with the Women's Institute once and they went on a pleasure-steamer and she came over ever so queer.

"Now, that's not the way to speak, Dorothy," said Mrs. Simnet, "and I'm sure I don't know what your husband will think of you, talking like that after all the good supper you've had."

"That's right," said Mr. Simnet's brother. "We all know what she is" and he tapped his forehead. "But she's a hand for fritters I never see better. Lovely and crisp outside and inside, well tasty's hardly the word," upon which Mrs. Simnet relented and said very handsomely that They did say that sometimes the ones that weren't all there could see further into a millstone than most, and all feeling was buried in another glass of champagne all round.

"And now you'd better take some of the plates and things into the scullery, Dorothy," said Mr. Simnet's brother, which his wife with perfect good-temper did and washed up so zealousy that she only broke two plates and dropped a saucepan, which gave the rest of the party time to have a finger of whisky all round.

"They do say," said Mrs. Simnet, "that we're as near Heaven on water as on land, but it doesn't make sense, not to my way of thinking. Salt water's unnatural, whoever says contrary, and there's some that shall be nameless as wouldn't be missed, and not a hundred miles from here do they live," which Plornish-like inversion deeply impressed her hearers. "And as soon as Dorothy's finished we'll all go in our sitting-room and have a nice cup of tea."

Comparisons are odious (though why we cannot think, nor do we see why saying a thing often enough should make it true, though it often does) so we will not draw any parallel between the Vinery kitchen and the Deanery dining-room. But we must confess that the Colonel's Lady (which rank we must assign to Mrs. Crawley) and Judy O'Grady (represented by Mrs. Simnet who would not have understood the allusion and would certainly not have taken it in good part) had on one subject a great deal of common. And we will not insult the intelligence of our reader by telling her that the subject was the Palace.

"We shall just have nice time to have dinner," said Mrs. Crawley as she, her husband, the Jorams and the usual visiting sons and daughters with wives or husbands as the case may be, sat down to table.

"*Benedictus benedicat*," said the Dean.

"And then," his wife continued, ignoring this interruption, "we will listen to the nine o'clock news. I daresay there is nothing of interest, there very rarely is, but you never know."

Her daughter Tertia, the one whose husband was the Rev. Anselm Beckett, said it was an extraordinary thing that it didn't matter what time you turned the wireless on, the news was always exactly the same as what you had heard when you last turned it on.

"I think, Tertia," said her father, "that you rather underrate the news. You should remember that the B.B.C. cater, which seems to me the most juste, for what doubtless they would call the cultural level of society—and when they say society they mean the large mass of good citizens who take their views from the wireless and never read a book till it has been a radio feature—as I believe it is called—and has been read aloud in unrelated snippets at intervals. Or even dramatised as they call it. Not that," he said, feeling that it was perhaps not fair to attack a body who had no representative present to defend it, "the dramatisation of, say, a novel of Miss Austen's would make anyone want to read it, for those who had read and loved it would resent hearing it mangled and vulgarised while those who hadn't read it would think they had; simply because," said the Dean, his long bushy eyebrows lowering over his deepset eyes, "they had heard a garbled and usually illiterate version of it read aloud in a breath-y voice with an eye on the clock. Con*tro*versy, they say," said the Dean with a scholar's bitter scorn. "And when they debate," he added, chewing the end of scholarly venom, "if debating you can call what are obviously unprepared chats, they begin every sentence with Well. Bah!" Which fascinating expletive, more often printed than spoken, made his family feel that father was going it.

"And how is that nice little Mrs. Parkinson?" said Mrs. Crawley to Mrs. Joram. "Her baby was such a charming little creature. What did she call him in the end?"

Mrs. Joram said Josiah, after Dr. Crawley who was going to stand godfather and Welk after Mrs. Parkinson's father and her son Francis had given the Parkinsons a refrigerator which everyone thought most suitable and Mrs. Joram, to her great pleasure, felt the Deanery opinion of Francis rising to Set Fair. For though she had never said a word the county grape-vine had conveyed to the Close that young Brandon (as older people still called him) was not being altogether satisfactory. But now that rumour had announced—and quite correctly for once—that he had come unscathed through the recent financial crisis and even (if the Treasurer was to be believed) made money out of it, his generosity was an added merit.

"Your daughter-in-law looked quite charming this evening Mrs. Joram," said the Dean. "I am told that she has had Parkinson's children at Stories while Mrs. Parkinson was in the nursing home. I hope your dragon of a nurse did not mind," for Nurse's capacity for taking umbrage which had grown with the years was quite celebrated among her employers' friends.

"Oh, Nurse is having a holiday and then she is going to Lady Cora Waring," said Mrs. Joram, "and Peggy has a nice girl from Grumper's End. It is such a good thing. She needs bullying and dear Peggy couldn't bully. Lady Cora will keep her in her place. And what do you think of Lord Lufton's engagement?"

"Excellent, excellent," said the Dean. "I have known Grantly all my life—we have a kind of cousinship you know through my mother's great-aunt who married Grantly's grandfather—or was it great-grandfather. At my age the generations seem to run together. Or else I am getting old and confuse them. But Octavia always sets me right," he added, looking with pride at his youngest child who had the whole county at her fingertips and would undoubtedly shove her husband into high clerical preferment very soon.

Octavia, who as usual showed every sign of adding to the population, said it was Mr. Grantly's great-grandfather. "They all married very young and had lots of children; just like us," she added in a voice whose self-satisfaction would have been extremely irritating had not her vanity—that of having a large healthy brood—been such an innocent and laudable one.

"And now Mrs. Grantly's daughter is marrying young Lord Lufton," said Mrs. Crawley. Not that there was an old Lord Lufton, but somehow the fact of his present Lordship having succeeded to the title after his father's too-early death made people think of him as much younger than he really was. Which is just the sort of thing people do think.

The conversation then veered to the proposed widening of Barley Street, and as the Corporation were (quite rightly) determined to widen it on the grounds of its being a bottleneck and all the really old houses being in a shocking state of decay and some of them condemned, while the National Trust and the Georgian Group were (quite rightly) equally determined that the traffic ought to go round by a new circular road connecting Ullathorne with Hogglestock and the fronts of the old houses be preserved as a National Monument, it is probable that the row, or friendly discussion as the newspaper called it, between those two bodies and the City Council will go on till the next War to end War makes all plans unnecessary. Meanwhile most people had lost interest in it and a good many regretfully withdrew their subscriptions to both those bodies because the late They had confiscated and surtaxed all their savings and not even Mr. Churchill himself could undo the deep wrongs done to this once proud and free country.

"Ten minutes to nine," said Mrs. Crawley suddenly. "I think we ought to go upstairs. What about you, Josiah? Or do you men want to talk?"

Dr. Joram, the Rev. Thomas Needham, and the Rev. Anselm Beckett politely looked to their host for a lead. Dr. Crawley said it would be a pity to hurry as it was that very good port that Secunda's husband had given him.

"I'm glad you like it, Dean," said Secunda's husband, who was, as we know, the editor of a small church-magazine. "I quite agree it would be a pity to hurry over it. Perhaps Mrs. Crawley wouldn't mind if we brought it upstairs."

It is quite possible that Mrs. Crawley might have objected, and when she objected no one rebelled. But the need to concentrate the whole strength of the Deanery on this evening's wireless news was more important and she let the innovation pass.

Upstairs a good fire was burning, supplemented (we are glad to say) by some central heating at the other end of the long drawing-room. The company seated themselves.

"Three minutes to nine," said the Dean, looking at his large old-fashioned watch. "Strange that so insignificant an apparatus should be able to put us in touch with the whole world."

"Well, Papa," said Secunda, always the most rebellious of his large brood, "you can't exactly call it insignificant. It cost fifty guineas and we all clubbed together for your last birthday because the old ones was so ghastly."

"Hush, Secunda," said her mother, as the time signal from Big Ben filled the room with an appalling boom.

"Dear, dear," said the Rev. Anselm Beckett and he turned the knob. A storm of cracklings burst out.

"That's not the way," said his wife and turned it again. Loud shrieks as of sirens in distress were heard.

Octavia Needham rose, adjusted the apparatus, and sat down again, while her husband gazed at her with loving admiration.

A voice, speaking with a friendly and *dêgagê* refinement calculated to rouse dislike in all reasonable bosoms, said that it was the B.B.C. speaking, and fluted through various announcements. The tension grew. The Dean silently refilled Dr. Joram's glass and his own and pushed the port towards his sons-in-law.

"That's the wrong way, Father," said his daughter Octavia in a loud whisper, but her very proper reproof was unheeded.

"Heah," said the voice, "is a message that has just come in. The motor cruiser *Anubis* which by earlier reports had trouble off the North African coast has arrived safely at Madeira. Among the passengers are the Bishop of Barchester and Mrs.—" at which point the Dean turned off.

There was a silence, compounded of such mixed elements that we shall not attempt to analyse them.

"I must say," said Mrs. Joram, looking pensively at old Mrs. Brandon's diamond on her lovely hand, "that after all these years it would be quite uncomfortable not to have someone at the Palace that one can really dislike."

COLOPHON

This book is being reissued as part of Moyer Bell's Angela Thirkell Series. Readers may join the Thirkell Circle for free to receive notices of new titles in the series as well as a newsletter, bookmark, poster, and more. Simply send in the enclosed card or write to the address below.

The text of this book was set in Caslon, a typeface designed by William Caslon I (1692-1766). This face designed in 1725 has gone through many incarnations. It was the mainstay of British printers for over one hundred years and remains very popular today. The version used here is Adobe Caslon. The display faces are Adobe Caslon Outline, Calligraphic 421, and Adobe Caslon.

Happy Returns was composed by Alabama Book Composition, Deatsville, Alabama and printed by Webcom Limited, Ontario, Canada on acid-free paper.

Moyer Bell
Kymbolde Way
Wakefield, RI 02879